Vachaspati Misra

Vivada Chintamani

SALZWASSER
VERLAG

Vachaspati Misra

Vivada Chintamani

Reprint of the original, first published in 1863.

1st Edition 2022 | ISBN: 978-3-37500-341-8

Verlag (Publisher): Salzwasser Verlag GmbH, Zeilweg 44, 60439 Frankfurt, Deutschland
Vertretungsberechtigt (Authorized to represent): E. Roepke, Zeilweg 44, 60439 Frankfurt, Deutschland
Druck (Print): Books on Demand GmbH, In de Tarpen 42, 22848 Norderstedt, Deutschland

VIVADA CHINTAMANI:

A SUCCINCT COMMENTARY

ON

THE HINDOO LAW

PREVALENT IN MITHILA.

FROM THE ORIGINAL SANSCRIT

OF

VACHASPATI MISRA.

BY

PROSSONNO COOMAR TAGORE.

CALCUTTA

1863.

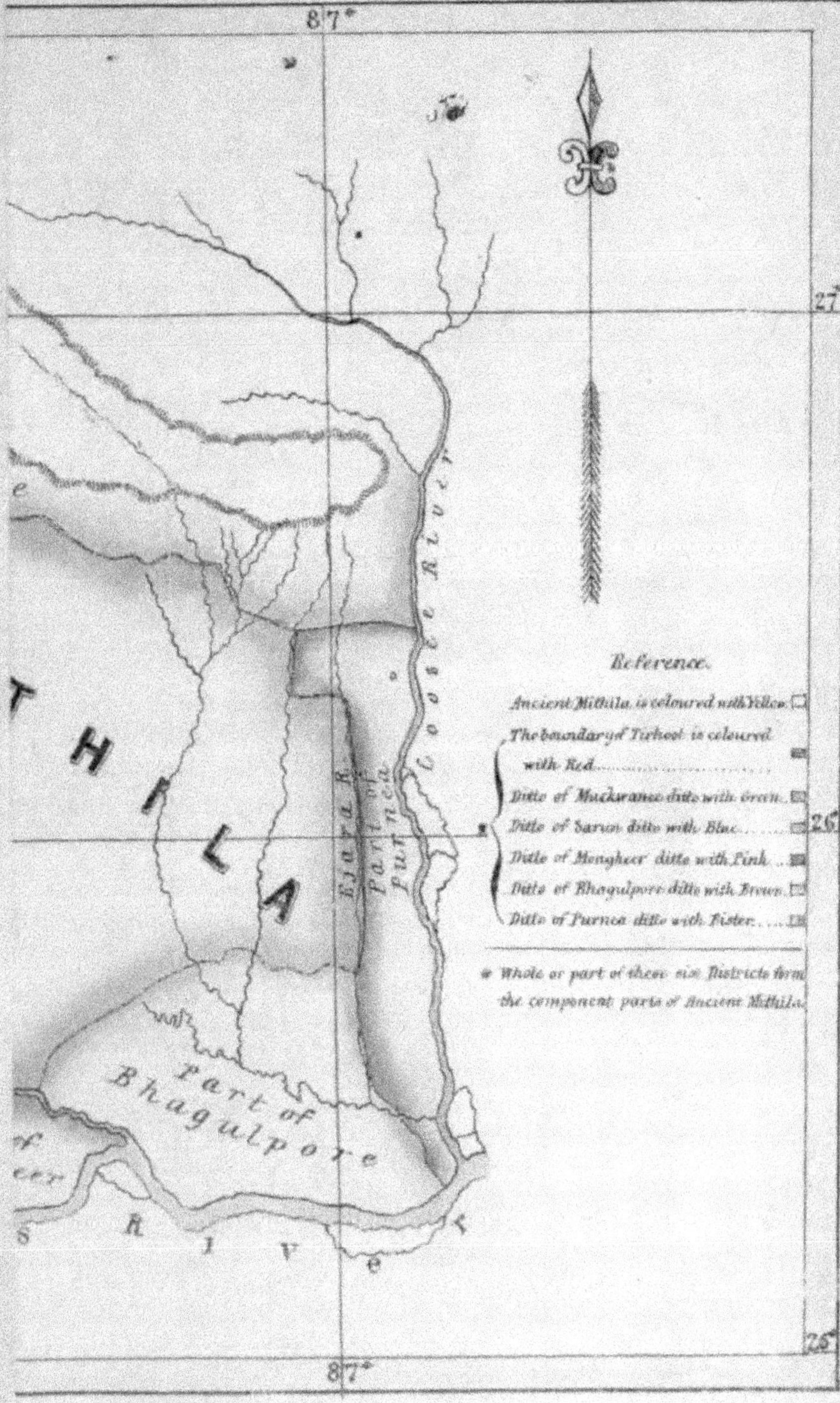

87°
27°
26°
25°
Coosee River
Part of Purnea
Part of Bhagulpore
Reference.
Ancient Mithila is coloured with Yellow
The boundary of Tirhoot is coloured with Red
Ditto of Muckwanee ditto with Green
Ditto of Sarun ditto with Blue
Ditto of Mongheer ditto with Pink
Ditto of Bhagulpore ditto with Brown
Ditto of Purnea ditto with Bister
* Whole or part of these six Districts form the component parts of Ancient Mithila.

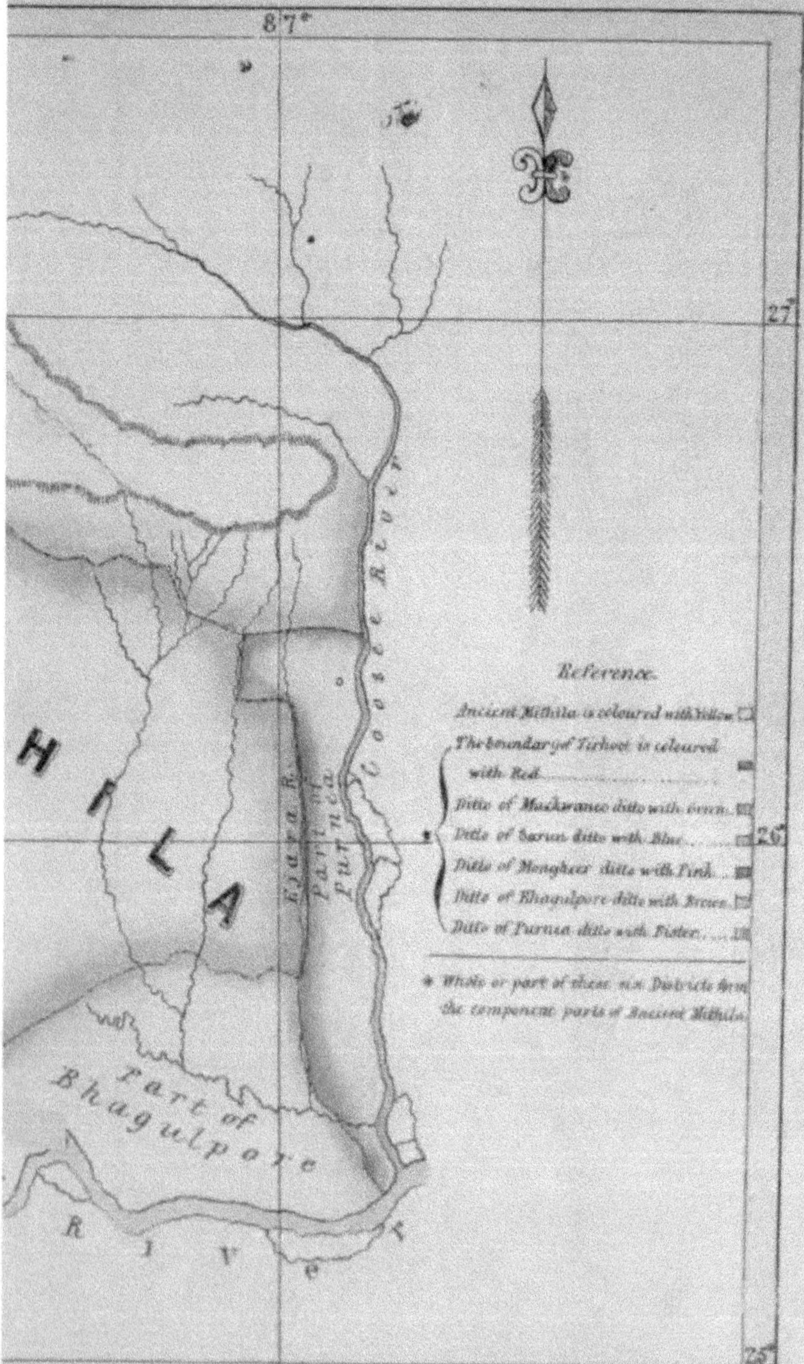

87°
27°
26°
25°
87°
Coosee River
Part of Purnea
Ejara R.
H I L A
Part of Bhagulpore
R i v e r
Reference.
Ancient Mithila is coloured with Yellow
The boundary of Tirhoot is coloured with Red
Ditto of Sarun ditto with Blue
Ditto of Mongheer ditto with Pink
Ditto of Bhagulpore ditto with Brown
Ditto of Purnea ditto with Bister
* Whole or part of these six Districts form the component parts of Ancient Mithila.

To the Honorable

Sir BARNES PEACOCK, Knight,

Chief Justice of the High Court of Calcutta.

Honorable Sir,

It affords me peculiar gratification to inscribe, on these pages, the name of one, who has deserved so well of India, and with whom it has been my happiness to be rather intimately associated, during the few but memorable years of the existence of the Legislative Council of India, as constituted under the presidency of the late lamented Marquis of Dalhousie. I gladly obeyed the summons of that enlightened nobleman to assist the labours of the Council, by affording it the benefit of my experience, derived from a long conversancy with the laws of the country, and intimate acquaintance with their general operation and especially their effect in forming the character and promoting the happiness of the Natives of India. The pleasure which I took, in rendering my services, was the greater from the close relation into which I was thus brought with one who had devoted himself to the cultivation of jurisprudence, and who had, in consequence of his great legal attainments, been selected to be the legal member of the Supreme Government.

On your elevation, at a subsequent date, to the office of Chief Justice of the Supreme Court, your diligent, faithful, and successful administration of justice, to the mixed population of the metropolis of India, could not fail to secure their esteem and confidence. But no one had better opportunities than myself of observing the zeal and assiduity, with which you discharged your high and responsible functions, as Member of the LEGISLATIVE COUNCIL, or the great talents, ardour, and diligence, which you brought to bear on the various subjects of its deliberations. Amidst the agitations which arose from the disturbed state of parts of the country, when the voice of law was silent and the authority of the magistrate was weakened or overborne, you gave an unrelaxed attention, as during a period of the utmost tranquility, to the revision of those Codes of Civil and Criminal Procedure, and substantive Criminal Law, which had years before been sketched out, but could not be reduced to a methodical, harmonious, and practical form, till your attentive and continued labours rendered them capable of being successively brought into operation.

The necessity of giving uniform laws, to the extensive dependencies of the British Empire in India, had been long felt, and was provided for at the last renewal of the East India Company's Charter for a fixed period. The Indian Law Commission, appointed for the purpose in the middle of 1835 submitted, at the close of 1837, an account of their labours with the drafts of laws which they had prepared. But such was the magnitude of the task, and so momentous the responsibility of giving effect to the suggestions of that body, that it was deemed necessary to obtain the opinions of the judicial officers of all parts of British India, whose experience enabled them to speak with authority on the subject. After years of hesitation, the Royal Commissioners in London rendered their Reports in 1845, and again in 1855 and 1856. When these were eventually referred to the LEGISLATIVE COUNCIL OF INDIA, and you undertook to preside over the Committee appointed to revise the various plans and suggestions, such was the earnestness which you and your colleagues displayed, that you presented your first Report on the subject at the close of 1856. On that occasion, the Committee concluded their remarks with "acknowledging the great assistance which they had derived from the extensive knowledge and experience of the Clerk Assistant to the Council, who acted as Clerk to them, and from his indefatigable exertions in carrying out their views,"—an expression of your commendation of the humble services rendered by me, which I cannot recall to memory without an emotion of sincere pleasure, heightened by the recollection of the kindliness of feeling invariably manifested towards me by you, in common with the other members of the Council. I record these facts, not simply with a view to commemorate them, as constituting some of the most gratifying incidents of my life. I refer to them more especially as incentives to the higher classes of my countrymen; to bring their information and abilities to the aid of those who are at the helm of the State, and thereby promote the welfare and happiness of this great community, who look up to them as the sources of general improvement and advantage.

The value and extent of your labours, in these and other respects, have been so well appreciated and so warmly acknowledged, by the Local and the Home Government, as well as by the unanimous and cordial testimony of the public, that it would have been presumptuous to attempt to join with theirs the expression of my individual sentiments, were it not for the satisfaction and pride which I feel in availing myself of this opportunity to record the humble share I had in those labours, the importance and advantages of which will be more and more sensibly felt every succeeding year.

The work, which I do myself the honor to present to you, though holding a distinguished place among the Hindoo law works of the Mithila School, is, I am aware, of a nature that must have less attracted your attention than any others, during the course of your judicial and legislative career in

India. I am certain, however, that it will not fail to receive from you such notice as may be permitted by the numerous and varied duties, imposed on you by your present very responsible position, as Chief Justice of the newly-constituted HIGH COURT, the success of which, as an experimental measure, will, it is acknowledged, principally depend on the ability, labours, and above all the example of the Judge appointed to preside over it, and the discretion with which he directs the labours, or stimulates the zeal, of his colleagues. Should you, amidst your multiplied duties, find time to examine the work, and consider it to be deserving of being given to the legal and literary world in an English dress, such an opinion, from so competent a judge, will afford me the greatest satisfaction I can derive from having undertaken to produce it, and it will contribute not a little to the favorable reception of the work by the public.

I have the honor to be,

Honorable Sir,

Your most obedient Servant,

PROSSONNO COOMAR TAGORE.

Calcutta, September 1863.

CONTENTS.

THE LAW OF INHERITANCE.

SUPPLEMENTARY.

PERORATION.

INDEX

PREFACE.

The learned Hindoo as well as the Anglo-Oriental Scholar is aware that, under peculiar circumstances, the people of India were induced to withdraw the legislative power from the hands of the executive authorities and entrust it exclusively to the holy sages. In offering to the public a translation of a work on Hindoo law, of some repute, it seems to be necessary to notice the state of the primitive law, and to show how at various times it underwent alterations at the hands of different compilers and commentators, till it has been reduced into the forms of what are termed the five distinct schools, prevailing in our days, wherein its provisions have been made locally applicable, and, as it were, peculiarly obligatory on the inhabitants of the provinces subject to their respective jurisdictions.

Rajah Rammohun Roy, whose information, talents, and judgment have secured the highest veneration for his name, and whose memory must for ever be connected with the progress of improvement in India, has thus described the causes of this remarkable revolution. At an early stage of civilisation, after the distinction of *casts* had been introduced among the inhabitants of Hindostan, the second class (the Kshatryas) were appointed to govern and defend the country. But, in consequence of the adoption of arbitrary measures, addiction to despotic practices, and abuse of primitive law, the other classes revolted against the tyranny, and, under the command of the celebrated Parasurama, the son of Jamadagni, and the grandson of Bhrigu, the promulgator of the Institutes of Menu, defeated the royalists in several battles, and put to death with signal cruelty almost all the males of the tribe. It was then resolved that the legislative authority should in future be confined to the first class, (the Brahmans,) who were, under no pretence, to take any share in the government of the State or the management of the revenues, while the second tribe (the Rajpoots) should exercise the executive authority. Under this system, India enjoyed peace, harmony, and good order, for many centuries. The sages of the sacred tribe, having no expectation or desire of holding public offices or possessing any political power, devoted themselves to literary and scientific pursuits, practised religious austerities, and lived in honorable poverty, safe from the agitations produced by the desire of riches and the intrigues and contests for power and ascendency. Freely associating with all the other tribes, they were able to understand the feelings and sentiments of the community, and to appreciate the justice of their complaints, and thereby to establish such laws as were required, and correct, as their labors proceeded, the abuses that had been created by the second tribe.

In token of the obligations generally felt to Parasurama, as the public benefactor and redeemer from political bondage, in having produced this auspicious change in the administration of the country, as well as of their veneration and regard for his character, the people nominated his grandfather, the sage Bhrigu, president of the supreme legislative assembly; and, according to that example, presidents were likewise appointed to all the other legislative assemblies, as they became established in the various parts of the land. We find it stated, accordingly, in Menu's Institutes, Chap. I. verse 60 :

"Bhrigu, great and wise, having thus been appointed by Menu to promulgate his laws, addressed all the rishis (sages) with an affectionate mind, saying, Hear!" The same practice is alluded to in the following passage: "Yagnyavalkya, grandson of Visvamitra (the sage), is described in the introduction of his own Institutes, as delivering his precepts to an audience of ancient philosophers, assembled in the province (legislative council) of Mithila. These Institutes have been arranged in three chapters, containing a thousand and twenty-three couplets. An excellent commentary, entitled Mitákshara, was composed by Vignyanesvara, a hermit, who cites other legislators in the progress of his work, and expounds their texts, as well as those of his author, thus composing a treatise which may supply the place of a regular digest."*

It is desirable to discover approximately the epoch of this great political revolution. But in making the attempt we must divest our minds of the fables and allegories of

---

* Colebrooke in Preface to Digest.—The following, according to Yagnyavalkya, are the names of twenty sages who have left works on legislation:—Menu; Atri; Vishnu; Harita; Yagnyavalkya; Ushana; Angira; Yama; Apastamba; Samvarta; Katyayana; Vrihaspati; Parasara; Vyasa; Sankha and Likhita, (these were brothers who each wrote one Smriti, and a third jointly, the three compositions being since regarded as but one work); Daksha; Gautama; Satatapa; and Vasisht'ha. Parasara also enumerates twenty legislators, but substitutes the names of Kasyapa, Bhrigu, and Prakheta, for those of Samvarta, Vrihaspati, and Vyasa. In the Padmá Purana the following names are given to complete the number of 36 legislators:—Marikhi; Pulastya; Prakheta; Bhrigu; Narada; Kasyapa; Visvamitra, of the Rajpoot tribe, whose devotions elevated him to the rank of a Brahman; Devala; Rishyasringa; Gargya; Baudhayana; Paithinasi; Jabali; Sumantu; Paraskara; Lokakshi; and Kuthumi. Of these some are cited in digests and compilations as authorities, but the names of others rarely occur in any compilation of law. Portions of their works are extant, but the greater part has probably been destroyed by the ravages of time. Nor is it easy to trace the times and places where their respective legislative assemblies were held, or ascertain the persons who presided over them respectively.

mythological writers.* We are happy to find that some vestiges have been left for our guidance. It has been observed that this revolution took place under the direction of Parasurama. Having effected the radical change in the constitution of the country, by which the legislative power was separated from the executive authority, that celebrated personage retired at an advanced age for devotion to a mountain called Mohendra, according to Sanscrit writers, in the vicinity of Cape Kumarika (Comorin,) where he established an era of his own to perpetuate, it is probable, the memory of the events of his life. As stated by Mr. James Prinsep, that era is yet used in that part of the Peninsula of India, (known among the natives under the name of Malayala,) extending from Mangalore, through the provinces of Malabar, Cotiote, and Travancore, to Cape Comorin. The era derived its name from him, and commences from 1176 B. C., and is reckoned in cycles of 1000 years. The year is solar or rather sidereal, and commences when the sun enters the sign Kanya

* The Pentateuch is believed to have been written about the close of the 15th century B. C. But its antiquity has not been examined with the rigour of criticism to which the Indian chronology has been subjected. Modern German theologians deny that it was written by Moses; and an English bishop and mathematician has published his grounds for asserting that its narratives "cannot be regarded as *historically true*," and rest on no other foundation than "ancient legends." The obloquy which the author has met with shows the prepossessions of the English, in behalf of the early objects of their veneration, to be too strong to permit a candid examination of their pretensions to remote antiquity.

Sir William Jones is very erroneously supposed to have been disposed to assert the superior age of the Hindoo sacred writings. He avowed himself "attached to no system, and as much disposed to reject the Mosaic history if it be proved erroneous, as to believe it if it be confirmed by sound reasoning from indubitable evidence." On the other hand, he declared that we could not "hope for a system of Indian chronology, to which no objection can be made, unless the astronomical books in *Sanscrit* shall clearly ascertain the places of the colures in some precise year of the historical age, by such evidence as our own astronomers and scholars shall allow to be unexceptionable." Evidence of the very kind he indicated was soon after found, as is stated in a subsequent place.

(Virgo,) answering to the solar month Asvina. There is also evidence that Bhrigu, who promulgated the laws of Menu, flourished about 1176 B. C.

It is observed by Sir William Jones in his Preface to the Institutes of Menu: "From a text of Parasara, discovered by Mr. Davis, it appears that the position of the vernal equinox had gone back from the tenth degree of Bharani to the first of Asvini, or twenty-three degrees and twenty minutes, between the days of that Indian philosopher, and the year of Christ 499, when it coincided with the origin of the Hindoo ecliptic; so that Parasara probably flourished near the close of the twelfth century before Christ. Now Parasara was the grandson of another sage, named Vasisht'ha, who is often mentioned in the laws of Menu, and once as contemporary with the divine Bhrigu himself," who promulgated the Institutes of Menu. This was the conclusion which Sir William Jones arrived at in 1790, and which was expressed in a paper in the Asiatic Researches, as well as in his translation of the Institutes of Menu published in 1794. It was since stated by Major Wilford, in the same Transactions, that "Mr. Davis, having considered the subject with the minutest attention, authorised him to say that the observation [of the place of the colures, referred to above] must have been made 1391 years before the Christian era," or about the close of the fourteenth century before Christ. Major Wilford added that the fact was "confirmed" by a passage from the same author, regarding "the *udaya*, or heliacal rising of Canopus."

On the principle laid down by Sir William Jones, that "the *Vedas* must have been written about 300 years before the Institutes of Menu," it will follow that the date of the latter is near the close of the 11th century before Christ.

Mr. Colebrooke, in 1801, alluding to a text of the Veda, which mentions the months in which the seasons occur, observes that "it may serve to prove that the Veda, from which it is extracted, (Apastamba's copy of the *Yajur-veda*, usually denominated the white Yajush,) cannot be much older than the observation of the colures recorded by Parasara, (see As. Res. vol. II. 268, 393,) which must have been made nearly 1391 years before the Christian era, (As. Res. vol. V. 288.)" The opinion is confirmed in a paper in the Asiatic Researches, (vol. VII. 283,) published by him in the ensuing year.

From references to the place of the colures contained in a hymn in the *At'harvana-Veda*, and a passage in one of the astronomical treatises which are annexed to the Vedas, it appears that the Hindoo calendar must have been regulated and consequently that Veda compiled, in the fourteenth century before Christ, as already stated on the authority of Mr. Davis's calculations.*

* It is remarkable that Mr. Mill, who alludes with apparent approbation to "the contempt with which judicious historians now treat the historical fables of early society," should nowhere have referred to these proofs, by which the early age of the *Vedas* is incontrovertibly established, and the determination of which contributes to the ascertainment of the age of Menu's Institutes. Attention to this point was peculiarly required from him. As he considered it "very evident that the institutions, described in the ancient books, are the model upon which the present frame of Hindoo society has been formed," it would have been a great point to determine, even upon probable grounds, the periods when the two works held in most reverence in India were penned. The investigations which we have briefly described place the matter beyond the reach of a doubt. They have, however, been unaccountably overlooked or misrepresented by several writers, who have professed to treat on the point.

Dr. Wilson, who opposed the conclusions of Mill regarding Hindoo institutions and manners, has left the evidence unnoticed.

Mr. James Prinsep has given a confused account of these researches, in saying, in his Useful Tables: "The situation of the equinoctial colure, in the time of the astronomer Parasara, is fixed by Davis in 1391 B. C.; by Sir William Jones, Colebrooke, and Bentley, in 1180; which latter closely accords with the epoch of the cycle of Parasurama, used in the Dakhan, and apparently unknown to these authors, B. C. 1176." Colebrooke, as we have seen, adopts and corroborates Davis's determination of the era of Parasurama.

On the foregoing grounds it is established, with all possible correctness, that this great revolution happened about the end of the twelfth century B. C., and that the legislative assemblies of Bhrigu, Yagnyavalkya, and other

Bentley should not have been named with them, for he has merely alluded to Davis's calculations, while the "great uncertainty and incongruity in many of his determinations of the dates of native princes and books," properly noticed, render his opinion in such matters quite unimportant. The remark, that the date (1180 B. C.) mentioned by Sir William Jones, closely accords with the epoch of the cycle of Parasurama (1176 B. C.) seems to imply that it rests on better grounds than the earlier one (1391 B. C.) But Mr. Prinsep has overlooked some important considerations. The revolution effected by Parasurama must have been twenty years previous to the commencement of his cycle. The *Vedas* must be assumed to have been promulgated and accepted as a divine dispensation some centuries anterior to the abuses committed by the Kshatrya sovereigns, in violation of its institutions, which led to that revolution. The era of those scriptures (in one of which Parasara's astronomical treatise is included) cannot, under these circumstances, be held to be too high by being fixed at the period (1391 B. C.) determined by Jones, Davis, and Colebrooke. In fact that date is to be considered as, properly speaking, the period in which the whole of the various portions of the *Vedas* were arranged by Vyasa in the form in which they appear. It is the publication of the Institutes of Menu that should be regarded as coeval with the origin of the cycle of Parasurama, became subsequent to the revolution which he effected.

Mr. Mountstuart Elphinstone, in his History of India, refers to Mr. Colebrooke as the person who incontrovertibly fixed the date of the *Vedas*. The point was, however, as shown above, first determined by the researches of Mr. Davis, from a reference to the position of the colures given in *two* Hindoo astronomical works. The conclusion from it announced by Sir William Jones was that the *Yajur-Veda* had been composed about 1181 B. C.; but Mr. Davis himself afterwards probably upon more careful examination, expressed an opinion that the work, in which the observation is to be found, must have been written not later than 1391 B. C. It is singular that the historian, though he has cited the two volumes of the Asiatic Researches (vols. II. and V.) in which those dates are laid down, should have failed to give credit to the authors who had preceded Mr. Colebrooke, particularly, as the latter, when demonstrating the same fact from the references in the *Atharvana-Veda* to the position of the colures, assumed the correctness of Mr. Davis's calculations. In doing justice to Sir William Jones and Mr. Davis, without overlooking the merit of Mr. Colebrooke's independent investigation in which the former, had he then been alive, would doubtless have acquiesced, by which he has confirmed the conclusions which his predecessors had arrived at upon distinct grounds, we should not omit to notice that Mr. Elphinstone is wrong in saying that Jones "supposed the *Yajur-Veda* to have been written in 1580 B. C.," as the latter merely took that to be "the highest age" which could be claimed for the work, and regarded the close of the 12th century before Christ as "the more probable of the two."

sages, assembled in different parts of the country at or near that time. The people of India have been so long accustomed to despotic government and profligate misrule, both under native and foreign princes, that they have subsided into apathy on political subjects, and regard the fate of dynasties and change of conquerors with equal indifference. It is, however, a matter of gratification to the minds of the Hindoos, even of the present generation, that, at so remote a period, their compatriots understood and asserted their political rights, and, though it cost the lives of many of the ancestors of the Brahmans and other races, caused the *separation* of the legislative and executive functions—a practice most judiciously adhered to in our days.

Taking the lowest dates, determined by the researches of Jones, Davis, and Colebrooke, as the era of the *Vedas*, and assuming the *Institutes* of Menu to be, if not of almost coeval date, 300 or even 600 years later, we find that the legislative assemblies, spoken of, promulgated their decrees at a period anterior to the establishment of every system of laws, the Mosaic perhaps excepted, of which any remains are extant.* Those decrees, still in force, with inconsiderable modifications, over one of the most extensive and remarkable divisions of the world, preceded, by nearly two centuries, the building of Rome and the

* We have seen that Sir William Jones, on a comparison of the style of the two works, considers the *Institutes* of Menu to be of a date posterior to the *Vedas*, that is, the close of the 11th century before Christ. Mr. Mountstuart Elphinstone is not satisfied with the *reasoning* on which this conclusion rests, "because there is no ground for believing that all languages proceed at the same uniform rate in the progress of refinement." In expressing this opinion he forgot that such reasoning is commonly adopted, for, in the absence of data, we have no other guide than analogy. But his own determination of the point, "very loosely," as he admits, must be still less satisfactory, as the ground on which it rests, "the difference between the law and manners there recorded and those of modern times," is altogether vague

enactment of the laws of Sparta by Lycurgus, and by three centuries the revision of those of Athens by Solon.

The Hindoo laws may advantageously be compared not only with the Mosaic laws, which are reputed to have been promulgated a few centuries previously, and still command the veneration of the race to whose forefathers they were delivered, but also with the fragments, that have been preserved by antiquarians, of the laws framed by Solon, on previous models and after observation of the systems of other countries. They do not, however, admit of a fair comparison with either the institutions of republican Rome or the more celebrated

---

and uncertain, and less capable of accurate appreciation. He would make the author of the Code to have lived about 900 B. C. But, in fact, there is no reason why his era should not be placed but a century later than that of the *Vedas*, that is, the 13th century before the Christian. "Revered by the Hindoos as the first of legislators," and placed on a footing with the Vedas by Vyasa, the son of Parasara, the author of a law tract as well as of the astronomical treatise annexed to the *Yajur-Veda*, Menu may have been a contemporary of the former at least, if not of the latter.

Mr. Morley states, in his account of the Hindoo law, (Introduction to his Digest of Reports of Indian Cases, published in 1850,) that "the arguments of Sir William Jones, who endeavoured to fix the date of the actual text [of Menu] at about the year 1280 before Christ, are almost as *inconclusive* as the traditions of the Brahmans; and the various epochs fixed by different authors seem to leave the question still undetermined. "It is manifest that he had taken as little trouble as the other authors to ascertain the facts, by reference to the proper sources of information. His account of the Hindoo law is chiefly derived from Mr. Colebrooke's writings. Hence, his silence on the results of that gentleman's investigations on the subject, (confirmatory of the previous researches of Jones and Davis,) is rather remarkable, especially since Elphinstone had summarised them as *conclusive* evidence, in his History of India, published in 1841, to which he himself has referred for its author's opinion. He is palpably guilty of carelessness in implying that Sir Graves Haughton has made a translation of Menu, and something worse in declaring that that imaginary version varies from Jones's "but slightly and no where importantly!" What the professor, did, he has thus stated: "the version of the learned translator has been carefully revised (reviewed?) and compared (with the original?); and as variations, though of trifling importance, have been discovered, they have been carefully recorded at the end of the work." He has *suggested* an improved rendering of a few passages, and offered some observations on points that seemed to require explanation, the perusal of which induces a regret that he did not attempt an independent version of the Institutes.

institutions of the empire. The laws of the Twelve Tables which absorbed or superseded the royal laws, were, notwithstanding their being eulogised as "the rule of right" and "the fountain of justice," gradually supplanted by the decrees of the senate and the annual edicts of the prætor. The uncertainty of the law was to some extent removed when, "instead of the Twelve Tables, the perpetual edict was fixed as the invariable standard of civil jurisprudence."* That *standard* had no greater permanence than the pre-existing systems. "During four centuries, from Hadrian to Justinian, the public and private jurisprudence was moulded by the will of the sovereign; and few institutions, either human or divine, were permitted to stand on their former bases." Three codes were successively composed by private lawyers and imperial command. The legal profession was a source of reputation and emolument; and the most eminent minds devoted themselves to the cultivation of law, and, by their labours, silently improved the institutions of their country, though, at the same time, by the variety and conflict of their opinions, they rendered a knowledge of the law a task of infinite difficulty. The Code, which was prepared by order of Justinian, was a compilation from the labours of preceding lawyers, not "a pure and original system of jurisprudence," like the Institutes of Menu. "The science of the laws is the slow growth of time and experience; and the advantage both of method and materials is naturally assumed by the most recent authors." But the Code which Justinian honoured with his name was so unsatisfactory, even to himself, as to be revoked within six years after its promulgation, and replaced with "a new and more accurate edition of the same work, which he enriched with two hundred of his own laws and

---

* The passages quoted in this and the following pages are from Gibbon.

fifty decisions of the darkest and most intricate points of jurisprudence." As the Code included but a small part of the Roman laws which guided the judgments of the courts, "a more arduous operation was still behind—to extract the spirit of jurisprudence from the decisions and conjectures, the questions and disputes, of the Roman civilians." The Digest, or Pandects, which embodied, in fifty books, with little order, the *dicta* of the lawyers; the Institutes, founded on those of Gaius, designed to form a manual for students; and the Novels, successively issued, completed the body of laws, which have shed a celebrity on the name of the emperor, unmerited either by his judicial labours or his political acts.*

The facts thus recapitulated indicate the wide disparity to be expected between the Hindoo laws, the production of nearly one and that a most remote period, and the Roman jurisprudence, the result of the labours of legislators and the most eminent lawyers, extending through a period of 1300 years, repeatedly recast after the experience of long intervals of time, and embracing the laws promulgated

* So little of the spirit of a legislator did this prince possess, that he is charged with venality, in making incessant and for the most part trifling alterations in the laws, and with "fraud and forgery," in inscribing with the venerable names of republican lawyers "the words and ideas of his servile reign," while the folly and iniquity of "denouncing the punishment of forgery" against those who should "presume to interpret or pervert the will of their sovereign," are apparent. The haste with which his patchwork legislation was produced, prevented the fusion of the heterogenous and incongruous materials into a harmonious system, as is evident from "the antinomies, or contradictions of the Code and Pandects."

"A prince, who sold without shame his judgment and his laws," by framing, in favour of certain churches, "a retrospective edict" to annul "established prescription," whether he was guilty of venality or bigotry, uxoriousness or favoritism, certainly acted in a manner "unworthy of a legislator and a man." Nor is his character redeemed from infamy because "an edict, so pregnant with injustice and disorder, was prudently abolished in the same reign" after it had served an "occasional purpose."

by the legislature as well as the decisions of judges and jurisconsults. Notwithstanding all the advantages on the side of the Roman system, it is equally exposed to the censure pronounced on the code of Menu, by the historian of British India, "that it is not easy to conceive a more rude and defective attempt at the classification of laws, than what is *there* presented." When Mill says that "the distinction of persons and things" is "the groundwork of the arrangement bestowed upon the Roman laws," he forgot that that division of subjects is peculiar to the Institutes of Justinian, deriving that advantage from its having been moulded on those of Gaius, and that it does not obtain either in the Codex or the Pandects, to which, therefore, the condemnation he pronounces against the Hindoo lawgiver, that "even this imperfect attempt at a rational division was far above the Hindoos," is quite as applicable. Moreover, it is not less true of the two compilations last named than of Menu's Institutes, that "in the order in which the titles follow one another, no principle of arrangement can be traced." In condemning the Institutes of Menu for want of classification, he has in reality condemned "the repositories of the Roman jurisprudence, which, (as observed by Stephens, the latest systematical writer on English law,) with the exception of the Institutes, are notoriously defective or confused in their arrangement." Such a defect is unpardonable in the compilers of those works, who might have better profited by the exemplars they had in previous codes, but is quite venial in a metrical work of the peculiar character of Menu's Institutes.

It may here be remarked that the speculations of the learned, about the ancient state of India, will be subject to much error and uncertainty if the account of the great political revolution above alluded to, be not borne in mind. The historian of British India, noticing the fact that, though the kingly power devolved on Kshatryas, and that, as such, they were the judges but could not exercise the judicial office without the aid of Brahmans, concludes that "the king is so far from possessing the judicial power, that he is rather the executive officer by whom the decisions of the Brahmans are carried into effect." He adds: "The uncontrollable sway of superstition, in rude and ignorant times, confers upon its ministers such extraordinary privileges that the king and the priest are generally the same person; and it appears somewhat remarkable that the Brahmans, who usurped among their countrymen so much distinction and authority, did not invest themselves with the splendour of royalty." Of this problem the author affords this solution—that the love of repose induced the Brahmans to part with the most laborious portion of their duties; but he at the same time owns that the anomaly remarked may have been caused by "accidental circumstances, of which little account was taken at the time, and which after a lapse of ages it is impossible to trace." On this the annotator on the historian makes the comment: "This is not a very liberal interpretation of the motives of the Brahmans, nor is it, in all probability, the correct one. We are too ignorant of the circumstances under which the system originated, to speculate upon the motives or purposes of those with whom it commenced. Apparently, however, it was contrived by a religious confederation, as the scheme best adapted to introduce order amongst semi-civilised tribes, and with no view to their own advantage or aggrandisement, or enjoyment of indolent ease." It is singular that Dr. Wilson, who had noticed in his note in a preceding page of Mill's History, that the Brahmans, "in early times, undertook to depose princes for tyranny and impiety," the accounts of which he styles "the legends of Vena, Parasurama, and

Devapi," and declared, in a contemporaneous work, (Preface to the Vishnu Purana,) that he found it "difficult to regard these legends as wholly unsubstantial fictions, or devoid of all resemblance to the realities of the past," should not have perceived that the true solution of the problem is to be found in the historical truth of the revolution declared to have been effected by Parasurama.* Such, however, was decidedly the view taken by Mr. Colebrooke, when he stated that, "since the memorable massacre of the Kshatryas, by Parasurama, the Kshatryas describe themselves from the same *gotras* as the Brahmans," (As. Res. Vol. IV. 206,) and no Anglo-Oriental can be named as higher authority on Hindoo antiquities.

The reform effected could not be rendered permanent. Though the making of laws was reserved to a separate class from the rulers, and the power of judicature was united with that of legislation, yet the kingly dignity could not thereby be "reduced to that of a dependent and secondary office." As the historian has remarked: "The Hindoo king, by commanding both the force and the revenue of the State, had in his hands the distribution of gifts and favours, the potent instrument, in short, of patronage; and the jealousy and rivalship of the different sets of competitors would, of their own accord, give him a great influence over the Brahmans themselves. The distribution of gifts and favours is an engine of so much power that the man who enjoys it to a certain extent is absolute, with whatever checks he may appear to be surrounded." Such was the case in this country.

* "The early history of most ancient states (as Heeren observes) is principally founded on traditions, which, however, colored or embellished by poets and rhetoricians, cannot be passed over in silence. That they contained truths as well as poetic fictions, is proved most evidently by the political institutions of which they narrate the origin."

After the expiration of several centuries, an absolute form of government again gradually prevailed. The first class, among whom were the descendants of the sages, having been induced to accept employments in civil and political departments, became entirely dependent on the second (the Rajpoots), and possessed so little consequence or independence, that they were obliged to explain away the laws enacted by their forefathers and to propound new rules according to the dictates of the reigning princes.* They became in fact merely the mouth-pieces of their rulers, and but nominal legislators; and the whole power, whether legislative or executive, was virtually exercised by the Rajpoot kings. Under these circumstances originated the division of the various schools of law, which prevailed for nearly a thousand years, till the Mahomedans from Ghazni and Ghor invaded the country, and, finding it divided among hundreds of petty princes, detested by their own subjects conquered them all successively, and introduced a despotic system of government, destroying the temples, the universities, and the other sacred and literary establishments of the Hindoos. To this change must be ascribed the decline of the arts and sciences, and the subversion of that ancient and remarkable state of civilisation, which existed among the Hindoos, at a time when the greater part of the known world was buried in comparative ignorance. The whole empire, with the exception of some few provinces, has since fallen under the dominion of Great Britain. Some advantages have already been derived from the prudent management of its latest rulers and administrators, based upon sound prin-

* In a similar case, Gibbon observed that, when "the institutions of the Arabian desert are ill-adapted to the wealth and numbers of Ispahan or Constantinople, the cazi respectfully places on his head the holy volume, and substitutes a dexterous interpretation, more opposite to the principles of equity and the manners and policy of the times."

ciples, from whose general character a hope of future quiet and happiness is justly entertained. But unfortunately the people have not yet arrived at that degree of advancement, adequate to their taking a share in the government of the country ; and the officers generally appointed are of foreign descent, and commence their career extremely young and consequently inexperienced, and at the same time unacquainted with the manners, habits, and customs of the people, who are composed of various tribes and races. To remedy this state of things, the British Government has recently introduced the system of appointing uncovenanted officers and trained lawyers to the highest posts in the judicial department. From their association with each other and with independent Native as well as European gentlemen, in the local Legislative Councils, and the necessary interchange of information on questions of jurisprudence and political and social economy, and on the wants of the country and the sentiments of the people, considerable improvement to all classes may be augured.

Having noticed the fact of legislative power having been vested in the sages, it is necessary to observe that those holy men, from their peculiar situation and the reverence they had for the sacred writings, rather assumed the character of the expounders and compilers of doctrines, established in the revealed religion of the Hindoos, than that of independent legislators and framers of original treatises. And since the Hindoos generally acknowledge the Vedas as of sacred authority, derived immediately from revelation, it follows that the propounders of the doctrines they set forth, have ever been held by the people in the highest veneration, and their expositions received as incontestable. Thus we find in a text translated by Sir William Jones according to the gloss of Sankara :—"God, having created the four classes, had not completed his work ; but in addition to it, lest the royal and military class should become insupportable through their power and ferocity, he produced the transcendent body of law ; since law is the king of kings, far more powerful and rigid than they ; nothing can be mightier than law, by whose aid, as by that of the highest monarch, even the weak may prevail over the strong." The motive ascribed for the revelation of law is most liberal and consistent with the opinions of modern jurists. It is to be hoped that such opinions will ever prevail among modern legislators. Instead of supporting power in the hands of the great, the law should even allow the "weak to prevail over the strong." The latter can in general take care of themselves without legislative aid. The former, naturally submissive and often trampled upon by the latter, require a helping hand for the preservation of life, liberty, and property.

The authoritative enactments of the primitive legislators have been, by the progress of time, subjected to a variety of comments, conformable to the special systems established in the different schools. This diversity of opinion among the commentators, together with the discrepancies in their interpretations, designed to meet the requisitions of the princes under whom they were indited,or suit the circumstances of the country at the time, accounts for the institution of the various schools. It is evident that the same passages of law have merely been modified, by peculiar constructions, to accommodate them to the features of the particular school in support of which they are adduced, just as the Koran and the Bible, though each is the same in substance among all professors of the respective creeds, have been variously interpreted to harmonise with the peculiarities of sectarianism.

On the subject of Hindoo law, there is (appended to Strange's Elements of Hindoo Law, vol. I.) an excellent paper, by that distinguished oriental scholar, Mr. Colebrooke, which may here advantageously obtain a place.

"The laws of the Hindoos, civil and religious, are by them believed to be alike founded on revelation, a portion of which has been preserved in the very words revealed, and constitutes the Vedas, esteemed by them as sacred writ. Another portion has been preserved by inspired writers, who had revelation present to their memory, and who have recorded holy precepts, for which a divine sanction is to be presumed. This is termed Smriti, recollection, (remembered law,) in contradistinction to Sruti, tradition, (revealed law.)

"The Vedas concern chiefly religion, and contain few passages directly applicable to jurisprudence. The law, civil and criminal, is to be found in the Smriti, otherwise termed Dharma Shastra, including duty, or means of moral merit. So much of this, as relates to religious observances, may be classed together with ancient and modern rituals, (bearing the designation of kalpa or paddhati,) as a separate branch; and forensic law is more particularly understood when the Dharma Shastra is treated of.

"That law is to be sought primarily in the institutes, or collections (sanhitas) attributed to holy sages; the true authors, whoever these were, having affixed to their compositions the names of sacred personages, such as Menu, Yagnyavalkya, Vishnu, Parasara, Gautama, &c. They are implicitly received by Hindoos as authentic works of those personages. Their number is great: the sages reputed to be the authors, being numerous—according to one list eighteen;

according to another twice as many; according to a third, many more—and several works being ascribed to the same author, his greater or less institutes, (Vrihat or Laghu,) or a later work of the author, when old, (Vriddha.)

"The written law, whether it be Sruti or Smriti, direct revelation or traditional, is subject to the same rules of interpretation. Those rules are collected in the Mimansa, which is a disquisition on proof and authority of precepts. It is considered as a branch of philosophy, and is properly the logic of the law.

"In the eastern part of India, *viz.*, Bengal and Behar, where the Vedas are less read and the Mimansa less studied than in the south, the dialectic philosophy, or Nyaya, is more consulted, and is there relied on for rules of reasoning and interpretation upon questions of law, as well as upon metaphysical topics.

"Hence have arisen two principal sects or schools, which construing the same text variously, deduce upon some important points of law different inferences from the same maxims of law. They are sub-divided, by farther diversity of doctrine, into several more schools or sects of jurisprudence, which, having adopted for their chief guide a favourite author, have given currency to his doctrine in particular countries, or among distinct Hindoo nations; for the whole Hindoo people comprise divers tongues, and the manners and opinions prevalent among them differ not less than their language.

"The school of Benares, the prevailing one in middle India is chiefly governed by the authority of the Mitakshara of

Vignyanesvara,* a commentary on the institutes of Yagnyavalkya. It is implicitly followed in the city and province of Benares, so much so that the ordinary phraseology of references for law opinions of Pundits, from the native judges of courts established there, previous to the institution of Adawluts superintended by English judges and magistrates, required the Pundit, to whom the reference was addressed, 'to consult the Mitakshara,' and report the exposition of the law there found, applicable to the case propounded.

"A host of writers might be named, belonging to this school, who expound, illustrate, and define the Mitakshara's interpretation of the law. It may be sufficient to indicate, in this place, the Viramitrodaya of Mitra-Misra and the Vivadatandava and other works of Kamalakara. They do not, so far as is at present recollected, dissent upon any material question from their great master.

---

*" Vignyanesvara, often called Vignyána Yogi, the author of the *Mitakshara* is known to have been an ascetic, and belonged, as is affirmed, to an order of *Sannyásis*, said to have been founded by Sankara-Achárya. No further particulars concerning him have been preserved. A copy of his work has indeed been shown to me, in which, at its close, he is described as a contemporary of Vikramáditya. But the authority of this passage, which is wanting in other copies, is not sufficient to ground a belief of the antiquity of the book; especially as it cannot be well reconciled to the received opinion, above noticed, of the author's appertaining to a religious order founded by Sankara-Achárya, whose age cannot be carried further back at the utmost than a thousand years. The limit of the lowest recent date which can possibly be assigned to this work, may be more certainly fixed from the ascertained age of the commentary; the author of which composed likewise (as already observed) the *Madana-Parijata*, so named in honor of a prince called Madanapala, apparently the same who gives title to the *Madanavinoda*, dated in the fifteenth century of the *Sambat* era (1431 Sambat, answering to the year of Christ 1375). It may be inferred as probable, that the antiquity of the *Mitakshara* exceeds 500 and is short of 1000 years. If indeed Dhareswara, who is frequently cited in the *Mitakshara* as an author, be the same with the celebrated Rajah Bhoja, whose title may not improbably have been given to a work composed by his command, according to a practice which is by no means uncommon, the remoter limit will be reduced by more than a century; and the range of uncertainty as to the age of the *Mitakshara* will be contracted within narrower bounds."—*Colebrooke's Preface to the Two Treatises on the Hindoo Law of Inheritance.*

"The Mitakshara retains much authority likewise in the south and in the west of India. But to that are added, in the Peninsula, the Smriti Chandrika and other works bearing a similar title, (as Dattaka Chandrika, &c.,) compiled by Devanda Bhatta, together with the works of Madhava Acharya, and especially the commentary on Parasara, and likewise the writings of Nanda Pandita, including his Vaijayanti and Dattaka Mimansa, and also some writers of less note.

"In the west of India, and particularly among the Mahrattas, the greatest authority after the Mitakshara is Nilakant'ha, author of the Vyavahara Mayukha and of other treatises bearing a similar title.

"In the east of India, the Mitakshara, though not absolutely discarded, is of less authority, having given place to others, which are there preferably followed. In North Behar or Mithila, the writings of numerous authors, natives of that province, prevail; and their doctrine, sanctioned by the authority of the paramount Rajah of the country, is known as that of the Maithila school. The most conspicuous works are the Vivada Ratnakara, and other compilations under the superintendence of Chandesvara; the Vivada Chintamani, with other treatises, by Vachaspati Misra; and the Vivada Chandra, with a few more.

"To these are added, in Bengal, the works of Jimutavahana and those of Raghunandana, and several others, constituting a distinct code of law, which deviates on many questions from that of Mithila, and still more from those of Benares and the Dekhan or southern Peninsula."

Sir W. Macnaghten, another high authority on the subject of law and the different schools composing it, says in the preface to his Principles of Hindoo Law :—

"There may be said to exist, in the present day, five distinct schools of Hindoo law, which differ more or less from each other. They may be termed the schools of Bengal, of Benares, of Mithila, of the Dekhan, and of the Mahrattas. The original Smritis are, of course, common to all; but they each assign the preference to particular commentators and scholiasts. In Bengal, the works chiefly followed are, the Dyabhaga of Jimutavahana, the Dayatatwa by Raghunandana, the Vyavaharatatwa by the same author, the Subodhini, a commentary of the Dyabhaga, by Srikrishna Tarkalankara, the commentary on the same by Acharya Chintamani, the Dayakrâma Sangraha of Srikrishna, and the compilations termed the Vyavastharnava, the Vivadarnavasetu, and the Vivadabhangarnava. In Benares, the preference is shown to the Mitakshara of Vignyanesvara, and its commentary by Vireshvara Bhatta, and Balam Bhatta, the Viramitrodaya by Mitra Misra, the Parasura Madhava, and the Vyavahara Madhava. In Mithila, respect is paid chiefly to the following authorities; the Vivada Chintamani, and Vyavahara Chintamani by Vachaspati Misra, the Vivada Ratnakara by Chandesvara, the Madana Parijata by Madanapadhyaya, the Dwaitaparisishta by Keshaba Misra, the Smritisara and Smritisamukhaya by Harinathopadhyaya, and the Vivada Chandra by Misaru Misra. The Mitakshara, the Smriti Chandrika, the Madhavya, and the Sarasvati Vilasa are the works of paramount authority in the territories dependent on the government of Madras; while the authorities chiefly referred to on the Bombay side are (besides the text books of Menu and Yagnyavalkya) the Vyavahara Mayukha, the Nirnayasindhu, the Hemadri, the Vyavahara Kustubha, and the Parasura Madhava. I do not mean to affirm that these are the only works of paramount importance recognised in the respective schools; but they are most frequently referred to; they are sufficient to solve the ordinary legal questions which arise; and suspicion may justly be excited, where an exposition of law is supported by citations from more recondite authorities. In questions relating to the law of adoption, the Dattaka Mimansa and Dattaka Chandrika are equally respected all over India; and where they differ, the doctrine of the latter is adhered to in Bengal and by the southern jurists, while the former is held to be the infallible guide in the provinces of Mithila and Benares."

The foregoing extracts from the writings of the eminent orientalists, Mr. Colebrooke and Sir W. Macnaghten, indicate that the Vivada Chintamani by Vachaspati Misra is a work of paramount authority in the province of Mithila or Behar. (A map of ancient Mithila is annexed for ready reference). But no translation of it having hitherto been published, the work now presented to the public is intended to supply the desideratum. Although our author in several points coincides with the writer of the Mitakshara, yet it is a matter of regret that, while Bengal has enjoyed an English version of an original treatise, the Dayabhaga; the western school, of the Mitakshara; and the Mahratta School (the Bombay Presidency) of the Vyavahara Mayukha; the Mithila or Behar province, (though known to have had in primitive times an independent legislative assembly under Yagnyavalkya,) has not been supplied with an English version of any original treatise, such as the Vivada Ratnakara, the Vivada Chintamani, and other works. We give the preference to the Vivada Chintamani over the Vivada Ratnakara, because the latter is the older work and its doctrine is followed in the former. Hence, by translating the Vivada Chintamani we got the essence of the Vivada Ratnakara.

The author of the Vivada Chintamani, having, in his introduction, particularly referred to the Ratnakara as one of the authorities consulted by him, has thereby enabled us to fix approximately the date of his work. The Ratnakara was compiled under the superintendence of Chandesvara, minister of Harasinha Deb, the king of Mithila, who was compelled by the Patan sovereign of Delhi to abandon his capital and take refuge in the Hills. When Simroun was destroyed by Tuglik Shah, in the year of Christ 1323, Harasinha Deb became its Rajah. The work of Vachaspati Misra must therefore have been compiled about a hundred years subsequent to that period, (say in the year of Christ 1423,) since he mentions the name of the Ratnakara in the introduction to it, and no Sanscrit writer ever thinks of quoting as an authority any work that has not passed the test of three generations. The author of the Dayabhaga, which is held to have been written in the beginning of the fifteenth century, boldly and freely controverts certain doctrines of Vachaspati Misra as those of a contemporary writer. Mr. Colebrooke, writing, in 1796, of the era of the *Vivada Chintamani* of Vachaspati Misra, observes that "no more than ten or twelve generations have passed since he flourished at Semaul in Tirhoot." It has been judicially determined (and it is in fact the general opinion) that in India 100 years would include the lives of three generations, which makes thirty-three years the average duration of Indian life or a generation. At this rate, the period of ten or twelve generations will amount to 400 years, which coincides with the era of this work, as we have on other grounds determined it.

The author of the Vivada Chintamani, following the authority of Menu, has divided his work into eighteen chapters, several of which are subdivided into sections. It is not necessary to state their titles in this place. But by referring to the table of contents for the principal heads, and to the work itself, it will be found that almost every subject connected with the dealings and transactions between man and man has been treated of. The legislation of a country progressing in civilisation can never be permanently fixed. The chief object of legislation is to meet the wants and necessities of the people. As their requirements increase, additional legislation becomes necessary, as is evident from the fact that when Menu divided his work, he found that eighteen heads were sufficient for the purpose, but the author of the Vivada Chintamani, who based his work on the original authority of Menu, has increased the sub-divisions to forty-five, to meet the existing wants of his day.

This work not only follows the arrangement of subjects found in the Institutes, but is as little methodical as the latter. The charge of defective classification of laws, brought by the historian of British India, is thus met by Dr. Wilson: "Confessedly the laws of Menu were intended for an early stage of society, when it is more important to devise than to classify. Classification is the business of high refinement, and then, according to our author's own showing, is never very successfully performed. As observed by a competent writer on this subject, (in the Asiatic Journal,) commenting on Mr. Mills' survey of Hindoo law: 'The most refined and enlightened countries in Europe partake with Hindostan in this symptom of barbarism. In England, till the appearance of Wood's Institutes, or Blackstone's Commentaries, the law lay over a mass of authorities, from which its principles were to be extracted by the practitioner as well as they could be. Yet who would have objected to England in the middle of the eighteenth century, that she had not arrived at an advanced state of civilisation, because her jurisprudence was dispersed and unmethodised?' By this test the attempt to classify would place the Hindoos higher in civilisation than the English. That the later writers on Hindoo law have not improved upon the method of Menu, is to be explained by the sanctity of the primitive code : it would have been irreverent to have disarranged the scheme there laid down, had it occurred to them as possible or advantageous to alter the classification." Here one erroneous principle is answered by another. A code of laws, such as that of Menu professes to be, cannot be compared with the laws of any country, that are known to be enacted from time to time. It can only be properly compared to another code. Now, if we compare it with the far celebrated work of Justinian, formed on the model of other pre-existing codes, we find no classification deserving of much praise, nor can any valid objection be made to the censure pronounced by Gibbon : "Among the various combinations of ideas, it is difficult to assign any reasonable preference ; but as the *order* of Justinian is different in his three works, it is possible that all may be wrong, and it is certain that two cannot be right."

We submit this translation of an original treatise, with much diffidence, and not without a solicitation of the learned readers' indulgence for the imperfections or errors which they may discover. Our purpose, in giving the world an English version of a Sanscrit treatise, is not to confine it to the perusal of those who are by birth strangers to the laws and institutes. We intend it also for the Anglo-Indian literati in general, who, being familiar with both languages and drinking deeply at the "living well" of its original language the Sanscrit, will be able to do justice to our labors. We have undertaken this translation for the benefit of the Mithila or

Behar Province. The judicial officers of that province, although it has some works of its own, have hitherto been content to refer solely to the Mitakshara. That production, being a commentary on the Institutes of Yagnyavalkya, who, as we have seen, (page vii.) was the first president of the legislative council of Mithila, was naturally held in high estimation by the jurists of that province, as also because its doctrines, in many respects, coincide with those promulgated in digests of local authority. If the work now offered prove useful even in a few cases, the decision of which may involve nice distinctions of law, we shall be sufficiently rewarded by the conviction that we have assisted in the administration of justice at least in that small degree.

The rules of inheritance occupy a principal part of the work, and have been prominently distinguished. The other subjects treated of by our author possess, however, not less interest, for the observer of mankind, than questions regarding succession in our days, for those invested with judicial office. "The laws of a nation form the most instructive portion of its history." But they who would study the character of a nation from its laws, are liable to arrive at erroneous conclusions, unless they take a very comprehensive view of the subject. This Mill, has attempted to do; but, from want of a thorough apprehension of the laws, and the character of the people, his conclusions are in some instances both absurd and unjust.

The circumstance which most strikes the observer of the Hindoo system of laws, and which has caused great scandal, is the division of the people into four tribes. An attentive consideration of the state of ancient society, in other parts of the world, will reconcile many seeming anomalies of that system, and prove that the same causes, which have been in transient operation in other countries, have permanently prevailed in this. Even the Anglo-Saxons, we are informed, were divided into four great classes, artificers and tradesmen, husbandmen, those who exercised the honorable profession of arms, and the clergy. "From the natural course of things it should seem that, in every country, where religion has had so much influence as to introduce a great body of ecclesiastics, the people, upon the first advance made in agriculture and in manufactures, are usually distributed into the same number of classes or orders. This distribution is accordingly to be found, not only in all the European nations, formed upon the ruins of the Roman Empire, but in other ages and in very distant parts of the globe. The ancient inhabitants of Egypt are said to have been divided into the clergy, the military people, the husbandmen, and the artificers. The establishment of the four great *casts*, in the country of Hindostan, is precisely of the same nature."* The people of Crete also were divided into classes, after the manner of the Egyptians, by the laws of Minos, whom, "represented under the emblem of the Minotaur," Sir William Jones seems willing to identify with "our MENU, with his divine Bull, and the MENUES of Egypt, with his companion and symbol *Apis*." Among the ancient Persians there were, according to the Zendavesta, four states, "that of the priest, that of the soldier, that of the husbandman, the source of riches, and that of the artisan or labourer." The institution was, indeed, of that early age, when, in the opinion of the eminent scholar just named, "the religion of the Brahmans, with whom we converse every day, prevailed in Persia." The professors of that faith held that "the first monarch of Iran, and of the whole earth, Mahabad, (a word apparently Sanscrit,) divided the people into

---

* Millar's Historical View of the English Government, quoted by Mill.

four orders, the *religious*, the *military*, the *commercial*, and the *servile*." The names assigned to them, it is added, were "unquestionably the same, in their origin, with those now applied to the four primary classes of Hindoos."

It is not the least remarkable that in Attica the people were divided by Cecrops into the four classes of priests, nobles, husbandmen, and artificers, and afterwards by Theseus into three, by the union of the sacerdotal class with that of the nobles. This alteration was made on the understanding, that the priests and archons and other magistrates should be elected out of the nobles, and that to these should belong the privilege of interpreting all laws, both civil and religious.

It was a general rule in ancient times that the offices of sovereign and pontiff should be more or less closely connected. The kings were originally the high priests of their nations, and personally offered sacrifices on solemn occasions. So we find the kings and heroes of Homer, though not denominated priests, performing sacrifices. In Egypt even a usurper needed to be consecrated to the priesthood, before commencing his reign. The two kings of Sparta, at their coronation, were consecrated priests, the one to the heavenly and the other to the national Jupiter. In many places the dignity of the priest was equal to that of the king. The religion of Rome was purely political; hence the chief priesthood appertained to the king, and was afterwards conferred on members of the patrician class, who engrossed to themselves, not only the priestly functions to the last age of the republic, but, until 366 B. C., all executive and judicial offices.

Such were the prevalent opinions of antiquity, here brought together to show that it is nothing remarkable that in India there should be distinct tribes. The Brahmans, as a class, were devoted to science and literature, which in the early ages were but the handmaids of religion, and were by birth and qualification eligible for priestly offices. Of the Kshatryas, the chiefs swayed the sceptre in times of peace, and led the forces when the country was to be defended from invasion, or when further acquisitions of territory were demanded, by increase of population or other political considerations. The Vaisyas were engaged originally in pasturage and agriculture, and in process of time in trade and the useful arts. The Sudras were to depend for subsistence on servitude and other laborious and menial occupations. The Brahmans, it should be carefully remembered, are not strictly speaking *priests*, though Sir William Jones has, in his translation of Menu, considered the two to be convertible terms. As observed by Dr. Wilson, "they conducted for themselves, and others of the next two castes, sacrifices, and occasionally great public ceremonials ; but they never, like the priests of other pagan nations, (or those of the Jews,) conducted public worship, worship for individuals indiscriminately, worship in temples, or offerings to idols. A Brâhman who *was employed to* make offerings to idols was held as degraded *(devala)* and unfit to be invited to religious feasts."

The *community* among the members of the first three classes is evident from their common privilege of studying the *Vedas* and the distinction of being *twice-born*. The low position of the Sudras, with the negation of such privilege and distinction, seems to indicate that they were not of the same race with the other classes, but the *aborigines* of the countries, into which the first three classes had *immigrated*, sections of whom had been reduced to subjection, while other sections, enjoying more or less civilisation, retained their independence and were under their own governments and laws. These facts are subversive of the theory of Dr. Wilson, that the Brahmanical religion was established by a colony of priests, "*perhaps* with a body of martial followers," or, as he says elsewhere, "contrived by a religious confederation, as the scheme best adapted to introduce order among semi-civilised tribes."* But they are quite consistent with the view of the original constitution of society in India, as composed of various classes, or rather the principal ones, and explain several features in the laws that cannot be accounted for on any other supposition.

I. The Brahmans are the highest in *rank* or rather estimation, but the *power* is vested in the Kshatryas. This could have proceeded from nothing but the actual circumstances under which the colonisation took place. The leaders would not have allowed themselves to be displaced by any rules devised by their religious guides; nor could these, owing to the paucity of their numbers and predilection for other pursuits, have undertaken to make new acquisitions of

* "A colony of priests, not in the restricted sense in which we use the term, but in that in which it still applies, in India, to an *agrah'ara*, or village, or hamlet, of Brahmans," &c.—"A society of this description, and perhaps with a body of martial followers, might have found a home in the *Brahmavartta* of Menu."—"Every thing in the Hindoo institutions indicates their originating not for political but religious principles."—Dr. Wilson even thinks that there are, in the *Vedas*, "allusions to the dangers undergone by some of the first teachers of Hindooism among the people whom they sought to civilise."—The professor has himself combated the notion of the Brahmans being in any sense *priests*. The supposition that a colony of priests, in command of a body of martial followers, would yield the supremacy to the latter, is self-contradictory. It is also certain that the Brahmans were in no sense *missionaries*, but a portion of a community who established themselves and their religion, like Mahomed, by the power of the sword.

territory or even protect the society from the attacks of aggressors. The chiefs of the second class are not only held up to view as gods among men, but are encouraged to attempt martial deeds, and foreign conquests, as the chief virtues of their position, by which their dominions were to be enlarged and the common advantage promoted.* Hence Menu recommends the "cordial union" of the two classes.

---

* Mill has remarked, without seeing the object and tendency of the policy: "Their very laws and religion encourage a spirit of restlessness and warfare. 'Fully performing all duties required by law, let a king seek to possess regions *yet unpossessed!*' This gives implicit encouragement to a spirit of conquest." Without making acquisitions the *immigrants* could not have obtained a settlement, in this part of the world, nor extended their empire and religion, and communicated the benefits of their superior policy and principles, to the utmost limits of the peninsula. He adds: "The gloss of Kulluka, the commentator, inserts the words *with justice*—a saving clause; but even then the practical effect of the law is but too visible." The commentator, it is evident, did not advert to the primitive period of Hindooism in India, but to the period in which that system had been fully established and when none but Hindoo kingdoms existed almost all over the country. On the other hand, Dr. Vincent observes: "It is confessed on all hands that Hindoo policy, both civil and religious, favours population, agriculture, and commerce." But, as it may be objected that "a tribe of military forms one part of the Hindoo system, and that war implies oppression," he refers to the Code of Laws as providing a remedy: "the produce of the field, the work of the artisan, the city without walls, and the defenceless village, are declared sacred and inviolable. Those only who used the sword were to perish by the sword." This is not a satisfactory explanation. The two seeming antagonistic principles are nevertheless easily reconciled. As *immigrants*, the professors of the *Vedas* desired the acquisition of territory. But they had no divine mission, such as the Hebrews are declared to have had, to exterminate the primeval inhabitants of the land, and deemed it an advantage to employ these, if in a low stage of civilisation, as ministers to their comfort. Nor did they desire the exclusive possession of the country. They even found it an advantage not to interfere with any aboriginal states, in which the arts of life had made sufficient advances to enable them to benefit the *immigrants*, and be ultimately benefited by imbibing the Brahmanical system. With such nations a conciliatory policy, and even mutual alliances, especially among the upper classes, would be most conducive to their object of final *annexation*. Thus the Romans, while they at once subjugated isolated and unallied states, entered into treaties with those who were too powerful to be overcome, till their ancient allies became separated from them. The principle of that people, which prompted them to spare the submissive and subdue the proud, is inculcated in Hindoo writings.

Mill remarks, from motives which are quite undisguised, that a "high and uncontrollable authority" is attributed to the monarch. But he forgot that, according to the laws of England, the king is "the vicar and minister of God on earth,"—"can do no wrong,"—is responsible to none for his acts, however oppressive,—but "the sovereign lord" and "the fountain of honour" of his subjects; while the subjects are bound to him by an intrinsic and indefeasible allegiance, not merely in his political capacity, but to his natural person and blood. The most ultra radical cannot deny that these are powers and distinctions far greater than Menu ever imagined. But with a rashness and inconsistency only to be equalled by that of recent writers, who echo his invectives against the Hindoo system, Mill asserts that the Brahmans, notwithstanding the apparent concession of *power* to the king, "secured to themselves a direct and no contemptible share of the immediate functions" of the executive, so that "the king was little more than an instrument in the hands of the Brahmans." He is however, immediately after, under the necessity of owning that "with this *inference* the *fact* does not correspond," and that the king's power over the army and the revenue was "sufficient to counterbalance the legislative and the judicative, and even a great part of the executive power, reinforced by all the authority of an overbearing superstition, lodged in the hands of the Brahmans."* A candid view of the law and an acquaintance with the manners of the people, reveal that the Hindoo government in any part of India was never tyrannical and oppressive, though despotic in theory. The king, as already shown, (page xxi.)

* Why should this author have laboriously constructed, solely to discredit the moderation of the Brahmans, with regard to secular power and influence, a theory of Hindoo government, which he is himself obliged to pronounce a baseless fabric?

was not above the law. He may occasionally commit excesses, (but they are not greater nor more numerous than those of which many kings of England were guilty,) yet he is far more controlled by the influence of religious feeling and public opinion, or rather by the deference habitually yielded to Brahmanical authority, than that of any, more strictly entitled to the description of constitutional or limited.

II. The Brahmans have the privilege of expounding the *Vedas*, but no more. This is attributed by Dr. Wilson, to a self-denying policy, but must rather have resulted from the circumstances of the case. "The whole tenor of the rules for the conduct of a Brahman is to exclude him from every thing like worldly enjoyment, from riches, and from temporal power. Neither did the Brahmans, like the priests of the Egyptians, keep to themselves a monopoly of spiritual knowledge. The Brahman alone, it is true, is to teach the *Vedas*, but the next two orders, the Kshatrya and Vaisya, are equally to study them, and were, therefore, equally well acquainted with the law and the religion." As the three classes were of the same stock, and spoke the same language, it was hardly possible to keep from them the knowledge of the sacred writings. On the other hand, the *aborigines*, without receiving instruction in the dialect of their conquerors, could not obtain that benefit. As stated in another place, the Kshatryas claimed to be derived from the same *gotra* or family with the Brahmans, (Menu expressly says "that the soldier originally proceeded from the Brahman,") and contended with them for the right of performing sacerdotal in addition to their military functions, or strictly speaking, in the language of Dr. Wilson, "for admission into the Brahmanical order." The Egyptian priests were obliged to devise a sacred *(hieratic)* alphabet, to conceal their theology from the knowledge of the profane vulgar, and also to initiate usurpers of royalty into the priesthood. Hence, the concession of the perusal of the *Vedas* to the other two classes was probably not optional.

III. To the same causes are undoubtedly traceable the different terms in which the Sudras are spoken of at times. Viewing the matter without the requisite discrimination, Mill pronounces the Sudra "an object of contempt and even of abhorrence, to the other classes of his countrymen." Even Elphinstone, after an examination of texts of Menu, and with the light he might have derived from a life-long residence in the peninsula, where he had seen a Holkar and a Sindhya on the throne, speaks of "the *degraded* state of a Sudra," and can only plead that his *condition* "was much better than that of the public slaves under some ancient republics," &c. This statement is coupled with an admission that "men of the first three classes were freely indulged in the choice of women (for wives) from any inferior *cast*," as it is made with a full knowledge of what Colebrooke had declared of the number of trades and professions open to the class. The opinion recorded by Dr. Wilson is the strangest of all. He remarks: "The law does not justify the term *abhorrence*. The condition of a Sudra, in the Hindoo system, was infinitely preferable to that of the Helot, the slave, and the serf, of the Greek, the Roman, and the feudal systems. He was independent; his services were optional: *these* were not agricultural, but domestic and personal, and claimed adequate compensation. He had the power of accumulating wealth, or *injunctions* against his so doing would have been superfluous." Dr. Wilson did not perceive that these injunctions must have been grating to the Sudra's feelings, as they proclaimed his degraded position, as much as those laws, that were in force in ancient states and are yet to be found among *quasi*-civilised nations, which declared the slave incapable of acquiring aught for himself. So far, the laws referred to indicate the Sudra to be of the class of the barbarous *aborigines*, whom the invaders, with the license claimed by all conquerors, had reduced to a condition only a few degrees better than slavery. The professor adds, that the Sudra "had the opportunity of rising to rank, for the Puranas record dynasties of Sudra kings, and even Menu mentions their existence." He failed to perceive that the *opportunity* must have been almost valueless, under the discouragements that stood in the way of the Sudras; that these dynasties must have had their origin at periods antecedent to the establishment of Hindooism in India, and were unconnected with Hindooism, since Brahmans were warned that they could not consistently reside in countries under such rule; and that there were independent nations, in a certain state of civilisation, who were termed Sudras, but with whose princely and noble families neither Brahman nor Kshatrya disdained matrimonial alliance, and who, consequently, when affiliated (so to speak) with Brahmanical communities, took rank with Kshatryas, and, like some Kshatryas of these times, claimed descent from other than Hindoo races.*

* This view of the characteristics of the first three classes, and of the Sudras, as distinguished into subjugated *aborigines* and the subjects of independent kingdoms of *aborigines*, may be compared with the present and accurate doctrine of the constitution of the patricians, their clients, and the plebeians, among the Romans. It is now acknowledged that the patricians, and their retainers, the clients, formed the original *people* of the republic, and, though socially distinct, shared the political power in different degrees. They who, by conquest or otherwise, became inhabitants of Rome and the surrounding territory, were not only separated from both classes by social laws, but specially distinguished from the former by being destitute of all political rights. On this view of things, it is intelligible that the clients, being attached to the patricians by the bonds of mutual interest, and, especially, by possessing a certain share of political power, should side with the aristocratic party in keeping down the plebeians, with whom they had no community of race or interest. The

The establishment of tribes implies that there should be no intermarriages among their members. The nobles among the Athenians jealously guarded the purity of their tribe: they not only accounted the progeny of mixed marriages as an inferior race, but are said, by the influence of Pericles, to have sold five thousand of such persons into slavery. In Rome the patricians not only arrogated the privilege of sitting in the senate and holding sacerdotal, magisterial, and judicial offices, but allowed no intermarriages with the plebeians, "who originally occupied a position little better than that of slaves."

---

plebeians, as newcomers, possessed only the right of occupying land and following other means of subsistence. But after they had acquired, under Servius Tullius, the privilege of the *suffrage*, they maintained a long struggle with the dominant party to be on an equality with them in all other respects. They acquired, immediately after the expulsion of the kings, the right of *appeal* from the decisions of the magistrates, and, about fifteen years later, that of appointing tribunes of their own, to interdict such acts of the senate as were prejudicial to their interests. It was not till fifty years after, that the law recognised *intermarriages* between the patricians and the plebeians. That critical event greatly aided the plebeians in being gradually declared equally eligible with the patricians, and ultimately even solely eligible for the office of consul.

When the social and political distinctions between the patricians and plebeians were levelled, the *clients* ceased to form a separate class. Even the term *plebs* lost its original signification, by being applied to the whole mass of persons of humble means and inferior station. The only distinction which remained was that of reckoning numerous ancestors, who had filled the most distinguished offices of the State.

The light thrown upon Roman history by the recognition of the true origin of the *plebs*, will be reflected on the state of ancient Hindoo society by distinguishing the two classes of persons confounded under the term *Sudras*. The subjugated *aborigines* are the class who are treated as a degraded race, whose highest ambition should be bounded by serving the *Brahmans*, who were within the pale of Hindooism, but not eligible to read the *Vedas* or receive more than elementary religious instruction, and intermarriage with whose class was consequently pollution. The *aboriginal* subjects of the kingdoms, with whom the Hindoo communities were sometimes at war and sometimes in alliance, are represented as professing no religion and opposing the practice of Hindoo rites, among whom Brahmans could not consistently reside, but with whom intermarriages were not uncommon, from policy on the part of the Kshatrya princes and chiefs, and for commercial or social advantages on the part of the Vaisyas. On the diffusion of Hindooism and the absorption of these Sudra kingdoms into Hindoo states, the whole of those of aboriginal race would come under

How probable then that, in India, where the sacerdotal class was, in theory, of a more sacred origin and therefore of peculiar sanctity, its members should be under certain restrictions as to intermarrying with those of lower origin! By the law the Brahman was specially directed to espouse a wife of the same class with himself. The duties of religion required this. The husband was one person with his wife, and performed religious rites together with her, and to her no sacrifice apart from him was allowed. The rule was, perhaps, neglected by some Brahmans, by taking wives only from the other

---

the general term *Sudra*, while the laws and practices, which refer to them as a degraded and servile race, could apply only to the subjugated barbarians and not to the other native tribes, who had attained a considerable degree of civilisation, and of whom many were in respectable and even opulent circumstances.

This view of the matter is confirmed by the references in the *Vedas* to "the *five classes* of men," explained by commentators to mean the four *casts* and the barbarian or *nishada*. The *dasyus* are in those writings constantly contradistinguished from the *aryas*. Dr. Wilson considers the former to signify "the indigenous *barbarian* races," "the uncivilised tribes of India, yet unsubdued by the followers of the *Vedas*, the *aryas*, the respectable and civilised race." It is, however, a gratuitous supposition that this fifth class were in any sense barbarous, except in that of difference of language, which is adverted to in the *Vedas* as marking difference of race, as the term *mlechcha* does in later times, and *barbarian* did in ancient Greece. The *dasyus* are represented as possessing *cities*, which, the professor admits, "indicates a people not wholly barbarous," but he qualifies the admission by adding that "the term may designate villages or hamlets," a supposition quite incompatible with the allusion to their "strong cities" and "hundred impregnable cities."

If we consult Menu, the best commentator we can have on the matter and language of the *Vedas*, we find (chap x.) that, besides the Brahman, the Kshatrya, the Vaisya, and the Sudra, there is not "a fifth pure class;" that the *nishada* are the offspring of the Brahman and the Sudra, and consequently one of the "mixed classes;" that the *vratya* and the *dasyus* are "outcasts of twice-born classes," and especially that "the twice-born classes, who become outcasts by neglecting their duties, are called *dasyus, or plunderers*, whether they speak the language of *mlechchas* or that of *aryas*." It would thus seem that the Sudras, though of aboriginal races, are according to the theory regarded as a pure tribe, perhaps also from being under the influence of Brahmanical doctrines, and that the fifth class was composed as well of the aboriginal races who had not been brought under that influence, and of course spoke their own languages, as of the pure and mixed tribes, who had renounced it, whether they spoke the language of the Hindoos, or that of the native races with whom they may have, from choice or necessity, associated themselves.

classes, even the lowest. Frequent mention is made in the *Vedas* of intermarriages between Brahmans and the daughters of Kshatrya princes. In one instance, a *rani* refuses her consent to her daughter's being united in marriage with a Brahman youth, whose distinguished appearance had won her husband's heart, on the ground of there being no precedent in their family of such union with one who had not acquired the superior dignity of *Rishi*. It is added that the Brahman resorted to the most orthodox methods of gaining that distinction, and, with it, the hand of his intended bride. There is also mention of kings bestowing their daughters by tens and fifties on individual Brahmans or *Rishis*, accompanied with ample gifts to the bridegrooms. Whether these are not, in the more remarkable instances, allegories, we need not attempt to decide. In fact, the *number* of the princesses, who are supposed to have remained unmarried till the appearance of the distinguished person, round whose neck they were garlanded in a single day, is a clear indication of the mythological character of the narrative. But, in any view of the matter, the legends speak very clearly of alliances, between the daughters of Rajpoot princes and eminent Brahmans, being, at first, sought as a peculiar distinction, and ultimately deemed a *sine quâ non*. The ground of such preference, on the part of the Kshatrya princes, was the peculiar rule of the Hindoo law, on the theory of the sacred origin of the four primitive *casts*, by which the offspring of *aniloma* marriages, *i. e.* of males of a superior *cast* with females of the next lower *cast*, held a rank below that of the father, but above that of the mother; while the offspring of a man of an inferior *cast*, begotten on a woman of a superior *cast*, was, by the rule of *biloma*, and the positive prohibition of such connections, degraded in proportion to the superiority of position of the female.

The intermarriages of Brahmans with Kshatrya females is thus accounted for. It is even recorded in the *Vedas* that the offspring of such marriages ranked as Brahmans, which must be accepted as an evidence of the *exceptional* instances, to be met with in the *unsettled times* of every institution. Analogy renders it probable that the Sudras, with whom the Brahmans occasionally intermarried, were not of the degraded class whom the nation held in subjection, but persons of the princely or noble ranks of such neighbouring kingdoms of the *aborigines*, as retained their independence and maintained amicable relations with Hindoo states. The alliances formed with such families, though not strictly in conformity to the sacred institutes, were not liable to the odium that would be incurred by intermarriage with the conquered and degraded Sudras. They may be compared to those, between Rajpoot and Moslem royal families, of which mention is made in the history of the early periods of the Mahomedan conquest of Hindostan.

While such a practice continued, the wife of the same class could alone "perform the duty of personal attendance and the daily business relating to acts of religion," and her son was recognised as the sole or chief heir of his property. But the paucity and inconvenience of these irregular connections, and the obloquy cast on them in Menu's Code, especially as regards Sudra wives, doubtless contributed to that strict conformity to law and propriety, which is insisted on and observable in modern times. While the practice was in vogue, it was not unlikely that there should be contests for distinction or supremacy, between the Brahmans and the next lower *cast*, the Kshatryas, who were equally permitted to read, though not to interpret, the *Vedas*. The offspring of a Brahman by a Kshatrya wife, who, in some instances, ranked as a member of the superior class, or of a Kshatrya by a woman of the higher *cast*, could not but be indignant at being superseded, both in rank and succession to hereditary property, by his half brother of unmixed parentage. The Roman law in such cases would have granted to a son of mixed descent the position enjoyed by his father. But, by the Hindoo law, ordinarily, the son of the Brahman by a Kshatrya woman was no Brahman, and the son of the Kshatrya by a Brahmani could not find a place even among the members of his mother's class, but descended to one much lower, because an alliance of this nature, where the woman was of a superior class, was strictly interdicted. Hence the dissensions and contents that we have supposed, which could not but tend to discourage the practice of intermarriages among persons of different *casts*, in proportion as Hindooism was extended over the country and the independent Sudra kingdoms successively disappeared.

It is observed by Dr. Wilson, (in his notes on Mill,) that there are several notices in Hindoo tradition of collisions between these two tribes, and that it is singular enough that the cause of dispute appears not to have been secular rank or power; the Brahmans not being described as seeking kingly dignity, or political ascendency, but the Kshatryas as contending for admission into the Brahmanical order, or rather of performing the duties of the priesthood, which exclusively belonged to the members of that order. In another work, however, the professor remarks "that there are several indications of Brahmanical *gotras*, or families, proceeding from Kshatrya races;" and that "the legend of Parasurama reveals a conflict even for temporal power between the two ruling *casts*." We shall not attempt to reconcile the inconsistency of these two statements of his, as to the object of the contest between the two classes. The Hindoo traditions are decidedly in favor of the disinterested and patriotic motive of the great Brahmanical leader, and the propriety of his object,—the establishment of the supremacy of the law, and the overthrow of arbitrary and tyrannical rule. Nor need we do more than point out the discrepancy between the foregoing remark, as to the origin of the *gotras* of the two classes, and that of Mr. Colebrooke, on the subject, quoted in a preceding page. It will be generally admitted, with reference to the acknowledged procession of the four *casts* from the body of Brahma, that there is more probability of the first two classes tracing their genealogy to the same *gotras*, than of the derivation of Brahmanical families from Kshatrya races. The fact of occasional, not to say frequent, intermarriages between Brahman and Kshatrya families, and of the sons of Brahmans by Kshatrya princesses ranking as Brahmans, adequately accounts for such contests as those referred to. The history of Rome affords an analogous instance. As long as there was no *connubium* (lawful intermarriage) between the patricians and plebeians, the former engrossed all the public offices, and no plebeian, however distinguished by wealth or abilities, could hope to attain consular dignity. The concession of the *connubium* established the eligibility of the plebeians to all offices. The strict observance of the legal interdiction of intermarriages between the several classes of Hindoos, put an end to such contests, by restricting each to its own rights and privileges.

When the position of the Brahmans, as explained in the INSTITUTES of Menu, is considered, and compared with the order of things visible in other portions of the globe, under other systems of religion, it will appear that there was no design, and certainly no means employed, to afford that class any undeserved superiority over the other tribes, either in respect to direct power, indirect influence, or wealth and secular advantages. Kingly power is reserved for the members of the second tribe, who, as soldiers, were assured of a certain degree of power and importance. As already observed, the Brahmans are not a priesthood. The sanctity of race and the study of the *Vedas* qualify them to expound those sacred writings, conduct the performance of sacrifices, and expound the law on all doubtful points, and thus to be the delegates of the king in dispensing justice to all classes. It is not their profession nor their duty, as a body, to serve at the altar, like the clergy of the Jewish and Christian religions, though the presence of some of them cannot be dispensed with, particularly at great ceremonials, especially the offerings at obsequies, the most important of the obligations that devolve on Hindoos.* Their duty consists in the study of sacred literature and in leading a life of gravity and even austerity, which none would be willing to pursue or assume unless actuated by the strongest motives. The celebration of the obsequies and other important ceremonies, must ever be accompanied by donations to Brahmans. The emoluments of these are dependent, not on birth or personal rank, but proficiency in the *Vedas* and reputation for sanctity of life and purity of manners. No acts of piety are so meritorious as

* One writer is so ill-informed as to say that "there have always been many races among us, living on this isolated condition, claiming only the name of Hindoos, but denying the authority of the *Vedas* and the *Puranas*, *disregarding the institution of casts*, and differing widely in most respects from the great bulk of the people." But he might have learned from Colebrooke that though the *Bauddhas* have no distinction of *cast*, yet the *Jainas*, who are assimilated to them in many respects, constitute a sect of Hindoos, who "admit the same division into four tribes, and perform, like religious ceremonies, termed *sanskaras*, from the birth of a male to his marriage, observe similar fasts, agree in the belief of transmigration, have priests who have entered into an order of devotion, employ *Brahmans* at their ceremonies, and, for want of *Brahmans* of their own faith, even have recourse to the secular clergy of the orthodox sect."

liberality to Brahmans. The sacred code nevertheless abounds with declarations of the impropriety of giving gifts to ignorant or depraved Brahmans. Hence, any individual of the class, who was under the influence of mercenary motives, had no prospect of success. A competency of worldly goods was solely to be gained by a laborious course of study and a consonant course of upright and ascetic demeanour and manners. It is invidiously remarked by Mill : "It is an essential part of the religion of the Hindoos to confer gifts upon the Brahmans. This is a precept more frequently repeated than any other in the sacred books. Gifts to the Brahmans form always an important and essential part of expiation and sacrifice." But let it be remembered that there can be no better criterion of the influence of pious principles than voluntary gifts to the teachers of religion.

If we look closely into the matter, we shall discover that the sneers of Mill and others, are merely the offspring of bigotry. Among the Jews, whose laws and institutions are accepted by Christians as of divine origin, the descendants of Levi were appointed to serve in sacred matters ; but many of them lost their lives for contending for an equal privilege with the sons of Aaron, the brother of Moses, the lawgiver, who were *exclusively* the *priests* of the nation, and for whom especially various emoluments were provided. Several cities, with their suburbs, were appropriated for their residence. They were exempted from all kinds of secular burdens or labours. They were entitled to a tenth of all that the Levites received from the nation, and to certain portions not only of all offerings and sacrifices in the temple, but of every animal that was killed for use. They were entitled to the first born of all animals, and to fees in commutation of their right to the first born of human beings, and had a share of all the spoils of war. But though the sacerdotal dignity was confined to a certain family, purity of person and sanctity of life were alike indispensable. They were necessarily to be well read in the law, and their superior learning and information caused them to be consulted as interpreters of the law and employed as judges in controversies.

It thus appears that the priests among the Jews, as regards sacredness of person, the learning which they were to cultivate, and the duties which they were to perform, were on the footing of Brahmans, among Hindoos. But the former had their temporal wants provided for, so that their descendants, however unworthy, had homes to live in, and lands to cultivate, and were sure of certain emoluments as long as the Jews were obedient to Moses. The latter had no provision made for their most ordinary necessities, and were entirely dependent upon their cultivation of religious knowledge, sacred law, and general literature, for the means of support, and were even bound to communicate their knowledge without reward. Hence it would have been an extraordinary omission in the legislator, not to have recommended them as the proper objects of the benevolence of the community, that so largely profited by their learned and spiritual labours. The Christian Scriptures* are not deficient in exhortations to the early converts to contribute to the necessities, not only of their spiritual teachers, but even of the nation, who were the *channel* of the communication to them of divine grace. Is it can-

* The standing rules laid down are: "Let him that is taught in the word *communicate* unto him that *teacheth* in all good things."

Obedience to the rule is thus commended: "No church *communicated* with me, as concerning giving and receiving, but ye only, (the Philippians.) Not because I desire a gift, but I desire that *fruit* that may abound to your account. But I have all, and abound: I am full, having received of Epaphroditus the things which were sent from you,—an odour of a sweet smell, a sacrifice acceptable, well-pleasing to God."

Even the obligation of Gentiles to contribute to the wants of believers of the Jewish nation, is insisted upon. "Now I go unto Jerusalem, to minister

did or generous to condemn similar directions in the Hindoo Scriptures, to relieve the worldly wants of the teachers of law and religion, or the priests who officiate at public and private solemnities? Is it not just to represent such liberality, to a venerable and useful body, as the appropriate and most commendable acts of piety? Besides, there is no hierarchy among Brahmans; and the liberality of the wealthiest monarchs could not much enrich a nation of Brahmans. Nor has it ever been known that any individual among them has ever acquired a pre-eminent station, except by the legitimate means open to all. On the other hand, as Dr. Wilson has noticed, "though acceptance of gifts is one mode of subsistence, Brahmans are prohibited from taking gifts indiscriminately, habitually, or excessively, and from receiving any reward for teaching, or any fixed wages or reward for sacrifices," and "if possessed of wealth, they are enjoined to give liberally." A Hindoo writer *emphatically* charges the Brahmans with degeneracy, because they "*sell their learning,* though it is reckoned a heinous crime in the Shastras." His prejudice has caused him to overlook very material facts. Sir William Jones had more candidly remarked: "To instruct others is the prescribed duty of learned Brahmans, and, *if they be men of substance,* without reward." But the learned are expected to give gratuitous instruction to those only who are of their own religion, in the degrees in which the several *casts* are entitled to it, and

---

unto the saints. For it hath pleased them of Macedonia and Achaia, to make a certain *contribution* for the poor saints which are at Jerusalem. It hath pleased them verily, and their debtors they are. For, if the Gentiles have been made partakers of their spiritual things, their duty is also to *minister* unto them in carnal things."

Nor must it be forgetten that "good works" are constantly mentioned as the necessary result and genuine evidence of *sincere* "faith." The happiness of the future world is to be in proportion to such good works: "He which soweth sparingly, shall reap also sparingly, and he which soweth bountifully shall reap also bountifully."

from whose liberality on ceremonial occasions the members of their own tribe were likely to profit. The rule certainly does not prevent their receiving remuneration either from foreigners, who cannot be expected to practise liberality towards Brahmans as such, or from institutions established by foreigners.* The author of the charge forgets, indeed, a circumstance not a little remarkable, and highly creditable to the Brahmans, taking into consideration their actual condition, and their destitution of those endowments which, in other countries, provide for the education of candidates for the clerical order. In other parts of the world, teaching has been a source of independence and even opulence. In India only are to be found not solitary but numerous examples of instruction, as well as *subsistence*, given gratuitously by *pundits* to students, whose numbers would exceed belief were they not a matter of notoriety.†

* Europeans, who desired instruction in Sanscrit, with a view to becoming acquainted with the religious writings of the Hindoos, at first experienced difficulty in prevailing on the *pundits* to communicate such instruction or supply copies of their sacred scriptures. Sir William Jones mentions that, "when the chief native magistrate at Benares endeavoured, at his request, to procure a Persian translation of Menu, before he had a hope of being at any time able to understand the original, the *pundits* of his court unanimously and positively refused to assist in the work." So Colonel Polier, who was the first European that obtained a complete copy of the four *Vedas*, in eleven large volumes, is said to have "had permission from the Rajah of Jayanagar to buy them." Major Wilford acknowledges that, though he was stationed at Benares, the centre of Hindoo learning, he could not have succeeded in collecting Sanscrit works, but for the friendship, encouragement, and support of Mr. Duncan, the resident, "which had a great effect on the Brahmans." Mr. Colebrooke, writing some years later, was disposed to question the prevailing belief, that "the religious prejudices of the Brahmans would prevent their imparting the holy knowledge to any but a regenerate Hindoo." But he overlooked the force of his official character, as well as the effect of time, in subduing those prejudices. Since then the Brahmans seem to have come to the just conclusion, that there was no prohibition, such as existed with regard to Sudras, against the communication of knowledge to foreigners, or the acceptance of gratuities for the same.

† The Rev. William Adam, who was deputed by Government to report on the state of education in Bengal and Behar, quotes Sir Thomas Munro, in his third Report, as aware that the sciences of theology, law, astronomy, &c.,

Thus in other systems of religion, the order of priesthood, whether hereditary or by election or appointment, was secure of certain privileges and immunities, without any particular reference to learning or sanctity. Among Christian nations, who have followed the example of the Jews, the priests have the assured enjoyment of the *tithes* appropriated for their maintenance. In the dark ages (and it is so to this day in some Christian countries) the chiefs of the priesthood enjoyed the most ample benefices, ranked with the highest nobles, and displayed almost princely magnificence. The temporal dominion, conferred by the piety of Charlemagne on the bishops of Rome, draws from the historian the natural reflection: "perhaps the humility of a Christian priest should have rejected an earthly kingdom, which it was not easy for him to govern without renouncing the virtues of his profession." But we cease to feel surprised at such inconsistencies of practice and profession, when we behold the cardinals "aspiring to emulate the purple of kings," and, in rational England, the primate of the church taking precedence of the most exalted of the nobility, and its dignitaries claiming a seat in parliament with the noblest of the realm, enjoying revenues rivaling those of princes, and thus leading the most pious to question, not merely the faith of these luxurious priests but the truth of the creed they coldly profess. Well might Gibbon say, alluding to the prelates of Armenia, who, "as soon as they have performed the liturgy, cultivate the

including the *Vedas* of course, were "usually taught privately, without fee or reward, by individuals to a few scholars or disciples." In the several districts, which he visited in the performance of his duty, he found Brahman. freely imparting, not only instruction, but subsistence, to students of Sanscrit. Even teachers of the vernacular schools, in the Bengal districts, some of whom were not of that class, afforded gratuitous instruction. The remark which he makes is no less creditable to the observer than to the parties: "It gives me great pleasure to mention these instances of unostentatious benevolence in the humblest ranks of native society."

garden," that "*our* bishops will hear with surprise that the austerity of *their* life increases in just proportion to the elevation of their rank." No Brahman could ever hope to be placed, by the most superstitious or the most liberal Hindoo king, in a position so enviable as that of the bishops of Europe. In the dark ages the priests claimed and enjoyed exemption from the jurisdiction of laymen, and were certain of being very leniently judged by the members of their own order. The Brahmans never aspired to immunity from the consequences of crime; and their exemption from capital punishment was the necessary consequence of their sacred origin. But, besides incarceration for life, they were punishable by infamy or banishment; of which the former was deemed adequate in Athens for many offences, and the latter in Rome for the highest. A comprehensive view of things renders it indubitable, to use the words of Dr. Wilson, that "the whole tenor of the rules for the conduct of a Brahman is to exclude him from every thing like worldly enjoyment, from riches, and from temporal power. Neither did the Brahmans, like the priests of the Egyptians, or those of certain religions in Europe, seek a monopoly of spiritual knowledge. The Brahman only, it is true, was to *teach* the Vedas, but the next two orders, the Kshatrya and Vaisya, were equally to study them, and were, therefore, (or might have been,) equally well acquainted with the law and the religion."*

* It has been justly observed by Professor Wilson: "A great mistake pervades all reasoning about the position of the Brahmans in Hindoo society. It must always be remembered that, whatever influence they may have exercised, it has been entirely personal, proportionate to their individual reputation for sanctity and learning. They are no priesthood. They have never had, as a body, any common purpose, any organisation, any head; and they can, never, therefore, have systematically prosecuted designs upon the liberties of the people. They are in fact the people; not separated from them as monastic or clerical sections, but making up a very large proportion of the population, and giving the whole force of the consideration, which their *cast* confers, to the security of popular rights."

There is no part of the subject on which so much and so general ignorance and prejudice prevail, in the most various and multiplied forms.* It was as much the duty of the next two classes to read the *Vedas* as that of the Brahmans. The general ignorance of the former has not been caused by the *laches* or the purpose of the latter, who, had they been equally negligent of their obligations on the point, would have been justly deserving of censure. But they are condemned even for having so far, and imperfectly, fulfilled their duty, as to preserve a certain amount of learning! Mr. Hodgson, from whom a little candour and honesty were to be expected, denounces, with amusing grandiloquence and odious bigotry, "the hostility of that *tremendous* PHALANX of *priestly* sages, which wields an *inscrutable* literature, *for the* EXPRESS *purpose of* PERPETUATING *the enthralment of the popular mind*," and designates them as "*dark* men" and "*dangerous* and powerful *pastors*." But, as we have seen, "the men of letters" in India are not *priests* or *pastors*, much less an embodied *phalanx* or *hierarchy*; and they have no monopoly of learning, except by the wilful neglect of duties and the culpable abandonment of privileges ascribable to the Kshatrya and Vaisya. The Rev. William Adam, who

* Such is the ignorance as to *cast*, that it is not surprising to find the writer of a prize essay, which was considered worthy of the second place, relying on a foreign authority, instead of the knowledge, which was accessible to him as a "native and to the manner born," and speaking of Brahmans as *priests* and of their *priestly office*, on which point Wilson corrects him. He is aware that the second and third primitive *casts* have "the sacred title of the *twice born*, and the privilege of *reading* the *Vedas*," yet expresses a virtuous indignation that the first class, "the descendants of those ancient sages alone, out of the whole body of the people, were to have an *exclusive* MONOPOLY of letters and religion." He goes on to say: "None but a Brahman, declared the Shastras, should *read* the *Vedas*, or *impart* religious instruction; and as the *Vedas* and their *angas* included all the literature and science of the country,—grammar, versification, arithmetic, *and* the mathematics—the law thus effectually enjoined ignorance *to* the rest of mankind." As the climax of misrepresentation, the writer adds: "The favored class alone were permitted *to read and write*; and this privilege they enjoyed undisturbed for ages."

was long an associate of Rajah Rammohun Roy, and specially investigated the condition of education in Bengal and Behar, has emphatically declared that the character ascribed by Mr. Hodgson to the Brahmans *is not deserved.*

It is singular that the efforts of the Brahmans of the present day, engaged as they *literally* are, in *the pursuit of knowledge under* DIFFICULTIES, should be a topic of *censure*, instead of praise. The condition of *Sanscrit* literature in Bengal was discussed by Lord Minto in his Minute, dated the 6th March 1811, which is considered by Mr. Adam to "possess the greater interest, because it bears the signature of Mr. H. T. Colebrooke, and because it is believed to have suggested the provision in the 53rd Geo. III. Chap. 155, Sect. 43," for "*the revival and improvement of literature and the encouragement of the learned natives of India*, and the introduction and promotion of a knowledge of the sciences among the inhabitants of the British territories in India." It was stated with truth and justice: "The principal cause of the present neglected state of literature in India, is to be traced to the *want* of that *encouragement*, which was formerly afforded to it by princes, chieftains, and opulent individuals under the native governments. Such encouragement must always operate as a strong incentive to study and literary exertions, but especially in India, where the *learned professions* have *little*, if any other, *support*." The strong prejudice which Lord Moira, afterwards Marquis of Hastings, as well as Lord William Bentinck had conceived against Brahmans, led them to decline the encouragement of Sanscrit learning, and thus defeat the unequivocal intention of the Imperial Legislature,—notwithstanding the arguments urged, particularly during the administration of the latter nobleman, by Sir William Macnaghten and other orientalists, for the special encouragement of oriental literature.

Whatever may be the views which ignorance or prejudice may form on the subject, the respectable position of the Brahmans, attributable *principally* to their own worth and talent, is (to cite Mr. Adam's testimony only) undeniable. "The teachers and students of Sanscrit schools constitute the *cultivated intellect* of the Hindoo people; and they command that respect which cultivated intellect always enjoys, and which, in the present instance, they peculiarly enjoy from the ignorance that surrounds them, the general purity of their personal character, the hereditary sacredness of the class to which most of them belong, the sacredness of the learning which distinguishes them, and the sacredness of the functions they discharge as spiritual guides and family priests. The only drawback on the influence they possess is the general, not universal, poverty of their condition, increased by the *frequent* (and *sweeping*) *resumption* of former *endowments*, (as well as their rent-free lands.) They are, notwithstanding this, a *highly venerated* and *influential* portion of native society." He adds: "There is no class of persons that exercise a greater degree of influence in giving native society the tone, the form, and the character, which it actually possesses, than the body of the learned, not merely as the professors of learning, but as the priests of religion." Nor must we omit to put, in juxtaposition, the remark of the same observer, that "Mahomedan schools of learning are not so *numerous* as those of Hindoos, but they are in general *more amply endowed*, and the teachers enjoy the same *high consideration* in Mahomedan society, and exercise the same *powerful influence*, that belong to the corresponding class of the learned in Hindoo society." Now, as the Mahomedan *literati*, whether priests or not, owe nothing to sanctity of person, but are placed by circumstances in a more advantageous situation than learned *Brahmans*, the respect paid to them and the influence exercised by them, can be due to nothing but the genuine fruits of learning and a disposition to apply it to the benefit of the community. It must be the height of illiberality not to take the same view of the respect paid to, and the influence possessed by, learned Brahmans. How could any class command the *veneration* of the more opulent, and possess *influence* over them, in the absence of rank and wealth, which have so great a power over the common mind, were its members not distinguished by their personal character and the sedulous but not interested cultivation of knowledge! The Brahmans do not indeed profess indifference to wordly honours and advantages. Their election of learning as a profession, to which their religion almost limits them, as *noblesse oblige* persons of birth in Europe, is *in fact* a vow "to scorn delights and live laborious days." But though they thus "strictly meditate the thankless Muse," they are constantly spoken of, even by persons not decidedly prejudiced against them, as "an ingenious and artful priesthood," who "rigidly monopolise learning." We should marvel at this perversity of judgment, were there not but too many examples, not only of the honors due to the worthy being gathered by the undeserving, but of men eminent for wisdom, piety, and beneficence, "of whom the world was not worthy," being treated with contempt, hatred, or even persecution.

If we look at the corresponding classes in Europe, whether in the dark ages, or in later times, this conclusion is strengthened. In the former period, the clergy were notorious for their ignorance and the profligacy which could not but result from the unnatural and irrational interdiction of marriage. The great subject of ridicule were the monks, who, though specially vowed to a life of poverty, devotion, and austerity, were more remarkable for ignorance, sensuality, and debauchery. Even in more enlightened periods, the clergy are held up to scorn as the opposites of what their profession required. The higher dignitaries are described as more engaged in the pursuit of rich benefices than in the discharge of their spiritual offices.* Bishoprics are asserted to be proper rewards for the cultivation of secular or rather classical learning, the diligent tuition of the sons of influential nobles, and even as the price of votes to be blindly given to unscrupulous ministers.†

* The possession of more than one benefice is forbidden by the relations between the pastor and his flock, and prohibited by the canons of the church, under the name of *plurality*. But the nepotism of pious bishops, and the piety of lay patrons, who destine their sons for the church, with a view to holding the benefices to which they have the appointment, lead to a general evasion of the law on this and other points. The *purchase* of benefices by or for clergymen, and the *sale* of them by the patrons, on whom it is incumbent to confer them *freely* on worthy ministers, for the promotion of piety, is a flagitious crime in religion, under the term of *simony*, but mildly punished by the law. Among other devices, resorted to with a view to defeat the law, it was the practice to take bonds, from the clergymen who were temporarily appointed to benefices, with the condition of resigning them when the *proteges* of the patrons were qualified to hold them. But the practice was so general that the highest courts of law could not be prevailed on to declare it simoniacal and illegal. When the question was finally decided by the house of lords, a law was passed to legalise the practice, if the party to be provided for with a church living were, either by blood or marriage, an uncle, son, grandson, brother, nephew, or grandnephew, of the patron. Thus the revenues appropriated, by the piety of former ages, for the promotion of religion, are the subjects of trade and policy with the present generation. Such are some of the transactions which take place in a nation that boasts to be foremost in civilisation and religion. No parallel to them, we venture to say, can be found among either the Brahmans or the purely laic classes of the Hindoos. Amongst these, endowments are sometimes misappropriated, as they are largely in England, but there is no systematic evasion of the law or *trade* in religion.

† There is so close a connection between the knowledge of the Hindoo scriptures and of the institutes of jurisprudence, as well as those relating to spiritual and civil duties, that none but such as have studied several of them are qualified to be ministers of religion and administrators of justice. But how poor the remuneration given to those who, after long and painful labours, qualify themselves to act creditably in these manifold capacities! How the small gifts received, by the most eminent of them, under anti-Hindoo establishments, are grudged, or envied, or misrepresented! On the other hand, Greek metres neither promote pious dispositions nor facilitate the instruction of the people in Christian knowledge and practice. Hence the pious are justly scandalised to see useless learning rewarded out of revenues, which were to be employed in contributing to the instruction, and relieving the necessities, of the poor. It was solemnly declared, "To the poor the gospel

Great is the contrast between the poverty and humility of the primitive teachers of the religion, and the wealth and arrogance of their successors of all classes,—most conspicuous in those who once maintained a right to set up and depose kings, and still contend for the possession of a temporal kingdom as a necessary adjunct to spiritual authority. But still more remarkable is the contrast between the ministers of the Christian religion and the Brahmans. The former profess to be the successors of teachers who disclaimed wealth, power, and even honour, and only required such a competency as should leave them free to attend to the duties of religion and the instruction of their flocks. They are expected to be versed in their sacred literature, and are, in general, amply provided for by the state, often by voluntary contributions, and style themselves or admit the style of reverend and even lord, in contempt of the most positive injunctions of the author of their religion. The latter are clothed with a sacred origin, and thereby entitled to the highest rank and supreme reverence; they are almost limited to learning as a profession; but no provision is made, even for their absolute wants. They neither possess temporal power, nor arrogate the disposal of earthly kingdoms. They are altogether dependent for their subsistence on voluntary gifts, and are not even at liberty to receive them from the inferior classes, among whom, in the present day, are included some of the wealthiest men, —or to act indiscriminately as priests, without forfeiting their position in the opinion of their brethren as well as that of the laity.*

is preached." A part of the collections of the early church (even in England) was for the benefit of that class. But a great authority has asserted that "the hungry sheep look up and are not fed!" This is true, in either sense. There are, besides, curates who can hardly say they are "passing rich with forty pounds a year," but who faithfully perform their duties, and bishops whose revenues far exceed ten thousand pounds *per annum*, with hardly any duty to perform.

* Is it ignorance or effrontery that leads Mill to describe the Brahmans as

This comparison is made, with a view, not to the reprobation of the habits or practices of the clergy of Europe, but to the exculpation of the Brahmans of India. They are, of all sacerdotal classes in the world, the most unassuming and the least grasping. At any rate, they have neither *aimed* at greater wealth, honour, or power, than the sacred law has allowed nor actually *gained* so much as they were entitled to by its decrees. It is asserted in works of authority, in which accuracy should be studied, that *Brahmans* "have maintained a more extensive *sway* than the priests of any other nation." Could these authors have forgotten to compare the commands of the author of the Christian religion, with the history of the papacy, or the position of the prince bishops of Germany and the lord bishops of England and France, to say nothing of those of Italy and Spain, or even the beneficiaries of most of the European states, with incomes a thousand times greater than any Brahman ever enjoyed, under the most liberal or most bigoted princes of this continent?

It will probably be urged that the crime of the *Brahmans* of Hindostan does not consist in possessing or claiming revenues, not averaging a thousanth part of those of the priests of Christendom; but in arrogating a *sacred* ORIGIN. Now, if to *reason* be to *distinguish*, the slightest consideration will suffice to convince the most prejudiced that,—whether we assume the theory of Dr. Wilson, that Hindooism owed its origin to "a colony of priests, *perhaps* with a body of martial followers," or, was "contrived by a religious *confederation*," or any other than what is deducible from the *Vedas*,—it is certain that the *Brahmans* of this day are not the *authors* of the system, but are under the same sacred obliga-

"a whole race of men set apart and exempted from the ordinary cares and labours of life?"

tions to maintain the doctrines transmitted to them as a divine revelation, which bind the Christians and other religionists to support the divine authority of their respective creeds. But there is this *material* difference between the two classes, that the *former* strictly conform to, and certainly do not diverge from, the line of *duty*, and the *benefits* dependent thereon, proscribed or allowed; but the latter, on the one hand, very much fall *short* of the precepts of their religion, and, on the other, *usurp* honours, privileges, and revenues, *immeasurably* in excess of what either the dictates or the practice of the apostles authorise. Hence, it is clear, that the *Brahman*, who stands upon the privileges of his *order*, as long as he strictly conforms to the precepts of the *Shastras*, is far less to blame than Earl Grey, who, about the time of the discussions on the Reform Bill, declared his intention to stand or fall with the *order* to which he had but just before been raised. The Christian minister, who enters the ranks of a clergy, among whose characteristics should be humility and poverty, cannot escape, either the censures of the world, or the reproaches of his own conscience, when luxuriating in the enjoyment of wealth, honours, and privileges. So great a departure from rule would be condemned by the author of the religion, and even the apostles who propagated it under all the disadvantages of poverty, reproach, and persecution.

It is remarked, with unique simplicity, by the writer on *cast*, in the *Calcutta Review*, that, "*if* the Brahman, the Kshatrya, and the Vaisya, did not really proceed from different parts of the Creator's person, the story is nothing short of *blasphemy*." The language savours of the *proverbial* zeal and asperity of the neophyte. In the short space of a couple of sentences, he satisfactorily settles the incontestable authority of the religion to which he has given his adhesion.

That is a question on which we cannot venture to offer an opinion. But there have been at least twenty opinions among Christians, of the early ages, as to who was the *Creator* of the world. Were the learned writer able to determine who was entitled to the distinction, it would not in the least contribute towards the identification of the person, who, in the opinion of Menu, was the great progenitor of the four principal *casts* of Hindoos. Till that point be settled, it cannot of course be decided whether the assertion in question be *blasphemy* or *truth*. The learned writer need not be reminded of the sentiments on the subject, expressed by Sir William Jones, which cannot be justly impugned, as nobody had a sincerer conviction of the Christian religion. "The Musselmans (as he remarked) are already a sort of heterodox Christians. They are Christians, if Locke reasons justly, because they firmly believe the immaculate conception, divine character, and miracles of the Messiah; but they are heterodox, in denying vehemently his character of Son, and his equality, as God, with the Father, of whose unity and attributes they entertain and express the most awful ideas; while they consider our idea as perfect *blasphemy*, and insist that our copies of the *scriptures* have been corrupted both by Jews and Christians." The diversified and clamorous or sanguinary contests of the early Christians, as to the person, the nature, and the reality of the Messiah, which occupied them, with vain endeavours to confound or separate his divinity and humanity, in a religious war for two hundred and fifty years, are perhaps better fitted to exercise this author's logical faculties, than a question so simple as the sacredness of the persons of *Brahmans*, which has never been questioned as savouring of blasphemy, or made the subject of controversy, among a people whose love of metaphysics is well established, who "were a nation of philosophers," and who could not be held in "the fetters of an intellectual tyranny."* They, who are so ignorant of the world, as not to have heard of the grand ceremony of *kissing the toe* or slipper of *his holiness* the pope, may be excused for being scandalised at "scenes, yet observable daily in the streets, of orthodox believers of all classes eagerly prostrating themselves before the Brahmans, as *they* pass, for *their* benedictions, receiving *their* feet on their heads, or scraping the dust therefrom with earnest devotion." When they are shocked to find that "the Brahman, with his prayers and his rites, must come to help the Hindoo at every emergency," they betray their ignorance of the constant and indispensable intervention of the Christian priest, at the birth, marriage, and burial of every believer in the system. What indignation is felt and expressed if the pastor refuse to perform the ceremony at the burying of the dead! What numbers of Christians believe that baptismal water effects the regeneration of the

* Such is the eulogium pronounced by Dr. Max Muller in his usual extravagant and mystical strain. The *imagination* of this author leads him to speak of *Buddhism*, which was merely a metaphysical speculation, such as the *Vedas* tolerate, as an attempt to eradicate Brahmanism. That Buddhists should not retain the distinction of *cast* is quite natural. The sect in India, which most resembles them, termed *Jainas*, observes the distinction. In other countries the religion was introduced after certain forms of civil society had been established. Hence the Brahmans, who may have migrated to them with persons of other *casts*, must have been at last absorbed into the promiscuous mass, preserving merely the respect which is paid to them as teachers, but as much elevated above the bulk of the people as the Brahmans are among the Hindoos and Hindoo sectaries.—The wildness of his theories would be quite astonishing, were they not the genuine result of his contempt of the first principles of inquiry. On *single* facts, or rather *myths*, he founds systems. From *incidents*, whether actual or allegorical, such as Draupadi's five husbands, king Dasaratha's killing a man, who was so obliging as to disclaim a pure birth, "in order to relieve him from the fear of having killed the son of a Brahman," he deduces wide and of course improbable conclusions, though, had he any canons of philosophising, he should have always remembered the remark he makes in one instance, that "cases like that of Maitreyi were *exceptions*, not the rule." Did it not occur to him that, among the inhabitants of a large continent, of various races, under different governments, there must be many practices irreconcilable with the laws, while even Menu declares custom to be transcendental law?

impure soul, that a few words of absolution by their ministers, or a few offerings to the church, atone for the most heinous crimes, or a few masses suffice to transfer the most guilty souls from hell to purgatory, and from purgatory to heaven!

The notion of propitiating the deity by the offering of human and other victims, is so contrary to reason that such sacrifices, though practised in remote times, as the *Vedas* enjoined, were absolutely prohibited by the sacred legislators of India from a very early date. In Grecian history, Agamemnon is represented as sacrificing his daughter Iphigenia. The Hebrew scriptures honor Abraham with the title of *friend of God*, (also ascribed to Mahomed,) for offering to prove his obedience, by sacrificing his son Isaac, when the odious character of the proposition should have induced him to doubt the justice of the author, and the possibility of its being the command of Heaven. In the Levitical law, however, sacrifices of animals are said to be of divine appointment. But the prophetical writers speak of them as of little or no efficacy, and even explicitly condemn the practice. This fact shows the progress of the mind, in correcting its early assumptions. As the practice "militates against our ideas of reason, and the absurdity of it has been represented in the strongest light by the sages of all nations," it is alleged that the divine appointment of it was with a view that it should be "typical of the last and greatest sacrifice." The whole Christian system turns upon the vicarious sacrifice of a superhuman being, for the expiation of the sins of all or a portion of mankind. Both parts of the doctrine are indefensible. Even the Christian writer in the Encyclopædia, whom we have just quoted, observes: "It may be fairly asked of those, who look for logical *reasons* for all divine appointments, whether, upon human principles, it seems the more probable that the sacrifice of Christ being predetermined, the notion should be familiarised to mankind by ordaining a previous practice; or that, the practice existing and having a meaning of its own in all minds, the new revelation should be *accommodated* to our notions by adopting that very practice for its foundation?" Certainly, in no government in the world would the punishment of innocent persons be regarded as an atonement for the sins of criminals. Is it consistent with reason that Heaven will accept what the justice of man rejects? Thus, it appears that the most ancient religions, which are accepted by the most intellectual and civilised nations, and by the greatest minds among them, as divine, reveal doctrines and authorise practices, which appear to others, when submitted to the examination of reason, to be in the last degree absurd and even impious.

It is not the object of these strictures to censure or even criticise any creed, to commend the Hindoo religion, or to eulogise or justify the Brahmans, but merely to describe things as they are, and reprove the malignity displayed towards Hindoos, and especially the *Brahmans*, their chiefs and representatives. Whatever be the merits of the several religions, all require ministers to teach doctrines and perform ceremonies. The Hindoo system declares the priest to be such by *birth*, provided he have qualified himself to act as such by a laborious study of some of the Shastras. His remuneration is nevertheless entirely dependent on his personal character and the voluntary contributions of his flock. On the Christian system, any one may be appointed a minister of religion, but he is supposed to receive a peculiar spiritual grace, by devolution from the apostles and from the founder of Christianity himself, of which he cannot be deprived either by his own misconduct or the act of those by whom it was conferred. His emoluments are not proportionate to his virtues or services, and may be enjoyed by him for life without reference to his conduct or merits.* It is therefore, evident, that, under both systems, the priest holds an inalienable and indefeasible sacred character ; but that the advantages of a worldly nature greatly preponderate on the side of the Christian. Wherein then consists the superiority of the Christian over the Hindoo doctrine and practice ? The invectives uttered against the Brahmans, whether by Christians or those who have renounced their ancestral religion, proceed either from ignorance or prejudice, or the mere affectation of superior discernment or piety. The accusations made are often too intangible to be analysed and exposed, a proof of the flimsy grounds on which they are uttered.†

* The reflecting part of Christians do not fail to see and condemn the anomalies and inconsistencies of the system exhibited to the world. Few have the courage to protest against them. Many in the upper classes, like certain slaveholders, who conscientiously regard slavery to be a crime, could not do so, without sacrificing the revenues, which they are accustomed to treat as the appanages of their manors. They silence the claims of religion by converting their advowsons to the profit of their relatives, whom they educate for the church, with as little scruple as, while professing patriotism, they obtain appointments in the gift of the ministry, to whom they pledge their votes in parliament and their power to return members to the lower house.

There have been some, whose scruples have led them to renounce a church, the ministers of which are appointed not for their piety and qualifications but through patronage and intrigue, rendering the sacred institution a mere political engine. Hence the spread of Dissent and the progress of Popery. A considerable part of the Scottish nation who long groaned under the yoke of lay patronage, have seceded from the establishment and formed the Free Kirk. But there are others who avow, with Dr. Paley, that they cannot afford to keep a conscience. The number is daily increasing of Christian ministers, who disbelieve certain portions of the Scriptures, and repudiate some of the fundamental articles of faith, but on one ground or another maintain their right to the revenues of a church which they declare to be in error. The members of such a Church, and particularly they who have embraced it from choice, should be the last persons to speak of the usurpations or priestcraft of Brahmans, who hardly obtain a competence by the greatest learning and the most zealous services in the cause of religion and education.

† Take an instance from Dr. Max Muller, who is so esteemed for his Sanscrit

Elphinstone, though disposed to take, in his History of India, a more liberal view than others, of the institutions of the country, has fallen into inextricable doubts by assuming that Menu's Code had been planned by the Brahmans. He ascribes the permanence of the Hindu institutions "to the union and consequent power of the priesthood, when once formed into a separate class, and to eir close alliance with the secular ruler." Had he kept in mind that the Brahmans were not a priesthood, and were not only without an hierarchy, but scattered over various kingdoms, or attended to the traditional accounts of the contests between that tribe and the one next below them, he would have perceived the unsoundness of these suppositions. But upon the view he has taken, he is of course unable to account for the little importance attached by them to the direction of public worship and religious ceremonies of all sorts, and the absence

---

knowledge and researches, though we have failed to discover what light he has thrown on the subject of which he treats. He speaks of the "hierarchical pretensions," and "hierarchical supremacy of the Brahmans," who never were a *priesthood* and consequently could not have had a *hierarchy*. It is probable from his saying, that king Janaka "asserted his right of performing sacrifices without the intercession (intervention?) of priests," that he takes *hierarchical* to be synonymous with *priestly*. But, again, he asserts: "Though the Brahmans *seem* never to have aspired to the *royal power*, their *cast*, as far as we know the history and traditions of India, has *always* been *in reality* the *ruling cast*." It is impossible, from the arbitrary style in which he employs words, to guess whether he means that the *Brahman* was the *chief cast*, or whether he would imply that the *Brahmans* possessed the greatest *influence* over the people. The words he immediately after uses—"their ministry was courted as the only means of winning divine favour, their doctrines were admitted as infallible, their gods were worshipped as the only true gods," &c., do not imply what would commonly be understood by "the *ruling cast*," and what Mill endeavoured, but fails, to establish,—that the *Brahmans* constituted the *executive* power of the country. Under any circumstances, how unmeaning are these remarks of his? May not every one say, of the Christian or any other clergy, with perfect truth, but quite *mal-apropos*, that "their ministry was courted as the only means of winning the divine favour, their doctrines were admitted as infallible, their gods were worshipped as the only true gods," and so forth? But who would not be laughed at for employing such language? In every religion, the priests and laity have a common faith, and common forms and objects of worship. In a word, were there no religion, there would be neither laity nor priests.

of recourse to "oracles and other means of deception." The facts, we have adverted to, show, on the contrary, the futility of the opinion, that the "main object" of the code was "to confirm and increase the power of the Brahmans." They cannot fail to satisfy the candid and unprejudiced, that no provision is made to secure to the Brahman either wealth or power, and that, whatever he may obtain of either must be dependent, not exclusively on his origin, but principally, if not wholly, on his own acquirements in sacred learning and the rectitude and beneficial tendency of his conduct and character.

Besides the particular professions and employments assigned to the several classes, others may be resorted to by them respectively, in case of necessity. Mr. Mill thinks that the alternatives authorised are all in favor of the superior classes. "The unfortunate Sudra, who has no resource, may be driven from his employments and his means of subsistence, mediately or immediately, by all the other classes of the community." He might have formed a juster notion on the point, had he referred to Mr. Colebrooke, whom he has cited as an authority, and who, in stating the succedaneous employments which may be resorted to by the several classes, remarks that, "although a man of a lower class is in general restricted from the acts of a higher, the Sudra is expressly permitted to become a trader or a husbandman." He thus sums up the details: "Hence it appears that almost every occupation, though regularly it be the profession of a particular class, is open to most other classes; and that the limitations, far from being rigorous, do in fact reserve only one peculiar profession, that of the Brahman, which consists in teaching the *Vedas* and officiating at religious ceremonies."

With the view already mentioned, we shall venture to notice one point more—the invective of Lord Macaulay on the character of the natives of Bengal, with special reference to the acts of Rajah Nundocoomar.

It was appropriately observed, in one of the anniversary discourses delivered before the Asiatic Society of Calcutta: "The ancients were accustomed to pronounce panegyrics on their own countrymen, at the expense of all other nations; with the political view perhaps of stimulating them by praise, and exciting them to still greater exertions. But such arts are here unnecessary." The virulence of Macaulay's attack will render its justice suspected; but its condemnation of the whole Italian nation as inferior to the English without exception, and of the Bengalees universally as beneath the former in point of morals, at once deprives it of its virus, and exposes the author of it to the contempt of the discerning. They who are the least capable of judging must admit that, in every nation, there must be specimens of the highest virtue and the lowest depravity. The accuracy of the noble writer has been repeatedly impeached. The love of truth indeed has but often been sacrified by him to paradox, the prejudice of party, and the glitter of a meretricious style.

When condemning the Italians as baser than the English, the Bengalees as baser than the Italians, and Nundocoomar as the worst of the Bengalees, he was *ignorant* that the object of his virtuperation was by descent of a different race. That, in the solitude of his closet, occupied in the preparation of articles for the *Edinburgh Review*, he had no opportunities at all of judging of the Bengalees, was to him a matter of secondary importance to the pleasure of *servilely* imitating a *conceit* in a well known ode of Anacreon. Were his opinion, under the circumstances, deserving of the least weight, it would suffer from contrast with that pronounced by Abul Fazel, the minister of the great Akbar. That statesman, who had a personal knowledge of the character of the Hindoo subjects of his sovereign, has drawn a character very different from the miserable *caricature* of the *Reviewer:* "Summarily, the Hindoos are religious, affable, courteous to strangers, cheerful, enamoured of knowledge, fond of inflicting austerities upon themselves, lovers of justice, given to retirement, able in business, admirers of truth, grateful, and of unbounded fidelity in all their dealings. Their character shines brightest in adversity, their soldiers know not what it is to fly from the field of battle. They have great respect for their rulers, and make no account of their lives when they can devote them to the service of God. If any person in distress flies to them for protection, although he be a stranger they take him by the hand, and will defend him at the expense of their property, reputation, and life."

Colonel Craufurd, from whom we have taken this quotation, in preference to Gladwin's translation of the Ayeen Akbery, remarks: "Though this character seems rather a list of good qualities, than a faithful portraiture of character, and though some of those qualities may perhaps be exaggerated, it must nevertheless be allowed that such praise from a Mahomedan, and from one who *possessed* so much *knowledge of the Hindoos* as Abul Fazel, speaks strongly in favour of their manners and character in general." It appears, however, from reference to a subsequent page of the Ayeen Akbery, that the praise is not indiscriminate. It is there added: "If a diligent investigator were to examine the temper and disposition of the people of each tribe, he would find every individual differing in some respect or another. Some among them are virtuous in the highest degree, and others carry vice to the greatest excess. But impartiality must allow that those among them, who dedicate their lives to the worship of the deity, exceed men of every other religion in piety and devotion. They are vigorous enemies and faithful friends, and, when driven to despair, make no account of their lives. They are renowned for wisdom, disinterested friendship, obedience to their superiors, and many other virtues. But at the same time there are among them men, whose hearts are obdurate and void of shame, turbulent spirits, who for the merest trifle will commit the greatest outrages. In short, some have the disposition of angels, and others are demons," (a proverbial expression.)

Having thus presented all the remarks of that judicious and observant minister, we may fairly assume that he would not have failed to record the *exceptions* in any large section of the people, had he met with such. We may also conclude, from his allusions to the love of knowledge and piety which he remarked among the Hindoos, and his statement of having frequently discoursed with many upright and learned men of that religion, that he did not discover, amongst the Brahmans, those odious qualities which prejudice and bigotry have imputed to them. Could Lord Macaulay have become aware of the sentiments of this eminent statesman, he would perhaps have blushed at having recorded, without having *observed* the character of the people, the remarks in question, which merely betray a lamentable weakness of judgment. The inconsistency of the writer is manifest from his own confession, immediately following his panegyric on the whole of his own nation, that one of the most lauded governors general of India had hired out the forces under his authority for the assassination of a brave and unoffending people, and had found a defender of his misconduct in a Christian clergyman: "Such a defence was wanting to make the infamy of the transaction complete.

The atrocity of the crime and the hypocrisy of the apology are worthy of each other."

The reproaches which are so undeservedly heaped on the *Brahmans*,* are not greater than the obloquy with which a large class even of the English treat the natives of India, who are, to use the language of Sir William Jones, "of great importance to the political and commercial interests of Europe, and whose industry has largely added to the wealth of Great Britain." Had Aristotle lived at the beginning of this century, and seen his countrymen held for several hundred years under a vile thraldom, by the Turks and even by Great Britain, he would have retracted his opinion that the Asiatics were intended by nature to be slaves. But it is strange that nations, whose countries have over and over submitted to the dominion of foreign races, should reproach the inhabitants of Hindostan for passing under other rulers, when these had never been under a common government and were not of homogeneous origin, nor enjoyed the benefits of assimilation, even by intermarriages. The defects in the character of this people or rather assemblage of nations, are not only ungenerously insisted upon, but magnified. Their best qualities are thrown into obscurity, seldom if ever

* They who inveigh against the *Brahmans* as the *authors* of the system for their personal advantage, exhibit an incredible confusion of ideas. Take the following as an instance in point: "If we see the *Brahman* in Hindostan *using* the superstition, he has *created*, to procure to himself and his order certain distinctions and privileges, we have seen the Christian priest doing the same." In fact, the Brahman is in the position of the English noble, whom no one blames for not being a republican or for sitting among the lords as an hereditary legislator, but who would be condemned were he to attempt the abolition of monarchy or *abuse* the privileges of his birth and station. While others speak of the Hindoo laws as a union of church and state, Dr. Buchanan Hamilton (whom Mill hailed as a congenial spirit) declares that they are "equally destructive to the prince and to the people," and that the Brahmans "have erected the dignity and power of the altar on the ruins of the state and he rights of the subject!"

acknowledged.* There is no question, however, but that, such is the excellence of the Hindoo system that it assures to all classes of the community, not only liberty, but freedom and security of trade, and the enjoyment of the fruits of their labours. Under the influence of the religion inculcated in the Shastras, humanity and policy, arts and commerce flourished, wealth abounded, agriculture prospered, and no poor laws were required to secure a wretched pittance to the destitute and infirm. The poorest are hospitable to strangers and travellers. "By their fruits ye shall know them," is undoubtedly a good test of religion and policy; and India, governed by her own laws and institutions, has always stood that test. Exceptions to the general prosperity and happiness may be found, but they are like spots in the sun. India is probably the only land where the principles of its religion and policy, combined, contribute to "the greatest happiness of the greatest number."† No higher praise can be desired for any country.

* In 1838, Mr. Adam wrote:—"I will not attempt to enumerate the benefactions that, within my own recollection, during the last 20 years, have flowed from the liberality of native gentlemen. Roads have been constructed, bridges built, and other public works executed. They are at this moment joining heart and hand with the European community for the relief of the Western Provinces. They have established, at their own expense, and in some instances teach, by their own labour, English schools, for the intellectual advancement of their countrymen. And they have from time to time, placed large sums at the disposal of the Committee of Public Instruction, for the objects of that body." These facts have never been recorded, nor those of a similar nature of subsequent dates. Even at the present time, the liberal acts of Native gentlemen receive no acknowledgment, while the most undeserved calumny of their motives and proceedings is propagated in every shape.

† It is undeniable that some atrocious doctrines and practices, of later times, have sullied the pristine purity of Hindooism. But they are quite parallelcd by the Romanist dispensations, to sanctify any enormity which the purchasers might wish to commit, and by the gifts of wax-lights to the churches, which absolve the Italian *banditti* from robberies and homicides actually committed. The Protestants feel themselves at liberty to disavow these as *corruptions*. The Hindoos, who regard the *Vedas* exclusively as revelation, are as much entitled to repudiate the modern abominations. But what apology can be offered for the *divines*, who, avowing that their religion breathes nothing but "peace on earth, good will towards men," justify the usurpations of their countrymen in India, which were not effected without the perpetration of numerous acts

As in this controversy, much depends on the *antiquity* and *authority* of Menu's Institutes, it is necessary to advert to certain strictures, by Mr. Ellis, on Mill's views of Hindoo laws, quoted by professor Wilson, in his edition of Mill's British India.

According to Mr. Ellis, the Code of Menu, "being a *mere text book*, is never used as authority, in Hindoo *courts*, but when accompanied by an explanatory commentary, or incorporated into a digest." Again: "For practical purposes, its use is very little, the original being a *text book* of the *oldest* date, without any commentary to adapt it to the circumstances of later times. A *mere text book* is considered by Indian jurists as of very little use or authority for the actual administration of justice. It may *almost* be said that the only conclusive authorities are *held* to be the Siddhantas, or conclusions of the authors of the digests and commentaries." Dr. Wilson, quoting the last passage, says in rather equivocal terms: "There can be no doubt that the work ascribed to Menu is a *very early* attempt at codification," and adds: "It is high authority, but is not all sufficient."*

Mr. Morley, who (as we have noticed, page xiii, *note*,) cites a translation that was never made, states, probably

---

of injustice and oppression, for the subjugation of the weak and trusting native princes, that rival the Machiavelian devices by which the unscrupulous Romans attained to universal empire? The plea urged is, at times, superiority of race, as if all nations were not made of one blood, or regarded with equal favour by the Lord of all! At others, it is progress in the arts of destruction of life, as if, contrary to the maxim of the Roman poet, superior knowledge were a release from the obligations of morality and a license to ferocity! The subjugation of unoffending nations is more frequently and specially represented, not as crime but a part of the plans of Providence. The ruler of the universe is *piously* described, by these ministers of the *gospel*, as inciting the people of Europe to acts of the greatest *wickedness*, for want of other means to facilitate the reception of his own *revelation* by the rest of the world!

* We have already (page xxii) seen Colebrook's opinion, that the Hindoo law "is to be sought *primarily* in the institutes, or collections (sanhitas) attributed to holy sages, such as Menu," &c.

from a private communication, which he did not quite apprehend: "Professor Wilson thinks that the work of Menu, as we now possess it, is not of so ancient a date as the *Ramayana*, and that it was most probably *composed* about the end of the third, or the commencement of the second century before Christ. This opinion of the highest living authority on the subject must be considered as *decisive*, so far as present materials can enable us to approximate the truth."* We have the professor's sentiments, under his own hand, communicated to Mr. Thomas, the editor of the *Indian Antiquities* (including Mr. James Prinsep's Useful Tables.) Without assuming carelessness or misapprehension, on the part of Mr. Morley, we could not account for his accepting, without remark, an opinion, so opposed to that of MM. Chezy and DesLongchamps, who pronounced the date of the Institutes to be "the thirteenth century previous to our era," and Schlegel, who considered it to have been in existence before the date of the invasion of India by Alexander the Great, to say nothing of that of Sir William Jones and Elphinstone, whose conclusions he seems to undervalue.

---

* Few persons, capable of judging for themselves, will coincide in this conclusion. A reference to these pages (to mention none of his own compositions) will show several instances of his inconsistency with himself—a proof of the little consideration which he bestowed on the subjects that he wrote upon, and the insufficient grounds on which he formed his opinions. We do not ask, whose votes adjudged the *precedence*, claimed for the professor by the writer's blind admiration. But we would fain learn whether the deliberate judgments, of those who have written on subjects with which they are intimately acquainted, are not entitled to more respectful attention than the decision *obiter* of one not conversant with them.

We would not be understood to imply any censure of the great diligence and accuracy which distinguish the author's compilation, and we cheerfully acknowledge the fairness and independence of his remarks on Indian legislation on the *lex loci*, as a surreptitious and unpardonable infringement of the parliamentary guarantee (to use the words of Sir William Jones) "to leave the natives of these Indian provinces in possession of their own laws, at least on the titles of *contracts* and *inheritance*."

The following are Professor Wilson's remarks: "Sir William Jones's estimate of the date of Menu, eight centuries before Christ, is based upon a very fanciful and inconclusive analogy, and not entitled to any weight whatever. In fact, the Laws of Menu are a compilation of the laws of very different ages: many are word for word the same as the *sutras* of some of the oldest *rishis*. There are various unquestionable proofs of high antiquity. The people of Bengal, Orissa, and the Draviras of the south, were not Hindoos when one passage was written; and Caldwell places Dravira civilisation, through the Brahmans, six or seven centuries before Christ. There is no mention of, or allusion to, Siva or Krishna, which places the work before the *Mahabharata*. There is evident familiarity with the *Vedas*, persons and legends being alluded to not found any where else. All such passages I *could* consent to consider at least as old as 800 B. C. On the other hand, there are many references to the merit of *ahinsa*, "non-injury of animal life," and these are probably later than Buddhism; and there is mention of the *Chinas*, a name that Sinologues say is not older than two centuries before Christ; but this may be an interpolation. However I should think the work may have been put together about that time, although very much of it is a great deal older."

The opinions thus expressed do not in reality differ much from those of Sir William Jones. Where they do, they are not entitled to the weight which is due to the conclusions of the latter. In the course of making a literal translation of the Code, after collation of many manuscripts and with constant reference to commentaries, the latter necessarily acquired a more intimate knowledge of its style and characteristics, than was to be expected from the cursory examination bestowed on it by the professor, who could not speak with confidence on juridical questions, and has, in fact, advanced nothing calculated to throw doubt on the judgment of the translator and others.

The professor's remark, that the Code is "a compilation of the laws of very different ages," is equivocal. It may mean that it is a compendium of laws of different periods, expressed in the author's own language, such as Blackstone's Commentaries for instance. In that case, we must suppose him to imply that the work was not composed earlier than two or three centuries before the Christian era. It may also mean that, though the body of the work was of an early date, and, according to him, "at least as old as 800 B. C.," yet it was "put together," (published,) in the form in which it appears, about the period first mentioned. His language is so vague that we really cannot venture to say which is his opinion.

If we may suppose the first, why does he speak of "interpolations," and of "various unquestionable proofs of high antiquity," and of the presumptions in its favour, on that point, from its not mentioning certain events and doctrines?—If we concede that it was the professor's intention to tell us that the Code was unquestionably as old as 800 B. C., but that passages had been foisted into it, then we cannot but feel surprised at the disparaging terms in which he has spoken of a man, equally celebrated as a linguist and a jurist. On the other hand, his theory of interpolations is quite inconsistent with the facts and with probability.

That the Code contains passages from the *sutras* of the *Vedas*, "changed only in a few sentences for the sake of the measure," is expressly stated by Sir William Jones. It is, therefore, quite a mistake, on the part of the professor and others, to mention the circumstance as a notable discovery.*

* In his introduction to the *Rig Veda Sanhita*, he cites Dr. Max Muller as his authority. See this learned writer's letter on the subject, *horribly*

The supposition of the Code having been interpolated is quite inconsistent with probability and unfounded in fact. Had the professor, or those who concur with him, had any familiarity with the different digests of Hindoo law, and commentaries thereon, they would have known how carefully the genuineness of every passage is scrutinised in rival works. Colebrooke, whose researches in all branches of Hindoo science and literature were extensive, has shown, in his essay on the *Vedas*, grounds for disbelieving those charges of fabrication and falsification which have often been "inconsiderately hazarded." Among other things he noticed that "the practice of reading the principal *Vedas*, in superstitious modes, tends to preserve the genuine text," a practice also applied, as he elsewhere notes, to the reading of "law, and other branches of sacred literature," and, as we are informed by Sir William Jones, scrupulously observed by "the *Brahman* who read *Menu* with him." Not less important, nor less applicable to the Institutes of Menu and other works of authority on law, is his observation: "It is a received and well-grounded opinion of the learned in India, that no book is altogether safe from changes and interpolations until it have been commented. But when once a gloss has been published, no fabrication could afterwards succeed; because the perpetual commentary notices every passage, and, in general, explains every word."

That no attempt at falsification has ever been made, we do not mean to assert. When Europeans were eager to penetrate the inaccessible fanes of Sanscrit learning, and entirely dependent on their *pundits* for access to the *adyta*, a few of these were tempted to impose on their ignorance. But

---

stuffed with *conjectures*, which Mr. Morley has inserted entire in his Analytical Digest, probably as a specimen of the *palpable obscure*.

such fabrications, the most remarkable of which are the deceptions practised upon Major Wilford, have generally been detected. With regard to Menu, with which we are immediately concerned, there can be no doubt that the care with which Sir William Jones collated the many manuscripts, which he had collected, and consulted the commentaries that were in his possession, would have enabled him to detect any considerable discrepancies among them, had such existed.*

What is the character of the supposed interpolations? There are allusions, it is thought, to the doctrines of Buddha, and mention is made of the *Chinas*.

The allusions are of a very questionable kind. The doctrine alluded to is common to the Buddhists and Jainas, as well as the Hindoos, and Colebrooke alludes to it as among "the received maxims for refraining from injury to any sentient being." The *Vedanta*, in attempting a refutation of the Sankhya philosophy, ("from which the sect of Buddha seems to have borrowed its doctrines,") notices "some of the sages of the law as having sanctioned the principles of the Sankhya." Yet when it condemns that philosophy "as at variance with the *Smritis*, as with the *Vedas*, it places the name of Menu at the head of *those Smritis*, "although the Institutes, which bear his name, will be found to afford seeming countenance to the Sankhya system." Thus, it is seen, that this notion of the

* Sir Graves Haughton, in his edition of the original and translation, alludes to the various readings of the manuscripts consulted by Sir William Jones. His "notes" testify to the groundless assumption of Dr. Wilson.

As an illustration, both of the attempt, and the difficulty of making interpolations in Menu that shall pass undetected, we may allude to Sir William Jones's finding a *verse* in a modern copy of that work, brought from Benares, in praise of the *Atharvana Veda*, which was not to be found "in the best copies, and particularly in a very fine one written at Gya, where it was accurately collated by a learned Brahman," and concluding, from the circumstances, that, "as Menu himself, in other places, names only three *Vedas*, we must believe this line to be an *interpolation* by some admirer of the *Atharvana*." (As. Res. I. 346.)

professor, of any actual allusion in Menu to Buddha, is quite chimerical.*

The mention of the *Chinas* by Menu is the only thing on which the notion of an interpolation can be made to rest. Were it possible to assign any *motives* for such an interpolation, the idea would still be discountenanced by the solid grounds urged by Sir William Jones, for believing that, notwithstanding the pretensions to antiquity advanced on its behalf, the Chinese are, to some extent, the descendants of colonies, detached from India, at an early period, intermixed with the progeny of the neighbouring Tartars, the race to whose authority it has ultimately succumbed.

It would have been more to the purpose had Dr. Wilson ascertained that there were considerable passages in Menu, dissimilar in style to the body of the work, the only rule by which, it is generally acknowledged, such questions can be decided. Sir William Jones, holding the poems of Kalidasa to have been composed before the beginning of the Christian era, considers it to be clear, "from the style and metre of the Dharma Shastra, revealed by Menu, that it was reduced to writing long before the age of Valmik or Vyasa, the second

* He says, in the work cited in the note preceding the above: "There is in Menu a faint intimation that Buddhistical opinions were beginning to exert an influence over the minds of men, in the admission that the greatest of virtues is abstinence from injury to living beings, which would make his laws posterior to the *sixth* century B. C." It is shown, in the text, that these opinions had long been "*received* maxims" among the Hindoos, and they indeed directly flow from the doctrine of the metempsychosis. The *Vedanta*, again, places Menu in a class perfectly the opposite of that imagined by Dr. Wilson, and it will no doubt be admitted to be a better judge on the point. It seems from the passage now quoted that the professor would determine the era of *Menu* from a single circumstance, in itself not very capable of leading to any positive conclusion. Hence we should not be surprised that his opinions are so fluctuating as well as indefinite—the eighth, sixth, and second century B. C. being severally fixed upon, according to the moment's mood of mind.

of whom names it with applause."* Hence he concludes that "we should not be thought extravagant, if we placed the compiler of those laws between a thousand and fifteen hundred years before Christ, especially as Buddha, whose age is pretty well ascertained, is not mentioned in them,"—an inference fully justified by the concurrent astronomical data already mentioned.

That he did not come to this conclusion without due consideration is certain. He was led, as we are assured by Lord Teignmouth, "to study the work of Menu, reputed by the Hindoos to be the oldest and holiest of legislators, and, finding it to comprise a system of religious and civil duties, and of law in all its branches, so comprehensive and minutely exact that it might be considered as the Institutes of Hindoo law, he presented a translation of it to the Government of Bengal." The task of *translating* the work was better calculated, than the repeated transcriptions of Thucidydes by Demosthenes, to render him a perfect master of the style of the author. We are therefore justified in placing the utmost confidence in his opinion on the subject, which is as follows: "The style and metre of this work (which there is not the

* Dr. Max Muller does indeed express an opinion on the point, but it is not such as to weigh against the authority of so elegant a writer and so good a judge of poetry as Sir William Jones. He says that Menu, "in transferring Vedic verses into epic *slokas*, is *sometimes* obliged to retain words and forms, which are not in *strict* accordance with the general character of his language." The opinion is seemingly given with some hesitation, and with good reason; for why should Menu have been *sometimes* obliged to use words unsuited to the composition with which he wished to incorporate them? When he speaks of it as "a fact, which accounts in some degree for the strange appearance of many of his verses, which are stiff and *artificial*, and very *inferior* in *fluency* to the older strains which they paraphrase," we are at a loss to guess his meaning. Very different are the *dicta* of the English translator of Menu: "That the *Vedas* are very ancient, and far older than other *Sanscrit* compositions, I will venture to assert from my own examination of them, and a comparison of their style with that of the *Puranas* and the *Dharma Shastra*. In the Manava Shastra the measure is uniform and melodious, and the style perfectly Sanscrit, or polished." See also what is stated on this point, in the text.

smallest reason to think affectedly obsolete) are widely different from the language and metrical rules of Kalidasa, who unquestionably wrote before the beginning of our era; and the dialect of Menu is even observed, in many passages, to resemble that of the *Veda*, particularly in a departure from the modern grammatical forms; whence it must at first view seem very probable, that the laws now brought to light were considerably older than those of Solon or even Lycurgus, although the promulgation of them, before they were reduced to writing, might have been coeval with the first monarchies established in Egypt or Asia. But, having had the good fortune to procure ancient copies of eleven Upanishads, with a very perspicuous comment, I am enabled to fix with more exactness the probable age of the work before us, and even to limit its highest possible age, by a mode of reasoning, which may be new, but will be found, I persuade myself, satisfactory, if the public shall on this occasion give me credit for a few very curious facts, which, though capable of strict proof, can at present be only asserted. The *Sanscrit* of the first three *Vedas*, (I need not here speak of the fourth,) that of the Manava Dharma Shastra, and that of the Puranas, differ from each other in pretty exact proportion to the *Latin* of Numa, from whose laws entire sentences are preserved, that of Appius, which we see in fragments of the Twelve Tables, and that of Cicero, or of Lucretius, where he has not affected an obsolete style. If the several changes, therefore, of Sanscrit and Latin took place, as we may fairly assume, in times very nearly proportional, the *Vedas* must have been written about 300 years before these Institutes, and about 600 years before the *Puranas* and *Itihasas*." Having already (pages ix, x*)

* Baboo Rajendralal Mittra, to whom oriental literature is under immense obligations, has kindly brought to our knowledge a letter of Archdeacon Pratt, (Journal of the Asiatic Society, 1862, page 49,) "on Colebrooke's determination of the date of the *Vedas*," which would otherwise have

referred to the fact, as determined on astronomical data, we shall not follow the author, in his attempt to discover "the greatest possible age of the *Vedas*," by an analysis of the series of preceptors and pupils, who are described, in one of "the *Upanishads* of the second *Veda*," as having "successively received and transmitted (probably by oral tradition) the doctrines contained in that *Upanishad*." The author proceeds to say: "The geographical part of the book, with most of the allusions to natural history, must indubitably have been written after the Hindoo race had settled to the south of the Himalaya. The name of Menu is clearly derived (like *menes*, *mens*, mind) from the root *men*, *to understand*; and it signifies, as all the *pundits* agree, *intelligent*, particularly in the doctrines of the *Veda*, which the composer of our *Dharma Shastra* must have studied very diligently; since great numbers of its texts, changed only

---

escaped our notice. The title of the letter involves an inaccuracy, implying a partial acquaintance with the subject; as it will have been seen, from the preceding pages, that the *determination* was made by Davis, from an astronomical tract of one Veda, and only *confirmed* by Colebrooke from a similar tract attached to another. The result obtained by the Archdeacon, making the approximative age of the *Vedas* to be 1181 B. C., is the same that was at first stated by Sir William Jones, probably from Davis's notes, (As. Res. II. 393,) but subsequently modified to 1391 B. C. (Ibid. V. 288,) in which *ultimate* determination Colebrooke concurred, as well as Sir William Jones, as we find the latter remarking, in his Discourse of the 28th February 1793: "we know, from an *arrangement* of the seasons in the *astronomical* work of *Parasara*, that the war of the Pandavas could not have happened earlier than the close of the twelfth century B. C.

We would suggest a reference to the earlier volumes of the Asiatic Researches, for the necessary data for calculation. The Archdeacon appears not to have referred to the several papers bearing on the subject, or he would have ascertained what stars were considered by Colebrooke to form the asterisms of the Hindoo lunar mansions.

It is singular with what *bias* and *reticence*, and on what limited acquaintance with Hindoo literature, authors have undertaken to settle the antiquity of astronomy in India, and other questions, and what reproaches they have, on imaginary grounds, heaped on the Brahmans. Without a knowledge of the Oriental languages, Dr. Buchanan Hamilton cites the English translation of the Ayeen Akbery "for an import which is not supported by the Persian or Sanscrit text." It was his purpose, from the history of Cashmere, to show that the Brahmanical system was of a late date; but, as Colebrooke remarks, the account "is so far from proving the priority of the

in a few syllables for the sake of the measure, are interspersed through the work and cited at length in the commentaries. The public may, therefore, assure themselves that they now possess a considerable part of the Hindoo scriptures. Whoever Menu may have been, he is highly honoured by name in the *Veda* itself, where it is declared that 'whatever Menu pronounced is a medicine for the soul.' And the sage Vrihaspati, now supposed to preside over the planet Jupiter, says, in his own law tract, that 'Menu held the first rank among legislators, because he has expressed, in his Code, the whole sense of the *Veda*; that no code was approved which contradicted Menu; that other Shastras, and treatises on grammar or logic, retained splendour so long only as Menu, who taught the way to just wealth, to virtue, and to final happiness, was not seen in competition with them.' Vyasa too has decided 'that the *Veda*, with its *angas*, or the six compositions deduced from it, the revealed system of medicine, the *Puranas*, or sacred histories, and the Code of Menu, were four works of supreme authority, which ought never to be shaken by arguments merely human.' Should a family of Brahmans omit, for three generations, the reading of Menu, their sacerdotal class, as all the *pundits* assure me, would in strictness be forfeited; but they must explain it only to their pupils of the three higher classes."

Jagannatha, the author of the Digest of Hindoo Law, translated by Colebrooke, (vol. I. 454,) declares Menu to be

Bauddhas that it directly avers the contrary," while the unsoundness of his views is manifest from various other considerations. Professor Playfair has shown, on scientific bases, that astronomy must have been cultivated, not merely about 3102 B. C., the beginning of the Kali Yug, but 1000 or 1200 years earlier, that is, 4300 B. C. The Vedas, there are grounds for believing, (which we cannot now enter into,) were in existence at even an earlier period, in an oral and traditionary form. The "determination of the date" above referred to is, consequently, to be understood as referring only to the proof of the single fact in question, the positions of the colures mentioned in certain astronomical treatises.

"the highest authority of memorial law." Almost every *vyavastha* of the *pundits* in these provinces places Menu at the head of the authorities cited by them; and we observe the *pundits* of the Rajah of Tanjore doing the same, when expressing their opinion on a point referred to them at the request of Sir Thomas Strange. It would be superfluous to adduce other arguments in refutation of the fantastical opinions advanced by Mr. Ellis and supported by Dr. Wilson.*

It was hardly possible that Sir William Jones's opinions, regarding the character of Menu's Code, should not in some degree be tinctured with the prejudice excited by a difference of race and religion. When he describes it as "a system of despotism and priestcraft, both indeed limited by law, but artfully conspiring to give mutual support, though with mutual checks," and that its "very morals, though rigid enough on the whole, are in one or two instances (as in the case of light oaths and of pious perjury†) unaccountably relaxed," he supplies an antidote to his prejudice, by adding: "nevertheless, a

* In illustration of our remark, (in a preceding page, xliv,)—that the offspring of a Brahman by a Kshatrya woman would, in some instances, rank as a member of the superior *cast*,—we omitted to refer to the fact, perhaps not generally known, that, in the Mithila and Benares provinces, there is, at this day, a race of that description. They are regarded as Brahmans, but of a low grade, and are commonly styled *bhooyar*, (properly *bhuhara*, lord of the land,) a term applicable to Kshatryas, and probably significative of their mixed origin.

† As these sheets are passing through the press, we observe a remark in a leading English review, that may, by comparison, serve to place this alleged *laxity of morals* in a proper light. The writer thinks "a statesman would be quite *right* in *showing* greater confidence than he *felt*;" and that, whatever may be his opinion, "he cannot afford to *say* so." Of these practices, the former is termed by Bacon *simulation*, and the latter by the schoolmen *suppression of the truth*. This public instructor of his country, doubtless from his knowledge of the conduct of politicians, declares both to be perfectly justifiable. If he *looked at home*, he certainly would not venture to condemn such acts as *failings* in the natives.

From the same source we learn some facts regarding the *impropriation* of tithes, which we cannot avoid alluding to, as completing the system of *laxity of morals*, of which *simony* and *plurality* (adverted to in a preceding *note*, page lviii) are remarkable features. The monks, who had fattened by the spirit of sublime devotion, of benevolence to mankind, and of amiable tenderness to all sentient creatures, pervades the whole work;—the style of it has a certain austere majesty, that sounds like the language of legislation, and extorts a respectful awe; the sentiments of independence on all beings but God, and the harsh admonitions even to kings, are truly noble." As a writer in one of the latest minor encyclopædias says: "many of the most learned Europeans are of opinion that, of all known works, there is none which carries with it more convincing proofs of high antiquity and perfect integrity," and, "as has been most frequently remarked, the most striking features by which the Code of Menu is distinguished are the rigour and purity of its morals." Nor shall we do amiss to quote the just and apposite remarks made by Sir Thomas Strange, near the conclusion of his work on Hindoo Law: "With some trifling exceptions, the Hindoo doctrine of evidence is distinguished, nearly as much as our own, by the excellent sense that determines the competency and designates the choice of witnesses, with the manner of examining, and the credit to be given them, as well as by the solemn earnestness with which the obligation of truth is urged and inculcated; insomuch that less cannot be said, of this part of their law, than that it will be read by every English lawyer with a mixture of admiration and delight, as it may be studied by him to advantage. Even the *pious perjury*, which it has been supposed to sanction, being resolvable, after all, into no greater liberty than what our juries (not indeed with

appropriation to themselves of a large portion of the *tithes*, were in turn despoiled by the *piety* of Henry VIII, the defender of the faith and the author of the Reformation. Their ill-got wealth, instead of being restored to the respective parishes, was distributed, not only among bishops and chapters and the colleges, but his personal favorites. At this day, *two-fifths* of the revenue, intended for the support of the parish clergy and parish poor, are "plundered" by the high dignitaries and beneficed clergy and the laity. Of this portion a moiety (£700,000 in round numbers) is absorbed by the laity, and more than three-fourths by the teachers of morals and religion.

perfect approbation) have long been allowed to take, where the life of a prisoner, on trial before them, is sometimes at stake,—credit is to be given to the pregnant brevity of the Hindoo oath, *viz.* 'What ye know to have been transacted in the matter before us, between the parties reciprocally, declare at large, and with truth;' as also to the noble warning, with which the subject, as detailed by Menu, is ushered in, that 'either the court must not be entered by judges, parties, and witnesses, or *law* and *truth* must be openly declared.'"

It might be interesting to notice, with a view to explain, various other points, connected with the laws or institutions of the Hindoos, which have been animadverted on, as questionable or even unjustifiable; but we should exceed the limits of a preface.

TABLE OF SUCCESSION

ACCORDING TO THE

Mitakshara, Vivada Chintamani, Vivada Ratnakara, Smriti-sara, Vivada Chandra, Madana Parijata, Viramitrodaya, and other works,

PREVALENT IN THE WESTERN SCHOOLS, INCLUDING MITHILA.

ON THE ORDER OF SUCCESSION TO THE ESTATE OF A DECEASED PROPRIETOR.

I. WHEN sons, after the death of their father, make a division of the paternal estate, the *portion* deducted for the eldest and other sons, as stated by MENU (Chap. IX. *v.* 112,) is not now authorised according to the *Mitakshara*, nor prohibited according to the *Vivada Ratnakara*. **Sons inherit equally.**

II. The *sons* of the deceased proprietor, on the division of his estate, receive equal shares. If any of them die during the life-time of the deceased proprietor, the division being made according to the number of the sons, the living sons receive a share each, and the fatherless *grand-sons* receive the shares of their respective fathers. **Sons inherit *per capita*.** **Grandsons *per stirpes*.**

III. An *adopted son* is entitled to a fourth part of the share of a son begotten by the deceased proprietor. **Adopted son.**

IV. When brothers make a division, their *sisters* are entitled to a fourth part of their shares. **Sisters.**

V. When sons make a division, their *mother* and *step-mother* receive shares like their respective sons. **Mother and Step Mother.**

VI. The *son of a Sudra* by his maid servant receives half the share of his son by a legal wife. If the owner have no legal wife, and no daughter by her, or daughter's **Sudra's natural son.**

son, such son becomes entitled to the whole. In default of sons, &c., and notwithstanding the existence of the legal wife, daughter, or daughter's son, he receives half.

Grandsons represent their fathers.

VII. When *grandsons* divide the estate of their grandfather, the division does not take place according to their number, but according to that of their fathers, that is, one of the sons leaving one son, another two, and a third three sons, the grandsons receive the shares of their respective fathers.

Grandmothers.

VIII. When grandsons divide the property of their grandfather, their *grandmothers* but not their mothers receive shares.

Great grandsons.

IX. According to the *Mitakshara*, *great grandsons* have no right to the property of the owner. But their right is mentioned in the *Vivada Chintamani*, *Vivada Chandra*, and *Vivada Ratnakara*.

Widow.

X. If the proprietor die without being *separated* from his brothers, &c., or, having been separated, after re-uniting with them, the *widow* cannot get his property. But if he die after *separation* or without re-union, she is entitled to it in default of nearer heirs.

Widow has a life-interest.

XI. A *widow*, inheriting her husband's property, can enjoy it for life, but cannot sell or make a gift of it at her pleasure.

Woman's peculiar property.

XII. Any property which a woman *inherits* is her *stridhan*, that is, peculiar property. Hence any property of her husband which she inherits shall, on her death, be received by the heirs of her peculiar property. But such property cannot, according to the *Smritisara*, be her *stridhan*. Hence the heirs of her husband shall receive it.

Son's property inherited by the mother is *stridhan*.

XIII. If the mother die after inheriting her son's property, such property becomes her *stridhan*. Hence the heirs of her peculiar property get it. This rule also holds good in the case of the property of grandmothers, great grandmothers, &c.

XIV. In the case of the inheritance of *daughters*, the unaffianced have precedence over the affianced. But there is no distinction according to the *Mitakshara*. Daughters.

XV. In the case of the inheritance of *daughters' sons*, they do not get shares according to the number of their mothers. Each of them receives an equal share. Daughters' sons inherit *per capita*.

XVI. According to the *Vivada Chintamani*, in default of the father of the owner, his *daughter's son* gets his property. Daughter's son.

XVII. According to NANDA PANDITA, in default of daughters' sons, *daughters' daughters* may get the property. But this does not coincide with the opinion expressed in the *Mitakshara*, &c. Daughters' daughters.

XVIII. According to the same authority, in default of uterine brothers, *uterine sisters* become entitled to the property. Uterine sisters.

XIX. If a *step-brother* be re-united and a *uterine* brother separated, each of them gets an equal share. Uterine and Step Brother.

XX. *Great grandsons* are not mentioned in the *Mitakshara*, as having a right to the deceased owner's property. In default of brothers' sons, the grandmother, grandfather, and the grandfather's sons and grandsons, and in their default, the great grandmother, great grandfather, and great grandfather's grandsons get the property. The right of seven generations of *sapindas* and fourteen generations of *sakulyas* has been mentioned. The great grandson is omitted in the *Smritisara*, from the list of *sapindas*, both from the texts quoted and the annotations. Great grandsons, according to the *Mitakshara*, do not inherit. *Sapindas* and *Sakulyas*.

XXI. The author of the *Vivada Chintamani*, like that of the *Mitakshara*, says that seven generations of *sapindas* and fourteen of *sakulyas* may inherit. But the right of great Great grandsons, according to the *Vivada Chintamani*, inherit.

Sapindas and *sakulyas.* grandsons is mentioned in that work, where the right of *sapindas* and *sakulyas* is spoken of. Thus four descendants may be entitled to property.

Great grandsons, *sapindas* and *sakulyas*, according to the *Ratnakara.* XXII. According to the *Vivada Ratnakara* and NANDA PANDITA, three generations are called *sapindas.* Hence three generations from father to great grandfather and their descendants down to great grandsons are successively entitled. In their default, *sakulyas*, and so forth, get the property.

Maternal uncles. XXIII. The authors of the *Vivada Chintamani* and *Viramitrodaya* have spoken of the right of *maternal uncles*, in default of *sakulyas*, where the right of *bandhu* is mentioned. But this does not coincide with the opinion of the author of the *Mitakshara.*

Unchaste widow. XXIV. An *unchaste widow* has no right to the estate of her husband, who, having been separated, did not re-unite with his co-heirs. But if she be merely suspected, she does not get the whole property, but is entitled to maintenance. So any woman suspected to be unchaste is not entitled to the whole property.

WESTERN SCHOOLS, INCLUDING MITHILA.

Heirs of the deceased Proprietor.*

	Order of Succession.		*Order of Succession.*
Son	... 1	Step Brother's Son	... 14
Grandson	... 2	Step Sister's Son	... *nil.*
Grand Daughter	... *nil.*	Step Brother's Grandson	... *
Great Grandson	... 3	Step Brother's Daughter	... ,,
Great Grand Daughter	... *nil.*	Step Brother's Daughter's Son.	,,
Son's Daughter's Son	... ,,	Grandmother	... 15
Grandson's Daughter's Son	.. ,,	Step Grandmother	... *nil.*
Great Grandson's Son	... *	Grandfather	... 16
Great Grandson's Grandson	... *	Father's Brother	... 17
Great Grandson's Great Grandson	... *	,, Sister	... *nil.*
Wife	... 4	,, Step Brother	... 18
Unmarried Daughter	... 5	,, Step Sister	... *nil.*
Married Daughter	... 6	,, Brother's Son	... 19
Daughter's Son	... 8	,, Sister's Son	... *nil.*
Daughter's Grandson	... *nil.*	,, Brother's Grandson	... *
Daughter's Daughter	... ,,	,, Brother's Daughter	.. ,,
Mother	... 9	,, Brother's Daughter's Son	... ,,
Step Mother	... *nil.*	,, Step Brother's Son	.. 20
Father	.. 10	,, Step Sister's Son	... *nil.*
Brother	... 11	,, Step Brother's Grandson	... *
Sister	... *nil.*	,, Step Brother's Daughter	... ,,
Step Brother	... 12	,, Step Brother's Daughter's Son	... ,,
Step Sister	... *nil.*	Great Grandmother	... 21
Brother's Son	... 13	Great Step Grandmother	... *nil.*
Sister's Son	... *nil.*	Great Grandfather	... 22
Brother's Grandson	... *		
Brother's Daughter	... ,,		
Brother's Daughter's Son	... ,,		

* The asterisks in this table refer to the heritable right of seven generations of *sapindas* and fourteen of *sakulyas*, which rests on the authority of the following passage of *Vrihat-Menu*, quoted in the *Mitakshara* :—" The relation of the *sapindas*, or kindred connected by the funeral oblation, ceases with the seventh person ; and that of *samanodakas*, or those connected by a common libation of water, extends to the fourteenth degree, or, as some affirm, it reaches as far as the memory of birth and name extends. This is signified by *gotra*, or the relation of family name."

	Order of Succession.
Grandfather's Brother ...	23
" Sister ..	*nil.*
" Step Brother ...	24
" Brother's Son ...	25
" Sister's Son ...	*nil.*
" Brother's Grandson ...	*
" Brother's Daughter ...	"
" Brother's Daughter's Son ...	*nil.*
" Step Brother's Son	26
Grandfather's Step Sister's Son ...	*nil.*
" Step Brother's Grandson ...	*
" Step Brother's Daughter's Son.	"
Great Great Grandmother ...	27
Great Great Step Mother ...	*nil.*
Great Great Grandfather ...	28
Great Grandfather's Brother.	29
Great Grandfather's Step Brother ...	30
Great Grandfather's Brother's Son ...	31
Great Grandfather's Brother's Grandson ...	*
Great Grandfather's Step Brother's Son ...	32
Great Grandfather's Step Brother's Grandson ...	*
Grandfather's Great Grandmother ...	33
Grandfather's Great Step Grandmother ...	*nil.*

	Order of Succession.
Grandfather's Great Grandfather ...	34
Great Great Grandfather's Brother ...	35
Great Great Grandfather's Step Brother ...	36
Great Great Grandfather's Brother's Son ...	37
Great Great Grandfather's Brother's Grandson ...	*
Great Great Grandfather's Step Brother's Son ...	38
Great Great Grandfather's Step Brother's Grandson ...	*
Grandfather's Great Great Grandmother ...	39
Grandfather's Great Great Step Grandmother ...	*nil.*
Grandfather's Great Great Grandfather ...	40
Grandfather's Great Grandfather's Brother ...	41
Grandfather's Step Brother ...	42
Grandfather's Great Grandfather's Brother's Son ...	43
Grandfather's Great Grandfather's Brother's Grandson	*
Grandfather's Great Grandfather's Step Brother's Son.	44
Grandfather's Great Grandfather's Step Brother's Grandson ...	*
Eighth Ascendant ...	45
His Son ...	46
His Grandson ...	47
His Great Grandson ...	*

	Order of Succession.		Order of Succession.
Ninth Ascendant	... 48	His Grandson	... 62
His Son	... 49	His Great Grandson	... *
His Grandson	... 50	Fourteenth Ascendant	.. 63
His Great Grandson	... *	His Son	... 64
Tenth Ascendant	... 51	His Grandson	.. 65
His Son	... 52	His Great Grandson	.. *
His Grandson	... 53	Father's Father's Sister's Son.	66
His Great Grandson	... *	Father's Mother's Sister's Son.	67
Eleventh Ascendant	... 54	Father's Mother's Brother's Son	67
His Son	... 55	Mother's Father's Sister's Son.	68
His Grandson	... 56	Mother's Mother's Sister's Son.	68
His Great Grandson	... *	Mother's Mother's Brother's Son	68
Twelfth	.. 57	The owner's Father's Sister's Son ..	
His Son	.. 58		
His Grandson	... 59	The owner's Mother's Sister's Son ..	69
His Great Grandson	... *		
Thirteenth Ascendant	.. 60	The owner's Mother's Brother's Grandson ...	
His Son	... 61		

On the Order of Succession to the Peculiar Property of Women.

I. Any wealth, movable or immovable, which *women* receive or inherit, is their *stridhan*, that is, peculiar property, which they have the power to give away, sell, or dispose of, at their pleasure. But they have no right to dispose of the immovable property inherited from their husbands or other relations.

Stridhan how far heritable.

II. According to the *Mitakshara* and other works, the *son* of a woman cannot inherit her peculiar property during the life-time of her *daughter*. But according to the *Vivada Ratnakara*, her daughter and son have an equal right to her whole property, excepting nuptial gifts (*parinaya*) *yautaca*, &c., received from her father.

Who may inherit *stridhan*.

Daughters' daughters represent their mothers.

III. In the case of the succession of *daughters' daughters*, their shares shall be determined according to the number of their mothers; in other words, if a daughter leave one daughter, and a second two, the grandmother's property shall be divided into two parts according to the number of the mothers. They who are not married have precedence over those who are.

The unmarried exclude the married.

IV. To the property of a woman, if married according to the forms called *Brahma*, &c., in default of her sons and grandsons, her *husband*, and, in his default, his *sapinda* (kinsmen) have right; but, if married according to the forms called *Asura*, &c., her mother and father, and, in their default, her *sapinda*, (kinsmen).

Co-wife's children.

V. According to the *Madana Parijata*, a *co-wife's daughter* or *daughter's son* is entitled to the wealth of a woman who dies leaving no children.

Sister's son, &c.

VI. In the *Vivada Ratnakara* mention is made of the right of the *sister's son*, husband's sister's sons, &c.

Heirs of the Separate Property of the deceased Proprietress.

	Order of Succession.		*Order of Succession.*
Unmarried Daughter	.. 1	Husband	.. *
Barren Widowed Daughter	.. 2	Husband's *sapinda*	.. *
Married Daughter	.. 3	" Sister's Son	.. *nil.*
Daughter's Daughter	... 4	Father	... *
Daughter's Son	... 5	Mother	... *
Son	... 6	Mother's *sapinda*	... *
Grandson	.. 7	Brother	... *nil.*
Co-wife's Son	... *nil.*	Brother's Sons, &c.	... "
Co-wife's Daughter	.. *nil.*	*If she die unmarried, her heirs are:*	
" Grandson	.. *nil.*	Uterine Brother	... 1
" Daughter's Son	.. *nil.*	Mother	... 2
" Great Grandson	.. *nil.*	Father	.. 3

* See Observation IV.

VIVADA CHINTAMANI.

INTRODUCTION.

THAT goddess, who is the genetrix of the universe, emerging from the sea of milk, looks askance at the assembly of gods, perceives by the glances of one of them that he would wed her, and bends down her head through bashfulness. The god, moved by love, which gave rise to the desire of embracing, holds the goddess with his perspiring hand, whereon she smiles. May that god vouchsafe protection from destruction!

Having prostrated himself before NARAYAN, and carefully studied the works styled *Krito Kalpa-druma*, *Párijáta*, *Ratnákara*, and others, the author, VACHASPATI MISRA, compiles the work, entitled VIVADA CHINTAMANI.

OF JUDICIAL PROCEEDINGS.

MENU says that (1) debt, on loans for consumption; (2) deposits, and loans for use; (3) sale without ownership; (4) concerns among partners; (5) subtraction of what has been given; (6) non-payment of wages or hire; (7) non-performance of agreements; (8) rescission of sales and purchases; (9) disputes between master and servant; (10) contests as to boundaries; (11) assault; (12) slander; (13) larceny; (14) robbery and other violence; (15) adultery; (16) altercations between man and wife, and their respective duties; (17) the law of inheritance; and (18) gaming with dice and with living creatures; are the eighteen heads of disputes.* Heads of disputes, according to Menu.

* Institutes, Chapter VIII. v. 4—8.

OF DEBT.

What are comprised under this head.

ON this subject NAREDA says:—"What may or may not be lent; by whom, to whom, and in what form; with the rules for delivery and receipt, are held *to be comprised under the title of* Debt.*

Loan on interest defined.

A loan on interest *(cusidá)* signifies that "contract of delivery and receipt, which is made with a view to gain *by the lender*, on the principal sum while remaining *with the debtor*, and money-lenders derive their subsistence from it."

Explanation.

"The principal sum while remaining with the debtor" means, while it remains or continues with the debtor.

"Gain" signifies interest, for which the principal is delivered and received.

Debt defined.

Consequently, that property, which affords a gain stipulated, in consideration of its remaining for a time with the debtor, is called a debt.

Loans upon and without interest.

When money is lent without charging interest, money-lenders cannot get their subsistence. But a loan upon interest and one without it have the same signification, so far as the repayment of them is concerned. What has been said here will be evident from the 4th Chapter of NYAYA.*

* The Author refers to his work under that title.

In matters of debt, that which is given, or something of the same species, is to be received back. Money employed for commercial purposes cannot, therefore, be called debt. Why money employed in commerce is not termed debt.

VRIHASPATI says that capitalists fearlessly receive four or eight times the capital from abject or indigent persons. Debt is, on this account, called *cusidá* (from *cu*, meaning abject, and *sidá*, indigent.) Why debt is termed *cusida*.

The word *or*, in the preceding sentence, does not limit the receipt of interest to four or eight times *the capital*. (The rate may be increased or decreased according to circumstances.) Rate of interest may vary.

KATYAYANA says, none should lend any wealth to women, minors, or slaves; for what is given to them can never be got back. Wealth not to be lent to women, &c.

VRIHASPATI speaks of the means of realising a debt. Lenders should deliver the things lent on taking *beneficial* pledges, or pledges to be merely kept in deposit with them, which may be equal in value to the capital and interest; on getting honest sureties; on agreements, or before witnesses. Debt how to be realised. Security for the payment of debt.

The meaning of the above is that recourse should be had to any of these, by which the confidence of the lenders may be established. For the confidence of the creditor.

A beneficial pledge signifies a pledge which may be made use of, according to agreement. Beneficial pledge defined.

Pledge kept in deposit.

A pledge *to be merely kept in deposit* means a pledge that cannot be used, according to agreement, such as gold, &c.

This, then, is the difference between a *beneficial* pledge and a pledge *to be merely kept in deposit.*

Rate of interest, according to Menu.

MENU speaks of the rate of interest which should be taken. The rate of an eightieth per cent. per month, allowed by VASISHTHA, should be adopted. "Hear the interest for a money-lender declared in the words of VASISHTHA: five *máshas* for twenty *palas* he may claim and should receive each month: hereby the law is not violated."

According to Vrihaspati.

VRIHASPATI says the twentieth of a *pala* is called *masha,* which weighs 16 *ratis.* Therefore a *pala* equals four *mohars* (80 *ratis* being equal to one *mohar*); or 20 *palas* yield an interest of one *mohar* (which represents an eightieth part of 20 *palas.*) Thus an eightieth part of the capital becomes the interest.

Exemplification.

According to MENU, 100 *mohars* yield an interest of one *mohar* and 20 *ratis* per month, that is, one and a quarter *mohar* becomes the interest.

This rate presumes security.

This rate of interest is allowed, if pledge be given; for YAGNYAWALKYA has particularly ordained an interest of an eightieth part of the principal, where a pledge has been delivered.

VYASA has also declared monthly interest to be "an eightieth part of the principal, if a pledge be given; an eighth part is added, if there be *merely* a surety; and if there be neither pledge nor surety, two in the hundred may be taken:" consequently, a monthly interest of 90 *ratis* may be taken, if 20 *palas* of gold be lent. Rate of interest according to Vyasa.

This rate of interest may be taken from *Brahmins*, and not from the members of any other class. This rate exigible from Brahmins.

MENU confirms this, in the following text:—"A money-lender may take two in the hundred from a priest; three from a soldier; four from a merchant; and five from a mechanic." As is also declared by Menu.

By taking two in the hundred, per month, a money-lender does not become a sinner. Two per cent. per month is allowable.

Even if there be a pledge, the rate of interest varies according to the direct order of the classes. Hence, the interest, charged to a soldier shall be one and a half, to a merchant twice, and to a mechanic two and a half times the amount taken from a priest. Rate of interest varies in the order of the four classes.

When a merchant takes interest at the rate allowed by MENU, he does not violate the law. Nor does a priest, soldier, or mechanic do so, if he take it in time of distress. Rates of interest allowed for merchants, priests, and others.

Higher rates of interest prohibited.

If any one take interest exceeding the abovementioned rate, this, being oppressive towards debtors, makes him a sinner.

Exceptions, for merchants and exigencies.

If any person, except a merchant, take the abovementioned rate, or at a rate exceeding it, when there is no distress, he becomes a sinner.

Rate of monthly interest, according to Harida.

HARIDA ordains a monthly interest of eight *panas* for twenty-five *kahonas*. Thus the principal becomes double after four years and two months.

Declared to be lawful.

The abovementioned rate being consonant to the rules of justice, does not make its receiver a sinner.

On the principal being doubled, interest ceases.

The principal being thus doubled after fifty months, it can no longer produce interest.

Various sorts of interest.

With reference to the various sorts of interest, VRIHASPATI says it is of four kinds; some say five, and others six. Correctly learn the following expressions: càyicà (corporal); càlicà (periodical); chàcràvridhi (compound interest); *càrita* (stipulated); *sichàvridhi* (daily interest); and *bhagalabha* (interest by enjoyment.)

Cayica (corporal) defined by Vyasa.

VYASA defines *càyicà* to be "that interest which arises from the body of a pledged female quadruped to be milked, or a male animal to work or carry burdens."

And by Nareda.

NAREDA defines *càyicà* to be "interest at the rate of one *pana*, or of half or other fraction of a *pana*," daily "paid without diminishing the principal."

In the work of HALAYUDHA, *pana-bajya* is read instead of one or half *pana*. Pana-bajya, according to Halayudha.

The meaning is that as long as the *pana*, that is, the principal, is not paid, interest may be charged even for a hundred years. Monthly interest exigible even for a century.

The interpretation of *cayica* by VYASA has been included in *bhagalabha* and is different from that by NAREDA. Another explanation of cayica.

Calica means interest paid monthly in full. Calica defined.

Chacravridhi means compound interest. Chacravridhi defined.

KATYAYANA defines *carita* to be that "interest which has been specially and voluntarily promised by the debtor, in a time of extreme distress, above the allowed rate." Such interest, if voluntary, must be paid. Carita defined.

If the promise of the debtor be obtained otherwise, that is, by compulsion, such interest is not to be paid. Promise on compulsion not binding.

VRIHASPATI defines *sikhavridhi* to be interest "received at the close of each day, or hair-interest, because it grows daily like hair." As hair cannot grow when the head is cut off, so interest cannot increase, if the principal be paid. Hence it is called *sikhavridhi*. Sikhavridhi defined by Vrihaspati.

Bhagalabha means "the rent *or use and occupation* of a mortgaged house or the produce of a mortgaged field. It is also called *adhibhaga* and includes the hire of other things." Bhagalabha defined.

Katyayana's definition.

KATYAYANA confirms this by saying that *adhibhaga* means a loan "made on an agreement that the whole use and profit of a pledge shall be the only interest."

Interpretations.

Cayica means annual, and *calica,* monthly interest. *Chacravridhi* signifies compound interest.

By *carita* is meant that interest which the debtor promises to pay in a time of distress.

Sikhavridhi means daily interest.

Bhagalabha means the enjoyment of the labor of slaves, and so forth.

Sikhavridhi, cayica, and bhagalabha may be received till the principal is paid.

VRIHASPATI says that the 5th, 1st, and 6th kinds of interest, namely *sikhavridhi, cayica,* and *bhagalabha,* may be received by the creditor as long as the principal is not paid.

More than twice the principal may be taken.

In these three cases, more than twice the principal may be taken, if it remain unpaid for a long time.

Loans, adhibhaga excepted, by whom to be repaid.

All sorts of loans except *adhibhaga* are to be repaid only by the debtor, his son, and his son's son.

Debt, secured by a written contract, by whom to be paid. Case of a debt secured by a pledge.

YAGNYAVALKYA says on the same subject :—"A debt, secured *merely* by a written contract, shall be discharged, *from a moral and religious obligation,* only by three persons, *the debtor, his son, and his son's son ;* but a pledge shall be enjoyed until actual payment of the debt *by any heir of any degree.*"

Consequently, even the great-grandson of a debtor is liable for a debt secured merely by a pledge.

VISHNU says that "even if the highest interest, *or that equal to the principal sum*, have accrued, the creditor *shall not be forced to* restore a pledge placed *in his hands*, unless there have been a special agreement."

A pledge not to be restored, even if the interest equal the principal, without special agreement.

If the creditor bind himself by special agreement to restore the pledge, when the highest interest has accrued, he shall then return it to the debtor.

Pledge to be restored if there be an agreement.

YAGNYAVALKYA says: "when a pledge has been given, *which the creditor* promised to return on *the debt being doubled*, then, surely, the interest having equalled the principal, the pledge must be restored on the double sum having been paid, or having been obtained from the use of the pledge."

Pledge to be restored, if the creditor promised to return it on the payment of principal, with interest equal to it.

This text also is applicable where "creditors promise to return the pledge on the debt being doubled;" because both this text and that of VISHNU may, consistently with brevity, be referrible to the same source.

This text is also applicable to a promise to return the pledge on debt being doubled.

Of the six kinds of interest, four should not be received "beyond the year."

Four kinds of interest not to be taken beyond the year.

GAUTAMA confirms this by saying that no lender should receive compound, annual, monthly, and stipulated interest, beyond the year, unless there be some other agreement.

Gautama's authority in support.

Annual interest, as explained by Nareda, may be received as long as the principal remains unpaid.

The text of VRIHASPATI, to the effect that annual interest may be received as long as the principal remains unpaid, is applicable to the annual interest, as explained by NAREDA, for the principal is not diminished. But annual interest, as explained by GAUTAMA, is that interest which is derived from enjoying the bodily labor of slaves, &c., because this meaning coincides with that given by VYASA. Consequently, pledged cows, &c., may be used for a year. But these four sorts of interest may be received, if there be an agreement, as has been declared by GAUTAMA.

These four sorts of interest may be received, according to agreement.

The receipt of interest double of the principal, &c., though culpable, is allowed.

The receipt of interest more than twice the amount of the principal by using the pledge, of compound interest, and of interest on principal which has been doubled by interest, is culpable, but is allowed. For VRIHASPATI says it is merely reprehensible to receive interest, when it has become more than double the principal, compound interest, and interest on principal which has been doubled by interest.

The receipt of interest double of the principal, is culpable.

In the *Grihasta Ratnakara* it is stated that it is culpable to receive interest more than twice the principal, compound interest, and the principal with the addition of the interest in the shape of principal.

Debts without agreement as to interest.

KATYAYANA speaks of debts contracted without an express agreement as to interest.

A debt not paid on demand by one

If a man go to a different country without paying a debt, in spite of the demand of his creditor, the debt will be liable to interest after three months commencing from the date of demand. Debt is here understood to be contracted expressly without stipulation of interest.

who goes to a distant country, liable to interest after three months.

If a person go to another country without paying for an article which he has purchased on credit, the price of it will bear interest after six months. Consequently, in cases of deposit, of a balance of interest, of the price of articles, and of that of articles purchased but not delivered, interest at the rate of five *panas* per cent. will be charged after six months, if they be not paid on demand.

Price of goods not paid for on demand when to bear interest and at what rate.

This rate shall be paid by Sudras. For it is proper to render this consistent with the provision of five per cent. interest on Sudras (mentioned above.)

The rate fixed, is payable by Sudras.

KATYAYANA says, interest cannot be charged on what is lent out of friendship, as long as it is not demanded.

No interest, unless demanded, on what is lent out of friendship.

If such loan be not discharged on demand, five per cent. interest is to be charged thereon. "Friendship" here signifies confidence.

Such a loan, not discharged on demand, bears five per cent. interest.

Such interest shall be charged after three months. For the text of KATYAYANA, above adverted to, should be maintained in consistency with this.

Such interest chargeable after three months.

Interest on what is lent out of friendship can be charged after six months.

NAREDA says, interest on what is lent out of friendship cannot be taken without special agreement. But, even without it, interest can be charged on such a loan after six months. "Lend" here means to deposit.

This text does not contradict any.

This text does not, therefore, contradict what has been said above about the charge of interest after three months.

Interest shall be charged, on the price of an article borrowed but not returned, after six months.

If a person go to a different country without returning an article which he borrowed for use, interest shall be charged on its price after six months.

Going to a different country is not essential.

Going to a different country is not essential; for even if a person, residing in his country, do not return any article borrowed for use, when it has been repeatedly demanded, interest becomes due, even if he be unwilling to pay it and there be no agreement to that effect.

Interest to be charged after six months, if the price be not paid, &c.

The meaning of the above is that if, under frivolous excuses, the aforesaid price be not paid and the deposit returned on the lender or depositor's demand, interest shall be charged thereon after six months; and if they are not fraudulently detained, interest shall be charged after one year.

Otherwise after one year.

On what, interest cannot be charged without previous agreement.

Without previous agreement, interest cannot be charged on the price of articles, salary, deposit, fine, money received by force or fraud, idly-promised gift, and wager laid in jest.

Idly-promised gift means a gift promised not for religious purposes.

Idly promised gift defined.

The text of KATYAYANA, that interest can be charged on the price of an article, or on deposit, even if there be no previous agreement, holds good, when they (the price and deposit) are not paid by persons who fraudulently go to another country.

Interest can be charged on the price of an article, &c., when they are not paid.

SAMVARTA says that the *peculiar property* of women, profit, deposit, doubtful money, and money due from a surety on account of his not producing the debtor, &c., cannot yield interest without previous agreement.

The peculiar property of women, &c., cannot yield interest, without previous agreement.

Here the *peculiar property* of women is understood to be spent from intimacy between the parties.

Peculiar property spent from intimacy.

Having referred to husbands, sons, and so forth, he adds that, if any of them enjoy the peculiar property of women against the consent *of the owner*, he shall be compelled to return it with interest and to pay a penalty. But if he do so with the permission of the proprietress, through affection, the payment of the principal, when he may have means, will be sufficient.

He who enjoys the peculiar property of women against consent, must return it with interest and penalty.

If enjoyed with permission, the payment of the principal will be sufficient.

VYASA says, money paid by a surety; pledged property, if used when it ought not to have been used; money not received by the creditor, when

Money, paid by a surety, &c., cannot bear interest.

it is willingly tendered by a debtor, who is his dependent; fines; earnest money; and idly-promised gifts; cannot bear interest.

A surety is not to pay interest more than twice the principal.

When a surety has to pay interest, he shall not have to pay more than twice the principal.

Money, not received by a creditor, should be kept with a third person, &c.

According to YAGNYAVALKYA, if a creditor do not receive money tendered by a debtor, it should be kept with a third person and should not be charged with interest.

Interest cannot be taken from a debtor from the day he is put in duress.

GAUTAMA says that interest cannot be taken from a debtor from the day on which he is put in duress.

Maximum limit of interest.

GAUTAMA speaks of the maximum limit of interest :—"The principal can be doubled by length of time only."

Interest, amounting to more than double the principal, cannot be received.

"*Length of time*" means that even when the time for trebling the principal arrives, interest, amounting to more than double the principal, cannot be received.

The rule is applicable in the case of gems, &c.

This rule is applicable in the case of gems, jewels, &c.

MENU particularly says that, when interest is received at one time, it should never exceed the double of the principal. But interest on rice, grain, the hair of animals, except *the wool of* sheep and beasts of burden, cannot exceed five times the principal.

According to Menu, interest, received at one time, cannot exceed the double of the principal, and on rice, &c., five times the principal.

If the principal and interest be received at one time, the interest on jewels, and so forth, may be double, and, on rice, and so forth, five times the principal. But if they be not received at once, the interest may be greater.

When interest may be double and when quintuple of the principal.

This is also the opinion stated in the *Ratnakara*, as expressed in the aforesaid interpretation put by NAREDA on *cayica*.

This is also according to the Ratnakara.

Interest on wool cannot exceed five times the principal; for KATYAYANA has said that jewels, pearls, coral, gold, silver, plough-shares, spun silk, and wool, cannot bear interest more than double the principal.

Interest on wool cannot exceed five times the principal.

GAUTAMA says, interest on *pashupaja*, hair, land, and beasts of burden, cannot exceed five times the principal.

Interest on pashupaja, &c., cannot exceed five times the principal.

Pashupaja means milk and other produce of kine, except clarified butter. For, according to KATYAYANA, all kinds of oil, wine, clarified butter, *gur*, and salt, yield interest eight times the principal.

Pashupaja defined.

VRIHASPATI says, gold yields interest twice, clothes and utensils of metal, except those of gold and

Gold yields interest twice the principal, &c.

silver, thrice; and rice and other products, beasts of burden, and hair, four times the principal.

Interest of fluids and female beasts.

VISHNU says, fluids yield interest eight times the principal. The offspring of female beasts of burden constitute the interest thereof.

Interest on vegetables, seeds, salt, &c.

VRIHASPATI says, vegetables yield interest five times; seeds and sugar-cane, six times; salt, oil-seeds, *gur*, wine, and honey, eight times the principal.

These rules always hold good.

These rules hold good even if the aforesaid articles remain for ever.

Interest of eight times the principal is applicable as regards salt, &c.

Interest amounting to eight times the principal on fluids is applicable as regards salt, &c., for this is provided for in express terms.

Interest on fluids, gold, rice, &c., according to Vasishtha.

VASISHTHA says, fluids other than salt bear interest three times the principal. Gold bears interest twice, rice and juices as well as flowers, fruits, &c., thrice, and what is sold by weight, eight times the principal.

Interest of eight times the principal is not applicable as to articles made of gold.

The last mentioned rate is not applicable in the case of articles made of gold, for a separate provision has been made as to them.

Grass, wood, &c., do not yield interest, without an agreement to that effect.

VRIHASPATI says that grass, wood, bricks, thread, and "substances from which wine or spirits are extracted," betel, bones, leather, weapons, flowers, and fruits, do not yield interest, unless there be an agreement to that effect.

If they be taken for use, interest must be paid.

Interest must be paid, if they be taken for use.

It is for this reason that KATYAYANA has ordained interest on plough-shares, spun silk, and hair, twice the principal; and VASISHTHA has allowed interest on flowers, seeds, and fruits, three times the principal.

Interest on ploughshares, &c., is twice, and on flowers, &c., three times the principal.

The various rates of interest on rice that have been already mentioned, are on account of difference in price.

The various rates of interest on rice are owing to difference in price.

Therefore, when rice is lent, it bears interest twice the principal, if its market price fall after a fresh crop. If the price fall still lower, the interest may be three times, and so on till it be five times the principal.

How interest on rice rises from twice to five times the principal.

This gradual increase of interest is applicable in the case of debt in general, for there is no fixed time for charging the various sorts of interest.

Gradual increase of interest is applicable in the case of debt in general.

HARITA says that rice which has been lent yields interest double of the principal. It may be thrice.

Rice yields interest double of the principal.

MENU has ordained interest according to the price. The rate fixed by navigators, travellers, and those who know the seasons and the peculiar institutions of countries, shall obtain. Knowing that shipments yield greater profit, they fix a larger interest.

Menu has ordained interest according to price.

HARITA has also treated of this subject.

According to some, one *kahana* shall yield interest of one *pana* per month.

One kahana yields interest at one pana per month.

Nareda declares this to be the universal rule.

NAREDA has likewise declared this rule to be prevalent throughout the world. The rates, fixed according to the peculiar usages of places, may be different.

Interest varies from twice to eight times the principal, according to usage.

Interest varies from twice, thrice, and four times to eight times the principal, according to the peculiar usages of different countries.

In what the knowledge of seasons and peculiar usages of countries consists.

Knowledge of the seasons and peculiar usages of countries consists in a knowledge of the fact, that four times the quantity of an article, to be got before a fresh crop, may be obtained after it at the same price, &c.

The provision of interest at twice the principal, &c., shall take effect in the direct order of the classes.

It is said in the *Ratnakara* that the provision of interest at twice the principal, &c., shall take effect in the direct order of the classes. The meaning may be that interest, amounting to twice the principal, shall be charged, within two or three months on grain, not freed from husk, and thrice on prepared grain and so on.

Persons of mixed parentage to pay interest of one pana on one kahana.

Interest of one *pana* on one *kahana* per month is charged on persons born of parents of different classes.

Rice may yield interest thrice or five times the principal.

Experienced persons say that rice may yield interest thrice or five times the principal, if the debt be of long standing.

RULES OF PLEDGE.

NAREDA says, what may be kept in one's possession, so that he may be its owner for a time, is called pledge. It is of two kinds, namely, a pledge that is to be released within a specified time, and a pledge that is to be retained as long as the debt is not liquidated. The rule regarding it is that, if the pledge be disfigured, or injured, through the negligence of the pledgee, he forfeits interest.

Pledge defined.

If the pledge be injured through the negligence of the pledgee, he forfeits interest.

"*Disfigured*" means broken, &c.

Interpretations.

"*Injured*" signifies spoiled.

KATYAYANA says, a pledgee forfeits interest by using a pledge that was to be only held in deposit. If a beneficial pledge be spoiled by use, interest shall be forfeited.

A pledgee forfeits interest, by using a pledge that was to be only held in deposit.

MENU says the use of the pledge *(adhi)* exempts it from interest.

Use of the pledge exempts it from interest.

The use of such pledge, as is to be released after a certain time, is the cause of its bearing no interest.

Use of the pledge is the cause of its bearing no interest.

Injury to the pledge is another cause of its being exempt from interest. Hence, if a pledge become useless through the carelessness of the pledgee, it shall be exempt from interest.

Injury to the pledge is another cause of its being exempt from interest.

An imprudent man using a pledge without the permission of the pledger, is excused by forfeiting half the interest.

If an imprudent man use a pledge without the permission of the pledger, he shall forfeit half the interest and shall thereby be absolved from the sin consequent upon such use.

According to Katyayana.

KATYAYANA says, if a person cause a living pledge to work without the permission of the pledger and against the will of the pledge, he shall forfeit the gain derived from such work or interest.

He who causes a living pledge to work against his will, shall forfeit the whole interest.

If a person cause a living pledge to work against his will, he shall forfeit the whole interest. But if the pledge voluntarily work, half the interest shall be forfeited.

The pledgee shall forfeit the whole interest, if he use a pledge, &c.

The pledgee shall forfeit the whole interest, if he use a pledge to be only held in deposit.

If a pledge be lost, the principal shall be forfeited, unless the pledgee be blameless.

NAREDA says, if a pledge be lost, the principal shall be forfeited. But if it be so by the act of God or of the king, the principal shall not be forfeited.

According to Vrihaspati.

VRIHASPATI says, if a pledge be wholly spoiled by use, the principal shall be forfeited. Where a valuable pledge is spoiled, the pledgee must satisfy the pledger.

Where these two rules are applicable.

These two rules are applicable in the case of loans bearing no interest.

VYASA says, if pledged gold, &c., be spoiled through the negligence of the pledgee, on the principal and interest being paid to him, the price of the spoiled pledge is to be taken from him.

If pledged gold, &c., be spoiled through the negligence of the pledgee, the price of the same is to be taken from him.

VRIHASPATI says, where a pledge is spoiled by the act of God or of the king, a second pledge is to be given or the debt liquidated.

Where a pledge is spoiled without the pledgee being in fault, a second pledge is to be given, &c.

NAREDA says, if a pledge, carefully kept, become useless in course of time, a second pledge is to be given or the debt liquidated.

If a pledge, carefully kept, become useless in course of time, a second pledge is to be given, &c.

VISHNU says if a pledger mortgage pledged land, even if it be equal in area to a *gocharma*, he shall receive bodily punishment.

Punishment of a pledger who mortgages pledged land.

If the land be smaller than a *gocharma*, the pledger shall be fined 16 *mohars*.

The meaning of the above is that the first pledge is valid, and the subsequent ones inadmissible.

The first pledge is valid, and not the subsequent ones.

A similar opinion is maintained in the *Parijata*, *Ratnakara*, *Smritisara*, *&c.* Hence, if a pledger sell his property, there can be no objection.

The opinion is corroborated by other authorities.

VRIHASPATI defines *gocharma* to be a piece of land, the produce of which can maintain a single individual for a year. It may be a little larger or smaller.

Gocharma defined.

In contests as to second pledge, occupation of the land without force gives title.

In contests about a second pledge, that pledgee who shall prove his occupation of the land without force, shall gain the cause. If it be occupied by both at the same time, both shall get it. This rule also holds good in the case of gift or sale.

This is generally the case.

If the evidence on both sides be equal, the case shall be decided by casting lots.

If the evidence on behalf of both the parties be equally strong, their claims shall be decided by casting lots.

If a pledge die, or be made useless through the carelessness of a third person, another pledge is to be given.

KATYAYANA says, if a living pledge die or be made useless through the carelessness of a person other than the pledgee, the pledger shall give another pledge and shall not be released from debt.

If pledged cows, &c., be accidentally destroyed, the principal shall be lost.

If pledged cows, &c., be accidentally destroyed, the principal shall be lost. This is according to the practice among persons of good manners.

The pledge to be submitted to the king on the death of the pledger.

If the pledger die, the pledgee shall submit the pledge to the king.

The pledge is to be publicly sold.

The pledge is to be publicly sold. The pledgee taking his principal and interest, the balance shall be deposited with the king.

VRIHASPATI says, where a house or land has been pledged for the use of the pledgee for a specified time, neither the pledgee will be competent to receive the money nor the pledger to take his property, unless the time expire. When the time has passed, the pledgee may receive his principal, and the pledger get back his property. If a house or lands be pledged for the use of the pledgee for a specified time, neither the pledgee can receive money nor the pledger take his property, till the time expire.

But the property may be released and the money taken by mutual consent, before the time expires. Except by mutual consent.

MENU says, a pledge, even if it remain for ever, cannot be sold or made *nesargo*, that is, pledged, by the pledger, for a larger sum of money, with another person. A pledge, even if it remain for ever, cannot be sold, &c.

According to HALAYUDHA, *nesargo* means gift. Therefore, gift of a pledge cannot be made. Nesargo defined to be gift.

The conclusion is that a pledge cannot be mortgaged or sold. A pledge cannot be mortgaged or sold.

Others explain the above passage in the following way. Pledgees, having no proprietary right, cannot make a gift of, or sell, the pledge to another. Therefore, formal prohibition is superfluous. When the time for the release of the pledge is specified, the debtor, having then no power over it, is not competent to make a gift of, or sell it to another. Another explanation of the passage.

The sale of a pledge in what case valid.

The rule, that the sale of a pledge becomes valid, is to be applied to such cases only in which the time for the release of the pledge is not specified.

A pledge if not released, may be given away or sold.

The remark that pledged property, unless released, cannot be made a gift of, or sold, has no foundation.

The foregoing passage of Menu supposed to be applicable to beneficial pledges.

It is in a manner mentioned in the *Kalpataru* that the foregoing passage from MENU is applicable to beneficial pledges.

But it may, for a similar reason, be applied to property kept in deposit and pledged without any agreement.

OF SURETIES.

Vrihaspati says, sages have mentioned four kinds of sureties in the system of jurisprudence: surety for appearance, for honesty, for paying a debt, and for delivering the debtor's effects.

Four kinds of sureties in the system of jurisprudence.

The fourth is for such articles as are taken as loan for use, and consequently for cases in which the surety undertakes to recover a thing taken by a person. Therefore, the fourth is for return only and not for payment. But money is to be paid by a surety of the third kind. This then is the difference between the third and fourth kinds of surety.

The fourth is for such articles as are taken as loan for use.

Difference between the third and fourth kinds of surety.

Sampradya, reading the above text in a different manner, thus explains the fourth:—The property of the debtor is to be given to the creditor.

The fourth explained by Sampradya.

The first surety declares he will produce the debtor; the second vouches for the debtor's trustworthiness; the third undertakes to pay for the debtor; and the fourth to recover the article taken.

The first surety declares he will produce the debtor, &c.

The first two sureties shall liquidate the debts with interest, if the debtors fail to pay.

The first two sureties shall liquidate the debts with interest.

The last two sureties, as well as their sons (after them,) shall pay the debt.

The last two sureties and their sons shall pay the debts.

Katyayana speaks of sureties for the settlement of differences.

KATYAYANA has made mention of sureties even for the settlement of differences, for the observance of oaths, &c.

This being one of the aforesaid four kinds, the number of sureties is therefore four.

Promises to pay, &c., require surety.

He says *dan* (promise to pay,) *uposthan* (promise to produce the debtor,) confidence, settlement of differences, and observance of oaths, require sureties.

Responsibility of sureties.

If those who have given sureties do not act properly, the latter shall be responsible.

The son of a surety when not obliged to pay the debt.

If a surety speak of a dishonest man as honest or cannot produce a debtor, he, but not his sons, shall pay the debt.

Yagnyavalkya confirms this.

YAGNYAVALKYA confirms this by saying that, when a surety, who vouches for the trustworthiness of a man or undertakes to produce the debtor, dies, his sons shall not be obliged to pay the debt.

The sons of a surety for payment liable for money.

Even the sons of a surety for payment shall be liable to pay the money.

A surety when to pay the debt.

If there be no act of God or of the king, and the time for the appearance of the debtor expire, the surety shall pay the debt.

If, after the time for producing the debtor has expired on account of the act of God or of the king, the surety carelessly refrain from producing him at a time when there is no act of God or of the king to prevent it, or if the debtor die, the surety shall pay the debt. The surety is to pay the debt, if he neglect to produce the debtor.

KATYAYANA confirms this in the following words. When a surety cannot produce the debtor at the proper place, and at the appointed time, when there is no act of God or of the king, he shall pay the debt. Katyayana confirms this.

If, on the expiration of the appointed time, the debtor cannot be produced, the surety shall pay the debt. This rule holds good when the debtor dies. The surety is to pay the debt, if the debtor be not produced at the appointed time.

If a person be surety for appearance, by taking a pledge, his sons also shall pay the debt. When the sons of a surety for appearance are to pay the debt.

This is confirmed by the following: If a creditor can prove that a person has become surety for appearance by taking a pledge, the sons of the surety also shall pay the debt. The rule confirmed.

The sons of the surety shall pay the principal only and not interest. The sons of the surety shall pay the principal only.

VYASA confirms it by saying that, when a person pays the debt of his grandfather and the son of a surety pays money due by the latter, both of them shall only pay an amount equal to the debt, but their sons shall not be liable to pay such debt. This is fixed. Vyasa confirms this.

Responsibility of several sureties.

YAGNYAVALKYA says that, in the case of several sureties, a debt shall be paid by them according to their respective shares. The creditor shall be competent to realise his debt from any of them, should there be a condition to that effect.

A creditor may realise his debt from any of the sureties, if there be such an agreement.

If a creditor, at the time of lending money, stipulate that he will realise his debt from any of the sureties according to his option, he shall be competent to do so.

Sureties may have time for inquiring after the debtor.

Sureties may have time for making inquiries after the debtor.

Vrihaspati confirms this.

VRIHASPATI confirms this by saying that creditors shall give the surety time for instituting inquiries after the absconding debtor.

The time varies according to the distance of places.

The time is to vary from fifteen days to a month and a half according to the distance of places.

A surety should not be harassed.

A surety shall not be harassed. A debt, due by him, is to be realised by mild measures.

If a surety be forced to pay a debt, he shall get its double.

A surety, who is forced to pay a debt, shall get its double after a month and a half (from the debtor.)

After a month and a half, interest shall accrue.

After that period, interest shall accrue, even if there be no previous agreement, and the principal shall be doubled in due time. It cannot be doubled till after a month and a half.

Any expense that a surety incurs for the debtor, shall be paid by the latter.

Any expense incurred by the surety, shall be paid by the debtor.

KATYAYANA confirms this by saying that, if a surety, harassed by a creditor, spend any thing for a debtor, he shall get it back by proving the same by witnesses.

Katyayana confirms this.

Before accepting a surety, it is proper for the creditor to ascertain whether the proposed surety is able to pay the debt, in case it cannot be liquidated by the debtor.

The creditor should ascertain if the proposed surety is able to pay the debt.

KATYAYANA confirms this by saying that a person, who cannot pay the debt to the creditor or a fine of an equal amount to the king, or is a stranger, should not be accepted as a surety.

Katyayana confirms this.

His ability to pay a debt, and so forth, should be ascertained by his public credit.

Public credit should decide the ability of the surety to pay the debt.

RULES FOR REALISING DEBTS.

When a debtor is to pay his debt.

VRIHASPATI says, a debtor shall pay his debt on demand, if there be no fixed time for payment, or on the expiration of the appointed time if there be any. Where no time is fixed, the debt is to be liquidated, on the interest rising to its highest point. On default of the debtor, his sons shall liquidate it.

On the death of a debtor, who is to pay his debt.

NAREDA says that, on the death of a debtor, his sons, if living separate, shall pay his debt in proportion to their respective shares; if not separate, it shall be paid by that son who takes the burden of the family on himself.

When a person goes to a foreign country, &c., his sons and grandsons are to pay the debt.

YAGNYAVALKYA says, when a person goes to a foreign country, dies, or is in great danger, his sons and grandsons shall pay his debt. If they question the justice of the claims of the creditor, they should satisfy them by receiving evidence.

According to Nareda.

NAREDA specially speaks of a man who goes to a foreign country. When a person goes to a foreign country, his son, nephew, or brother, shall not pay his debt until twenty years have elapsed.

Interpretation.

The words "twenty years," that occur in the following text of VISHNU, refer to cases in which persons reside in foreign countries ; or else there will be inconsistent opinions.

When a debtor dies, becomes an anchoret, or remains abroad for twenty years, his sons or grandsons shall pay the debt. It is optional to his great grandsons to pay it or not ; in other words, they cannot be compelled to pay. When a debtor dies, becomes an anchoret, &c., his sons and grandsons shall pay the debt.

Debts contracted under an agreement, shall be paid by the debtor, his sons, or grandsons. Obligation as to debts, under an agreement.

A pledge cannot be redeemed without paying the debt. How a pledge may be redeemed.

The passage is explained in the *Ratnakara* and by some others as follows. If a debt, contracted by a person, be for the benefit of an undivided family, his sons, nephew, or brothers shall pay it twenty years after he has gone to a foreign country. How the passage is explained in the Ratnakara and by others.

According to the author of the *Smritisara*, a debt contracted by the members of a family, after partition, for themselves, shall be paid by their sons, if they go to foreign countries. The rule as to time refers to the above case. But it cannot be applied in the case of a debt contracted for the benefit of the family before partition, for all its members are then debtors. This explanation renders the provisions made by the sages free from obscurity. Consequently, when a debt is to be paid in obedience to the orders of the sages, and not for contracting it, the period of twenty years is applicable. But a debt, contracted for the benefit of the family, is to Debt contracted by the members of a family after or before a partition.

be paid before twenty years have elapsed. For YAGNYAVALKYA says, a debt contracted for the benefit of the family before partition, is to be paid by all of them, when the debtor dies or goes to a foreign country. They should not, in this case, require time, since there is no necessity for it. Time should be allowed when a debt is contracted after partition.

When time is not necessary for the payment of a debt.

Time is not necessary when a debt is paid during the life-time of the debtor, because VRIHASPATI says, if a person be blind, deaf, mad, or afflicted with some incurable disease, his sons shall pay his debts established by evidence, even when he is near them.

Who shall pay the just debt of a poor man.

The *Parijata* explains it as follows. When a person is unable to pay his just debt owing to poverty, his sons, who live separate from him and have means, and, on their default, his grandsons, if they have means, shall pay it.

Debt contracted by several men.

When a debt is contracted by several men, and one of them survives the rest, the survivor shall pay it for all. On his default, his son shall pay only his share of the debt.

The surviving joint debtor or debtors shall pay the entire debt.

If there be an agreement to the effect that the creditor shall be competent to realise his money from any of the joint debtors, the surviving one or ones shall pay it. For it is at the option of the creditor to take it from any of them.

If one of the joint debtors go to a foreign country, his son shall pay the whole of his debts. If he die, his son shall pay his share and not that of any other debtor.

Responsibility of son of one of the joint debtors.

As such debt must be paid, these texts are mentioned in disallowance of time.

Why time is disallowed in these texts.

On the death of any of the joint debtors, his share of the debt shall be paid by his son.

Who shall pay the debt of a deceased joint debtor.

KATYAYANA says, what is promised by a man for religious purposes, be he in health or sick, must be paid. On his death, his son shall pay it.

What is promised for religious purposes must be paid.

NAREDA particularly says, a minor is not to pay a debt, even when he is independent.

A minor is not to pay a debt.

KATYAYANA asserts that, on the death of their father, minors shall pay his debt in due time according to law. If they do not pay it, they shall dwell in hell.

Minors shall pay the debt of their dead father in due time.

A child of eight years of age is equal to one in the womb. A child under his sixteenth year is called *bala* or *paganda*. After his sixteenth year, the child attains majority, and, if he have no parents, becomes independent.

Definition of minority.

KATYAYANA says that persons shall pay the just debts, or the balance of the debts, of their grandfathers. But if the debts were contracted for gambling or drinking, and were not acknowledged by their fathers, they are not liable to pay such debts.

Just debts, &c., of grandfathers.

Particular debts of fathers.

GAUTAMA speaks of the liquidation of particular debts incurred by fathers.

What debts of their father, sons are not liable to pay.

Their debts, due for being sureties, for losses sustained in mercantile transactions, the purchase of spirituous liquors, gaming, and fines, do not devolve on their sons.

Debt due for being surety defined.

Debt due for being surety means that *incurred for being* surety for appearance and for confidence.

According to Vrihaspati.

VRIHASPATI says that sons are not liable for such debts of their fathers as are due for the purchase of spirituous liquors, for gaming, idly-promised gifts, love, anger, surety, fines, tolls, and the balance of tolls or fines.

Vyasa confirms this.

VYASA confirms this. Fines, tolls, or their balance thereof, and debts for irregular conduct, due from fathers, shall not be paid by their sons.

Debts through love and anger.

KATYAYANA speaks of debts incurred through love and anger.

Debt through love defined.

Debt through love means what is promised to a harlot.

Debt through anger defined.

Debt through anger means what is promised to a man as compensation for any injury done him.

Idly-promised gift defined.

Idly-promised gift means what is promised without effect. For how can a man be prevented from giving a thing which *has been already given?*

Debt by a surety defined.

Debt by a surety means a debt due for being surety for appearance and confidence.

NAREDA speaks of some cases in which even paternal debts are not to be liquidated by sons. Paternal debts.

Where the property of a man is taken by one *man*, and his wife by another, and he has a son, his debt shall be paid by the first; and, on the default of the first two, by the son. Debt to be paid by him who takes the property of the debtor.

On default of the first and third, the second shall pay the debt. When to be paid by him who takes his wife.

Though there be a son who is competent to pay the debt, but is in distress, he who takes the property shall be liable for the debt. He who takes property shall pay the debt.

On the default of a person who has taken his property or one who has taken his wife, his son, though he be in distress, shall be liable to pay. When the son is to pay his father's debt, without getting his property.

On the default of a person taking his property and a son competent to pay money, he who takes his wife shall pay his debt. When he who takes the wife of the debtor is to pay the debt.

Therefore, if there be a person who has taken his estate, neither his son nor he who takes his wife shall pay it. The person taking the estate, shall alone pay the debt.

VRIHASPATI says, if the son of a debtor be in distress, he who takes his estate shall pay the debt, and, on his default, he who has taken his wife shall pay it. According to Vrihaspati.

A father's debt to be paid under certain circumstances.

KATYAYANA says that a person shall pay his father's debt, if he be not in distress and if he be able to discharge it, or else he shall not pay it.

Who shall pay the debt of a person, when his son is in distress, &c.

Where the son is in distress, or is a minor, the debt is to be paid by him who has taken his father's property, and, on his default, by him who has taken his mother.

According to Yagnyavalka.

YAGNYAVALKYA says that a son shall pay his father's debt on the default of him who has taken his father's property or taken his mother.

The heirs of a debtor shall pay his debt.

If the debtor have no son, his heirs shall pay his debt.

The son who gets the post of his father, shall pay the debt.

Therefore, a person, whose father's estate has not been taken by others, shall pay his debt even though he have no means to do so. Therefore, that son who gets the post of his father shall bear his burden, and consequently he, and not his brothers, shall pay his father's debt.

Explanation.

In short, the son who has taken the post of his father, and is competent to pay, shall liquidate his debt, even if there be one who has taken his father's property or wife.

Who is to pay the debt on default of such a son.

On the default of such a son, he who has obtained the estate shall pay the debt.

When the person who takes the debtor's wife is to pay the debt.

If no one take his estate, he who has taken his wife shall pay the debt, even if there be sons other than those who are competent to pay it.

On the default of these, sons, who are unable to pay and who have not taken the post of their father, shall be liable to pay his debt. When sons unable to pay the debt, &c., shall be liable.

Of several sons, he who has been appointed to the post of the father shall pay his debt. The son appointed to the post of the father shall pay the debt.

NAREDA says that persons, other than sons, shall pay the debt. According to Nareda, who is to pay the debt.

A debt, contracted by an uncle, a brother, or mother, before partition, for the benefit of the family, shall be paid by all its members. Debt contracted for the benefit of the family.

MENU says that a debt, contracted for the benefit of the family by a dependent of its dependents, whether in the native country or abroad, cannot be disowned by the head of the family. According to Menu.

VRIHASPATI says that a debt, contracted for the benefit of the family, by an uncle, brother, son, wife, servant, pupil, or dependent, shall be paid by the head of the family. According to Vrihaspati.

If a debt, contracted by the servant of a family, should be paid, it is plain that what is incurred by one of its members should also be paid. For it is a common saying that a debt, incurred by the members of a family who live together, shall be paid. A debt incurred by the joint members of a family shall be paid.

Certain of the debts of a son are to be paid by his father. For instance, such debts as are approved of by his father or such as the father shall pay out of affection, or else he shall not pay it. Certain debts of a son may be paid by his father.

Women are not liable for the debts of husbands and sons.

According to VISHNU, women shall not pay debts due by their husbands and sons; nor shall husbands and sons pay such as are due by their respective wives and mothers.

A woman's debts do not fall on her husband, &c.

NAREDA affirms that the debts of a woman do not fall on her husband, unless they be for the benefit of the family. For a debt, contracted for the benefit of the family, must be paid.

But the debts of the wives of washermen, &c., shall be paid by their husbands.

But the debts of the wives of washermen, fowlers, milkmen, and wine-vendors, shall be paid by their husbands. For the latter depend entirely on, and their families are supported by, the former.

This rule holds good where the women manage families, &c.,

This rule holds good where the women manage families, and the men are simple and without any distinction of caste.

Exemplification.

The above is merely an instance. For the debts incurred by the wives of Brahmins, and so forth, for the benefit of the family, are likewise paid.

What debts to be paid by women, according to Yagnyavalkya.

YAGNYAVALKYA speaks of debts that are to be paid by women. He says that the debts of a man which his wife has consented to pay, and those incurred by both of them, shall be paid by her.

According to Katyayana.

KATYAYANA says that debts, contracted by a woman, with her husband and son, and what she incurred herself, shall be paid by her.

According to Narda.

NAREDA says, a woman is not bound to pay the debts due by her husband or son.

If a man, on his death-bed, enjoin his wife to pay his debt, she must pay it.

When a woman is to pay her husband's debt.

In short, a woman shall pay such debts as she agrees to pay.

Debts which a woman agrees to pay.

If she inherit the family estate, she must pay the debts, even if she do not agree to do so. For she has taken the property.

Debts devolve on women with family estates.

NAREDA makes special mention of some of those who take others' wives.

Nareda on the responsibility of those who take others' wives.

He who takes possession of the fourth or last of the *shairinis*, or first of the *punorbhus* (widows,) shall pay debts due by the husband.

He who takes the fourth or last of the shairinis, &c., shall pay the debts of the husband.

He who takes the wife of a poor and childless dead man, shall pay his debts, for the wife is the dead man's property.

He who takes the wife of a poor and childless dead man, shall pay his debts.

NAREDA speaks of the fourth *shairini* and first *punorbhu*. By the fourth *shairini* is meant a woman, who, having come from a different country, or having been purchased by wealth, or being pressed by hunger or thirst, takes shelter with a man by saying that she will belong to him. By the first *punorbhu* is meant a woman, who, having lost her husband before she attained puberty, is married a second time.

Fourth shairini and first punorbhu defined.

Debts of poor and childless wine-vendors, &c., shall be paid by those who take their wives.

KATYAYANA says, debts due by poor and childless wine-vendors, &c., shall be paid by those who take their wives.

Explanation.

Wine-vendors, &c., mean such as depend on their wives for support.

Debts due by those who live abroad, &c., shall be paid by those who take their wives, &c.

KATYAYANA says, debts due by those who live abroad for a long time, who are childless, who are void of the senses, who are mad, and who are anchorets, shall be paid by those who take their wives and property, even when they are alive.

How they shall pay debts.

These persons shall pay debts in the same manner as sons pay their paternal debts; but the difference is that they do not pay interest, since no provision has been made to that effect.

Who shall get the dues of a dead and childless Brahmin creditor.

NAREDA says that, on the death of a childless Brahmin creditor, his dues shall be paid to his kinsmen, and on their default, to his relations.

Other Brahmins shall get them.

But if there be neither kinsmen nor relatives, his dues shall be given to Brahmins.

When they shall be thrown into the water.

On their default, they shall be thrown into the water.

If the creditors be soldiers, &c., their dues shall be paid to the king.

If the creditors be soldiers, &c., their dues shall be paid to the king. For it is understood that all wealth, save that of Brahmins, devolves on the king. Therefore, what belongs to Brahmins shall not be received by the king.

MENU speaks of the means to be taken by a creditor, if the debtor do not pay the debt on demand. **Menu on the means of realising a debt.**

A creditor should be allowed to realise his debt by whatever means he can do so. **A debt is to be realised by any means.**

Dharma (mode of recovery consonant to moral duty), *vyavahara* (suit in court), *chhal* (artful management), *acharita* (distress), and *bal* (legal force), are the five means whereby a debt may be realised. Each of these shall alternately be used on the failure of the other. **Five means of realising a debt.**

VRIHASPATI defines *mode consonant to moral duty* to be the mode of recovery "by the interposition of friends and kinsmen, by mild remonstrances, by importunate following," or by performing *dharna* before the house of the debtor. **Mode consonant to moral duty defined.**

If the debtor be a poor Brahmin, a debt shall be gradually realised from him according to his income. **A debt shall be gradually realised from a poor Brahmin.**

KATYAYANA defines the mode of recovery by suit in court to be the mode of recovery by arresting a debtor, openly dragging him before the public assembly, and confining him "until he pay what is due, according to the immemorial usage of the country." **Mode of recovery by suit in court defined.**

Artful management defined.

Artful management means the act of realising a debt by borrowing a thing of the debtor with an artful design, or withholding a thing deposited by him, or the like.

Distress defined.

Distress signifies the realisation of the debt by confining the wife, son, or the cattle of the debtor, or preventing egress from, and ingress into, his house.

Legal force defined.

Legal force means the realisation of the debt by binding the debtor, carrying him to the house of the creditor, and beating him, or other means.

Demand should at first be made.

Before adopting any of these means, it is necessary to make a demand.

A debt from a king, &c., is to be realised by mild expostulation.

KATYAYANA says, if a king, master, or priest be the debtor, a debt is to be realised by mild expostulation.

Debts from shareholders, &c., to be realised by artful management.

Debts from shareholders and friends are to be realised by artful management.

Debts from merchants, &c. to be realised by suit in court.

BHRIGU says, debts from merchants, agriculturists, and artisans are to be realised by suit in court, and those from wicked men by legal force.

How debts are to be realised from poor wine-vendors, &c.

VRIHASPATI speaks of cases where debts cannot be realised by suit in court. If the debtors be poor wine-vendors, &c., the creditor shall bring them to his house and force them to liquidate their debts by bodily labor.

If they be poor Brahmins, debts shall be gradually realised from them. From poor Brahmins.

YAGNYAVALKYA says, if they be poor and belong to low castes, they shall be forced to liquidate their debts by bodily labor. Low caste debtors shall be forced to liquidate their debts by bodily labor.

But if they be poor Brahmins, debts shall be gradually realised from them with reference to their income. Debts from poor Brahmins to be gradually realised.

KATYAYANA speaks of the penalty for using legal force at the outset. Penalty for using legal force at the outset.

If the debtors be, in the beginning, forced to do any thing which is disadvantageous to them and advantageous to the creditors, the latter shall be fined the *first sahasa* (250 *panas*,) and the former shall be freed from their debts. When the creditor shall be fined, and the debtor freed from his debt.

NAREDA says, if the debtors become poor owing to some unforeseen events, debts shall be gradually realised from them according to their income. Debts shall be gradually realised from persons becoming poor by some unforeseen events.

When the interest of a loan reaches its highest point and the debtor cannot liquidate it, he can, if he like, renew it on compound interest. When the debtor can renew a loan on compound interest.

VRIHASPATI confirms this by saying that creditors shall realise money with interest on the expiration of the appointed time; or the debtors shall agree by writing to give compound interest. Vrihaspati confirms this.

When interest, exceeding twice the principal, may be received.

VRIHASPATI says, when the interest has risen to its highest point, and it has been added to the principal, interest exceeding twice the principal may be received.

When the principal comprises principal with interest, compound interest may be charged, &c.

When the principal comprises principal with interest, compound interest may be charged on twice the principal and some other interest may be enjoyed; and the principal shall consist of the interest and principal.

When a debt of valuable articles having been doubled, the debtors have died, &c., their movables shall be taken, &c.

He speaks on the subject of the absence of the debtors. When a debt of valuable articles having been doubled, the debtors have died or absconded, their movables shall be taken and disposed of with the knowledge of witnesses. Their price being fixed, they shall be laid open to public inspection. The dues of the creditors being taken after the adjustment of accounts, the balance shall be given to the debtors.

Creditors are not to blame, if debts be thus realised before the debtors' kinsmen.

If money be realised in the abovementioned manner before the kinsmen of the debtors, no blame can be attached to the creditors.

A creditor is not to be punished, even if he realise the debt by legal force.

The king should not punish a creditor, even if he realise the debt by legal force.

Vishnu confirms this.

VISHNU confirms this by saying that the king should not prevent a creditor from realising his dues by any of the aforesaid means.

YAGNYAVALKYA says the king cannot prevent a creditor from realising his dues that have been admitted by the debtors.

A creditor cannot be prevented from realising his dues admitted by the debtors.

If such a debtor bring a suit against his creditor, the former shall be fined and shall pay the debt.

The debtor shall be fined, if he bring a suit against his creditor.

A *kryabadi* debtor, who does not admit the claim of the creditor, cannot be forced to pay the debt by any of the aforesaid means and cannot be arrested.

A kryabadi debtor.

VRIHASPATI confirms this by saying that a *kryabadi* debtor cannot, in doubtful cases, be (*sangdhirdhata*), arrested.

Vrihaspati confirms this.

He who causes the arrest of such a man becomes liable to just punishment.

Arrest of such a man punishable.

A *kryabadi* debtor means one who undertakes to pay what is legally due by him.

A kryabadi debtor defined.

Doubtful cases (*sangdhirdhata*) means cases where the nature of the coin lent, its number, &c., the amount of interest, and the payment or non-payment, are disputed.

What are doubtful cases.

MENU says, the king shall impose, on wicked creditors and debtors, a fine of twice the amount which any of them endeavors to gain by cheating.

Wicked creditors and debtors shall be fined.

This rule is applicable to the case of rich men.

The rule applicable to the rich.

Menu fixes a penalty for debtors who, at first, declining to pay debt, afterwards promise to pay it.

MENU also enjoins that a person who, at first declining to pay a debt, afterwards promises to pay it, shall be fined five per cent. But if his debt be proved by evidence, he shall be fined ten per cent. This rule applies to the cases of men.

A debtor who refused to pay his debt, &c., shall be punished.

YAGNYAVALKYA says, if the debt of a man who refused to pay it, be proved by evidence, he shall not only pay the debt but also an equal amount of fine.

A creditor bringing a false suit to be fined.

If a creditor bring a false suit, he shall pay a fine of twice the amount claimed therein.

Where this rule is applicable.

This rule is for him who has failed in *karanabad* and *pragnaobad* (two sorts of reply).

Middle class men.

It is for men of the middle classes.

A rich man wickedly withholding payment of others' dues shall be fined.

YAMA says, if a rich man wickedly withhold payment of the dues of others, the king shall cause them to be paid by fining him twice the amount of the debt.

If a creditor prove his claim, the debtor shall be fined.

VISHNU says, if a creditor, by instituting a suit, prove his claim, the debtor shall pay it, and a fine equal to a tenth of the same.

A twentieth of the debt to be given to the king.

On realising a debt, the creditor shall give the king a twentieth part of the amount.

KATYAYANA says that a man, who is indebted to several parties, shall pay him first, from whom he got the first loan. If the king or a Brahmin be one of the creditors, he should be paid before others. A debtor shall first repay the first loan, or the king or a Brahmin.

If all the bonds have been written in one day, the debts, payments, balances, and interest, shall be equal; otherwise, according to the order of time. Bonds of the same date, to be treated as equally valid.

That creditor, who can prove that the debtor acquired money by means of his principal, must be paid before any other creditor, if the debtor have no means of liquidating all his debts. What creditor must be paid before any other.

YAGNYAVALKYA says that the bond shall be torn upon payment of the debt. Where no deed exists, let one be prepared by way of a release. But a debt which was contracted before witnesses must be paid also before witnesses. The bond shall be torn upon payment of the debt, &c.

DEPOSITS.

Deposit defined by Nareda.

NAREDA defines deposit to be the entrusting of one's property with another person from confidence and without suspicion. The wise have included it in the category of subjects of dispute.

With whom articles may be deposited.

MENU says that articles shall be deposited with a person, who is "of high birth and of good morals," who is virtuous, who speaks truth, who has many kinsmen, and who is wealthy and respectable.

What is upanidhi.

YAGNYAVALKYA says that "a thing enclosed *under seal* in a box or casket, which the owner delivers into the hands of another, without mentioning *its kind, form, or quantity,* is called *upanidhi,* and must be restored in the same condition."

Two sorts of deposits.

NAREDA says that "deposits are declared to be of two sorts, attested and unattested." They should be returned in the same condition in which they were delivered. Otherwise, the depositary shall be tried by ordeal.

He who consumes a deposit, &c., commits a heinous deed.

VRIHASPATI says, he who consumes a deposit or from neglect spoils it, commits a deed as heinous as the murder of a son or friend by a man, or the damage done by a woman to her husband.

A depositary shall not destroy a deposit.

A depositary shall not destroy a deposit. For it is infamous to do so. He shall keep it with great care, and restore it on the first demand.

As long as the depositor is alive, the deposit shall not be restored to any but him.

Deposit not to be restored to any but the depositor.

VRIHASPATI confirms this, by saying that a deposit shall be restored to the depositor in the condition in which he left it, and not to his sons.

Authority of Vrihaspati on the above.

MENU says, if a depositary delivers a deposit to the sons of a depositor after his death, neither the king nor the kinsmen of the deceased shall harass him.

A depositary shall not be harassed for delivering a deposit to the sons of a deceased depositor.

NAREDA says, if a deposit be lost with the property of the depositary, the loss will be the depositor's. Such will also be the case, if the deposit be lost by the act of God or of the king, "unless there was a fraudulent act on the part of the depositary."

If a deposit be lost with the property of the depositary, or by an act of God or the king, the loss will be the depositor's.

But the depositary shall bear the loss, if the act of the king were occasioned by his fault, in which case the loss is attributable to him.

The depositary shall bear the loss, if the act of the king were occasioned by his fault.

This is also the opinion of MENU :—If the deposit be stolen, "washed away by water, or consumed by fire," the depositary shall not make it good, unless he himself took a part of it.

Menu's opinion.

If, a portion of a deposit being appropriated, the remainder be neglected, or kept with some other person, in the hope that he may not be required to restore it, the depositary must restore the whole deposit.

When the depositary is to restore the whole deposit.

The depositary shall make good what is lost by his fault.

KATYAYANA says, the depositary shall make good what is lost by his fault. Further, he, by whose fault a deposit is lost or taken away, shall be compelled to make good the value of it with interest, unless it be lost by the act of God or of the king.

The depositary shall bear the loss, if the act of the king were occasioned by his fault.

But if the act of the king were occasioned by his fault, the depositary shall bear the loss.

The value of a destroyed article when to be made good by the borrower.

KATYAYANA speaks of articles that are borrowed. He says that if a borrowed article, which is not returned on demand, when there is no further occasion for it, or the time of its return has expired, be destroyed even by the act of God or the king, the value of it shall be made good by the borrower.

This rule is applicable to deposits for delivery, &c.

NAREDA says that this rule is applicable to "deposits for delivery and the like, bailments with an artist, sealed deposits, bailments in the form called *nyasa*, and mutual trusts."

In what manner judges shall ascertain whether any article was or was not kept with a person.

If a person deny that any article was left with him, the judges shall ascertain the point in the following manner. They shall cause something to be lodged with him. If they get it back on demand, they must conclude that he is not dishonest; otherwise they must consider him such.

This rule is applicable in the case of a loan for use.

This rule is applicable in the case of a loan for use *(yachita.)* It has not been mentioned in a proper place in the *Ratnakara.*

VRIHASPATI says, if the depositary spoil a deposit by keeping it separate from his own articles, or through carelessness, or do not return it on demand, the value of it shall be made good with interest. If the depositary spoil a deposit, &c., the value of it shall be made good with interest.

The meaning of the above is that, if a depositary take care of his own articles by keeping them in a particular place, and neglect the deposit, he must pay the value of it with interest. Explanation.

If the deposit be not restored on demand, and then be taken by the king, the depositary shall make good the value of it. If a deposit, not restored on demand, be taken by the king, the depositary shall make good its value.

NAREDA confirms this by saying that he, who does not return a deposit on demand, shall be punished by the king. If it be, in the mean time, spoiled, the value of it is to be paid. Nareda's authority on the point.

If the depositary, without the permission of the depositor, use a deposit for gain, he shall be punished and compelled to surrender it with the gain derived. If the deposit be used without permission for gain, the depositary shall be punished.

VYASA says that, if a deposit be used, it shall be restored with interest. But if it be injured through carelessness, the value of it must be given. If it be fortuitously spoiled, a moderate price shall be given. If a deposit be used, it shall be restored with interest.

MENU says that he, who takes possession of others' property on false pretences, shall, with his accessaries, be tortured to death in a public place. Those who take possession of others' property on false pretences, shall be tortured to death.

This rule is applicable in other cases of the kind.

This rule also holds good in other cases of this description.

Vrihaspati's authority on the point.

VRIHASPATI confirms this by saying that, if a bailment for delivery *(anvahita)*, a loan for use *(yachita)*, bailments with an artist *(shilpinasha,)* &c., be taken, this rule obtains.

Explanation.

" Bailments with an artist" means gold, &c., given to workmen to be manufactured into ornaments, &c.

Workmen punishable in the same manner.

If workmen take them on false pretences, they shall be liable to the aforesaid punishment.

If an article be injured, while it is with a workman for repair, the value of it must be made good by him.

If an article be left with a workman for repair in a specified time, and be injured after the expiration of that time, by accident or otherwise, the value of it must be paid by the workman.

Explanation.

The meaning of the above is that, if it be injured after the expiration of the fixed time, the artisan shall make good its value, and not otherwise.

He who does not return a deposit, &c., shall be punished as thieves.

MENU says, he who does not return a deposit and he who demands something which he did not deposit, shall be punished as thieves, and fined in an amount commensurate with what they endeavour to gain by deceit.

How this passage is rendered in the Matsya Purana.

In the *Matsya Purana*, this *sloka* is read in the following manner :—Instead of being equal to the amount attempted to be taken by deceit, the fine shall be twice that amount.

The last reading is applicable to mean and dishonest rich persons. To whom the last reading is applicable.

But the injunction of MENU is applicable to poor and honest persons. Menu's injunction applied to poor and honest persons.

KATYAYANA says that he, who uses, neglects, or unconsciously spoils any deposit, and so forth, shall himself pay for it. His sons, and others who were not concerned in injuring it, shall not be responsible. He who spoils any deposit, shall alone be responsible.

GAUTAMA confirms this by saying that "the necessity of making good a deposit, a thing bailed for delivery to a third person, a pledge on a thing borrowed or hired, and the like, if destroyed by the fault of the bailee, shall not fall upon any of his heirs, if they were free from blame; but it falls on the bailee, by whose fault the thing was destroyed." Gautama's authority on the point.

"A thing bailed for delivery to a third person" means an article left with one in order to be given to another. Explanation.

KATYAYANA defines *upanidhi* to be an article which has been sold but not delivered, or which is left with another person on the owner's going to another country, a pledge, a bailment for delivery, (*anvahita*,) a loan for use, or money advanced to tradesmen for gain. Upanidhi defined by Katyayana.

The deposit and restoration of articles, the care with which they should be kept, and the penalties, &c., for neglect, are dealt with according to the rules of deposit. The rules of deposit, where applicable.

SALE WITHOUT OWNERSHIP.

Sale or gift of articles by persons without title, inadmissible.

NAREDA says that, according to the rules of Judicial Proceedings, the sale or gift of articles by persons, who have no title thereto, is inadmissible.

Sale, gift, or pledge by others than the owners, prohibited.

KATYAYANA says that the sale, gift, or pledge of articles by persons who are not the owners, are prohibited.

He who sells the property of another, without permission, is to be treated as a thief.

MENU says that he, who sells the property of another man without the consent of the owner, shall not be admitted as a competent witness, but shall be treated as a thief, who pretends that he has committed no theft. If he be a near kinsman of the owner, he shall be fined 600 *panas*. But if he be neither kinsman, nor able to produce a written document transferring the proprietary right to him, he shall be punished like a thief.

Punishment for selling property without the knowledge or against the will of the owner.

If the property of any person be sold without his knowledge, the vendor shall be fined 600 *panas;* but if it be done against the will of the owner, the vendor shall be punished like a thief, that is, his hands shall be cut off.

Vrihaspati on the measures to be adopted, when one demands a thing honestly purchased.

VRISHAPATI speaks of the measures to be adopted by an honest man, when a person demands from him a thing which he has purchased.

When the actual owner claims the purchased article, the purchaser may be freed from trouble by producing the vendor.

When the owner claims a purchased article, the purchaser may produce the vendor.

KATYAYANA says that a purchase shall be publicly made, or the vendor produced. If the vendor reside at a distant place, a certain time shall be allowed for every four miles.

Purchases to be publicly made, or the vendor produced.

If a person declare that he had purchased the article, and agree to produce the vendor, he shall, first of all, be required to do so. The validity of the sale may be known from the vendor. Consequently, when he cannot be found, inquiries shall be instituted into the validity of the purchase, that is, whether it was publicly made or not.

A person pleading purchase should produce the vendor.

VYASA speaks of the measures to be adopted when the vendor is produced.

According to Vyasa, when the vendor is produced, the purchaser not to be harassed.

When the vendor is produced, the purchaser shall not be harassed. But a suit may be carried on between the owner and the vendor.

VRIHASPATI says, if the vendor, on being produced, lose the suit, he shall satisfy the purchaser, pay a fine, and return the disputed article to its actual owner.

If the vendor lose the suit, he shall satisfy the purchaser, &c.

If the purchase have been fraudulently made, the purchaser shall, in addition, be punished.

If the purchase be fraudulent, the purchaser to be punished.

Purchaser under suspicious circumstances, equally guilty with the vendor.

NAREDA says that he, who purchases a thing from a slave who received no order from his master to dispose of it, or from a wicked man, privately, at a very inadequate price, or at an unseasonable hour, is equally guilty with him who sells others' articles.

Such a purchaser is guilty even if he produce the vendor.

Such a purchaser is guilty, even when he produces the vendor.

Purchaser who conceals his vendor, punishable.

NAREDA says that the purchaser shall not keep the vendor concealed, for he may be relieved by producing him. Otherwise, he is equally guilty with the vendor, in other words, shall be punished like him.

Punishment of the purchaser, who cannot produce the vendor.

NAREDA also says that, if the purchaser cannot produce the vendor, or give a satisfactory account of the purchase, he shall pay money to the actual proprietor, and suffer a pecuniary penalty in proportion to the claims set forth in the suit.

Case where the vendor cannot be produced, but the purchase seems to be fair.

MENU says that, when the vendor cannot be produced, but the purchase seems to have been publicly and consequently fairly made, the purchaser shall not be liable to a fine, but shall pay the actual proprietor.

Explanation.

Where the purchase has been publicly made, and the claim of the actual proprietor is proved, and the vendor cannot be produced on account of his having gone to a distant place, the king shall not punish the purchaser, but shall cause him to pay the actual proprietor.

According to KATYAYANA, the real proprietor shall recover his property, if those, who can identify it, say that he did not make a gift of, or forsake, or sell it.

Owner to recover his property, if it be proved that he did not dispose of it.

VRIHASPATI speaks of what is to be done to a man, who, having publicly purchased an article, cannot produce the vendor, because his place of residence cannot be ascertained. In the absence of proper evidence, the king shall pronounce the purchaser partially guilty, taking his character into consideration.

A purchaser to be held partially guilty, when there is not proper evidence, but the purchase was publicly made.

When a person purchases any thing, in a place surrounded by the shops of tradesmen, and with the knowledge of the public officials, and the vendor cannot be found in consequence of his living in an unknown place, or of his death, the actual proprietor shall establish his title by proof, and take possession of it on giving the purchaser half the value.

Case in which the proprietor may take possession of an article, by giving the purchaser half the value.

In such a case both the actual proprietor and the purchaser lose half *each*, according to the rules of judicial proceedings.

The actual proprietor and the purchaser lose half in such a case.

The purchase of an article without knowledge of its owner, and its neglect, are the causes of the injury of articles.

Causes of the injury of articles.

Where the actual proprietor cannot prove his title, he, who has publicly purchased the property, shall get it, and the proprietor shall be punished according to law.

When he who has publicly purchased the property, shall get it, and the proprietor be punished.

Katyayana's authority.

KATYAYANA confirms this:—If the proprietor cannot prove his title to the property by witnesses, he shall be punished like a thief, to prevent his bringing such a suit again.

Certain purchases, not valid.

Certain purchases, even from the actual proprietor, are not valid.

A fraudulent purchase equivalent to theft.

VRIHASPATI speaks on the subject. He says, if the purchase be made before others, by giving the vendor a reasonable price, it is valid; but a fraudulent purchase makes a man guilty of theft.

Fraudulent purchase defined.

By fraudulent purchase is meant the purchase of articles within a room, without the precincts of a village, at night, in solitary places, from wicked men, or at very inadequate prices.

Fraudulent purchase subject to the rules of invalid sale.

The rules as to the sale of property by one who has no right thereto are applicable to fraudulent purchases.

Vishnu's authority.

VISHNU confirms this by saying that, if a man purchase a thing privately at a low price or in a solitary place, he shall be punished like a thief.

Penalty for not giving notice to the king, of recovery of stolen property.

YAGNYAVALKYA says, if a man, whose property has been stolen or who misses it, give no notice of its recovery to the king, he shall be fined 96 *panas*.

The reason of the penalty.

This penalty is imposed on him for his attempt to defraud the king of his gain from the recovery of missing articles.

CONCERNS AMONG PARTNERS.

YAGNYAVALKYA says that those tradesmen, who jointly carry on business for gain, shall share the profit and loss according to their shares in the stock, or the conditions of their agreement.

Joint traders shall share the profit and loss according to their shares in the stock.

The meaning of the above is that, in the absence of an agreement, the shareholders shall receive profit or bear loss according to their respective shares in the stock. Where an agreement exists, the business shall be carried on agreeably to its conditions.

Explanation.

VRIHASPATI says, if the stock or the profits be diminished owing to the act of God or of the king, such a loss must be borne by all the shareholders according to their shares. He makes special mention of the following:—That shareholder, who causes a loss to the firm by acting against the wishes or without the assent of the others, shall alone bear it. The partner who, by his own exertions, saves the common stock from the act of God or of the king, shall be allowed a tenth part of it, and the remainder shall be divided among all according to their shares in the stock.

If the stock, &c., be diminished, owing to the act of God or of the king, such loss shall be borne by all the shareholders.

NAREDA says, he who, by his own exertions, preserves the goods of the partnership from the act of God, from robbers, from the king, from fire, and so forth, shall get a tenth part of them.

He who, by his own exertions, preserves the stock, shall get a tenth part of it.

According to Katyayana.

According to KATYAYANA, he who preserves goods from robbers, water, or fire, is entitled to a tenth part of them. This rule is applicable to all sorts of property.

Some say a tenth part is due, even when the article preserved belongs to an individual.

Some say that a tenth part is receivable, even when the article preserved belongs to an individual. But this cannot be the case, inasmuch as this rule occurs in the case of joint trade. This opinion is maintained in the *Ratnakara* and by others.

How joint traders shall carry on business.

Joint traders should carry on business without deceiving each other. KATYAYANA confirms the above, by saying that joint traders shall honestly purchase and sell goods, whether in the presence of each other or not.

Katyayana's authority.

A sharer, suspected of fraud, may be cleared by ordeal.

VRIHASPATI says, if a shareholder be suspected of fraud, he may be cleared by ordeal.

This rule is applicable in every case.

Explanation.

Ordeal here means evidence. For it is probable that evidence may be obtained from customers, and so forth.

A fraudulent partner may be expelled on returning his stock.

YAGNYAVALKYA says, a fraudulent partner may be expelled on returning him his stock. If the business cannot be transacted on account of his expulsion, another partner may be admitted.

Explanation.

The meaning of the above is that, if the remaining shareholders be unable to manage the business, a new partner should be admitted.

NAREDA says that, on the death of one of the partners, his business shall be undertaken by his heir. On default of one, some other competent man or all the shareholders shall transact it.

The business of a deceased partner shall be undertaken by his son.

The meaning of the above is that, on the death of a partner, his heir shall get a tenth part of the profits, if he preserve the stock. On his default, he who may preserve it shall get it. If there be no such person, those shareholders who may preserve it, shall get a tenth part of the profits.

Explanation.

NAREDA says, if a merchant, from a foreign country, die, the king shall preserve his goods till his heirs appear.

The king shall keep the goods of a deceased foreign merchant

VRIHASPATI says, if a partner die for want of proper care, the officers, appointed by the king, shall render his goods to the king.

The king is the heir of a partner who dies for want of proper care.

When a person appears, describing himself as the heir to the deceased, and proves that he is so, he shall get the goods.

The heir to the deceased shall, on proof, get the stock.

NAREDA says, if the deceased have no heir, his relatives and kinsmen shall get his property.

On failure of direct heirs, the relatives and kinsmen get his property.

On their default, it shall be carefully kept for ten years.

What shall be done if no relatives appear.

What the king shall receive from the property of a Sudra, &c.

VRIHASPATI says, that the king shall receive a sixth part from the property of a *Sudra,* a ninth from that of a *Vaisya,* a tenth from that of a *Kshatrya,* and a twentieth from that of a Brahmin.

When the king may take the whole property.

But after three years have elapsed, "if no owner of the goods appear, let the king take the whole; but the wealth of a Brahmin he must bestow on Brahmins."

The king may take the property of all persons except Brahmins.

BAUDHAYANA says, that the king shall take possession of the property of all persons, except Brahmins who have no heirs, after keeping it for one year.

Cause of the difference in time.

This difference in time is owing to the different degrees of distance from which the heirs are to come.

When the king may appropriate the property of another.

NAREDA says that, when there is no probability of the appearance of any heir of the deceased owner, immediately or hereafter, the king shall appropriate the property to his own use, after keeping it for ten years. Such conduct of the king does not make him a sinner.

An acting priest shall receive the stipulated share of the specific fee.

If any of the priests, engaged in a worship, be unable to perform his duty, another shall be appointed to act for him, who shall receive the stipulated share of the specific fee.

VRIHASPATI says, it is a general rule that, if one of the partners be in distress, and consequently unfit for business, his kinsmen or partners shall act for him.

If one partner be unfit for business, his kinsmen, &c., shall act for him.

YAGNYAVALKYA says, if a partner be dishonest, he should be expelled by returning him merely his stock. If his work cannot be managed by the remaining shareholders, a new partner should be admitted.

A dishonest partner should be expelled by returning nim merely his stock.

This rule is applicable in the case of the priests engaged in performing a sacrifice, agriculturists, laborers, &c., who jointly carry on business.

This rule is applicable in the case of priests engaged in performing a sacrifice, &c.

MENU says, if a priest be forced by sickness to abandon his work, his partners shall allow him his share of the sacrificial fee according to his work.

A priest forced by sickness to abandon his work, shall be allowed to take his share of the sacrificial fee.

If he abandon his work before the sacrificial fee be given, he may have his full share, provided he caused the work to be finished by another.

When he may have his full share.

The meaning of the above is that if, during the sacrifice called *madhyahnik*, &c., one of the priests abandon his work from sickness, when the sacrificial fee had not been given, as it should have been, he may have his share of it, and he shall cause the remaining work to be finished by his sons, &c.

Explanation.

What the several different priests shall have.

Of the priests engaged in a sacrifice, those who are the chief shall have half the fee. The second set shall have half, the third a third part, and the fourth a quarter of the first share.

The sacrifice called jyotishstoma should be completed by a hundred offerings.

It is mentioned in the *Vedas* that the sacrifice called *jyotishstoma* should be completed by a hundred offerings. Consequently, provision has been made for a hundred cows for this sacrifice. It is here necessary to determine the manner in which they should be distributed amongst the priests.

Fees of the chief priests.

The chief priests, namely, the *hota*, or reader of the *Rigveda*, the *adharjya*, or reader of the *Yajurveda*, the *Brahma*, or superintending priest, and the *udgata*, or chanter of the *Shyamaveda*, shall have half the number of cows *minus* two, that is forty-eight, for the sake of distribution among all. Consequently the first four shall have forty-eight cows.

Fees of the second set.

The second set, namely, the *maitrabaruna*, *prastota*, *brahmanachchhangsi*, and *pratiprastota* shall have half of the first share, that is, 24 cows.

Fees of the third set.

The third set, namely, the *achbaca*, *neshta*, *agnidhra*, and *protihota*, shall have a third part of the first share, that is, 16 cows.

Fees of the fourth set.

The fourth set, namely, the *gravana*, *unneta*, *pota*, and *subrahmanya*, shall have a fourth part of the first share, or 12 cows.

These classes are described in the Vedas.

The fourth classes of priests are fully described in *adharju grihapatima*," &c., of the *Vedas*.

Is every priest to receive the fee awarded for *the performance of* his duty, or are all the priests to divide the whole fee among themselves? It is a matter of doubt whether the priests shall receive the fee awarded for *the performance of* their respective duties, such as two pieces of gold at the time of bathing for the reader of the *Yajurveda*, and so forth, or shall divide the whole fee among themselves.

Are priests to receive the fees awarded to them respectively or divide the whole amount?

To clear this doubt, MENU says: "Let the reader of the *Yajurveda* take the car, and the *Brahma*, or superintending priest, the swift horse; or, *on another occasion*, let the reader of the *Rigveda* take the horse, and the chanter of the *Shyamaveda* receive the carriage, in which the purchased materials of the sacrifice had been brought."

Distribution of fees according to Menu.

The meaning of the above is that in the *adhan* ceremonies of certain Vedic Brahmins, the reader of the *Yajurveda* gets the car, the superintending priest the swift horse, and the reader of the *Rigveda* the common horse.

Explanation.

Therefore, the conclusion is that every priest shall have the fee assigned to his duty.

Conclusion.

SANKHA and LIKHITA say that, on default of one of the appointed priests, another shall be employed in his place, who shall receive a portion of the fee according to his work, and the balance shall be received by the person before engaged.

On default of one of the appointed priests, another shall be employed in his place.

The sacrificer should wait till the return of the priest, who goes to a distant country, after being engaged.

If a priest, who is first engaged, go to a distant country on account of urgent affairs, the sacrificer should wait till he returns, and should not, in his absence, perform the sacrifice. But if he hear a rumour of his death, he can have it performed by another priest, who shall have the fee. But if the first priest come back, something should be given to him.

A priest who goes to a distant country at the time of the sacrifice, although forbidden by the sacrificer, and the person who recommended him, to be fined 100 panas each.

If a priest repair to a distant land at the time of the sacrifice, when he is forbidden by the sacrificer, he shall be fined 100 *panas*. The chief priest, who recommended so wicked a man, shall also be fined 100 *panas*.

If a man, who is sick, &c. be engaged as a priest, he shall be gratified with presents, &c.

If a man, who is sick, wicked, mad, or in any other way, disqualified, be engaged as a priest, he shall be gratified with presents, and another appointed with his permission.*

A priest wilfully rejecting a blameless sacrificer, to be fined.

If a priest wilfully reject a blameless sacrificer, he shall be fined 200 *panas*.

A sacrificer willingly forsaking a blameless priest, to be fined.

If a sacrificer willingly forsake a blameless priest, he shall be fined 200 *panas*.

A vicious or ignorant priest or vicious or miserly sacrificer.

If a priest be vicious or ignorant, he may properly be discarded. If the sacrificer be vicious and miserly, he may properly be discarded by the priest.

* Provided he be competent to express a wish on the point.

MENU says if a sacrificor forsake a competent priest, or the latter discard an innocent sacrificer, each of them shall be fined 100 *panas*.

According to Menu.

The rule as to the fine of 200 *panas* is applicable, where either the priest or the sacrificer willingly discards or forsakes the other, or does so by reason of his wealth.

Where the rule as to the fine of 200 panas is applicable.

NAREDA speaks of the three kinds of priests, namely, the hereditary priest, one who is appointed by the party himself, and one who voluntarily performs the sacerdotal functions from choice.

Three kinds of priests.

The priest, "who discards a sacrificer, though he be not a grievous offender, nor otherwise faulty, and the sacrificer who discards a priest, though guilty of no grievous offence, shall each be fined."

A priest rejecting a sacrificer, though not faulty, and a sacrificer forsaking a priest though guilty of no grievous offence, shall each be fined.

"This is the law for hereditary priests, and for those who are engaged by the party himself; but there is no offence in discarding a priest, who officiates of his own accord."

This law applies in the case of hereditary priests and of those engaged by the party himself.

VRIHASPATI says that sales and purchases shall be conducted according to local rules.

Sale and purchase shall be conducted according to local rules.

What has been jointly given, shall also be jointly received. He who does not demand the return of his loan, forfeits interest. This rule of loans has been already mentioned, and, on this account, is briefly touched upon here.

Any thing jointly given is to be jointly received.

Rules for the guidance of agriculturists.

Hear the rules for the guidance of the agriculturists.

"Prudent men conduct cultivation, in partnership with those who are equally provided with beasts of burden, labourers, seed, land, and the implements of husbandry."

He, who causes a loss in the joint cultivation, shall indemnify all cultivators.

"He, who, through his deficiency in cattle and seed, causes a loss in the joint cultivation, shall indemnify all the cultivators."

Explanation.

The meaning is that the loss, which is sustained on account of a land that becomes waste, owing to the deficient supply made by a cultivator, shall fall to his share.

Artisan defined.

The sages define an artisan (*silpi*) to be a person who can manufacture articles of gold and other metals, thread, wood, stone, and leather.

Goldsmiths, &c., working together, shall share the remuneration according to their work.

When goldsmiths, and so forth work jointly, they shall share the remuneration according to their work.

What young apprentices and able work men are to receive.

KATYAYANA specially speaks of these :—If four artisans work together, namely, a young apprentice, a more experienced learner, a good artist, and an instructor, they shall receive, in the order, in which they are mentioned, one, two, three, and four shares, of the pay *divided into ten parts.*

The superintendent of the builders of a house, &c., is entitled to a double share.

VRIHASPATI says, the superintendent of the builders of a house or temple, or of those who make articles of leather, is entitled to a double share.

"This has been ordained by wise legislators for a band of musicians: let him who marks the time skilfully (*tala*) take a share and a half, and let the singers have equal shares." Share of singers, &c.

"If, *in time of war*, any property be brought from a hostile territory by pillagers, under the authority of their lord, they shall give a sixth part of it to the king, and divide the rest among themselves in proper proportions. How property, brought from a hostile territory by pillagers, shall be divided.

The chief of the pillagers shall have four shares; he who is very valiant, three; he who is superior in strength, two; and the rest one each. Shares of the chief pillager, &c.

The chief of the pillagers means one who exerts mind and body. Chief pillager defined.

KATYAYANA says, pillagers shall divide the property brought from a foreign country, according to the fixed rule respecting their shares, and give a tenth part to the king. According to Katyayana.

If the king countenance the pillagers, he shall have a sixth part. But if he be in a distant place from which he cannot support them, he shall receive a tenth part. The king, if he countenance the pillagers, shall have a sixth part.

If any of the pillagers be seized, the sum paid by him as ransom shall be made good by all. The ransom of such as are captured, to be made good by all.

These rules hold good with regard to merchants, agriculturists, pillagers, artisans, and others, whose shares have not been defined. Where these rules hold good.

SUBTRACTION OF WHAT HAS BEEN GIVEN.

Subtraction of what has been given, defined.

NAREDA defines it to be the recovery of an article which was not given in due form. It is one of the heads of contests.

Four kinds of gifts.

In law there are four kinds of gifts, namely, what may not be given, what may be given, valid gifts, and invalid gifts.

Of what may and may not be given.

There are eight kinds of things that may not be given; what may be given is of one kind; valid gifts are of seven, and invalid gifts of sixteen sorts.

When a gift is said to be not given in due form.

A gift is said to be not given in due form, when it is composed of things which should not be given, when it is imprudently made, when it is made to a wrong party, when it is made without the assent of the parents of the donor, or when the donor is aged.

According to Vrihaspati, what things may not be given.

VRIHASPATI says, joint property, a son, a wife, a pledge, one's whole wealth, a deposit, an article borrowed for use, and one that has been promised to another, are the eight kinds of things that may not be given.

Interpretation.

Here joint property means what belongs to several persons.

What sorts of gift are void.

Of these eight kinds, the gift of joint property, a son, and a wife, is void, for none has any right over them according to common sense. The gift of a son and a wife against their will, that of the whole wealth of a person who has a son, and that of an article promised to another, are void according to the rules ordained by the *Shastras*.

No one has any power over a pledge, a deposit, or a borrowed article. Pledge, deposit, and borrowed article cannot be given away.

Even if a person have any power to make a gift of his son, wife, whole wealth, and what has been promised to others, the exercise of it has been prohibited by an injunction in the *Shastras*. Gift of son, &c., has been prohibited in the Shastras.

According to the author of *Smritisara*, the gift of the whole wealth of a man is valid, if he be the sole owner of it. But such a man commits wrong by doing a prohibited act. The gift of the whole wealth of a man is, according to the author of Smritisara, valid.

NAREDA says that an article bailed for delivery, a thing lent for use, a pledge, joint property, a deposit, a son, a wife, the whole wealth of a man who has a son, and that which has been promised to another, cannot, according to the sages, be given away even by a person who is oppressed with a grievous calamity. Things which may not be given are therefore of eight kinds, the son and the wife being taken as one. What can not be given away, according to Nareda.

A son and a wife cannot be given by a man without their assent, nor the whole of his property without that of his heirs, even in time of distress. A son and a wife cannot be given without their assent.

KATTAYANA says a person's son and wife can be given with their assent. They cannot be sold or given without their assent. According to Katyayana.

The whole estate of a man can be sold in time of distress only.

The whole of his estate should be kept by him. But it may be given or sold in time of distress. Otherwise it can never be sold or given. "This has been settled in codes of law."

A person's son and wife cannot be sold or given, if they object.

If the sale and gift of a person's son and wife be objected to by them, they must be kept by him. But they can be made over to others with their assent.

The whole of a man's estate cannot be given or sold, even with the assent of his heirs.

Others assert that the whole of a man's estate cannot be given or sold even with the assent of his heirs, for the very existence of the *whole* estate is a bar to its sale or gift.

Both the parents can sell, give, or desert the son.

Vasishtha says that "a son is formed of seminal fluids and of blood proceeding from his father and mother as an effect from its cause;" consequently both the parents have a right to sell, give, or desert him.

An only son should neither be given nor taken.

But there is a slight difference in the case of an only son. Vasishtha adds, that an only son should neither be given nor taken, "since he must remain to raise up a progeny for *the obsequies of* ancestors." A woman has no power to give or take a son but with the assent of her husband.

Why a woman cannot adopt a son even with the assent of her husband.

An only son should not be given, even with his assent, to guard against the extinction of the family. A woman has no power to adopt a son, even with the assent of her husband, for she cannot perform the rites of adoption.

The common saying that a woman has no power to take or give a son, but with the assent of her husband, shews that, as she can give a son with the assent of her husband, so she has power to adopt one with his assent. Consequently it might be argued that she has power to perform the rites of adoption. As a woman can give a son with her husband's assent, so she can adopt one with his consent.

This argument is reasonable. She has a right to do so in association with her husband, but not alone, since in such a case the rule, which empowers her to take a son with her husband but not to perform the rites of adoption, will be infringed. A woman can adopt a son with her husband.

VRIHASPATI says, what remains after defraying the expenses of the maintenance of his family, a man may give to others. What a man can give to others.

He who acts contrary to this rule practises such a virtue as converts the honey which he tastes into poison. To act contrary to this rule is wrong.

KATYAYANA states what may and what may not be given. A person may give what remains after maintaining his family, and he may give property excepting his dwelling-house, but he cannot give his whole estate. What a person can or cannot give.

He who exercises charity by putting his family to inconvenience, commits a sin; whereas he who helps the poor, out of what remains after maintaining his family, performs a good deed. He who exercises charity by putting his family to inconvenience, commits sin.

By the violation of the above rule, a person not only fails to practise virtue but commits sin.

But such charity cannot be reclaimed.

Such charity is admissible, since it is exercised in a legal manner. Consequently, any thing given in this way, cannot be taken back.

A gift of the goods of others is invalid.

Therefore a gift of the goods of others is invalid.

Such a rule also holds good with regard to immovable property.

It is mentioned in the *Smritisara* that such a rule also holds good with regard to immovable property.

A gift of joint property requires the assent of all the partners.

A gift of joint property requires the assent of all the partners, but that of personal property does not require such assent.

Vrihaspati's authority.

VRIHASPATI confirms this by saying that a gift made out of the seven virtuous means of acquiring property, house and land, whether ancestral or self-acquired, is valid.

Self-acquired property can be disposed of, at the option of its owner.

Self-acquired property can be given by its owner at his pleasure.

How a pledge may be transferred.

A pledge can be given (transferred) according to the rules of mortgage. The whole of the ancestral property, or what is received in time of marriage, cannot be given.

Seven virtuous means of acquiring property.

MENU says that "succession, occupancy, or donation, and purchase or exchange, conquest, lending at interest, husbandry or commerce, and acceptance of presents from respectable men," are the seven virtuous means of acquiring property.

Succession means what is inherited. Interpretations.

Occupancy or *Donation* means waif.

Purchase means what is bought.

Conquest means what is acquired by war.

Lending at Interest means a loan for interest.

Husbandry or *Commerce* means tillage or trade.

Acceptance of presents from respectable men means the receipt of gifts made by virtuous men.

Other means of acquiring property.

Besides these, there are several other means of acquiring property. An article, obtained by any means, may be disposed of according to the choice of the owner.

Joint property may be given by assent.

What belongs to many may be given with their assent.

Joint ancestral immovable property how given.

Joint ancestral immovable property may be given with the assent of all the heirs.

When a gift of saudaic ancestral property is valid.

It is said that a gift of *saudaic*, ancestral property, and what has been gained by strength, is valid, when it is made by a man with the assent of his wife, kinsmen, and master respectively.

Saudaic defined.

Saudaic means what is received in time of marriage for the use of the bride.

Consent of the wife is not necessary for giving clothes, &c.

If a man wish to make a gift of it, it is proper that he should obtain the consent of his wife, which, however, is not necessary, when he makes a gift of the clothes, &c., which he received for his own use.

If her assent in the latter case be necessary, the meaning of the law becomes obscure.

Joint ancestral property, whether movable or immovable, can be given with the assent of all the heirs.

The assent of all the heirs is required for a gift of joint ancestral property, whether movable or immovable.

What gifts require the assent of the king.

The assent of the king is required for a gift of elephants and other valuables obtained by war, for it is understood that they belong to him. But it is not required, when clothes, &c., are given, for soldiers generally get them.

What gift requires the assent of a conquered king.

Others say that the assent of a conquered king is required for a gift of horses, &c., which were given by him to his soldiers, and conquered and returned by the victor.

What is meant by a pledge being given according to the rules of mortgage.

By the saying that a pledge shall be given by the rules of mortgage, is meant that it should be given in the following manner :—" Such an article has been pledged to me (pledgee). I transfer it to you. You may deliver it to its owner on receiving the principal, interest, &c."

A single kinsman cannot dispose of immovable property.

Kinsmen, whether joint or separate, have equal power over immovable property. Consequently, one of them is not competent to sell, give, or pledge it.

Partners cannot give, sell, or pledge that property which has been divided, but not distributed.

According to this passage, where the whole property has been divided but it is yet unknown what portion will fall to whose share, separate partners have no power to give, sell, or pledge that property, because it belongs to all.

When an individual shareholder may act independently.

When the whole property is actually divided, the individual action of the shareholders is valid.

Here shareholders means sons.

Others say that here shareholders signify sons. Consequently, sons have no power over immovable property, even when it is divided during the lifetime of their father. They are, therefore, competent to make a gift of the aforesaid seven means of income.

Gift not to be recalled.

A gift of an article which belongs to the donor, cannot be recalled.

The punishment of a person who does not give what he promised, &c.

HARITA says that, if a person do not give what he had promised, or if he take back what he has given, he becomes liable to different kinds of torments and becomes a bird or the like in the next world.

A promise not performed is a debt both in this and the next world.

If a promise be not performed, it continues as a debt both in this and the next world.

He who does not give a priest what he promised of his own accord, shall be fined.

KATYAYANA says, he who does not give a priest what he promised of his own accord, shall be forced by the king to pay it as a debt and fined 250 *panas*.

He who does not give what he has promised, shall be fined a mohar.

It is said in the *Matsya Purana* that a person who does not give what he has promised, shall be fined a *mohar*.

Gifts should not be made to wicked persons.

GAUTAMA specially says, a gift, even if it were promised, should not be made to wicked persons.

Wicked persons defined.

Here wicked persons means such as are declared by the law incapable of receiving gifts from their want of religious instruction.

VALID GIFTS.

VRIHASPATI says, "Things once delivered on the following accounts cannot be resumed, such as wages for the pleasure *of hearing poets or musicians and the like*, the price of goods sold, a nuptial gift to a bride *or her family*, an acknowledgment to a benefactor, a present to a worthy man, from natural affection or from friendship."

What things cannot be resumed.

These eight valid gifts are, properly speaking, only seven, since what is given out of friendship is included in the other gifts.

Seven kinds of gifts.

INVALID GIFTS.

What sort of gifts shall be considered not given.

NAREDA says, "What has been given by men agitated with fear, anger, lust, grief, or *the pain of* an incurable disease, or as a bribe, or in jest, or by mistake, or through any fraudulent practice, by a minor, an idiot, a person not his own master, a diseased man, one insane or intoxicated, an outcast, or in consideration of work unperformed, must be considered as ungiven."

Katyayana on the subject.

KATYAYANA says, what has been given by mistake in jest, by a person not his own master, or agitated with lust, anger, or the pain of an incurable disease, by an hermaphrodite or an idiot, must be considered as ungiven.

A bribe is by no means to be given.

"If a bribe be promised for any purpose, it shall, by no means, be given, although the consideration be performed.

Bribes to be restored by force.

"But if it had at first been actually given, it shall be restored by forcible means; and a fine of eleven times as much is ordained by the son of GARGA and by the son of MENU."

A gift made by a diseased man from virtuous motives, is valid.

If a diseased man make a gift with virtuous motives, it shall be considered as valid. For KATYAYANA says, what a person, whether he is healthy or not, has given, or promised to give, for virtuous deeds, shall be paid even by his sons after his death.

Bribe defined.

KATYAYANA defines *utcocha* (bribe) to be any thing "received for giving information of a thief or a robber, of a man violating the rules of his class, or of an adulterer, for producing a man of depraved manners *ready to commit thefts or other crimes*, or for procuring a man to give false testimony." The giver shall not be fined, but an arbitrator or intermediate person, *receiving a bribe*, shall be held guilty."

Gifts for arresting robbers, or speaking the truth, may be taken back.

What is given to persons for arresting robbers, and to witnesses for inducing them to speak the truth, may be taken back, even when they perform the required act.

A gift made under the influence of lust or anger.

A gift of a thing made under the influence of lust or anger, has been touched upon under "Debt."

Gifts made by a man under the influence of wrath, &c., are according to Vrihaspati, void.

VRIHASPATI says, "What is given by a person in wrath or excessive joy, or through inadvertence, or during disease, minority or madness, or under the impulse of terror, or by one intoxicated or extremely old, or by an outcast, or an idiot, or by a man afflicted with grief or with pain, or what is given in sport; all this is declared ungiven, or void." But what is given by these persons with virtuous motives, is valid. "If any thing be given for a consideration unperformed, or to a bad man mistaken for a good one, or for any illegal act, the owner may take it back."

What is given from virtuous motives is valid.

Menu's authority on the above.

MENU confirms this, by saying that what a person has promised for a virtuous action, can be taken back, if it be not performed.

A donee who returns a gift out of pride or avarice, is punishable.

If such a gift be made, and it be returnod by the donee out of pride or avarice, the king shall fine him one *mohar*.

He who receives what is *deemed* ungiven, or gives what cannot be given, should be punished.

NAREDA says, "He who foolishly receives what is *deemed* ungiven, and he who gives what may not be legally aliened, should be punished by the king, who knows the law."

NON-PAYMENT OF WAGES OR HIRE.

VRIHASPATI says, what may not be given, &c., having been mentioned, the rules for servants will now be touched upon.

Rules for servants.

The breach of a contract for service is a head of dispute.

Breach of contract for service, a head of dispute.

The disputes that arise between a master and his servant for wages will be mentioned in course. Servants are of three kinds, according to their respective amounts of wages.

Three kinds of servants.

NAREDA speaks of the different kinds of servants. The learned have spoken of five kinds of "persons bound to obedience:" four are servants or labourers, and the remaining one is a slave. There are again fifteen kinds of slaves.

Nareda on the same subject.

NAREDA says, "A pupil, an apprentice, a hired servant, and, fourthly, a commissioned servant, perform work; slaves are those born of a *female slave* in the house, or the like."

Difference between servants, &c., and slaves.

The wise have said that all these owe a certain degree of dependence.

All these owe a certain degree of dependence.

VRIHASPATI speaks of the four kinds of servants. These four accept service for science, human knowledge, love, or pay.

Servants accepting service for science, &c.

Science defined.

Science signifies a knowledge of the three *Vedas*, for the acquisition of which a pupil serves his preceptor, according to the rules laid down in the *Shastras*.

How long a pupil should obey his preceptor.

According to NAREDA, a pupil should obey his preceptor, as long as he cannot acquire science. He should equally obey his preceptor's wife and son.

What are called human sciences.

VRIHASPATI describes an apprentice :—" Arts consisting of *work in* gold, husbandry, and the like, and the art of dancing and the rest, are called human sciences ; let him who studies these, perform work in his teacher's house."

He who wishes to acquire his own art should reside near an instructor, fixing a certain period of apprenticeship.

NAREDA says, " Let him who wishes to acquire his own art, with the assent of his kinsmen, reside near an instructor, fixing a certain period of *apprenticeship*. Let the teacher instruct him, keeping him in his own house, and not employ him in other work, but treat him as a son."

A pupil is not allowed to desert a good instructor.

A pupil shall not be allowed to desert a good instructor. If he do so, he shall be compelled by forcible means to reside near him, and is liable to " stripes and confinement."

How long a pupil must reside with his preceptor.

A pupil must reside with his preceptor during the fixed time, even if he acquire the art before the expiration of it.

How long the instructor may take the profit of the work of his pupil.

The instructor shall take the profit of the work of his pupil, as long as the latter is in his apprenticeship.

Having acquired human knowledge within the fixed time, the pupil shall offer to the teacher "the best reward in his power," and depart with his permission. **When and in what manner the pupil may leave his master.**

VRIHASPATI says, that he who commits adultery with the female slave of a person is called *(burro-babrita)* lover of another's female slave. Such a man shall labor for the master of the female slave, in the same manner as other slaves do. **A lover of another's female slave shall labor for her master.**

The servant for pay is declared to be of many sorts; another is the servant for a share of the profits. **Servant for pay.**

These shall work and get wages according to contract. **These shall work and get wages according to contract.**

Husbandmen and herdsmen have servants of two kinds. They get a share of the grain and the milk of cows. Those who work for a share of the profits have been included among servants, who work upon wages. Therefore there are four kinds of servants or labourers. **Husbandmen and herdsmen have servants of two kinds.**

NAREDA says there are three kinds of labourers *(bhritaka)* and refers to others. The hire of their labour should be fixed according to "their strength and to the benefit *derived from their exertions.*" A soldier is the highest of these; a servant employed in husbandry is middlemost; a carrier of burdens is the lowest. **Three kinds of labourers.**

A commissioned servant.

"He who shall be commissioned for affairs, or for the superintendence of the family, should be considered as a commissioned servant; and he is also called a family servant in some instances."

According to Vrihaspati, such servant is included in the class of paid servants

VRIHASPATI has included the abovementioned servant in the class of servants who work upon wages. But NAREDA has considered him different for a slight distinction.

Four kinds of servants perform pure work, and the fifteen kinds of servants perform impure work.

VRIHASPATI says that the four kinds of servants perform pure work. The fifteen kinds of servants perform impure work.

Pure and impure work.

Work is said to be of two sorts, pure and impure. What is done by the servant is pure, and what is done by the slave, impure.

What is to be considered impure work.

"Cleaning the house, the gateway, the necessary, and the road, removing the dirt and rubbish, and all other impurities, attending the master at his pleasure, and rubbing his limbs, are to be considered as impure work; and all other work as pure."

Fifteen kinds of slaves declared by the law.

"One born *of a female slave* in the house *of her master*, one bought, one received *by donation*, one inherited *from ancestors*, one maintained in a famine, one pledged by a *former* master, one relieved from great debt, one made captive in war, *a slave* won in a stake, one *who has* offered *himself* in this form, 'I am thine,' an apostate from religious mendicity, *a slave for a* stipulated *time*, one maintained in consideration of service, a slave for the sake of his wife, and one self-sold, are fifteen kinds of slaves declared by the law."

An apostate from religious mendicity shall be the slave of the king, &c.

NAREDA says that an apostate from religious mendicity shall be the slave of the king, and cannot be emancipated, for there is no penance for him.

How men of the three twice-born classes, who renounce religious mendicity, are punished.

KATYAYANA says, "where men of the three twice-born classes forsake religious mendicity, let the king banish a man of the sacerdotal class, and reduce to slavery a man of the military or commercial class."

How a man, who renounces religious mendicity, is punished.

DAKSHA says, "if a man, after assuming religious mendicity, abide not by his duty, let the king cause him to be lacerated by the feet of dogs, and immediately banish him."

Slaves who may and who may not be emancipated.

NAREDA speaks of those slaves who may and who may not be emancipated from slavery. "Of those *slaves*, the first four (one born in the house, one bought, one received, and one inherited) are not *of right* released from slavery: unless they be *emancipated* by the indulgence of their masters, their servitude is hereditary."

Interpretation.

By slaves are meant these four. Others are called slaves, because they resemble these four in their dependence.

In a following text to the effect that the wife of a slave shall also be the slave of the master of the bridegroom, one of these slaves is referred to.

The vilest of slaves is he who, being independent, sells himself.

"That low man, who being independent, sells himself, is the vilest of slaves; he also cannot be released from slavery," but by the indulgence of his master.

The speech of Hurrischunder in Markandea Purana, about the natural servitude of a Sudra, is merely indicative of his vileness.

The speech of Hurrischunder in *Markandea Purana* to the effect that, "a Sudra, though emancipated by his master, is not released from a state of servitude, for, of a state which is natural to him, by whom can he be divested?" is merely indicative of the vileness of a Sudra. For if their bondage be natural, how can the *slokas* with regard to their purchase stand?

A second person cannot acquire absolute dominion over the slave, who, having given himself in this form, "I am thine" goes to him.

"Over the slave, who, having given himself in this form, 'I am thine,' goes to another, the second master does not acquire *absolute dominion*; the former owner may at pleasure reclaim him."

The king shall liberate those who are stolen and sold by thieves, &c.

"They who are stolen and sold by thieves, and they who are enslaved by force, should be liberated by the king; their slavery is not admitted."

A slave who rescues his master from imminent danger of his life, to be emancipated and rewarded.

"Among those whoever rescues his master from imminent danger of his life, shall be released from slavery, and shall receive the share of a son."

"One maintained in a famine is released from servitude, on giving a pair of oxen; for, what was consumed in a famine, is not discharged by labour alone."

When one maintained in a famine is released from servitude.

"One pledged is also *released*, when his master redeems him by discharging the debt; but, if *the creditor* take him in payment *of his demand*, he becomes a purchased slave."

A pledged slave is released by his master's discharging his debt.

A debtor is relieved from bondage by the payment of the debt with interest.

When a debtor is released from bondage.

From the statement that a debtor may be forced to labor, it is clear that a slave for debt has been already mentioned.

He who becomes a slave for a fixed time for liquidating his debt, is emancipated on the expiration of the time.

When he, who becomes a slave for a fixed time for liquidating his debt, may be emancipated.

"One who offered himself in this form, 'I am thine,' one made captive in war, and a slave won in a stake, are emancipated on giving a substitute equally capable of labour."

Emancipation of other kinds of slaves.

"One maintained in consideration of service is immediately released on relinquishing his subsistence, and a slave for the sake of his bride is emancipated by divorcing his wife."

When one maintained in consideration of service may be released.

KATYAYANA says, "if a man approach his own female slave, and she bear him a son, she must, in consideration of her progeny, be enfranchised with

When a female slave of a man may be emancipated.

her child." In the *Prakasha, Parijata,* and *Ratnakara,* it is said that if the man, who approaches his own female slave, and has a son by her, have no other son, she must be enfranchised with her child. Otherwise, her emancipation cannot be secured.

Nareda on the form of emancipating a slave.

NAREDA says that "a benevolent man, who desires to emancipate his own slave," should "take a vessel of water from off the shoulder of the slave, and instantly break it. Sprinkling the head of the slave with water from a vessel containing rice and flowers, and thrice calling him free, the master should dismiss him with his face towards the east."

Privileges of one emancipated from slavery.

Thenceforward let the slave be called "one cherished by his master's favour:" the food prepared by him may be eaten, and gifts from him may be accepted; "and he is respected by worthy men."

A wife, a slave, and a son, have no property.

These three persons, a wife, a slave, and a son, have no property. Any thing, which they may acquire, belongs to the person to whom they themselves belong.

When sons may divide their father's estate.

DEVALA says that sons may, on the death of their father, divide his estate among themselves, for they have no claim upon it during his life-time, if he be blameless, and MENU has declared that women, during the life-time of their husbands, and slaves during that of their masters have no rights.

Brahmins may take things from Sudras.

Brahmins may, without apprehension, take things from Sudras, for these have claim over nothing, since their property belongs to their master.

KATYAYANA says that a man has dominion over the estate of his slave. But he has no right to the goods given out of kindness to the slave by him or obtained by the slave by the sale of his freedom. The slave's estate subject to the dominion of his master.

The wife of a slave shall also be the slave of his master, for her husband being her master, she must be the slave of her master's master. The wife of a slave is the slave of his master.

The wife of a slave, even when she is the slave of another, must also be the slave of her husband's master. Consequently, a female slave requires the permission of her own master for her marriage, because it is the cause of her emancipation from bondage to her own master. If she marry without the permission of her own master, her marriage cannot be valid, and she cannot be relieved from servitude to him. Even when she is the slave of another.

PERSONS LIABLE TO SLAVERY.

Slavery is not legal in the inverse order of the classes.

NAREDA says that, "in the inverse order of the classes, slavery is not legal, excepting in the case of one who forsakes his duty; *in this respect,* the condition of a slave is held similar to *that of* a wife."

A member of a superior class cannot be the slave of one of inferior class.

A member of any superior class cannot be the slave of one of any inferior class. But he who forsakes his duty, may be.

A Brahmin can never be a slave.

KATYAYANA says that a Brahmin can never be a slave. Slavery should be limited to the three inferior classes.

A Brahmin should never be the slave even of his equal.

A Brahmin should never be the slave even of his equal. "A gentle and learned man may employ in labour one inferior to himself in those qualities."

A Brahmin versed in the Vedas should not cause an inferior of his own class to perform impure work.

A Brahmin versed in the *Vedas* should not cause an inferior of his own class to perform impure work, "for the glory of a king is obliterated by the slavery of a Brahmin." VRIHASPATI has declared that "the law permits the servitude of men of the military, commercial, and servile classes, to one of an equal class, on some accounts, but on no account let a man compel a Brahmin to perform servile acts."

The meaning of the above is that a learned man may cause an ignorant man of his class to labor, and that a very learned man may make his inferiors work for him. But they should never engage them in impure work, such as removing filth, and so forth.

A learned man may cause an ignorant man of his class to labor, &c.

MENU says that poor soldiers and merchants should be maintained by the Brahmins, if they come for employment. But they shall perform their own duties.

Poor soldiers and merchants should be maintained by the Brahmins, if they come for employment.

The king shall impose a fine of 600 *panas* on that Brahmin who improperly compels men of his own class to do the work of a Sudra.

A Brahmin compelling his equals to do the work of a Sudra, to be fined.

A Sudra, whether he is purchased or not, shall do all kinds of work. For God has made him a slave.

A Sudra shall do all kinds of work.

A Sudra, even when he is emancipated by his master, cannot be free; for bondage being natural to him, who can deliver him from it?

A Sudra can never be free.

VISHNU says, he who enslaves a Brahmin shall be fined 1000 *panas*.

He who enslaves a Brahmin, is to be fined.

KATYAYANA says, the king shall punish a man, who seizes a Brahmin woman or sells her, or who "enslaves a woman of family, impelled by lust, or causes her to be approached by another." The bondage of a Brahmin woman or a woman of family is invalid.

The king shall punish a man, who seizes a Brahmin woman, &c.

He who treats as a slave the nurse of an infant child, &c., shall be fined.

He who "treats as a slave the nurse of an infant child, or a free woman, or the wife of his dependent," shall be fined 250 *panas*.

He who attempts to sell an obedient female slave.

He who attempts to sell "an obedient female slave, who resists the sale, and he is not in distress, but able to subsist, shall pay a fine of 200 *panas*.

WAGES AND HIRE.

Wages of servants to be paid according to contract.

NAREDA says that a man shall pay wages to his servant, in proportion to work done, at the beginning, middle, or end of the work, according to contract.

What wages are due to the servant of a merchant, a herdsman, &c., when the same is not fixed.

Where the amount of wages is not fixed, the servant of a merchant, a herdsman, and the servant of a husbandman, shall respectively get a tenth part of the profits of goods sold, of the milk, and of the grain.

A servant shall be paid according to the work performed by him.

YAGNYAVALKYA says, that a servant shall be paid according to the work performed by him.

The man who guides the ploughshare shall receive a third or a fifth part of the crop.

VRIHASPATI says, that "the man who guides the ploughshare" shall receive a third or a fifth part of the crop.

What ploughman shall get a fifth and what ploughman a third part of the crop.

The meaning of the above is that the ploughman who gets food and clothes shall receive a fifth part, and he who does not get them, a third part of the crop.

Where Nareda's rule as to wages is applicable.

NAREDA's provision of a tenth part of the produce as wages for the servants of husbandmen, is applicable in the case of all save the ploughman.

A ploughman forsaking his work, and thereby destroying the crop, is punishable.

APASTAMBA says that, if a ploughman forsake his work, and the crop be thereby destroyed, he shall be beaten with a rod. If a herdsman forsake his work, he shall be beaten with a rod and his own animals shall be seized.

What wages the servants of a merchant shall receive, when nothing has been settled.

VRIDHA MENU says that, when nothing has been settled, the servants of a merchant shall receive such wages as will be recommended by those who understand commercial affairs, and know what articles are procurable in what season and in what country.

He, who, receiving wages, does not perform his work, when he can do so, is punishable.

VRIHASPATI says that he, who, having received his wages, does not perform his work, when he is able to do so, shall be fined twice the amount of his pay, and shall return the wages to his master.

Yagnyavalkya on the point.

YAGNYAVALKYA says that he, who, having received his wages, forsakes his work, shall be fined twice the amount of his pay; and he who forsakes the work he has undertaken without taking wages, shall be fined the amount of his wages, and his implements, &c., should be kept by the other servants.

He who does not perform a work contracted for, shall be first paid, and then forced to do it.

NAREDA says that he, who does not perform a work contracted for, shall be first paid, and then forced to do it.

A servant, who does not work, is to be fined.

VRIDHA MENU says that, if a servant do not work, he shall be fined 200 *panas*.

Where the rule holds good.

This rule is applicable where the servant, having commenced the work, does not finish it.

A servant, who does not work from wantonness, is punishable.

MENU says that a servant, who does not perform his work, not from inability to do so but from wantonness, shall be fined eight *krishnalas* of gold and shall not receive his wages.

If work, engaged for, be not performed by a servant, whether he is in health or not, wages shall not be given to him, even if but a small portion of his work remain to be done.

Wages shall not be given to a servant, unless he perform the work engaged for.

If a servant, having recovered from sickness, finish his work even after a long time, wages shall be paid to him.

Wages to be paid, if a sick servant finish his work, even after a long time.

NAREDA says that wages shall not be paid to that servant, who abandons his work, before the expiration of the appointed time. But if he do so in consequence of the fault of his master, he shall get wages for the work which he has already performed.

Wages shall not be paid to that servant, who abandons his work before the expiration of the appointed time.

According to VISHNU, if a servant neglect his work before the expiration of the appointed time, he shall forfeit the whole of his wages and pay a fine of 100 *panas*. If his master dismiss him, without any reasonable cause, before the expiration of the fixed time, the whole of his wages shall be given him, and a fine of 100 *panas* shall be paid by the master.

Vishnu on the point.

VRIDHA MENU says that a servant shall make good the loss which he has caused by his carelessness. But if he had caused it with a view to do wrong, he shall pay twice its value.

A servant shall make good the loss caused by his carelessness.

But if any thing be stolen, burned, or drowned, its value is not to be made good by the servant, that is, what has not been lost on account of his fault, shall not be made good by him.

The value of any thing stolen, or destroyed, is not to be made good by him.

The master is responsible for offences, committed, by his order, by his servant.

VRIHASPATI says, that if a servant steal or do any improper act, pursuant to the order of his master, the latter shall be responsible for it.

He, who does not impart instruction, shall return the wages paid him.

It is mentioned in the *Matsya Purana* that he, who, having received wages, does not impart a knowledge of letters, nor teach the arts, shall be forced by a good king to return the wages.

The remuneration to be given to the servant of a merchant, who dismissed him after he had performed half the journey.

VRIDHA MENU says, that if a merchant dismiss a servant whom he engaged to sell his goods in the course of a certain journey, he must pay full wages to the servant for the part of the way which they travelled, and half of the wages for the part which they did not travel over.

If the goods be seized or stolen on the way, what wages the servant is to receive.

KATYAYANA says, if the goods be seized or stolen on the way, wages shall be given to the servant for the part of the way which he travelled over.

He who does not pay wages to his servants is punishable.

VRIHASPATI says, that a man, who does not pay wages to his servants even when work has been done, shall be forced by the king to pay, and severely punished.

A man on a journey, who does not take care of a wearied or sick servant, is punishable.

KATYAYANA says, that if a man on a journey leave a tired or sick servant and do not take care of him, (by keeping him) in a village for three days, he shall be fined 250 *panas*.

OF PROSTITUTES.

NAREDA says, if a prostitute forsake her paramour after taking an advance, she shall be fined twice the sum she may have taken. But if the paramour refuse to receive her, he shall merely lose the money he advanced. If, however, the prostitute do not attend when sent for, because she is unwell, afraid, tired, or employed in the service of the king, she is not to blame.

A prostitute, forsaking her paramour, after taking an advance, is punishable.

It is said in the *Matsya Purana* that a prostitute, who, having received money from one man, goes to another and does not return it, shall be compelled to do the latter.

A prostitute, receiving money from one man and going to another, shall be compelled to return it.

If a man unnaturally abuse a prostitute's person, or cause her to be approached by many, he shall be compelled to pay eight times the amount of the money promised and a fine of an equal amount.

A man unnaturally abusing a prostitute's person, &c., shall be fined.

He who brings a prostitute for a man other than the one for whom she was engaged, shall be fined a *masha* of gold.

A man bringing a prostitute for a man, other than the one for whom she was engaged, shall be fined.

If a man do not pay a prostitute, he shall be compelled to pay her twice the amount she ought to have received, and a fine of an equal amount to the king.

A man who does not pay a prostitute is punishable.

What a prostitute approached by several men is to receive.

If several men approach a prostitute, each of them shall pay her twice the amount which she would have received, had only one of them approached her, and a fine of an equal amount to the king.

The principal harlot shall determine disputes arising among the frequenters of her house.

NAREDA says, that if " a dispute arise among the lascivious frequenters of her house, in respect of matters occurring there, the wise have declared that it shall be determined by the principal harlot."

OF RENT AND HIRE.

He, who lives in a house built on a tenanted land, shall, at the time of removal, take away his straw, bricks, and so forth. But if he do not pay rent, he cannot take away the straw, and so forth, without the permission of the proprietor of the land.

He, who quits land on which he had built a house, may, on paying the rent, take away his materials.

Katyayana says, if a person, having hired a house, tank, bazar, and so forth, do not give up possession thereof, he shall pay the rent until he do so.

The tenant of houses and lands shall pay rent, until he give up possession thereof.

Tank in the abovementioned sentence means one that has not been devoted to charitable purposes.

Definition of tank.

Nareda says, he who having hired elephants, horses, cows, asses, camels, and so forth, does not return them, after he ceases to require them, shall pay for them as long as he keeps them.

A hirer of certain animals shall pay for them as long as he keeps them.

Vridha Menu says that he, who, having hired a carriage for the purpose of going to any place, does not pay the hire, shall be compelled to pay it even if he do not use the carriage.

The hire of a carriage, to be paid, even if it have not been used.

By *carriage* is here meant also a boat or any other conveyance.

Interpretation.

Things yielding rent revert to the owner on the expiration of the appointed time.

NAREDA says, things yielding rent come to the possession of the owner on the expiration of the appointed time.

If any article be injured, &c., owing to an unavoidable cause the hirer shall repair it.

If any article be injured or broken owing to a cause other than the act of God or of the king, the hirer shall repair it after the fixed time.

If it be not returned on the expiration of the appointed time, &c., the loss is to be made good.

If it be not returned on the expiration of the appointed time, and if it be injured even by the course of time, the hirer shall make good the loss.

OF DISPUTES BETWEEN MASTER AND SERVANT.

MENU says that a cowherd, who does not get food and clothes, may take the milk of the best of ten cows with the permission of their owner. What a cowherd who does not get food and clothes is to receive.

This rule is applicable in the case of persons who tend cows that have calves. Where this rule is applicable.

NAREDA speaks of the tending of cows in general. He who tends 100 cows shall annually have a calf three years old, and he who tends 200 cows, shall get a cow with a calf. Both of these herdsmen shall have every eighth day the milk of all the cows. Nareda on the remuneration of persons tending cows.

VRIHASPATI says, cowherds shall get the milk every eighth day. Cowherds shall get the milk every eighth day.

NAREDA says that cowherds shall, at day break, take the cows to pasture, and every evening return them to their owner, when they have eaten grass and drunk water. Duties of cowherds.

YAGNYAVALKYA says that a cowherd, receiving wages, shall pay the price of a cow that may have been lost or stolen through his negligence. A hired cowherd to pay for a cow lost or stolen through neglect.

MENU says, cowherds are to blame for any injury done to the cows in the day. But the blame falls on their owner, if they be injured during the night in his house. But if they be kept out of the house at night, the herdsmen are to blame. Cowherds are to blame for injury done to cows in the day.

A cowherd is not to blame, if cows be taken by robbers.

MENU and NAREDA say that a cowherd cannot be blamed, if the cows be forcibly taken by robbers, and if he give notice to the owner, in a proper place and season.

The cowherd is not to blame, if any of the cattle be seized, &c., during his captivity.

According to VAS, the cowherd "is not chargeable, if he be made captive, if the village be overpowered, or if the district be thrown into confusion, and any of the cattle be seized or destroyed."

Cowherds shall defend cows from insects, &c.

VRIHASPATI says cowherds shall try their utmost to defend cows from insects and reptiles, robbers and tigers, and protect them from falling into pits and caves. They should call out for help, when any accident happens, or inform the owner of it.

Cowherds shall make good the loss sustained by their not defending the cows from insects, &c.

The cowherds shall make good the loss sustained by the owner owing to their not defending the cows from insects and reptiles, calling out for help, or informing the owner of any accident, and shall pay a fine to the king.

If cows be taken away by robbers, &c., through the carelessness of the herdsman, he shall pay the value of them.

MENU says if the cows be taken away by robbers, destroyed by insects and reptiles or dogs, or die by falling into caves or pits, or stray owing to the carelessness of the herdsman, he shall pay the value of them.

Cowherds, through whose neglect cows have strayed, &c., shall pay the price of them.

The meaning of the above is that the cowherds shall pay the price of cows that have strayed or have been killed owing to their want of proper care.

YAGNYAVALKYA says that, if cows die owing to the negligence of their keeper, he shall pay their price and a fine of thirteen *panas* and a half.

If cows die through the neglect of their keeper, he is punishable.

VISHNU says if cows stray, when they are taken without the permission of their owner, their keeper shall be fined twenty-five *kahanas*.

If cows stray, when they are taken without the permission of their owner, their keeper shall be fined.

It is said in the *Brahma Purana* that the king shall torture that cowherd to death, who, having taken wages, comes to the interior of the village, leaving the cows in a desolate forest.

Cowherds, who leave cows in a desolate forest, shall be tortured to death.

If a cow die, of some disease, in the stall of her owner, he shall be fined and forced to pay wages to her keeper.

If a cow die, through disease, in the stall, the owner shall be fined, &c.

NAREDA says, the rules prescribed for cowherds are applicable in the case of all other herdsmen.

The rules prescribed for cowherds are applicable in the case of other herdsmen.

On the death of a cow, its keeper becomes free from every responsibility, if he carry its horns, tail, or the like, to its owner. The death of the animal requires proof.

On the death of a cow, her keeper becomes free, if he carry the horns or tail to the owner.

NON-PERFORMANCE OF AGREEMENTS.

Villagers and others to frame certain rules for public purposes.

VRIHASPATI says that the villagers, workmen, Brahmins, &c, shall frame certain rules for redressing public grievances and performing good deeds.

The oppression of the king and robbery can be put down by a body of men.

The oppression of the king and robbery, being common dangers, can be put down by a body of men, but not by an individual.

In public movements, business to commence on mutual confidence being established.

In such public movements, mutual confidence being first established by wealth, agreement, or the attestation of witnesses, business shall be commenced.

Some persons to be appointed by the villagers as counsellors.

Two, three, or five persons shall be appointed by the villagers as their advisers. Those shall be pure, versed in the *Vedas*, polite, prudent, the offspring of noble families, and competent to do every description of work, and their advice shall direct the villagers.

Their advice to be attended to.

YAGNYAVALKYA says, all should listen to the advice of these men. He who will disobey it shall be fined 250 *panas*.

He who disregards advice, &c., is punishable.

KATYAYANA prescribes a penalty of 250 *panas* for him, who disregards reasonable advice, interrupts speakers, and talks unreasonably.

According to NAREDA, the king shall keep the infidels, citizens, merchants, soldiers, and the like, in order, both in a place difficult of access and in a frequented spot. All classes of persons should be kept in order.

All classes of persons should be kept in order.

YAGNYAVALKYA says, that every person shall perform a duty, ordained for the good of all, if it be not against his own duty, as the favor of the king should be monthly secured.

Every one is bound to perform a duty, ordained for the good of all, if it be not against his own duty.

The orders of the king shall also be obeyed, as the performance of any work appointed by the king for public welfare.

The king's orders also to be obeyed.

KATYAYANA says, he who insolently disobeys the orders of the king, shall be punished.

A person insolently disobeying the king's orders, is to be punished.

YAGNYAVALKYA says, that he who takes the property of the public, and does not obey the orders of the king, shall be deprived of his property, and driven out of the country.

He who takes public property &c., is punishable.

KATYAYANA says, it is the opinion of BHRIGU that a highway robber, a violator of the rules of the community, and a waster of public wealth, shall be put to death with the permission of the king.

Highway robbers and disorderly persons to be put to death.

VRIHASPATI says, he who having power to obey the orders of the king, does not obey them, shall be deprived of all his property and banished.

He who disobeys the king's orders to be punished.

He, who excites disputes and disobeys the rules of the community, shall be fined six *nishkas*, each of which is equal to four gold mohars.

He who excites disputes, &c., shall be fined.

According to Menu.

MENU adds silver weighing 320 *ratis* to the above-mentioned fine.

Nishka defined.

The word *nishka* signifies four gold mohars. The reason of this explanation is to prevent its being understood for 150 or 5 mohars, to which it is equal according to some sages.

He who wounds the feelings of others, &c., to be soon banished.

He who wounds the feelings of others, excites quarrels, commits violent deeds, and acts maliciously towards all and the king, shall be soon banished.

He who discontinues eating in the same line or pot with another, without any fault of the latter, shall be punished.

KATYAYANA says, he, who eats in the same line or pot with another and discontinues doing so without any fault of the latter, shall be punished.

Tradesmen, who conspire to deprive the king of his dues, to be punished.

VRIHASPATI says, the tradesmen who conspire to abscond and deprive the king of his dues, shall be compelled to pay eight times that amount.

He, who, being engaged in public business, reaps any benefit, shall forfeit it.

YAGNYAVALKYA says that he, who, being engaged in a public business, reaps any *private* benefit therefrom, shall pay it for the public welfare. If he object to do so, he shall be forced to pay eleven times the amount.

Gain derived from any public business belongs to the community.

VRIHASPATI says that gain, derived from any public business, shall belong to the community.

A public servant shall pay the debt, incurred on the public account for his own benefit.

KATYAYANA says, a public servant shall pay the debt, which he has incurred on the public account for his own benefit.

The meaning of the above is that, since the debt has not been incurred for the public welfare, it is to be paid by him who has contracted it. Why it is to be paid by him.

A man, who is subsequently admitted into a joint business, with the consent of all the shareholders, shall participate in the receipts as well as the debts of the business. A subsequent partner shall participate in the receipts as well as the debts of the joint business.

"He who remains" in the firm "is a sharer in all matters relating to provisions, partible stock, gifts and duty; but he who forsakes it, is entitled to no share." He who remains in the firm is a sharer in all matters relating to provisions, &c.

RESCISSION OF SALE AND PURCHASE.

He who does not deliver immovable things shall pay the loss suffered, &c.

NAREDA says, he who does not deliver the things he has sold, shall pay the loss suffered, if they be immovable, as the loss of crops, &c. But if cows, bulls, or other animals that are capable of motion, be sold and not delivered, the loss of milk, labor, and the like, sustained through their non-delivery, shall be paid by him.

Who shall make good the loss owing to a fall in the price.

If the price of a thing become gradually reduced, the loss owing to the reduced price shall be made good by the vendor.

The rule applicable in the case of persons, who reside where the sale takes place.

This rule is applicable in the case of persons who reside where the sale takes place. But if a thing were purchased to be conveyed to another place, the profit, which the purchasor might have gained, shall be made good by the vendor.

He who taking the price does not deliver an article to its purchaser, shall be punishable.

VISHNU says that he who, taking the price, does not deliver an article to its purchaser, shall be forced by the king to do so, with interest, and to pay a fine of 100 *panas*.

Where this rule is applicable.

This rule is applicable, where the full price has been received.

Goods may be detained till the price be paid.

A person is not to blame for detaining articles for the price.

NAREDA says that the aforesaid rules are applicable, where the price is paid. Where it is not paid, the purchaser is not to blame, if there be some arrangement. These rules are applicable where the price is paid.

NAREDA says, if an article, which has been sold but not delivered, be destroyed, burnt, or stolen, the loss shall be borne by the vendor. If an article, sold but not delivered, be destroyed, &c., the loss shall be borne by the vendor.

YAGNYAVALKYA says, if a purchaser do not get articles on demand, and they be destroyed by the act of God or of the king, the vendor shall bear the loss. But if they be not taken on delivery, any loss owing to this, must be sustained by the purchaser. If a purchaser do not get articles on demand, and they be destroyed, the vendor shall bear the loss.

MENU says, he who repents, after selling or purchasing an article, may take or give it back within ten days, after which he cannot do so. He who repents selling or purchasing an article, may take or give it back within ten days.

If any one demand or return it after ten days, the king shall fine him 600 *panas*. Any one demanding or returning it after ten days shall be fined.

The king shall, by the abovementioned rule, keep him, who repents after doing a thing, in the path of duty. The king shall thus keep him, who repents after doing a thing, in the path of duty.

KATYAYANA says that he, who, taking possession of a purchased article, returns it, and he who, selling it, does not give delivery of it, when it is in a proper state, shall respectively get the price and the article, on giving a tenth part of the former. He, who, taking possession of a purchased article, returns it, and he, who, selling it, does not deliver it, when it is in a proper state, shall respectively get the price and the article, on giving a tenth part of the former.

Where the article was not taken possession of, and evidence and agreement exist, a tenth part of the price is not to be given by the purchaser, if he return it within ten days. After that period, it cannot be returned.

A bad article, clandestinely sold, may be returned even after ten days.

A bad article, clandestinely sold, may be returned, even after ten days, by proving its blemish.

He who sells a bad article, without letting the purchaser know its blemish, shall pay double its price, &c.

VRIHASPATI says, that the foolish man who sells a bad article, without letting the purchaser know its blemish, shall pay double its price; and a fine equal to it.

Articles sold by a drunkard, &c., shall be returned by the purchaser and taken back by the vendor.

The article which is sold by a drunkard, a mad man, a dependent or stupid person, or at an inadequate price through fear, shall be returned by the purchaser and taken back by the vendor.

He who delivers an article to a person, who has not been engaged by its purchaser, is punishable.

He who, selling an article to a person, delivers it to another, who has not been engaged by the purchaser, shall pay twice the price and an equal amount of fine.

Who is subject to the abovementioned fine.

The *Ratnakara* says, the abovementioned fine is imposed on such as purchase or sell articles in a place other than that in which the settlement of price was made.

When a vendor may sell articles to a person other than the purchaser.

If a purchaser do not take the delivery of purchased articles, the vendor is not to blame, if he sell them to some other person.

YAGNYAVALKYA says, if a person, purchasing an article, do not receive it, the vendor is competent to put it up for re-sale. Any loss in this shall be made good by the purchaser.

When a vendor may put up an article for re-sale.

If a person, having taken earnest money from an intending purchaser, sell an article to another, he shall pay the first customer double the earnest money.

What a person, who does not get an article on giving earnest money is to get from the intending customer.

NAREDA says, merchants deal in all kinds of articles. They gain profit in proportion to the amount of the price. Therefore, he, who understands business, shall sell articles at a fair price, considering the place where, and the season when, they are sold.

Merchants gain profit in proportion to the price.

This way of dealing is profitable.

Ten days' time, allowed for returning or taking back articles, when they are sold, is applicable to roots.

Roots can be returned, &c., within ten days.

This is confirmed by VYASA and NAREDA.

Hides, wood, bricks, thread, rice, wine, liquids, cloth, gold, silver, and other metals, shall be tried the moment they are purchased.

What articles shall be tried the moment they are purchased.

Animals that give milk shall be tried within three days from the date of purchase.

How long animals that give milk shall be tried.

Beasts of burden shall be tried within five days.

And how long beasts of burden.

Pearls, diamonds, jewels, and corals shall be tried within seven days.

And jewels and valuables.

How long men and women shall be tried.

Men shall be tried within fifteen days, and females within a month.

Roots shall be tried within ten days.

All kinds of roots shall be tried within ten days.

Iron and cloths in a day.

Iron and all kinds of good cloths shall be tried in a day.

How long roots, iron, &c., shall be tried.

YAGNYAVALKYA says, roots, iron, beasts of burden, jewels, and so forth, women, animals that give milk, and men, shall be tried within ten, one, five, seven, eight, three, and fifteen days respectively.

Vrihaspati confirms the above.

VRIHASPATI is also of this opinion.

Vendor to take back articles and return the price to the purchaser.

If the articles prove, within the specified time, to be of bad quality, the vendor shall take them back and return the price to the purchaser.

Articles invariably to be returned within the prescribed time.

Even if the articles were bad at the time of sale, they shall be returned within the prescribed time.

A bad article, purchased by mistake, to be returned within the appointed time.

If a bad article be purchased by mistake, it shall be returned within the appointed time.

Nareda on cases where an article is purposely spoiled.

NAREDA speaks of cases in which the purchaser purposely spoils an article.

A cloth, become dirty by use, cannot be returned.

A cloth, become dirty by use, cannot be returned by a man, even if it had been purchased in a damaged state.

The different times, above adverted to, are applicable to cases in which the articles are purchased without trial.

The different times mentioned hold good where the articles are purchased without trial.

YAGNYAVALKYA confirms this.

The same confirmed.

If experienced merchants repent after purchasing articles, they shall be fined a sixth part of their price.

Experienced merchants, who repent after purchasing articles, are punishable.

According to NAREDA, an experienced merchant shall not repent after purchasing an article. He knows what articles may yield profit and what may cause loss.

The reason why they should not.

The purchaser of an article shall try its qualities and blemishes. He is not competent to return it, if he had purchased it after trial.

The purchaser of an article cannot return it, if he purchased it after trial.

VRIHASPATI says, a man, before purchasing a thing, shall look to it himself and show it to others. He cannot return it to the vendor, if he take it after proper trial.

Vrihaspati on the above.

NAREDA specially speaks of the advisableness of returning purchased articles even before the time assigned for trial.

Purchased articles returnable even before the time assigned for trial.

He who, purchasing an article, thinks that he has been cheated, shall return it to the vendor in the state in which he took it on the day of purchase.

What a person should do, if he think he has been cheated in the purchase of an article.

What a person shall forfeit if he return an article on the second day from the date of purchase, &c.

If he return it on the second day from the date of purchase, he shall forfeit a thirtieth part of the price; if, on the third day, he shall forfeit a fifteenth part of it. After that it cannot be returned.

Where this rule holds good.

This rule is applicable where an article is taken after three days' trial.

The forfeit to be paid on the return of a good animal that gives milk.

KATYAYANA says, he, who returns a good animal that gives milk, within the specified time, shall pay a tenth part of its price.

Where this rule holds good.

This rule is applicable where the purchaser does not receive an animal which he did not take possession of.

Explanation.

The aforesaid rule is applicable where the animals have not come under the control of the purchaser.

Where the following rules are applicable.

The following rules are applicable, where they have come under their control. Consequently there is no inconsistency.

The forfeit to be paid for returning a thing after taking possession of it.

BHRIGU says, he who repents and returns a thing after taking possession of it, shall give a sixth part of its price to the vendor.

What article may be returned even after a long time.

The article, sold by the vendor by concealing its blemish, may be returned even after a long time.

Menu's authority on the above.

Menu confirms this, by saying that, if a good article be mixed with one of inferior quality, if it be licked by dogs, &c., if it be less in weight, if it be not weighed in the presence of the purchaser, or if it be covered with another, it cannot be sold.

Articles having certain blemishes may be returned at any time.

The meaning of the above is that articles, having the abovementioned blemishes, may be returned at any time.

CONTESTS REGARDING BOUNDARIES.

When contests regarding boundaries shall be settled.

MENU says, if the boundary of two villages cause a contest, it shall be settled in the month of Joista, when the landmarks may be distinctly traced out.

Certain trees to be planted on the boundaries as landmarks.

Vatas, *pipulas*, *palasas*, *salmalis*, *salas*, or *talas* trees, that yield milky sap, "clustering shrubs, *venus* of different sorts, *sami* trees, and creepers, or *saras*, and clumps of *cubjacas*," should be planted on the boundaries, "and mounds of earth" raised "on them, so that the landmarks may not easily perish."

Other means of denoting the common limits

"Lakes and wells, pools and streams, ought also to be made on the common limits, and temples dedicated to the gods."

Certain articles should be placed under ground in the centre of the boundaries to guard against disputes.

To guard against contests that often arise on account of the boundaries, let stones, bones, tails of cows, ashes, bricks, dried cow-dung, charcoal, bran, and other articles that are not destroyed by time be placed under ground in the centre of the boundaries.

How the king is to decide contests regarding boundaries.

The king shall decide the contests regarding boundaries by the abovementioned marks, by previous possession, or by the course of a stream.

The boundary lines of villages denoted.

VRIHASPATI says that a tank, well, pond, large tree, garden, temple, mound, channel, the course of a river, stones, reeds, or clustering shrubs shall form the boundary lines of villages.

Should any doubt arise, notwithstanding the abovementioned marks, it is to be removed by the depositions of witnesses.

Witnesses to be heard, if doubts arise, notwithstanding such marks.

In default of these, four men, who reside on the four sides of the two villages, shall decide the contest in the presence of the king.

Or neighbours from the four sides of the two villages.

Should there be no such men, men who live in forests, such as hunters, fowlers, milkmen, fishermen, "diggers for roots," snake-catchers, and gleaners, shall be examined. Their declarations shall direct the king *how* to decide the contest.

Or certain descriptions of persons of the neighbourhood.

VRIHASPATI says that the witnesses, "putting earth on their heads, wearing chaplets of red flowers, and clad in red mantles," shall "be sworn by *the reward of* all their several good actions, to give correct evidence concerning the metes and bounds."

How the witnesses shall be sworn.

The king shall fix the boundaries according to the statements of the aforementioned men and write down their names.

How the king is to fix the boundaries.

NAREDA says that no man, however trustworthy or experienced he may be, should alone fix the boundaries. This duty, being a responsible one, ought to be performed by many.

No man should alone fix the boundaries.

If a person wish alone to fix them, he should do so by fasting, putting earth on his head, wearing a chaplet of red flowers, and clad in a red mantle.

Except according to a prescribed form.

Here fasting is an addition.

r

Who is competent to decide a dispute in default of witnesses, &c.

VRIHASPATI says, that a person, who is respected by both the parties to the dispute, is competent to decide it alone in the absence of witnesses and landmarks.

Wicked men not to be witnesses.

KATYAYANA says that, according to the sages, a king shall not make wicked men witnesses.

The king shall, in conjunction with the moula, decide contests on boundaries.

Leaving aside wicked men, the king shall, in conjunction with the *moula*, decide contests on boundaries.

Veracious witnesses are blessed.

Witnesses secure God's blessing by making true statements regarding the boundaries.

False witnesses to be fined.

If they utter falsehood, they shall be fined 200 *panas* each.

If the inhabitants on the four sides of the villages utter falsehood, they shall be fined.

If the inhabitants on the four sides of the villages utter untruth, they shall be fined 500 *panas* each by the king.

Boundaries of villages, fields, &c, to be fixed.

KATYAYANA says that the boundaries of villages, fields, or houses, shall be fixed by the declarations of those who dwell around them.

Moula defined.

Pundits define *moula* to be persons who have changed their habitations. They are called *moula*, because they were the aborigines.

When the king should fix the boundaries.

NAREDA says that, in the absence of witnesses and landmarks, the king shall fix the boundaries.

VRIHASPATI says, that the possession of a piece of land, yielded by a river or given by a king to a village, on taking it from another, cannot be disputed.

The possession of alluvion and land given by the king cannot be disputed.

The land, left by a river, is acquired by those who reside on the bank, which it forsakes, and the land given by the king belongs to him who gets it. If this be not admitted, then men cannot gain by the act of God or of the king.

To whom such rightfully belong.

Ruin, prosperity, and life depend on the act of God and of the king. Therefore what is thereby done, cannot be overruled.

The reason of the rule.

Where a canal has been dug, as the boundary-mark of two villages, the disjunction and junction of land by the encroachment or recess thereof cannot cause any dispute. If any dispute arise, the parties, who raise it, shall be punished.

The encroachment or recess of a canal, dug as the boundary of two villages, cannot cause any dispute.

In such cases fortune and misfortune shall be considered.

Points to be considered.

Who shall get the land left by the river?

Proposition.

A river increases on one side and decreases on the other. This cannot be helped.

Alluvion and diluvion inevitable.

The land, forsaken by a river owing to its taking a different course, falls to the share of him who is the owner of the land adjacent to the bank. When a land is divided into two or more parts by the violent course of a river, it shall belong to the former owner.

Who acquires land, forsaken by a river, owing to its changing a course.

Gift by the king of certain land is illegal.

A gift of land made by the king, by taking it from its proprietor through anger or avarice, or under a pretext, is illegal.

When the king's gift of land is valid.

If the king take a piece of land from a person and give it to a superior, his present shall be valid.

Explanation.

The meaning of the above is that the boundaries, fixed by the king through anger, shall be invalid. In all other cases they shall be valid.

Contests about the boundaries of gardens, &c., shall also be decided.

YAGNYAVALKYA says, that contests about the boundaries of gardens, temples, villages, ponds, groves, houses, and water-courses, shall also be decided according to the foregoing rules.

How the centre of the boundaries of lands, wells, &c., is to be determined.

MENU says, that the centre of the boundaries of lands, wells, ponds, gardens, and houses, shall be determined by the people dwelling around them.

When a person cannot be deprived of the use of a house, &c.

VRIHASPATI says, that a person cannot be deprived of the use of a house, pond, market, or any such property, in whatever manner it may have been acquired, provided he has been using it from the day of his residence near it.

Windows, &c., cannot be forcibly removed.

Windows, water-courses, verandahs, bungalows, cornices, cannot be forcibly removed. The foundations of houses, water-courses, and thoroughfares, and windows, cannot be blocked up.

Blocking up water-courses, &c., punishable.

He who blocks up water-courses and dwelling-houses shall be punished.

No one shall be at liberty to open a window in a place, after he has resided there for a long time. A person cannot open a window in a place, after residing there for a long time.

Windows and water-courses cannot be made by a person, on the side of another's house. Windows, &c., cannot be made on the side of another's house.

VRIHASPATI says, that a privy, fire place, or hole, cannot be made, nor can the leavings of boiled rice, &c., be thrown by a person near the house of another. A privy, &c., cannot be made, &c., near the house of another.

KATYAYANA says that a privy, fire-place, hole, or water-course may be made, or an oil-machine, &c., placed, by a person leaving free two cubits of land from the house of another. A privy, &c., may be made, at two cubits distance from another's house.

VRIHASPATI says that *(sangsaran)* a passage uninterruptedly used, by men as well as animals, cannot be blocked up. A passage uninterruptedly used by men and animals, cannot be blocked up.

KATYAYANA says that, if a number of trees grow on the *common* boundary of two villages, and their flowers and fruits fall in both, they shall be enjoyed by the inhabitants of both of them. Who shall enjoy the flowers and fruits of trees on the common boundary of two villages.

If the branches of a tree, growing on the land of one person, fall on that of another, the latter shall take them. Who shall take the branches of a tree, growing on the land of one and falling on that of another.

MENU says that he, who, not being in distress, throws filthy substances into public thoroughfares, shall pay a fine of 2 *kahanas* or 32 *panas* and remove them without delay. He, who wantonly throws filth into thoroughfares, shall be fined.

Infirm persons defiling a thoroughfare, to be warned.

If a distressed or old man, a pregnant woman, or a boy, defile a thoroughfare, they shall be warned and shall clean the place.

A person, throwing filth into streets and public places, shall be fined.

VISHNU says, if a person throw bones, sweepings, or other impure things, into the public streets, or by the sides of gardens or water-courses, he shall be fined 100 *panas* and compelled to remove them.

The penalty of 2 *kahanas*, mentioned by MENU, is applicable in the case of a person who partially defiles a thoroughfare, &c. There is therefore no inconsistency.

He who defiles ponds, and public places, shall be fined.

KATYAYANA says, that he who defiles ponds, gardens, and *ghats* with impure things, shall be compelled to cleanse them and fined 250 *panas*.

This penalty is to be imposed on such as are often guilty.

This penalty is for such as often defile ponds, &c.

He who seizes upon lands, by intimidating their owners, shall be fined.

MENU says he who takes gardens, houses, ponds, or land, by intimidating their owners, shall be fined 500 *panas*. But if they be taken under the impression that they belong to him, he shall be fined 200 *panas*.

He who does not observe boundaries, and destroys landmarks, shall be fined.

VRIDDHA MENU says that, he who does not observe the boundaries, and cuts down trees planted for distinguishing the boundaries of two villages, shall be fined 200 *panas*.

He who forcibly takes possession of lands or destroys trees planted on the boundaries of two villages, shall be fined 1000 *panas*.

He who seizes upon lands or destroys trees, that form landmarks, shall be fined.

SANKHA says, he who destroys landmarks shall be fined 108 *panas*. But he who takes land more than he actually owns, shall be fined 1008 *panas*.

He who destroys landmarks, shall be fined.

He who takes the water of a field shall be fined 108 *panas*.

He who takes the water of a field shall be fined.

NAREDA says that, if a man erect a bridge on the ground of another, he should not be obstructed, for the bridge benefits many and the owner of the ground sustains a comparatively slight loss.

Why a person erecting a bridge on the ground of another, should not be obstructed.

It is desirable that the public good be promoted *even* at the expense of the owner of the land.

The public good should be promoted even at the expense of the owner of the land.

YAGNYAVALKYA says that, if a mound be raised on a land without the knowledge of its owner and it increase the crop of the fields of others, the builder of the mound shall not obtain profit therefrom, but the owner of the land. If he neglect it, the king shall take it.

Who shall obtain the profit of the increase of crops, owing to the raising of a mound on a land without the knowledge of its owner.

OF CULTIVATED AND UNCULTIVATED FIELDS.

Who shall get the produce of a field cultivated by another person in the absence of its proprietor.

NAREDA says, if the proprietor of a field be poor, die, or go to a distant country, and if the field be uninterruptedly cultivated by another person, the latter shall get its produce.

How the proprietor may get back the field.

If the proprietor return when the field has been, or is being, cultivated, he shall get it back by paying the expenses incurred.

What the proprietor should get if unable to pay the expenses.

KATYAYANA says, if the proprietor have no means of paying the expenses, the cultivator shall receive the produce *minus* an eighth part of it, which shall be given to the proprietor.

When the field should be given back to the proprietor.

After eight years' occupation of this description, the field shall be given back to the proprietor of it.

How long an eighth part of the produce may be taken by the proprietor.

An eighth part of the produce shall be taken by the proprietor, and the remainder by the cultivator, continually for eight years, after which the proprietor shall get back the field without paying any costs.

Where this rule is applicable.

This rule is applicáble to *khila*, a field that cannot be cultivated without great difficulty.

A field that is not cultivated for one year is called *ardha khila*, and that which has lain uncultivated for three years, is called *khila*.

Ardha khila and khila defined.

Ground uncultivated for five years is the same as a desert.

Ground uncultivated for five years is a desert.

VRIHASPATI says, that leased ground shall be cultivated by the lessee in proper seasons. If he fail to do so, he shall pay the proprietor as much as the latter would have received, had there been a tolerable crop.

What a lessee should pay to the proprietor of ground, if he fail to cultivate it at the proper seasons.

OF RENT OF LAND.

He who does not cultivate leased land, &c., shall pay its owner the stipulated quantity of produce, &c.

According to Vyasa, he who does not cultivate land taken by him on lease, nor cause it to be cultivated, shall pay its owner the stipulated quantity of produce and an equal amount of fine to the king.

What the hirer of a land that lies uncultivated for years is to give to its owner.

The owner of land that lies uncultivated for years, shall receive the value of a tenth portion of its produce from him who hires it.

What the owner of cultivated land is to receive.

The owner of cultivated land shall receive an eighth part of its produce from its cultivator.

What the owner of very fertile lands is to receive.

The owner of very fertile land shall receive a sixth part of its produce.

The gain of the owner shall be fixed according to the nature of the land.

The gain of the owner shall be fixed according to the nature of the land.

Where the abovementioned rules are applicable.

The abovementioned rules are, according to Vrihaspati, applicable to lands of tolerable fertility.

What the cultivation of land that resembles a desert and yields a tolerable crop shall receive.

Therefore, if land that nearly resembles a desert in quality, yield a tolerable crop, its cultivator shall give the owner of it a tenth part of its produce.

What the owner of khila or ardha khila land shall receive.

The owner of *khila* land shall get an eighth part of its produce, and that of *ardha khila*, a sixth part.

If the lessees do not cultivate the leased lands, the king shall cause them to pay the value of the aforesaid parts of the produce thereof to their proprietors.

The liability of lessees, who do not cultivate leased lands.

MENU speaks of the disposal of the crops of fields cultivated without the permission of their owner.

The crops of fields cultivated without the permission of their owners.

He, who, having no fields, sows seeds in those of others, does not get the produce.

He, who sows seeds in the fields of others, does not get the produce.

The produce of seeds thrown from one field into another by a storm or a deluge, is enjoyed by the proprietor of the field.

Who is to have the produce of seeds thrown into a field by a storm.

He who sells bad seeds, destroys those that have been sown, or forcibly takes possession of land, shall be mutilated.

Punishment of certain agricultural offences.

OF THE PRESERVATION OF GRAIN.

What quantity of land is to be kept for pasturage.

YAGNYAVALKYA says, that land measuring 100 *dhanus* or 400 cubits (a *dhanu* being equal to 4 cubits) shall be kept for pasturage between the village and the fields according to the pleasure of the villagers, to the quantity of land, or to the order of the king. If the village be very large, the pasturage shall extend to 200 *dhanus* or 800 cubits. In a town it shall measure 400 *dhanus* or 1600 cubits.

Menu on the point.

MENU says, that land, measuring 100 *dhanus* or "three casts of a large stick," shall be left on every side of a village. In a town, the said quantity of land shall be left.

When herdsmen are not to be fined for damage done by cattle to grain.

If cattle damage grain in unfenced fields near pasture land, the king shall not fine the herdsmen.

Vishnu on the point.

VISHNU says, if cattle feed for a short time on grain in a field that lies unenclosed with a hedge at the extremity of pasture land, or near a thoroughfare, the herdsman is not to blame. But if they feed upon it for a long time, the herdsman shall incur blame, for the damage may have been intentionally done.

Yagnyavalkya's authority.

YAGNYAVALKYA confirms this, by saying that, if cattle consume grain produced in fields situate near a highway or within the limits of pasture land, and if the loss be caused without any such intention on the part of the herdsmen, they are not to blame. But if the cattle be purposely allowed to graze there, they shall be punished like thieves.

If cattle eat up the grain in a distant field, the herdsmen shall be fined.

According to MENU, if cattle eat up the grain in a distant field, the herdsman shall be fined 25 *gandas*.

The owner of the land to get his share of the produce.

In all cases the owner of the land shall get his due share of the produce.

Fines shall be imposed according to the species of the cattle.

SANKHA and LIKHITA say, that fines shall be imposed according to the species of the cattle. The herdsmen who let loose cattle by night shall be fined 5 *mashas*. But if they are let loose during the day, the herdsmen shall be fined 3 *mashas*.

Fines to be in proportion to the neglect, &c.

But if they be let loose for a short time, the herdsmen shall be fined one *masha*. They cannot be fined, if the cattle be let loose near the village.

What sort of masha is meant.

The *masha* referred to above is made of silver, for VASHYAKARA says that a golden *masha* may be used for the payment of fines, and so forth, but a fine for damage done to grain by cattle shall be the silver *masha*, which, according to MENU, is equal to two *kristalas*.

Cattle shall graze night and day at pleasure.

It is understood that cattle shall graze night and day at pleasure.

The cowherd to be fined if a cow eat up grain.

KATYAYANA says, if a cow eat up grain, the cowherd shall pay a fine of four *panas*.

The owner of a buffalo eating up grain, to be fined.

If a buffalo eat up grain, its owner shall be fined eight *panas*.

The owner of a goat, &c., eating up grain, to be fined 4 panas.

If a goat, sheep, or calf eat up grain, the owner of each of them shall be fined four *panas*.

Gautama on the punishment of the owners of cattle that eat up grain.

According to GAUTAMA, the owner of a cow shall be fined five, that of a camel six, that of a buffalo or horse ten, and that of a sheep or goat two *mashas*.

Sankha and Likhita on the point.

SANKHA and LIKHITA say, that the owners of all calves eating up grain shall be fined one *masha*.

Nareda on the same.

According to NAREDA, a herdsman, who lets his cattle loose and these feed on the grain of others, shall be fined twice the value of the grain consumed.

How the herdsman whose cattle feed on grain all night, is to be fined.

If cattle feed on grain during the whole night, the herdsman shall be fined four times the amount, of the grain consumed.

When herdsmen are to be punished like thieves.

Herdsmen, who tend cattle in the fields in the presence of their owners, and suffer them to eat up grain, shall be punished like thieves.

If cattle entirely destroy grain, how the owners and herdsman are to be punished.

According to NAREDA, if cattle entirely destroy grain, their owners shall pay its price to the loser, the herdsman shall be flogged, and the owner shall pay a fine to the king.

The owner of grain that is consumed, to receive its value.

According to VISHNU, the owner of grain that is consumed shall receive its value in all cases.

If cattle, when tended or not, eat up grain, their owner shall pay its value and shall be fined.

If cattle eat up grain, their owner how to be punished.

NAREDA says that he, who demands compensation for the consumption of grain, shall be paid that quantity of grain which, in the opinion of the neighbouring farmers, might have grown there.

What compensation is due to a person whose grain has been consumed.

The owner of a cow, eating up grain, shall pay the landlord the value of the plants or the grain. The husbandman shall be paid in grain. This penalty is to be imposed for damage done by cows.

The owner of a cow, consuming grain, shall pay the landlord the value of the plants or the grain.

It is not proper to take the value of grain eaten up by cows, for the receipt of it makes a man a sinner.

Receipt of value of grain eaten up by cows, is improper.

USHANA confirms this by saying, that the gods and the ancestors of the man who takes the value of what is consumed by cows, do not accept his offerings.

Ushana's authority on the above.

Herdsmen are responsible for any loss caused by the cattle, when these are under their charge. Otherwise their owners are so.

When herdsmen are responsible for loss caused by cattle.

VISHNU speaks partly on the same subject. The owners of cattle that are *not* tended, and the herdsmen of those that *are* tended, shall pay a fine for any loss caused by them.

Vishnu on the point.

When herdsmen or proprietors of cattle eating up grain are not punishable.

NAREDA specially says, if cattle eat up grain, when their herdsmen or proprietors are confined by the king's officers, killed by thunderbolts, snake-bites, tigers, and so forth, or die by falling from trees, or are afflicted with any disease, they cannot be punished.

What animals eating up grain shall be set free.

YAGNYAVALKYA says, if bulls or other animals that are consecrated to the gods, or those which have brought forth young ones ten days before, or have suddenly come, or are astray, eat up grain, they shall be set free, for they are impelled by God or the king.

Menu on the point.

MENU says, a cow that has brought forth a calf only ten days before, or is about to bring forth one, a bull or any other animal that has been consecrated to the gods, whether these are tended or not, cannot be punished.

Why elephants and horses are not to be punished.

USHANA says, that elephants and horses shall not be punished, since they assist the king in the protection of his subjects.

What persons and cattle shall not be punished.

Blind or lame men and bulls marked with some religious symbols, shall not be punished. Nor should cows that have suddenly come, or have recently brought forth young ones, or *(byabhicharini)* that are running fast, consecrated cows in general, and cows brought for sacrifice, be punished.

Where the penalty ordained by Gautama, holds good.

The penalty of ten *mashas,* ordained by GAUTAMA, as to the owners of horses and buffalos, holds good in the case of those of merchants, and others. There is consequently no inconsistency.

Blind and *lame* men, above referred to, mean such as are quite helpless. **Blind and lame defined.**

In the *Parijata*, *obisharini*, which signifies lustful, is used instead of *byabhicharini*. **Obisharini is used in the Parijata instead of byabhicharini.**

According to SANKHA, young animals, calves, elephants, and horses, cannot be prevented from eating up grain. **Young animals, calves, &c., cannot be prevented from eating up grain.**

KATYAYANA says, if the owners of large, middle-sized, and little animals, complain against one who pursues them, the pursuer shall be fined. **The pursuer of animals of various sizes, is to be fined.**

According to VRIHASPATI, if the animals are driven or punished, when they enter a garden house, pasture land, house, fold, and so forth, they may be confined or punished without subjecting the person to any penalty. **Animals trespassing on cultivated or inhabited places, may be confined or punished.**

ABUSE.

Abuse defined.

NAREDA defines abuse *(bakparushya*)* to be the reviling of a person's country, nation, race, and so forth, in vehement and abusive terms.

This meaning is confirmed in the Mitakshara.

This is its general meaning, and the *Mitakshara* confirms it. The meaning given to it by others is incorrect, for abuse does not injure the person reviled.

Three kinds of abuse.

It is of three kinds, namely, *nishtur, aslila,* and *tibra.* The punishment of persons guilty of these shall be light or heavy according to the nature of the abuse.

Definition.

Pundits define *nishtur bakparushya* to be insulting language, *aslila,* language that should not be uttered, and *tibra,* language that deeply wounds the feelings of others.

Two kinds of parusha.

According to VRIHASPATI, *parushya* is of two kinds, namely, abuse *(bakparushya)* and assault *(dandaparushya).*

Each of these is subdivided into three kinds, &c.

Each of these is subdivided into three kinds and has as many kinds of punishment.

Abuse of the first kind defined.

Abuse of the first kind means the use of false and abusive language, attacking the country, circumstances, race, and so forth of persons, and declaring them to be vicious.

---

*This word is generally rendered *slander*, as in the passage, translated by Sir W. Jones, in the Introduction to this work.

The tenor of the whole of this Section proves that the proper rendering is *abuse*.

Pundits say, that abuse of the second kind means the unjust abuse of persons, by speaking in bad terms of their mothers, sisters, and other *relations*, and declaring them to be vicious.

Abuse of the second kind defined.

Abuse of the third kind means the use of language charging a man with eating and drinking forbidden articles and committing some heinous crime; or in short, of language that wounds the feelings of others. It is understood to imply great vice on the part of the person abused.

Abuse of the third kind defined.

If two persons of the same class abuse each other, both of them shall be equally punished. If a member of an inferior class abuse one of a superior class, he shall receive double the punishment fixed for the offence. If the member of a superior class abuse one of an inferior class, he shall receive double the fixed punishment.

How two persons of the same or different classes, abusing each other, should be punished.

According to YAGNYAVALKYA, language used in attacking mean or stupid persons, makes the abuser liable to half the punishment.

The abuse of mean or stupid persons is liable to half the punishment.

If a person abuse the wife of another or a respectable man, he shall be doubly punished.

Punishment for abuse of a man's wife or a respectable man.

According to KATYAYANA and USHANA, he who repents for abusing any one, promises not to do so again, and declares that his offence arose from inadvertence, carelessness, jocularity, or fun, shall receive only half the punishment.

He who repents for abusing any one &c. shall receive only half the punishment.

How persons of the same class and qualifications are to be punished.

VRIHASPATI says that, if persons of the same class and qualifications abuse each other, they shall be fined 13½ *panas*.

Vishnu on the punishment for abuse.

VISHNU, speaking of the punishment for abuse, says that half the prescribed punishment shall be inflicted on a member of a superior class who abuses one of an inferior class, and that double that punishment shall be inflicted when a member of an inferior class abuses one of a superior class.

How a man abusing his equal is to be punished.

But, if a man abuse his equal, he shall be fined twelve *panas*.

How a man abusing an inferior, or a person disabled, is to be punished.

When a man abuses his inferior or those who are blind or lame, or otherwise disabled, he shall be fined six *panas*.

Punishment for abuse imputing gross iniquity.

YAGNYAVALKYA says, if a person abuse another by stating that he has committed fornication with his mother or sister, the king shall fine him twenty-five *panas*.

Menu on the punishment for abuse.

MENU says, "a soldier abusing a priest shall be fined a hundred *panas*; a merchant so *offending*, a hundred and fifty or two hundred; but for such an offence, a mechanic or servile man shall be whipped."

Punishment of a priest for abusing a soldier, merchant, or Sudra.

"A priest shall be fined fifty *panas*, if he abuse a soldier; twenty-five if he abuse a merchant; and twelve if he abuse a man of the servile class."

If a priest and soldier exchange abusive words, the former shall be fined 250, and the latter 500 *panas*.

How a priest and a soldier are to be punished, if they exchange abusive words.

The above rule also holds good when a merchant and a mechanic exchange abusive words. This rule is applicable in the case of gross abuse.

Where this rule holds good.

According to VRIHASPATI, if a mechanic give religious instruction to a person, utter words of the *Vedas*, or grossly abuse a Brahmin, his tongue shall be cut off.

The tongue of a mechanic to be cut off, for certain offences.

If a mechanic grossly abuse any member of the twice-born classes, his tongue shall be cut off, since he is of mean descent.

The reason of the punishment.

Red-hot iron, of the length of ten fingers, shall be thrust into the mouth of that mechanic, who abuses any member of the twice-born classes by name.

Punishment of the mechanic who abuses any member of the twice-born classes by name.

Hot oil shall be dropped by the king into the ears and mouth of that mechanic, who through pride gives religious instruction to the twice-born classes.

Punishment of the mechanic, who through pride gives religious instruction to the twice-born classes.

In the *Kalpataru*, gross abuse is defined to be the use of words indicative of the vices of the abused.

Gross abuse defined.

Punishment of a Sudra abusing or assaulting any member of the twice-born classes.

GAUTAMA says, "if a Sudra abuse or assault any member of the twice-born classes, he shall be deprived of the organ with which he offends. In other words, his tongue shall be cut off if he abuse; his hands or any other limb shall be maimed, if he assault.

Punishment of a mechanic for hearing the words of the Veda.

If a mechanic hear words of the *Veda*, his ear shall be sealed with lead.

Uttering them.

If he utter words of the *Veda*, his tongue shall be cut off.

Or learning them.

If he learn words of the *Veda*, his body shall be injured.

Punishment for false aspersions.

MENU says that he, who proudly throws false aspersions on the learning, nativity, race, profession, or body of another, shall be fined 200 *panas*.

Explanation.

The meaning of the above is that if a man insolently call another ignorant, or say that he was born in a bad place, or is not a Brahmin, or has not done any good deed, or has been circumcised, he shall be fined 200 *panas*.

Vyasa on the punishment for degrees of abuse.

VYASA says, that a man shall be fined 250 *panas* if he abuse another by calling him vicious; 500, if he call him very vicious; 1000, if most vicious.

NAREDA says, "he, who declares the king to be negligent of his duties, shall have his tongue cut off and shall be deprived of all his property."

Punishment of one who declares the king to be negligent of his duties.

According to YAGNYAVALKYA, he who maligns the king or discloses his counsels shall be driven out of the country, having had his tongue cut off.

Yagnyavalkya on the punishment of offences against the king.

USHANA says, penalties for crimes, for which no provision has been made, by ancient legislators, on account of their diversity, shall be fixed after consideration.

Ushana on penalties for crimes, punishment for which has not been fixed.

Abuse has been treated of in the NITI CHINTAMANI.

Reference to the Niti Chintamani.

ASSAULT.

Vrihaspati on the punishment of a man guilty of the first kind of assault.

VRIHASPATI says, that a man shall be fined one *masha*, if he be guilty of the first kind of assault, which consists in throwing dust *and other things* on, or lifting a hand or foot against another.

On whom such punishment is to be inflicted.

The abovementioned punishment is, according to the *Pundits*, inflicted on men who assault persons of their own class.

He who throws dust, &c., on the wife of another &c., shall be punished.

A man shall be fined two or three *mashas*, if he throw dust *and other things* on the wife of another, or on a respectable man, or lift his hands against or kick any such persons.

Yagnyavalkya on the point.

According to YAGNYAVALKYA, he who throws dust and other things on others and defiles their bodies, shall be fined ten *panas*. But if he kick, or spit or throw impure things on another, he shall be fined double.

Explanation.

This punishment is inflicted when persons of the same class are thus illtreated. When superiors or the wives of others are thus used, double the punishment shall be inflicted; and when inferiors are thus offended, half the punishment shall be sufficient. If this ill-treatment be inadvertently caused by a drunkard or insane person, and such like, no punishment shall be inflicted.

Punishment of one who defiles the lower or middle members of a person of the same class.

KATYAYANA says, if a man urine or vomit on the lower members of the body of a person of the same class or soil them with filth, he shall be fined forty *panas*; but if the middle members be thus soiled, he shall be fined sixty *panas*.

Of one who defiles the head of a man.

He who urines on *or defiles* the head of a man, shall be fined eighty *panas*.

Of one who pulls the limbs or dress of an equal.

YAGNYAVALKYA says that the person who pulls the hands, feet, or cloth of an equal, shall be fined ten *panas*.

Of one who, having bound and dragged an equal, applies his feet to his body.

The person who, having bound an equal with a piece of cloth and cruelly dragged him, applies his feet to his body, shall be fined 100 *panas*.

Of one who lifts his hand against or beats an equal.

KATYAYANA says that, if any one lift his hand against his equal, he shall be fined twelve *panas*. But if he beat him, he shall be fined 24 *panas*.

Where this rule holds good.

This rule is applicable in the case of such members of the *twice-born classes* as are equal.

Punishment of one who throws stones and sticks at his equal.

VRIHASPATI says, if a person throw stones and bits of wood at his equal, he shall be fined 250 *panas*.

Of one who lifts his hands against or attempts to kick an equal.

If a person lift his hands against his equal, he shall be fined ten *panas*. But if he attempt to kick him, he shall be fined twenty *panas*.

Punishment of one who lifts his hands or feet against others, or otherwise assaults them.

VISHNU says that he, who raises his hands against others, shall be fined ten *panas*. He who raises his feet against others shall be fined twenty *panas*. He who uses pieces of wood, shall be fined 250 *panas*. He who uses offensive weapons, shall be fined 1000 *panas*.

Explanation.

This last rule is applicable where an inferior behaves in the abovementioned manner towards his superiors.

Punishments for several kinds of mutual assaults.

YAGNYAVALKYA says that, if two persons lift their hands against each other, they shall be fined ten *panas*; but if they raise their feet, they shall be sentenced to a fine of twenty *panas*. If they use offensive weapons, they shall be fined 500 *panas*.

The rule applies to Brahmins.

This rule is applicable where the parties are Brahmins.

Menu on the punishment of assaults with the hands, clubs, or feet.

MENU says that, if a person angrily beat others with hands or clubs, his hands shall be cut off. But his feet shall be cut off, if he spurn others.

Punishment of an inferior who desires to sit with his superiors on the same bedstead.

If an inferior desire to sit with his superiors on the same bedstead, he shall be banished after having his buttocks stamped, or shall be deprived of them.

Of an inferior spitting on his superior.

If an inferior spit on his superior, the king shall cut off his lips.

Of defiling his person.

But if he urine on his superior, his organ shall be cut off by the king.

If he insult his superior by breaking wind on any member of the body, his anus shall be cut off by the king.

Of breaking wind on any member of his body.

If any person lay hold of the feet, hair, beard, or testicle of his superior with his hands, the king shall cut off his hands.

Of seizing certain members of his body.

The abovementioned penalties are for the misconduct of Sudras towards Brahmins.

These penalties inflicted on Sudras.

VRIHASPATI says, that they, who use weapons against each other through anger, shall be fined 500 *panas*.

Punishment for assaults with weapons.

Legislators say that if, in an affray, two persons wound each other, they shall be beaten in proportion to the severity of the wound inflicted.

In case of mutual wounding the punishment is to be in proportion to the wounds.

If any one throw stones and sticks at others, he shall be fined two *mashas*.

Punishment for throwing stones, and sticks at others.

Legislators say that, if blood be shed in an affray, the person so offending shall be fined four *mashas*.

The fine for shedding blood in an affray.

VISHNU says that, if a person be severely wounded without bloodshed, the person so offending shall be fined 32 *panas*.

For severe wounding without bloodshed.

But if blood flow out of the wound, the person inflicting the wound shall be fined 64 *panas*.

For wounding with bloodshed.

For a wound whereby the skin is torn off with blood.

MENU says that, if the skin be torn off with blood, the person who causes the wound shall be fined 100 *panas.*

And if the flesh be visible.

But if the flesh be visible, the person who causes the wound shall be fined 24 *mohars.*

Punishment for breaking the bones.

He who breaks another's bones shall be banished.

Vrihaspati on tearing the skin and the flesh.

VRIHASPATI says, that the person who tears the skin shall be fined 250 *panas;* but he who tears the flesh shall be fined 500 *panas.*

On breaking the bones.

The man who breaks bones shall be fined 1000 *panas.*

Capital punishment for killing with weapons.

He who kills another with offensive weapons shall be capitally punished.

The fines for breaking or cutting off certain members.

If a person break the teeth, feet, ears, noses, or hands of others, he shall be fined 500 *panas.* But if he entirely cut off any of them he shall be fined 1000 *panas.*

Punishment for slitting or violently breaking certain members.

KATYAYANA says that, according to BHRIGU, he who divides the ear, nose, lip, feet, eyes, tongue, male organ, or hands, shall be fined 1000 *panas.*

He who violently breaks any one of them shall be fined 500 *panas.*

YAGNYAVALKYA says, that he who breaks the hands, feet, or teeth of another, cuts his nose or ear, breaks open a *sore*, or beats one till the man is half-dead, shall be fined 500 *panas*. Yagnyavalkya on the punishment for certain injuries.

VISHNU says that he, who wounds one of the eyes, the shoulders, the arms, or the thigh of another, shall be fined 1000 *panas*. Vishnu on the punishment for wounds on certain members.

But if he wound both the eyes, the king shall confine him for life and shall wound both his eyes. For wounding both eyes.

YAGNYAVALKYA says that he, who wounds both the eyes or obeys the orders of the king's enemy, or a Sudra who maintains himself by putting on the sacred thread, shall be fined 800 *panas*. Yagnyavalkya on the punishment for certain offences.

The abovementioned punishment is for slightly wounding the eyes. The punishment is for slight hurt to the eyes.

The different kinds of penalties for the same offence are for the different degrees of wounds. Explanation.

MENU confirms this, by saying that they, who wantonly beat men or animals with cruelty, shall be punished, considering the extent of their suffering. Menu on the punishment for cruelty to men or animals.

But if a person unconsciously injure a man or animal, he is not to blame. Unconscious injury to man or animal is excepted.

NAREDA says that a Sudra's offence is atoned, when the member with which he beats a Brahmin is lopped off. He who beats even a guilty king, How the offence of a Sudra may be atoned for.

shall be impaled and burnt alive, since such a man is worse than a murderer of a hundred Brahmins.

Even a very wicked Brahmin is not to be put to death.

This punishment is for all except Brahmins. For the execution of even a very wicked Brahmin is prohibited.

The member of a Sudra, with which he strikes one of the twice-born classes, to be cut off.

MENU says, that that member of a Sudra's body, with which he may strike any of the twice-born classes, shall be cut off.

The hand or feet of a person striking another, to be cut off.

If a person strike another with his hand, foot, or stick, his hand or foot shall be cut off.

The punishment for wishing to sit with a superior on the same bed.

If a person wish to sit with his superior on the same bed, he shall be banished after his buttocks have been stamped with a hot iron, or one of his hips shall be cut off.

For spitting or making urine on a superior.

If a person spit on a superior through pride, the king shall cut off his lips. If he urine on him, his organ shall be cut off.

For breaking wind on him.

If he break wind on any member of his body, his arms shall be cut off.

Committing any other outrage on him.

If he take hold of his hair, feet, beard, neck, or testicle, his hands shall be cut off.

To whom these penalties apply.

The abovementioned penalties are applicable to Sudras, when they misbehave towards any member of the twice-born classes.

Certain acts of misbehaviour, committed by a Sudra towards a superior, to be punished.

APASTAMBA says, that a Sudra, who interrupts members of the twice-born classes in conversation, walks together with or goes before them, or sits or lies on the same bed, shall be punished.

The penalties inflicted on Sudras for abusing Brahmins, and *vice versâ*, are also applicable in cases of assault.

KATYAYANA says, that the penalties inflicted on Sudras for slandering Brahmins and *vice versâ* are likewise applicable in cases of assault.

The compensation due to a person wounded or plundered.

VRIHASPATI says, that he who wounds others in an affray shall pay the cost of their cure. He who plunders any article shall render its value.

Severer punishment due when several persons wound or plunder an individual.

YAGNYAVALKYA says that, if several persons wound an individual, each of them shall receive double the prescribed punishment. If they plunder any articles in an affray they shall not only return them but shall pay a fine of double their amount.

How a person may punish his wife, and certain other persons, for acting wrong.

MENU says that, if the wife, son, servant, pupil, or uterine brother, do any wrong, the person injured shall lash the back, but not the head, with a rope, or a slip of bamboo. The person who acts contrary to this rule shall be as guilty as a thief.

Yama on the point.

YAMA says that, when a wife, son, slave, male or female, or pupil, do any wrong, the person offended shall lash with a rope or a piece of split bamboo, the lower parts of their body, but never the head. He who acts contrary to this rule shall be punished.

How a pupil shall be checked.

NAREDA says that, if a pupil do any wrong, he shall be checked by words, by any other means save punishment, or with a thin rope or split bamboo.

He shall never be severely punished. Nor shall he be punished on his head or breast.

Gautama on the point.

GAUTAMA says that a pupil shall be checked without being beaten.

If he be punished in any other way, the king shall punish the instructor.

Apastamba on the point, and the means to be taken if the pupil cannot be checked by reprimand.

APASTAMBA says, if a pupil do any wrong, he shall be reprimanded a hundred times. If he cannot be thus checked, his instructor shall threaten him with punishment, throw water on him in winter, or deprive him of food, according to his strength, until he be corrected.

A father, punishing his son for any wicked deed, shall not be punished.

NAREDA says that, if a father punish his son for any wicked deed, he shall not be liable to punishment.

A person shall not be responsible, if his servant engage in an affray.

When a servant engages himself in an affray and beats others, his master shall not be liable to punishment.

When the owners of dogs shall be fined.

YAGNYAVALKYA says that, if the owners of dogs do not prevent the animals, when they can, from attacking others, they shall be fined 250 *panas*. If the attacked person request the owners to take away the dogs, and they do not, they shall be fined 500 *panas*.

KATYAYANA says that, if the marks of assault cannot be perceived, the dispute shall be determined by proof, and, in default thereof, by oath.

How a dispute is to be determined, if marks of assault cannot be perceived.

NAREDA says, that the aggressor in a dispute shall certainly be deemed guilty. If the aggrieved party return the abuse or beating, he also shall be guilty. But the former shall be severely punished.

A difference to be made between the aggressor in a dispute, and the aggrieved if he retaliate.

KATYAYANA says that he, who wounds others with a sword, or such other weapon, even if he had been first wounded, shall be punished.

A person wounding others with swords shall be punished, even if he be not the aggressor.

VRIHASPATI says that he, who abuses the person who abused him, returns a beating, kills a murderer, or checks him by censure or flogging, is not to blame.

Aggressors and guilty persons may be lawfully punished by the sufferer or others.

If *Sudras*, and the like, be checked by harsh measures by any member of a superior class who was abused by them, the king shall not punish him.

Any member of a superior class checking Sudras shall not be punished.

NAREDA says that if a *shvapaka*, an eunuch, a *chandala*, a prostitute, a fowler, a groom of elephants, any member of the twice-born class who has not been invested with the sacred thread after the expiration of the proper time, or a slave, insult the king, instructors, or superior men, or violate rules fixed by the king, each of them shall be immediately punished according to his guilt.

Persons of inferior grades insulting persons of the twice-born classes, or the king, or superiors, are to be immediately punished.

They who punish such persons shall not be deemed guilty.

Legislators say, that they who punish the aforesaid persons shall not be deemed guilty.

Such persons need not be brought before the king, but shall be punished by the superiors whom they insult.

Any of the aforesaid persons need not be brought before the king when they insult their superiors, who shall themselves punish them. For these are the dregs of society, and their property is also like rejected articles. They shall be punished by the king in their persons, but not fined.

Ugra defined.

The son born of a *Sudra* mother and *kshatrya* father is called *ugra*.

Kshota defined.

The son born of a *kshatrya* mother and *ugra* father is called *kshota*.

Shvapaka defined.

The son born of a *kshota* mother by a *ugra* father is called *shvapaka*.

Chandala defined.

The son born of a *Brahmin* mother and *Sudra* father is called *chandala*.

Who shall be punished in person and not fined.

KATYAYANA says, he who should not be touched, a cunning person, a slave, a very vicious person, he who is born of a mother of a superior class and a father of an inferior class or a *chandala*, shall be punished in person, but not fined, when they are guilty.

How a person, killing certain animals, shall be punished.

VISHNU says, that a hand and foot of that man who kills a goat, horse, or camel, shall be cut off.

He who sells uneatable flesh, or kills domestic animals, shall be fined one hundred *panas*, and shall have to pay the price of the animals killed.

Selling uneatable flesh, or killing domestic animals, to be punished.

They who castrate animals and kill wild animals shall be fined fifty *panas*.

Punishment for castrating animals and killing wild ones.

They who kill birds and fishes shall be fined ten *panas*.

For killing birds and fishes.

This punishment is for those who kill them not for food.

Explanation

MENU says, that they who maliciously lop off trees belonging to others, shall be fined according to the nature of the loss done.

Persons maliciously lopping off other men's trees shall be fined.

YAGNYAVALKYA says that he, who cuts off the branches of large and useful trees, such as *vat*, *pipula*, by which a man supports himself, shall be fined twenty *panas*, he who cuts their trunks shall be fined forty *panas*, and he who cuts their roots shall be fined eighty *panas*.

Yagnyavalkya on the punishment of persons cutting off the branches of trees and otherwise injuring them.

Double of the abovementioned punishment shall also be inflicted on those who cut the branches, trunks, or roots of trees the base of which is covered with stones, which are in sepulchres, near places of sale, or celebrated holy places.

Double the punishment when to be inflicted.

Half of the aforesaid punishment shall be inflicted on those who cut the branches, trunks, and

And when but half.

roots of creeping plants of different kinds in the abovementioned places.

Vishnu on the punishment of persons who cut down fruit-trees.

VISHNU says that he, who cuts down trees that yield fruits, shall be fined 1000 *panas*. A fine of 500 *panas* shall be inflicted on those who cut down trees that bear flowers; and that of ten *panas* on those who cut down creeping plants and the like.

Fine for cutting straw, &c.

He who cuts straw and such produce, shall be fined fifty *panas*.

The price of the articles destroyed to be paid.

The aforesaid offending parties shall also pay the price of the articles destroyed.

LARCENY.

Menu says, that the king, on satisfying himself by inquiries as to their guilt, shall punish thieves according to the value of the articles stolen. How the king shall punish thieves.

Vrihaspati says, that the king, ascertaining through his officers the guilt of thieves, by their associating with known thieves, and by *having in their possession* instruments for breaking into houses or stolen articles, and causing the articles to be returned to their owners, shall punish the thieves according to law. Vrihaspati on the point.

Menu says, that the king shall very diligently restrain thieves. For the suppression of theft increases his fame and power. The king shall diligently restrain thieves.

That king who bestows exemption from fear "shall always be honored," since he performs, *as it were,* a perpetual sacrifice, giving exemption from fear as a constant sacrificial present. What the king gains by suppressing theft.

The king, who takes revenue without protecting his subjects, weakens his dominions and loses a seat in heaven. What he forfeits by not doing so.

There are two kinds of thieves, namely, *(prakasha) known* and *(aprakasha) unknown.* Two kinds of thieves.

Known *(prakasha)* thieves are tradesmen, and the like, unknown *(aprakasha)* thieves are house-breakers, and the like. Known and unknown.

PUNISHMENT OF KNOWN THIEVES.

Vyasa on known thieves.

VYASA speaks of thieves of the first sort. He says that tradesmen steal by giving a smaller quantity of things in weight and measure, by putting down in books a greater quantity than is actually given, by raising the prices of articles by their own men when customers come to purchase them, and by the fluctuation of prices. There are some tradesmen who mix articles of the same description but of a lower price with those of a higher price.

The fine for giving an eighth less in weight or measure.

YAGNYAVALKYA says that he, who steals an eighth part in weight *or* measure, shall be fined two hundred *panas.*

Explanation.

Or in the preceding sentence signifies that, by whatsoever means the theft is committed, the thief shall be fined two hundred *panas.*

For a ninth part.

He who steals a ninth part shall be fined two hundred *minus* one-eighth *panas.*

And for a seventh part.

He who steals a seventh part shall be fined two hundred *minus* one-eighth *panas.*

For giving less than an eighth or one thing for another.

KATYAYANA says, that he who steals (more than *an eighth* part) in weighing or measuring articles, by giving one thing for another, and so forth, shall be fined 250 *panas.*

This provision does not, therefore, contradict the rule of YAGNYAVALKYA.

Fine for selling adulterated goods.

MENU says that he, who sells adulterated articles at a price equal to that of good ones, shall be fined 250 *panas* where he shall cheat one-seventh part, or 500 *panas* where he shall cheat one-fifth part, and so forth.

Certain crimes punishable by mutilation.

He who sells counterfeit seeds, forcibly takes possession of the field sown by another with seed, or violates the rules of the place, nationality, race, learning, or the king, shall be disfigured, or in other words his nose or ears shall be cut off.

The punishment for selling articles by concealing their defects.

VRIHASPATI says that he, who sells articles by concealing their defects, such as are adulterated or that have been polished up, shall pay the purchaser double the price given by him, and shall pay a fine equal to it.

For one who sells adulterated medicines.

YAGNYAVALKYA says, that he who sells adulterated medicines, oils, and the like, salt, articles emitting a sweet scent, rice, *goor*, and the like, shall be fined sixteen *panas*.

Explanation.

The punishment fixed by VRIHASPATI shall be inflicted on such as cheat in selling valuable articles; and those that cheat in articles of moderate price shall be liable to the punishment prescribed by YAGNYAVALKYA. Therefore there is no inconsistency.

A person falsely stating the weight or measure of articles for sale, &c., shall be fined.

YAGNYAVALKYA says that he, who falsely states the weight or measure of articles for sale, sells articles out of the market with bad motives or trades fraudulently, shall be fined eight times the value of the things sold.

The punishment for attempting to sell things furtively.

VISHNU says that he, who attempts to sell things out of the market from bad motives, shall be fined his whole property.

Explanation.

This fine is imposed on one who repeatedly does this.

The punishment fixed by YAGNYAVALKYA shall be inflicted on one who occasionally does this. Therefore there is no inconsistency.

How the trader who often uses false weight, &c., is to be punished.

SANKHA says that the trader, who often sells articles by false weight or measure, shall be punished in person or his limbs shall be cut off.

How a person who often does so, is to be punished.

The head of him who often acts in the abovementioned manner shall be shaved, and the ear or any other limb of him who always does this shall be cut off.

Where these two kinds of punishment are held to apply.

Others say, that the aforesaid two kinds of punishment shall be inflicted according to the value of the articles sold.

The punishment for preparing and using counterfeit weights, &c.

YAGNYAVALKYA says that they, who prepare and use counterfeit weights, measures, licenses, and coin, shall be fined 1000 *panas*.

And practising impositions with regard to coins.

The abovementioned fine shall also be imposed on those who examine coins, and so forth, and, from bad motives, call good coins bad and *vice versâ*.

VISHNU says that he, who sells counterfeit pearls and so forth, by describing them as true, shall be fined 1000 *panas*. The punishment for selling counterfeit pearls, &c.

YAGNYAVALKYA says, that the merchants, who conspire to sell articles at such prices as press heavily on those who prepare idols and so forth, or raise or lower the prices of things settled by the ruler, shall be fined 1000 *panas*. For selling articles at high prices, &c., to idol makers, and varying the prices fixed.

The same fine shall be imposed on those who conspire to purchase articles at reduced prices or sell them at advanced rates from wicked motives. And for conspiring to purchase articles at low rates, and sell them at high ones.

MENU says that they, who sell elephants, horses, &c., worthy of the king's use, or, through avarice, deal in articles, the trade in which is prohibited by the king, without his permission, shall be fined at the price obtained by them. Persons selling elephants, or dealing in prohibited articles, shall be fined.

MENU says, that the king shall, by way of customs, take one-twentieth part of the value of goods, fixed by those who understand mercantile business and know the prices of goods. The duty to be paid to king on the value of goods.

VISHNU says, that one-tenth of the prices of country goods and one-twentieth of those of foreign ones shall be taken by the king. Vishnu on the duties payable on home and imported produce.

The meaning of the above is, that one-tenth of the profit of goods purchased and sold in the country, and one-twentieth of that of goods purchased from a foreign land and sold in the country, shall be taken by the king. Explanation.

Gautama on the duty on articles of commerce, &c.

GAUTAMA says, that the tax on articles of commerce shall be one-twentieth of their prices, but that on roots, flowers, medicines, rice, and the like, honey, flesh, straw, and wood sold in the country by purchase from a foreign one, shall be one-sixth of the profit.

What goods shall not be taxed.

VASISHTHA says that legislators quote MENU on the subject of taxes.

The proceeds of goods, the price of which falls short of one *kahana*, of trades and of the sale of children, fees of ambassadors, what is gained by begging, the profit of articles, a portion of which has been stolen away, of any thing sold by learned Brahmins, or things brought for performing sacrifices *(yogas,)* shall not be taxed.

How physicians shall be fined, for improper treatment of persons of various grades.

VISHNU says, that those physicians, who treat respectable persons in a bad manner from unfair motives, shall be fined 1000 *panas*. But if they treat men of the middle classes in the above-mentioned manner, they shall be fined 500 *panas*. A fine of 250 *panas* shall be imposed on them, when they cause the ill-treatment of insignificant persons.

Vyasa on prostitutes and other inciters to crimes.

VYASA says, that prostitutes, rogues, and artisans entice persons to commit wicked deeds, of which they are perfectly ignorant, against their will. They deceive those who place confidence in them.

Vrihaspati on punishment of culpable officers of court.

VRIHASPATI says, that the officers of court, who act unlawfully or live by bribery, and they who betray confidence, shall be expelled from the country.

YAGNYAVALKYA says, that bribe-takers shall be deprived of their whole property and be banished.

The punishment for bribe-takers.

If washermen put on the clothes of others, they shall be fined three *panas*. But if they sell, hire out, mortgage, or lend them, they shall be fined ten *panas*.

For washermen, who put on others' clothes, &c.

VRIHASPATI says that they, who pretend to be hermits by taking staves (in their hands) or putting on skins, and maliciously injure others, shall be confined by the officers of police.

For pretended hermits.

MENU says that the goldsmith, the most wicked of all dealers, who does any wrong, shall be mangled to pieces with razors by the king.

A goldsmith doing any wrong, to be mangled to pieces.

Legislators say that the abovementioned punishment is imposed, when he repeatedly does wrong.

Explanation.

YAGNYAVALKYA says that he, who deals in articles alleged to be made of gold and adulterated flesh, shall be fined 1000 *panas* and deprived of the three members of his body: in other words, he who publicly deals in gilt articles describing them as golden and sells dog's flesh for that of deer, shall be fined 1000 *panas* and deprived of his nose, teeth, and hands.

The punishment for dealing in articles alleged to be made of gold and flesh unfit for food.

He, who sells bad articles by describing them as good, shall be fined eight times their price; in other words, when a bad article is made showy in appearance and sold at a very high price, the person so doing shall be fined eight times the excess of the (proper) price.

The punishment for puffing bad articles, and selling them at high prices.

Persons selling or mortgaging boxes, &c., with false descriptions, to be punished.

They, who sell or mortgage boxes, and the like, other than those shown at first, or counterfeit musk, and the like, shall be punished according to law.

The punishment for selling articles at high prices.

He, who sells an article worth less than one *pana* at a high price, shall be fined fifty *panas*. But when the price of such an article is one or two *panas*, the vendor shall be fined one hundred or two hundred *panas* respectively. In like manner the punishment shall be heavier according to the nature of the crime.

A person selling or depositing a box of things of little value, as containing valuables, &c., to be punished.

He, who sells or deposits a box or chest full of things of little value, stating that it contains valuables, or counterfeit musk, and the like, for pure articles, shall suffer legal punishment.

The punishment for deceiving others by depositing or selling articles at high prices, &c.

He, who deceives others by depositing or selling an article worth half a *pana* at a higher price, or by stating it to be very valuable, shall be fined fifty *panas*.

The punishment shall be one hundred times greater than the price.

But where its price is one *pana*, the depositor or vendor shall be fined one hundred *panas*. In this manner the punishment shall be one hundred times greater than the price.

Selling things of little value by describing them as very valuable, to be punished.

VRIHASPATI says, that they, who sell things of little value by describing them as very valuable, or deceive women and boys, shall be punished in proportion to the amount they may have taken.

The king shall cause those who sell counterfeit gold, pearl, coral, and the like, to give the purchasers the price taken from them and to pay a fine of double the amount. Persons selling counterfeit gold, and valuables, how to be punished.

YAGNYAVALKYA says, that pure gold does not diminish, if it be kept in fire days and nights. Pure gold does not diminish, even if always kept in the fire.

If silver weighing one hundred *palas* be put in a fire, there is a diminution of two *palas* at the utmost. Silver is diminished two per cent.

If one hundred *palas* of pure tin or lead be put in a fire, there is a diminution of eight *palas*. Pure tin or lead eight per cent.

If one hundred *palas* of copper be put in a fire, a diminution of five *palas* takes place. Copper five per cent.

If one hundred *palas* of iron be put in a fire, a diminution of ten *palas* takes place. Iron ten per cent.

He, who says that a greater diminution has taken place in putting any of the aforementioned metals in the fire, shall be punished. He who declares the contrary shall be punished.

YAGNYAVALKYA says, that if 100 *palas* of coarse cotton or woollen thread be given, 110 *palas* of cloth shall be prepared. The quantity of cloth prepared out of 100 palas of coarse thread.

If the thread be somewhat coarse, the cloth shall be 105 *palas*; but if it be fine, it shall extend to 103 *palas*. And what quantity if the thread be coarse or fine.

PUNISHMENT FOR UNKNOWN THIEVES.

The punishment of house-breakers.

MENU says, the king shall impale those who break into houses at night, by cutting off their hands.

Of thieves.

VAS says, thieves acquire many kinds of treasure by house-breaking. The king shall cause their owners to receive them and then impale the thieves.

Of those who repeatedly steal or rob passengers.

VRIHASPATI says, they who repeatedly steal shall be impaled: they who rob passengers shall be executed and suspended on trees.

Of persons stealing males.

VRIHASPATI says, the king shall burn those who steal males with fire made of straw, and so forth.

Of those who steal females.

They who steal females shall be burnt by being dragged them over red hot iron or with fire made of sticks, and so forth.

On whom this punishment is to be inflicted.

This punishment is for the stealing of men and women descended from respectable families.

Menu's authority on the point.

MENU confirms this by saying that they, who steal men or women in particular who are the descendants of respectable families and they who steal emeralds, shall be executed.

The punishment of him who steals human creatures.

VYASA says, he who steals human creatures shall be kept at the junction of four streets, after his hands and feet have been cut off.

This punishment is for the theft of persons of the middle classes. What persons are referred to.

He who steals men shall be fined 1000 *panas*. The punishment for stealing men.

This punishment is for the theft of mean persons. What persons are meant.

He who steals women shall forfeit all his property. A person stealing women to be fined.

He who steals virgins shall be put to death. A person stealing virgins shall be executed.

The fine of the whole property is imposed, when mean women are stolen. Mean women referred to above.

MENU says, half of the foot of that man shall be cut off who pierces the noses of cows belonging to *Brahmins* and steals beasts. The punishment for piercing the noses of cows belonging to Brahmins, &c.

The king shall punish him who steals animals of great size, arms, and medicines, considering the time and necessity. For the theft of animals of great size, arms, and medicines.

Animals of great size signify elephants, horses, and so forth. Time means a time of war. Necessity signifies the time when the animals are required for riding, and so forth. Explanation.

NAREDA says, they who steal animals of great size, shall be fined 1000 *panas*, they who steal animals of moderate size 500 *panas*, and they who steal little animals 250 *panas*. Nareda on the point.

Vishnu's laws on the matter to be valid.

The laws prescribed by VISHNU in this matter shall be valid.

The punishment for theft of horses.

VYASA says, the stealer of horses shall be killed, his hands, feet, and waist being cut off.

The punishment for heinous thefts and assassination.

YAGNYAVALKYA says, they who steal prisoners, horses, and elephants, and suddenly murder persons, shall be impaled.

For those who break into granaries, &c.

They, who break into granaries, arsenals, and temples, and steal horses, elephants, and cars, shall be killed without trial.

The punishment prescribed by Vishnu for stealing cows, &c.

VISHNU says, they who steal cows, horses, elephants, or camels, shall be deprived of a hand, foot, and so forth: they who steal goats, and the like, shall have a hand cut off.

Explanation.

Such horses and elephants are understood to be of inferior kind, as belong to persons who do not know how to manage them or are stolen in time of peace.

The punishment prescribed by Vyasa for stealing animals.

VYASA says, one foot of that man who steals animals shall be cut off with a sharp weapon, such as a spade, &c.

By Menu for persons loosing or unloosing animals to steal them, or destroying slaves and cattle.

MENU says, they who tie loose animals, or unloose chained ones, with the motive of stealing them, and destroy slaves, horses, and cars, shall be punished like thieves.

MENU says, two fingers of those, who unloose chained animals for the purpose of stealing them, shall, in the first instance, be cut off. In the second instance one hand and foot shall be cut off. In the third instance they shall be killed.

And for persons unlooing animals to steal them once or oftener.

YAGNYAVALKYA says, a thumb and the finger just next to it on the right side of that person, who pursues or unlooses animals for the purpose of stealing them, shall be cut off.

For pursuing or unloosing animals to steal them.

VRIHASPATI says, those who steal rice measuring more than ten *kumbhas* shall be killed.

For stealing more than ten kumbhas of rice.

But those who steal less than the abovementioned quantity shall be forced to give compensation to the owners and fined eleven times the quantity stolen.

A stealer of less than the aforesaid quantity shall be fined.

According to the *Ratnakara* and others one *kuraba* is equal to twelve times the quantity of rice that can be held in the hollow of the hands of a full grown man. Four *kurabas* make one *prastha*, twenty *prasthas* one *kumbha*.

Kuraba defined.

The legislators of *Mithila* call ten *kumbhas* a *khari*, which is equal to the rice required for the support of a full-grown man.

Khari how understood in Mithila.

Others say that, in measuring rice, each of the following measures, *pala*, *kuraba*, *prastha*, *araka*, and *dron*, is inversely four times greater than the other.

Several measures of rice, defined.

Baha defined. Sixteen *drons* make one *khari*, twenty *drons* make one *kumbha*, ten *kumbhas* make one *baha*.

Explanation. The *kumbha*, as defined here, is the quantity above referred to.

The punishment for a crop destroyed through the cultivator's fault. If the crop be destroyed through the fault of the cultivator, he shall pay a fine of ten times his share.

But it is less, if destroyed through the fault of his servant. If it have been done through the fault of his servant and without his knowledge, he shall be fined five times his share.

The owner of the land shall nevertheless take his share. In addition to the aforesaid penalty it is proper that the owner of the land shall take his proper share.

The punishment for stealing camphor, nuts, rice, &c. NAREDA says that he, who steals any of the undermentioned, camphor and other aromatics, nuts and other spices, rice and other grain, shall be fined ten times its value.

The stealer of 100 palas of camphor, or precious metals, to be put to death. MENU says, he who steals camphor, and other aromatics, or gold, silver, and other precious metals, weighing more than one hundred *palas*, shall be put to death.

Also the stealer of more than 100 pieces of cloth. The same penalty is inflicted on one who steals more than one hundred pieces of cloth.

But if more than fifty *palas* of camphor, gold, and the like, and as many pieces of cloth, be stolen, the hands of the thief shall be cut off.

The hands of the stealer of more than 50 palas of camphor, &c., to be cut off.

If less than the abovementioned quantity and number be stolen, the thief shall be fined eleven times the value of the articles stolen.

The stealer of less than the abovementioned quantity and number shall be fined.

The owners of the stolen articles shall also be paid.

The owners shall also be indemnified.

SANKHA says, he who steals gold and silver shall be either punished in person or any one of his limbs shall be cut off.

The stealer of gold and silver shall be punished in person.

The meaning of the above is that if he, who steals a small quantity of gold and silver, be a respectable man, he shall be punished in person. But if he be of a mean caste, his ear shall be cut off.

Explanation.

VISHNU says, he who steals jewels of inferior quality shall be fined 1000 *panas*.

The fine for stealing jewels of inferior quality.

He who steals tools of husbandry, such as ploughs, spades, and the like, at the time of cultivation, shall be fined 108 *panas*, and shall pay the value of the stolen articles.

He who steals tools of husbandry at the time of cultivation shall be fined.

MENU says, he who steals a small quantity of prepared rice from a store-house or vegetables and fruits, shall be fined fifty *panas* if he be in any way related to the owner, otherwise he shall be fined 100 *panas*.

Menu on the punishment of a stealer of a small quantity of prepared rice.

The stealer of a small quantity of safflower, &c., shall be fined.

He who steals a small quantity of safflower, paddy, unprepared rice from a store-house, a plant or tree, or common articles of these descriptions, shall be fined one *masha* of gold.

The stealer of a small quantity of rice, milk, &c., how to be punished.

VYASA says that he, who steals a small quantity of rice, milk, or articles made of milk, shall pay their owner the value thereof and a fine of double their value.

The punishment prescribed by Menu for the stealer of a small quantity of certain articles.

MENU says, a fine of double the value of the following articles shall be imposed on him who steals a small quantity of them :—thread, cotton, refuse of wines, cow-dung, *goor*, curd, milk, and the like, water, straw, and so forth, bamboo, bamboo-baskets, salt, earthen utensils, earth, ashes, fish, birds, oil, *ghee*, flesh, honey, articles made of the skin, and other parts of beasts of all kinds, or other articles of this description, wines, boiled rice, and fruits of all kinds.

Explanation.

The abovementioned penalty is imposed, if a small quantity of any of those articles be stolen.

To be varied if the things have been kept for use.

He, who steals any of the aforesaid articles that have been kept by their owners for use, shall be fined one hundred *panas*.

The stealer of sacred fire shall be fined.

He who steals sacred fire from another's house shall be fined one hundred *panas*.

The punishment prescribed by Nareda for the theft of certain articles.

NAREDA says, he who steals any of the articles mentioned below which are of moderate price shall be fined five times their value.

Wooden vessels, straw, and the like, earthen-ware, bamboo, bamboo baskets, strings, bones, hides, vegetables, ginger, esculent plants, flowers, fruits, articles made of milk, and the like, *goor*, salt, oil, sweetmeats, boiled rice, wine, and other things for consumption.

This punishment is imposed, when a large quantity of the abovementioned articles is stolen. When this penalty is imposed.

MENU says, he who steals a water-pot or a rope from a well, or breaks a water distributing place, shall be fined one *masha* of gold, and shall make good the damage. The punishment for stealing a water-pot or a rope from a well, &c., or destroying a watering place.

VISHNU says that he, who steals any other articles of which no mention is here made, shall pay a fine equal to their value. How the stealer of unenumerated articles shall be punished.

NAREDA says, that the three kinds of penalties which the sages have fixed for robbery are also applicable in the case of theft. The three kinds of penalties for robbery applicable in a case of theft.

The fine of 250, 500, or 1000 *panas* shall be imposed on a man according as he steals articles of inferior, ordinary, or superior quality. Fine to be in proportion to the quality of articles.

This punishment is for the theft of articles which have not been mentioned. Explanation.

KATYAYANA says, the king shall cut off those limbs of the thieves with which they injure others, to prevent them from so doing again. How thieves are to be punished according to Katyayana.

A person taking articles without permission shall be deprived of his hands.

VRIHASPATI says, the hands of him who takes the articles of others without their permission, whether they be wood, straw, flower, or fruit, shall be cut off.

Explanation.

This punishment is for such as take the articles of their superiors.

Brahmins cannot be punished in person.

GAUTAMA says, Brahmins cannot be punished in person.

How a Brahmin thief is to be punished.

If Brahmins steal, they shall not be received into the company of pure Brahmins, and the theft shall be made known by making them ride on asses. They shall also be expelled the country and shall be branded like thieves.

How a Brahmin stealing from necessity is to be punished.

But if he have committed theft from necessity, a Brahmin shall atone for it, that is, he who, being unable to support himself, steals, shall have his hands cut off, but shall be required to return the articles to their owners to atone.

Murderer and other criminals not being Brahmins shall be executed.

APASTAMBHA says, he who commits murder, steals gold, or forcibly takes possession of others' land, shall be executed if he be not a Brahmin.

How a Brahmin murderer, &c., shall be punished.

If he be a Brahmin, his eyes shall be put out.

Explanation.

This provision is for mean Brahmins.

NAREDA says, a thief of the abovementioned description shall not be fined but punished in person, because his property is like filth owing to its being acquired by foul means. This thief is understood to be not a Brahmin.

Why a thief of the abovementioned description shall not be fined.

SANKHA says, if Brahmins, who perform *(yogas)* sacrifices, steal, their heads shall be shaved. But if Kshatryas and middle class Brahmins steal, they shall be made to ride on asses.

Sankha on the punishment of superior Brahmins who steal, &c.

VISHNU says, the king shall cause the stolen articles to be returned to their owners and punish the thieves according to law.

How the king shall dispose of the stolen articles and punish the thieves.

YAGNYAVALKYA says, the king shall cause thieves to give back the stolen articles to their owners and then torture them to death. But if the thieves be Brahmins, they shall be branded on the forehead and driven out of the country on camel or ass-back.

Yagnyavalkya on the above.

This penalty is for Brahmins.

Explanation.

KATYAYANA says, a Brahmin shall be arrested when the charge of theft is proved against him, whether he be found with the stolen goods or not, deprived of all his property, and branded.

Katyayana on the punishment of a Brahmin charged with theft.

KAUSHIKA says, that he shall be kept in irons till his death and shall receive a small allowance of rice ; and should he be able to do any work, he shall do such work for the king.

Kaushika on the point.

Explanation. The first-named penalty is for such Brahmins as have wealth but do not perform the duties of Brahmins. The last-named one is for such as are poor and do not perform the duties of Brahmins.

How a virtuous Brahmin stealing is to be punished. VRIHASPATI says, if a Brahmin, who performs his duties, steal, he shall be required to give back the stolen articles to their owner and atone for his crime; if he do not make atonement, he shall be imprisoned for life.

How a Sudra who steals, knowing the guilt of stealing, shall be punished. MENU says, a *Sudra* who steals, knowing the guilt of stealing, shall be punished eight times greater than the prescribed punishment.

How a Vaisya who steals, knowing the guilt of stealing, shall be punished. If a *Vaisya*, who knows the criminality of stealing, steal, he shall be punished sixteen times greater.

How a Kshatrya stealing under such circumstances shall be punished. A *Kshatrya* who steals under such circumstances shall be punished thirty-two times more.

How a common Brahmin shall be punished for a similar offence. A common Brahmin shall be punished sixty-four times more for a similar offence.

How a talented Brahmin shall be punished. A talented Brahmin shall be punished a hundred times more for a like offence.

How a very learned Brahmin is to be punished. A very learned Brahmin shall be punished one hundred and twenty-eight times more.

OF HARBOURING THIEVES.

MENU says, the Brahmin who takes any thing from thieves, even when it is for performing sacerdotal duties or those of an instructor, shall be guilty like a thief.

A Brahmin who takes aught from thieves is as guilty as a thief.

The king shall kill like thieves those who assist thieves with fire,* boiled rice, house-breaking instruments, and leather, or keep with them stolen goods.

Those who assist thieves with fire, &c., shall be killed like thieves.

YAGNYAVALKYA says, he who assists such as are known to be thieves or murderers with rice, shelter, fire, water, instruction, house-breaking instruments, or travelling expenses, shall be fined 1000 *panas*.

The punishment for harbouring thieves and murderers.

NAREDA says, they who assist thieves with rice or a place of shelter, or do not arrest them when they can do so, shall be punished like thieves.

Nareda on the point.

They who invite or order men to steal, give them shelter, or conceal their guilt, shall be punished like thieves.

Excitors and harbourers of thieves to be punished as thieves.

KATYAYANA says, they who purchase stolen goods, take them as gifts, or conceal them, knowing them to be such, shall be punished like thieves.

The same punishment for receiving stolen goods.

* Fire here means fire which assists the thief in his act.

W

Harbourers of great thieves to be executed.

VISHNU says, they who give shelter to enormous thieves shall be executed by the king.

But no punishment for assisting thieves for self-preservation.

But if such thieves, as cannot be checked by the king, be assisted for the sake of self-preservation, no penalty is to be imposed.

The punishment of those who, having the power, do not check village-affrays and other offences.

MENU says, that the king shall punish like thieves police officers or the inhabitants of the frontiers of a country having the charge of its police, when they neglect their duties. They who, having the power, do not check village-affrays or persons who destroy landmarks, and so forth, or corn, or take away from others stolen goods, shall be expelled the country with their property, whether they be in the service of Government or not.

SOME PARTICULARS REGARDING THEFT.

Certain travellers not to be punished for taking produce from fields.

IF a traveller, belonging to one of the twice-born classes, and having no passage money, take two sugar-canes, roots, or the like, from the field of another, he shall not be punished.

According to Menu persons taking fruits, &c., not to be called thieves.

MENU says, he who takes fruits or roots of trees, wood for making oblations to fire, and grass for cows, cannot be called a thief.

Explanation.

The fruits in the abovementioned sentence mean such as have not been taken by others; for the taking of rejected fruits does not, according to GAUTAMA, constitute theft.

The king shall appoint suitable persons to protect his subjects.

APASTAMBHA says that the king shall appoint noble, good, and trustworthy persons to defend his subjects both in town and country from wrong.

The subordinate officers should be equally qualified.

The subordinate officers should be equally qualified. These shall defend the residents of a town and places eight miles from it on each side, or be required to make good what shall be stolen. They shall also make good any thing stolen from a village and places within two miles from it.

Officers, who fail to apprehend thieves, to pay the value of the stolen goods.

KATYAYANA says, if the thief-catchers, officers of police, and defenders of the frontiers cannot apprehend thieves, the king shall make them pay what has been stolen.

The village headman to pay for what may be stolen within the village.

KATYAYANA says that he, who is in charge of a village, shall pay what may be stolen within the village.

The king shall make good any thing stolen in forests.

But if any thing be stolen in forests, the king shall make it good. If any thing be stolen in a place other than a forest, he who shelters thieves shall give it. The king shall make good any thing stolen in his kingdom. If after inquiry the king recover the stolen article, he shall take it.

Searching inquiries shall be made for stolen articles.

Searching inquiries shall be made for stolen articles. If they are not recovered, their price shall be paid by the king. If he neglect this he shall be guilty before God.

The whole stolen property to be recovered from him with whom a part is found.

VRIDDHA MENU says, a person shall get the whole stolen property from him with whom a part has been found, if, in the absence of all proof, he swear that all is with the thief.

Missing or stolen articles, recovered by officers, to be confiscated, if not claimed within a year.

YAGNYAVALKYA says, if collectors of customs and police officers, and so forth, recover any mislaid or stolen article, the owner shall have it if he demand it within a year. After that the king shall take it.

Such articles shall be carefully kept by the Government servants.

MENU says, such mislaid or stolen article shall be carefully kept by the Government servants. If it be stolen, the king shall cause such a thief to be killed by an elephant.

ROBBERY AND OTHER VIOLENCE.

NAREDA says, *(sahosa)* robbery means what is daringly done by those who are proud of their strength. For *sahosa* means force; theft is one of its elements. **Robbery defined.**

Robbery *(sahosa)* signifies oppression by means of strength; and theft, injury done to others under pretext. **Difference between robbery and theft.**

The oppression practised by force with the knowledge of the oppressed is called *(sahosa)* robbery, and that done without his knowledge theft.

Robbery *(sahosa)* is divided by NAREDA into three sorts, namely, robbery of the first class, meaning injury done to others by spoiling their fruits, water, ground, and so forth; robbery of the second class, or the spoiling of others' eatables, drink, domestic animals, and household articles; and robbery of the third class, or injury done to others by poison, weapons, rape, and murder. **Three kinds of robbery.**

MENU speaks of robbery of the first and second classes. **Menu on robbery of the first and second classes.**

He who spoils the implements of husbandry, fruits, flowers, and bridges, shall be fined one hundred *panas* and upwards.

A fine of 200 *panas* and upwards shall be imposed on him who injures animals, clothes, eatable and drinkable things, and household furniture.

Menu on robbery of the third class.

MENU speaks of robbery of the third class.

He who forcibly takes away women, men, cows, gold, gems, the treasures of gods and Brahmins, silken clothes and all sorts of good articles, shall at first be fined their price, then twice their price considering his character, and killed, on a repetition of the crime, to prevent him from committing it again.

Nareda on robbery of the first class.

NAREDA says, the fine for robbery of the first class shall be according to the nature of the crime, but it shall not be less than one hundred *panas*.

Penalties for robbery of the second and third classes.

According to the legislators, the penalty for robbery of the second class shall be 500 *panas*, and for that of the third class, execution, sale of the whole property, transportation, disgraceful branding, or the cutting off of the limbs with which injuries are committed.

The guilt of robbers of the first and second classes is atoned for by fines.

The guilt of those who commit robbery of the first and second classes, is atoned for by the fine imposed on them, and they may be admitted into society.

A robber of the third class is to be punished.

He who commits robbery of the third class shall be excommunicated even when he suffers an adequate penalty.

The punishment for injuring or taking common property.

In short, he who injures or takes common property shall be fined one hundred *panas* and upwards.

He who destroys landmarks, and the like, forcibly or stealthily, shall make compensation to the loser. If the criminal belong to a low caste, he shall be fined twice the value of the articles spoiled, and so forth.

A destroyer of landmarks, &c., to make compensation to the loser.

He whe commits robbery of the third class should not be admitted into society, even after he is adequately punished.

A robber of the third class is to be expelled from society.

MENU says, he who spoils the goods of others, knowingly or not, shall satisfy them and pay a fine equal in value to the articles injured.

He who spoils the goods of others shall be punished.

YAGNYAVALKYA says, the injury of others' property is an act of robbery for which a fine double the value of the injured article shall be inflicted.

He who injures others' property shall be fined.

He, who having injured or stolen articles, declares that he has not done so, shall be fined four times the value of the articles in question.

The punishment for not confessing to having injured or stolen articles.

If a man loosen the walls of the house of another, he shall be fined fifteen *panas*. He shall be fined twenty *panas* if he loosen the fastenings. But if he divide a house or break it, a fine of forty *panas* shall be imposed on him, and he shall be required to repair them; for according to MENU, he should satisfy the party endamaged.

For loosening the walls, &c., of the house of another.

He who injures hides or articles made thereof, wood, or earth, or fruits, roots, and flowers, shall be fined five times their value.

For injuring hides, &c.

Explanation. The penalty of not less than one hundred *panas*, prescribed by MENU, for destroying flowers, &c., regards such as are of superior quality.

The owner to be satisfied. The owner must in all cases be satisfied.

The punishment for injuring crystalline articles. KATYAYANA says, he who injures a portion, a moiety, or the whole of articles made of crystalline substances, shall be fined 250 *panas* and satisfy the owner of them.

For throwing thorns, &c., into another's house to annoy him. YAGNYAVALKYA says, if a man throw thorns and the like into another's house to annoy him, he shall be fined sixteen *panas*. But if he throw snakes, and the like, with the same motive, he shall be fined 500 *panas*.

For breaking the walls of others' houses, &c. VISHNU says, he who breaks the walls of others' houses, and so forth, shall be fined 500 *panas*, and be required to repair them.

For annoying others by throwing noxious articles into their houses. He, who annoys others by throwing any noxious articles into their houses, shall be fined one hundred *panas*.

Explanation. The annoyance referred to in the abovementioned sentences must be understood to be very great.

The punishment for abusing one's superiors, and certain other offences. YAGNYAVALKYA says, it is a settled point that he who abuses or insults his superiors or beats his brothers' wives, does not deliver over to proper parties the articles entrusted to him, breaks into houses locked up with padlocks, does not receive neighbours and kinsmen on occasions of marriage, and so forth, shall be fined fifty *panas*.

He, who has sexual intercourse with widows without getting permission to beget sons; does not reply to calls for help by a man in difficulty, as for instance when he is being robbed; abuses men without cause; being a *Chandala*, touches his superiors of other classes; entertains *Sudras* and *Sudra* ascetics on the occasion of any poojah or ceremony, takes improper oaths, such as imply incestuous connection with a mother, and so forth; engages in doing things above his power through vanity; deprives trees of the power of producing fruits and common animals of that of producing young ones; swindles public property; or causes the abortion of maid-servants, shall be fined one hundred *panas*. For certain offences.

The same fine shall be imposed on fathers and sons, friends and brothers, wives and husbands, instructors and pupils, if any of them leave the other, without some heinous cause of offence. For forsaking fathers, sons, &c.

MENU says, mothers, fathers, wives, and sons cannot be forsaken. The person who does so without heinous offence on their part shall be fined 600 *panas*. Menu on the point.

Forsake here means not to support them. Explanation.

SANKHA says, if a person willingly forsake any of them, he shall be fined two hundred *panas*. Sankha on the point.

The penalty on this head prescribed by YAGNYAVALKYA is for ignorant persons. Explanation.

The provision of MENU is applicable where an ignorant person forsakes another who is learned.

The penalty prescribed by SANKHA is applicable where ignorant persons willingly leave each other.

Two learned persons forsaking each other, to be punished.

If two learned persons forsake each other, they shall be punished according to the rule laid down by SANKHA.

The limb with which father, mother, or instructor is struck, to be cut off.

If a person beat his mother, father, or instructor, the king shall cause that limb with which he committed the injury to be cut off.

The punishment for defiling Brahmins.

VISHNU says, if Brahmins be defiled by means of things that should not be eaten, the person doing so shall be fined sixteen *mohars*.

For rendering a Brahmin impure by causing him to take onions, &c., or to drink.

If a person make a Brahmin impure by causing him to eat onions, and so forth, which destroy caste, he shall be fined one hundred *mohars*. But if he cause him to drink, he shall be killed.

For so acting towards a Kshatrya or Vaisya.

If a *Kshatrya* be made impure in the abovementioned manner, half of the aforesaid penalty is to be inflicted. If a *Vaisya* be thus injured, half of the last mentioned penalty is to be imposed.

Explanation.

This provision applies to the case of good Brahmins.

Yagnyavalkya on the above.

YAGNYAVALKYA says, if a Brahmin be made impure by things that should not be eaten, the person causing it shall be fined 1000 *panas*.

The punishment for defiling Kshatryas, Vaisyas, or Sudras.

He who acts thus towards *Kshatryas* shall be fined 500 *panas*; and a fine of 250 *panas* shall be imposed on him who makes *Vaisyas* impure in this way. If *Sudras* be made so, the guilty person shall be fined 125 *panas*.

This provision regards inferior Brahmins, &c. **Explanation.**

MENU says that he, who causes a Brahmin, *Kshatrya*, or *Vaisya* to eat or drink things that should not be eaten or drunk, shall be fined 1000, 500, or 250 *panas* respectively. **Menu on the point.**

He who acts in the abovementioned manner towards a *Sudra* shall be fined fifty-four *panas*. **The punishment for defiling a Sudra.**

This provision regards very common *Sudras*. Misconduct towards others should be visited with the punishment fixed by YAGNYAVALKYA. **Explanation.**

VISHNU says, if a Brahmin eat such things as destroy caste, such as onions, and so forth, he shall be banished. **A Brahmin eating things that destroy caste, to be banished.**

YAGNYAVALKYA says that a person, who charges the paramour of any of his female relatives with theft, shall be fined 500 *panas*. If he let him go on receiving a bribe, he shall be fined eight times the last mentioned fine. According to others the fine shall be eight times the bribe taken. **The punishment for charging the paramour of a female relative with theft, &c.**

He who sells blankets with which dead bodies had been covered, declaring them to be good, ill-treats superiors, and rides in the king's carriage, and so forth, without his permission, shall be fined 500 *panas*. **For selling blankets that covered dead bodies, ill-treating superiors, and riding in the king's carriage, &c.**

MENU says, in all cases of the performance of religious ceremonies for injuring innocent persons, the preparation of medicines by the ignorant, or the performance of a part of those ceremonies, a fine of 200 *panas* has been fixed. **For performing religious ceremonies to injure innocent persons, or preparing medicines without being qualified.**

For mixing good with bad articles, or injuring gems.

He who mixes good articles with bad ones, breaks hard things, such as gems, and the like, or pierces, at the wrong places, gems, and the like, which require to be perforated, shall be fined 250 *panas*.

For Sudras who support themselves by following the profession of Kshatryas.

If *Sudras* support themselves by following the profession of *Kshatryas*, and so forth, they shall be deprived of all their property and sentenced to be banished.

For Sudras who do so by pretending to be Brahmins.

YAGNYAVALKYA says, if *Sudras* support themselves by putting on the appearance of Brahmins, they shall be fined 800 *panas*.

For breaking bridges, &c.

MENU says, he who breaks bridges, flags, posts, or images of the gods, shall repair them and be fined 500 *panas*.

For cutting, stealing, or burning idols, or destroying temples.

KATYAYANA says, he who cuts, steals, or burns the images of the gods, or destroys temples, shall be fined 250 *panas*.

For selling uneatable articles, or breaking idols.

VISHNU says, he who sells articles that should not be eaten or sold, or breaks the images of the gods, shall be fined one hundred *panas*.

Explanation.

This difference in the penalty for the breaking of idols is with reference to their being good or bad, or the wealth of the offender.

Sankha on the punishment for injuring gardens and certain other offences.

SANKHA says, he who injures gardens, idols, wells, bridges, flags, landmarks, and so forth, or drinking-places of animals near wells, shall be compelled to restore them to their former state and fined 800 *panas*.

VISHNU says that they who break large bridges shall be killed.

They who break large bridges to be killed.

SANKHA says, he who defiles tanks, ponds, or other water places, puts thorns, and so forth, on thoroughfares, poisons liquids, and presents free women to slaves, shall be either put to death or deprived of his limbs.

The punishment for defiling tanks and certain other offences.

YAGNYAVALKYA says, the woman who administers poison, sets houses on fire, kills men, or breaks bridges, shall be thrown into water with a stone about her, if she be not pregnant.

For a woman for poisoning or committing certain other offences.

The woman who is particularly guilty, who kills her husband, parents, or child, shall be deprived of her ears, hands, nose, and lips, and caused to be destroyed by bulls.

For a woman guilty of killing husband, parent, or child.

The person who sets fields, houses, forests, villages or granaries on fire, or has criminal intercourse with the wife of the king, shall be burnt with fire made of reeds.

He who sets fire to houses, &c., or debauches the queen, shall be burnt.

MENU says, he who breaks the walls of towns, and so forth, blocks up the tanks surrounding them, or breaks the doors thereof, shall be put to immediate death.

He who breaks the walls of towns, &c., shall be killed.

They who steal from the king's treasuries, mutiny, or instigate the king's enemies, shall be tortured to death.

Persons robbing the king's treasuries, or guilty of mutiny or sedition, shall be killed.

YAGNYAVALKYA says, a Brahmin guilty of an offence deserving of capital punishment, shall be fined one hundred *mohars*.

A Brahmin, deserving of capital punishment, shall be fined.

How his punishment is to be commuted.

If he commit an offence deserving of the amputation of his limbs, he shall be fined fifty *mohars*.

If he commit an offence, the punishment of which is banishment, he shall be fined twenty-five *mohars*.

The punishment for extorting bribes from suitors.

They who extort bribes from suitors in courts of justice shall be banished and their whole property confiscated.

For Government officers injuring the causes of suitors.

If officers employed by Government injure the causes of suitors, they shall be deprived of their property, the source of their pride.

How the king shall treat honest and dishonest officers.

YAGNYAVALKYA says, the king shall reward his honest officers and kill the dishonest by trying their character through thieves.

The punishment for bribe-takers.

Persons who take bribes shall be deprived of their property and transported.

How learned men shall be induced to settle in the country.

Learned men shall be induced by gifts, regard, and veneration, to settle in the country.

The punishment for misconduct of Government officers.

He who, being a Government officer, arrests one who has been proved to be innocent, allows the guilty to escape, or arrests or releases those whose innocence or guilt has not been ascertained, shall be fined 1000 *panas*.

For persons playing the king, robbing or abusing him.

KATYAYANA says, they who play the king, steal Government revenue, or abuse him, shall be put to death.

They, who dress like the king, dance or sing, neglecting Government duty, exact fines greater than have been inflicted, or steal the king's property, shall be tortured to death. For other offences touching the king.

VISHNU says that they who, not being of the royal family, desire to assume ruling power, shall be executed. For pretenders to royalty.

YAGNYAVALKYA says, that they, who write more or less than what is ordered by the king, or release persons who commit adultery or steal, shall be fined 1000 *panas*. For neglect of duty of public officers.

SANKHA says, they who act without authority, giving out that they are thus acting under Government orders, disobey royal commands, or use false weights and measures, shall be executed or deprived of their limbs, according to the nature of their crime. For assumption of authority, disobedience, and using false weights and measures.

KATYAYANA speaks of insignificant crimes. Insignificant crimes.

He who uses fabricated documents or seals shall be fined 1000 *panas*. Using fabricated documents or seals.

MENU says, he who issues fabricated royal orders, falsely accuses officers, serves the enemies of the king, or kills boys, women, or Brahmins, shall be put to death. Menu on the punishment for certain offences.

VISHNU says, *prakriti* means king, master, friend, wealth, troops, kingdom, and fort. They who injure any of these shall be put to death. Persons injuring the king, &c., shall be put to death.

A person corrupting any of the elements of State to be put to death.

These seven being the elements of the State, he who corrupts any of these, shall be put to death.

The punishment for throwing offensive weapons or causing abortion.

YAGNYAVALKYA says, he who throws offensive weapons to injure others or causes abortion shall be fined 1000 *panas*.

For homicide.

He who is guilty of killing a man or a woman shall be fined 1000 or 250 *panas*.

Explanation.

The abortion above adverted to is of all women except those of the Brahmin class.

The punishment for abortion, terminating fatally or otherwise.

If the sufferer die of the pain, the guilty person shall be fined 1000 *panas*; otherwise a fine of 250 *panas* shall be imposed.

Ushana on the punishment of persons causing abortion.

USHANA says, he who causes the abortion of women by forcing them to labour, shall be fined 250 *panas*. But if it be caused by drugs, a fine of 500 *panas* shall be imposed; but if it be owing to beating, a fine of 1000 *panas*.

Vrihaspati on murder and murderers.

VRIHASPATI says, there are five kinds of violent acts, of which the principal is murder. Murderers shall not be punished by fine. They shall be executed.

Murderers and assassins shall be tortured to death by the king.

Katyayana on murderers.

KATYAYANA also says that murderers shall be punished with death.

The king, who has the interest of his subjects at heart, shall not release such as are the terror of all, even for the sake of gaining friends or riches. A good king should not release persons who are the terror of all.

The king, who, for the sake of riches or through fear, does not destroy wicked men, degrades his government and loses it. The king's duty to cut off the wicked.

He, who kills others by closely binding them, by fire, poison, or weapons, through anger, and so forth, is called *(sahosa)* robber. Robber defined.

BAUDHAYANA says, if *Kshatryas* and the like kill Brahmins, they shall be executed and their whole property shall be confiscated. The punishment of Kshatryas, &c., for the murder of Brahmins.

If they take away the lives of men equal or inferior to them, they shall be fined in proportion to their wealth, and physically punished according to their strength. For the murder of men equal or inferior to them.

If Brahmins murder *Kshatryas, Vaisyas,* or *Sudras,* they shall pay a fine of a thousand cows and a bull, a hundred cows and a bull, or ten cows and a bull respectively. For Brahmins murdering persons of other classes.

In the murder of *Sudras* is included that of women who are not menstruating, and the killing of cows, except those which have brought forth calves, and of bulls. Explanation.

Those who kill women and cows of the kinds mentioned shall perform the penance called *Chandrayana.* Penance to be performed by those who kill such women and cows.

The punishment for the murder of menstruating women.

The penalty for the murder of women who are menstruating is the same as that of *Kshatryas.*

For killing certain creatures that should not be killed.

The punishment inflicted on the murderer of *Sudras* is also inflicted on him who kills a goose, jackdaw, peacock, red goose, crane, crow, owl, frog, weasel, shrew, and other creatures that should not be killed.

When several persons beat a man, he who inflicts the fatal blow, to be deemed the murderer.

VRIHASPATI says, where several persons beat a man through anger, he, among them who inflicts the death-blow, shall be deemed the murderer and punished as such.

The guilt of those who assist the murderer.

Those who assist him shall be guilty in part.

Trials for murder how to be conducted.

The trial of a murderer shall be conducted by ascertaining the following points: the severity of the wound, the part where it has been inflicted and whether a wound in such a part can be fatal, the strength of the murdered person, single or repeated wounds.

Explanation.

The meaning is that the punishment of murder shall be imposed on him who has inflicted a fatal wound. He who first inflicts the wound or assists the murderer shall receive punishment half of that inflicted on the latter.

How a wound is known to be fatal.

The fatal nature of the wound shall be determined by its severity, by its infliction on a tender part of the body, the strength of the murdered person, or repeated cuts.

NAREDA says, that the abovementioned punishment is applicable in the case of all men except Brahmins without distinction of class. For Brahmins cannot be put to death, but their heads may be shaved, they may be banished, branded on the forehead, and caused to ride on asses.

All men except Brahmins may be capitally punished.

YAMA speaks of robbery and theft.

Yama on robbery and theft.

Brahmins shall never be punished in person. They shall be confined in secure places, where they shall be fed, or, being bound with ropes, shall be made to labor. They shall labor for a month or fifteen days. The king shall cause them to do things unworthy of their position according to their offence.

Brahmins shall never be punished in person.

YAGNYAVALKYA says, they who instigate others to commit violent deeds, shall receive punishment double that of the latter. But they who encourage men to act in the aforesaid manner, by entertaining them with hopes of defraying all the expenses of lawsuits, shall be punished four times more.

The punishment for instigating the commission of violent deeds.

KATYAYANA says, he who instigates or assists one who is ready to do a violent deed, gives him advice concerning it, shelters him, helps him with weapons, rice, or advice at the time of detection, orders him to administer poison, does not help one who is in terror of a robber or causes him to be helped, oppresses others in the guise of a Government servant, accuses the sufferer, or approves of the deed of the said wicked man, or does not,

Katyayana on the point.

when he is able, check him, and is guilty of any of these thirteen violent deeds, shall be fined in proportion to his wealth.

The repentant criminal liable to half the penalty but he who denies his guilt to severer punishment.

NAREDA says he, who, committing some violent deed, craves pardon from the king or acknowledges his guilt, shall be liable to half the penalty. If he do not confess his guilt or support himself by violent deeds, he shall be severely punished even for a very common offence. If he, being guilty, declare that he is not so and that he will, on conviction, receive punishment, he shall, if convicted, be liable not only to the punishment for his offence but also to that which he agreed to receive.

INQUIRY AFTER MURDERERS.

YAGNYAVALKYA says, that inquiries shall be made of the sons, friends, or prostitute of the murdered, or prostitutes as to whether he had any quarrel and so forth with any body; and of the residents of the place where the murder has taken place, as to whether he, influenced by avarice, accompanied any body. Inquiries after the murderer to be made in certain quarters.

VRIHASPATI says, where the corpse is found but the murderer cannot be discovered, the king shall trace him out from the enmity that the murdered person might have had with any one. How the murderer is to be discovered, when the corpse is found.

Government officers shall also make inquiries regarding him of the people of the place where the murder took place, and from the friends and kinsmen of the deceased, by friendly means, rewards, threats, and torture.

Wicked persons may be known from bad company, weapons, or stolen property. How wicked persons may be known.

The means of finding out thieves and murderers have been mentioned.

He who has been arrested on suspicion and does not confess his guilt shall be released on oath. Suspected persons, who do not confess, to be released on oath.

This provision is applicable in all cases.

The murderer and his accomplices to be tortured to death.

VYASA says, the murderer being convicted the king shall torture him and his accomplices to death.

The innocent to be released on oath, the guilty executed.

VRIHASPATI says, the innocent shall be released on oath; the guilty shall be executed.

The renown of the king will thereby increase.

The fame and virtue of the king increase by the abovementioned mode of release of the virtuous and punishment of the vicious.

ADULTERY.*

VYASA says, that there are three sorts of adulterous acts. He has also thus defined them. An adulterous act of the first class consists in speaking with the wife of another in a private place or forest, and at an unseasonable time, ogling at her, smiling at her, sending pimps to her, or touching her ornaments or clothes. Three sorts of adulterous acts.

NAREDA says, there are three kinds of adulterous acts; namely, sitting, speaking, and amusing one's self with others' wives in solitary places and at unseasonable hours. Nareda on the subject.

The meeting of a man and a woman at the junction of two rivers, at a ghaut, in a garden or forest, is also called a kind of adulterous act. The meeting of a man and woman at certain places, deemed an adulterous act.

An adulterous act signifies the means by which the object of the attachment of the said man and woman may be known. An adulterous act defined.

The means are such, as conversation, and the like, as do not indicate any thing but lust. The means of determining it.

It may therefore appear from their words and movements that they are influenced by lust.

---

* The word *sangrahan* has been rendered *adultery* by Sir William Jones and others; but, like the Arabic *zina*, it seems properly to denote illicit *commerce*. The word has accordingly been rendered variously here, according as the passages required.

When such meeting is not to be deemed an adulterous act.

Conversation and the like between a man and woman in solitary places through ignorance, simplicity, or pressure of business, without bad motives, cannot be called an adulterous act.

Who may converse with others' wives and where.

The following passage of MENU bears the same signification. Beggars, encomiasts, priests, or artisans, shall be allowed to converse with others' wives at the houses of the latter.

An adulterous act of the first class defined.

An adulterous act of the first class signifies the means whereby it may be known that the minds of both the man and the woman have been attached to each other.

An adulterous act of the second class defined.

VRIHASPATI says that, according to lawgivers, an adulterous act of the second class means the sending of fragrant articles, garlands, fruits, wine, victuals, or cloths, or conversation in solitary places, and the like.

Vyasa on the point.

VYASA defines it to be the sending of fragrant things, garlands, incense, ornaments, or cloths, or seduction by victuals and drinking materials.

Explanation.

Conversation in an adulterous act of the second class is understood to be closer than that in the first. Presents of the aforesaid articles is attended with expense, therefore an adulterous act of the second class appears to be viler than that of the third class.

An adulterous act of the third class defined.

VRIHASPATI says, that legislators define an adulterous act of the third class to be a man and woman sitting on the same bed, dallying with, and kissing or embracing each other.

VYASA defines it to be their sitting on the same bed in a place apart, and handling the hair of each other. Further explained.

It also means the exchange of benefits, sports, touching of clothes or ornaments, or sitting on the same bed.

The touching of the breasts of the wife of another by a man by mutual consent, and their silence when they unbecomingly touch each other's persons may also be called an adulterous act of the third class. What may also be called an adulterous act of the third class.

Instead of *exchange of benefits* the word *upachar*, which means the sending of betel, and the like, to each other, occurs in some books. Different version.

NAREDA says, if a man declare from pride, ignorance, or the hope of glory, that he has embraced a certain woman, that is also a sign of an adulterous act. Boast of having embraced a certain woman, also a sign of an adulterous act.

A man's holding the feet and clothes of prostitutes, and asking them to stop in streets, may be called an adulterous act. The holding of the feet and clothes of prostitutes, &c. may be called an adulterous act.

The word "prostitutes" is here mentioned by way of illustration. Explanation.

The abovementioned conduct of a man towards any other woman than his own wife is called an adulterous act. Adulterous acts are of nine sorts: first, exchange of benefits; second, sudden meeting in solitary places; third, taking hold of the neck, hair, and so forth; fourth, of the ear; fifth, of Such conduct towards any other woman than one's wife, is called an adulterous act. Nine sorts of adulterous acts.

the nose ; sixth, of the hands, and the like ; seventh, loitering in the same place ; eighth, sitting on the same bed ; and ninth, taking food from the same pot.

Vrihaspati on the punishment for adultery.

VRIHASPATI says, a fine of 250, 500, or 1000 *panas* shall be imposed on persons guilty of adultery of the first, second, and third classes respectively.

A rich man to receive a greater punishment.

If a man be rich, he shall receive a greater punishment than this.

The punishment for conversing with a woman in spite of prohibition.

MENU says, he who converses with a woman with whom he has been forbidden to do so, whether in a solitary or other place, shall be fined 250 *panas*.

A man conversing with a woman through necessity is not guilty.

The guilt of adulterous inclination, according to Menu.

If a man converse through necessity with a woman with whom he was not forbidden to speak, he shall not be guilty, for his motive is not wicked. If he converse with her in a solitary place he shall be guilty ; as MENU says, he who converses with the wife of another at a ghaut or in a forest, within a chamber, or at the junction of rivers, shall be *held* guilty of adulterous inclination.

The punishment for conversing with a woman in spite of prohibition.

MENU says, a man ought not to converse with a woman by whose husband and other *relatives*, he may have been forbidden to do so. If he do it he shall be fined a *mohar*.

Yagnyavalkya on the point.

YAGNYAVALKYA says, if a woman converse with a man after she has been forbidden to do so, she shall be fined one hundred *panas*. If a man do this after he has been forbidden, he shall be fined two hundred *panas*. If both the man and the woman do it after they have been forbidden, they shall be fined 250 *panas* each.

MENU says, he who converses with a woman kept by one master, or with his maid servant, or a female ascetic, in a solitary place, shall be punished with a small fine, that is, less than a *mohar*.

The punishment for conversing in private with certain women.

SANKHA says, the limbs of all men, except Brahmins, with which they may do any wrong shall be cut off, or the offenders shall be fined 8000 *panas*. Brahmins cannot be punished in person.

Excepting Brahmins, the limbs with which any wrong is done, shall be cut off.

MENU says, the king shall banish such *Kshatryas*, *Vaisyas*, and *Sudras* as are addicted to lewdness, by branding them with marks of disgrace and cutting off their ears and noses.

The punishment for libidinous persons of the lower classes.

If a member of an inferior class have connection with a female of a superior class, he shall, according to MENU, be executed.

For the man who has connection with a woman of a superior class.

The man who brings about this wicked connection, or gives place for it, shall receive a similar punishment.

The pander to such crime shall be similarly punished.

If a man converse with women, the caste of whose husbands cannot be ascertained, he shall not be punished in the abovementioned manner.

Conversing with the wives of common men, not so punishable.

MENU confirms this, by saying that the aforesaid rule is not applicable in case of conversation with the wives of public dancers or singers, or of those who are supported by their wives, for these allow

Adultery, but not conversation, with certain women, punishable, according to Menu.

their wives to prostitute themselves. But if adultery be committed they shall be punished, as will be seen from the chapter treating of adultery with corrupt women.

Adulterous acts when held to be crimes and when not.

NAREDA says, adulterous acts with married women in their houses are crimes. But if they be done in the houses of the men, and the women go there, such acts are not held to be crimes.

Conversing or committing adultery with a woman under certain circumstances not punishable.

VISHNU says, if a man converse or commit adultery with a woman who has been forsaken by her husband, or whose husband is a hermaphrodite or impotent, or who is willing, he shall not be liable to punishment even if the conversation or adultery take place in her own house.

PUNISHMENT OF ADULTERY, FORNICATION, AND RAPE.

MENU says, he who violates an unmarried woman shall, immediately on conviction, be put to death.

Rape of an unmarried woman a capital crime.

If a man have connection with a willing unmarried woman he shall not be put to death, if both of them belong to the same class.

But not commerce with a willing unmarried woman of equal class.

If a member of an inferior class have connection with an unmarried woman of a superior class, whether she be willing or not, he shall be put to death.

Rape or fornication committed by a man of an inferior class, a capital crime, if the woman be unmarried and of a superior class.

But a man, who has connection with an unmarried woman belonging to the same class with her, or at her father's desire, shall give him the regular marriage fees. On paying these the man and the woman may be married.

The punishment of rape or fornication, where the woman is unmarried and of equal class, avoided by marriage.

NAREDA says, on the same subject, if a man have connection with a woman of the same class to which he belongs, with her consent, he shall marry her after adorning her with ornaments and paying attention to her.

Nareda on the point.

Such a woman shall be married by a man on giving double marriage fees, ornaments, and peculiar property.

Double fees, ornaments, and presents required.

The fingers used in the defloration of an unmarried woman of equal class, to be lopped off, &c.

If a man deflour an unmarried woman of the same class by touching her private parts with his two fingers, these fingers shall be lopped off and he shall be fined 600 *panas*.

Only a fine to be imposed if the man acted with her consent.

But if this be done with her consent, the fingers shall not be cut off, but he shall be fined 200 *panas* to prevent him from repeating the crime.

Treatment of an unmarried woman having connection with a man of a superior or inferior class.

NAREDA says, if an unmarried woman commit fornication with a man of a superior class, she shall not be punished. But if she do so with one of an inferior class, she shall be bound and kept at home.

Punishment of an unmarried woman guilty of the defloration of another.

If an unmarried woman deflour another by touching her private parts with two fingers, she shall be fined 200 *panas*, shall pay double marriage fees, and receive ten stripes.

And of a married woman guilty of the same crime.

If a married woman act in the abovementioned manner, her head shall be shaved and her two fingers shall be cut off, and she shall be paraded mounted on an ass.

Her punishment for repeatedly doing so.

Her fingers shall be cut off and she shall be mounted on ass-back, if she repeatedly do this.

The punishment for defiling a woman adorned for marriage or otherwise.

YAGNYAVALKYA says, if a man defile a woman adorned with ornaments for her marriage, he shall be fined 1000 *panas*; if she be not adorned with ornaments for marriage, he shall be fined 250 *panas*.

This penalty is for persons of the same class. But if a member of an inferior class so misbehave towards a woman of a superior class, he shall be executed.

If the woman be of a superior, the crime is punishable with death.

If a man thus misbehave as regards a willing woman of an inferior class, he shall not be punished.

But no punishment is incurred, if the woman be willing and of inferior class.

If a man thus act towards a woman of a superior class, his hand shall be cut off and he shall be put to death.

The punishment applies, if the woman be of a superior class.

The woman, who, being proud of the beauty and so forth of her brothers and other relations, dishonors the bed of her husband, shall be caused by the king to be killed by dogs, and her paramour shall be burnt to death in a bed of red-hot iron on which the public executioners shall throw wood.

The punishment due to brother and married sister guilty of incest.

MENU says, if a Brahmin violate a *Kshatrya*, *Vaisya*, or *Sudra* woman who has no guardian, he shall be fined 500 *panas*.

The punishment of a Brahmin for rape on an unprotected woman of an inferior class.

If he thus misbehave as regards the wife of a person of a mean class, such as a washerman, a shoe-maker, and the like, he shall be fined 1000 *panas*.

For rape on a woman of a mean class.

If a man, who was once convicted of having connection with a woman, be charged with a similar misconduct with the same woman after a year, he shall be liable to double the punishment that was at first inflicted on him.

For repetition of fornication after a year.

For commerce with a Chandala or other mean woman.

If he have connection with a woman of the *Chandala* or *Bratta caste,* he shall be fined 1000 *panas.*

Bratta defined.

Bratta means a woman descended from a *Bratta,* or one who does not practise virtue, but acts disreputably, for, according to HARITA, he, whose virtue is declining and whose conduct and acts are becoming bad, is called *Bratta.*

The same defined by Halayudha.

HALAYUDHA defines *Bratta* to be such a woman as, being of an age beyond the time of marriage, has not been married.

The punishment for repetition of fornication with a Chandala woman, &c.

If fornication be committed with a *Chandala* woman or *Bratta* for the second time, the adulterer shall be fined double.

Or a woman of the same class.

Therefore, if fornication be repeatedly committed with a woman of the same class, the offender shall also be doubly punished.

For twice-born men who have connection with mean women.

YAGNYAVALKYA says, if a twice-born man have connection with a mean woman, he shall be banished after his body has been branded with the figure of a headless man.

For a Sudra so acting with a mean woman.

If a *Sudra* thus act towards a mean woman, his body shall only be branded in the abovementioned manner.

For a Chandal having connection with a woman of the twice-born classes.

If a *Chandala* have connection with a woman of the twice-born classes, he shall be put to death.

From the provision that a *Sudra's body* shall only be branded with the figure of a headless man, it is to be understood that he shall not be banished. Explanation.

Therefore, there is no inconsistency in the provision of death in case of a *Chandala* having connection with a woman of the twice-born class.

If a *Sudra* have connection with a woman of one of the twice-born classes, whether she have a guardian or not, one of his limbs shall be cut off, and he shall be deprived of a portion of his property if she have no guardian. But if she have one, he shall be deprived of all his property. How a Sudra having connection with a twice-born woman shall be punished.

By one of the limbs is meant the male organ, for GAUTAMA says, if a *Sudra* have connection with a woman of one of the twice-born classes, he shall be deprived of his male organ and all his property. But if she have a guardian, he shall also be put to death. Gautama on the point.

If a *Vaisya* have connection with a Brahmin woman who has a guardian, he shall be imprisoned for one year and fined 1000 *panas*. How a Vaisya having connection with a Brahmin woman, who has a guardian, shall be punished.

But if a *Kshatrya* act in the abovementioned manner, his head shall be shaved with the urine of asses and he shall receive the aforesaid penalty. How a Kshatrya so acting shall be punished.

If a *Vaisya* or *Kshatrya* have connection with a Brahmin woman who has no guardian, the former shall be fined 500 and the latter 1000 *panas*. How a Vaisya or Kshatrya having connection with a helpless Brahmin woman, shall be punished.

Explanation.

The smaller penalty on the *Vaisya* is in the case of connection with a Brahmin woman equal to a *Sudra*. But in the case of connection with a good Brahmin woman, he shall be punished like the *Kshatrya*.

How a Kshatrya or Vaisya having connection with a Brahmin woman, who has a guardian, shall be punished.

If a *Kshatrya* or *Vaisya* have connection with a Brahmin woman who has a guardian, he shall be punished like a *Sudra* guilty of the same offence, or shall be burnt to death by his body being covered with straw, and so forth.

Explanation.

By the *Brahmin woman* in the preceding sentence is meant a talented one.

Therefore, there is no inconsistency in the provision of a fine of 1000 *panas*, and so forth, made above.

Punished like a Sudra means deprived of his entire property and male organ, and put to death.

Burnt to death, &c. VASISHTHA says a *Vaisya* shall be covered with red *kusha*, and a *Kshatrya* with reeds, and burnt.

The punishment of a Brahmin for violating or having connection with a Brahmin woman who has a guardian.

If a Brahmin violate a Brahmin woman who has a guardian, he shall be fined 1000 *panas*. If he have connection with her with her consent, he shall be fined 500 *panas*.

Capital punishment how and when commutable.

Where the punishment of death is necessary, there the Brahmin's head shall be shaved.

Men of other classes shall be put to death.

If a Brahmin be guilty of crimes of every description, he shall be expelled the country, but allowed to take his property, without being wounded. How a Brahmin guilty of all kinds of crimes shall be punished.

He shall be thus expelled, if he have been repeatedly guilty. The punishment is for being repeatedly guilty.

There is not a greater vice than the murder of a Brahmin. Therefore the king shall not even think of the execution of one. Execution of a Brahmin prohibited.

If a *Vaisya* have connection with a *Kshatrya* woman who has a guardian, or a *Kshatrya* with a *Vaisya* woman, each of them shall be punished in the same manner as if they had so acted with a Brahmin woman who has no guardian, or in other words the *Kshatrya* shall be fined 1000 *panas*, and the *Vaisya* 500 *panas*. How a Vaisya committing adultery with a Kshatrya woman, who has a guardian, shall be punished.

This small punishment for the *Vaisya* is in the case of a talented man and an untalented woman. In other cases both of them shall be punished 1000 *panas*. Explanation.

If a Brahmin have connection with a *Kshatrya* or *Vaisya* woman, who has a guardian, he shall be fined 1000 *panas*. A Brahmin, having connection with a Kshatrya or Vaisya woman who has no guardian, shall be fined.

If a *Kshatrya* or *Vaisya* have connection with a *Sudra* woman who has a guardian, each of them shall be fined 1000 *panas*. A Kshatrya or Vaisya, having connection with a Sudra woman, shall be fined.

The punishment for a Kshatrya having connection with a Kshatrya woman.

If a *Kshatrya* have connection with a *Kshatrya* woman, his head shall be shaved with the urine of asses.

A Brahmin, having connection with a helpless woman of any inferior class, shall be fined.

If a Brahmin have connection with a *Kshatrya*, *Vaisya*, or *Sudra* woman, who has no guardian, he shall be fined 500 *panas*.

And two-fold if he do so with a Chandala or other mean woman.

But if he do the same with a woman of the *Chandala* or other inferior caste, he shall be fined 1000 *panas*.

The punishment for forsaking mother, father, wife, or son, without cause.

Mother, father, wife, and son cannot be forsaken. Should a man forsake any of them without any offence which deserves forsaking, he shall be fined 600 *panas* by the king.

For a sacrificer forsaking a priest, and *vice versâ*.

If a sacrificer forsake such a priest as is competent and innocent, or if the priest forsake an innocent sacrificer, each of them shall be fined one hundred *panas*.

For a person taking a woman or man to a certain place for adultery, or giving such place.

It is said in the *Matsya Purana* that the person, who takes a woman or man to a certain place for adultery, or gives a place for it, shall be liable to a fine equal to that imposed on an adulterer.

For a person violating an unwilling woman.

VRIHASPATI says, he who violates an unwilling woman shall be deprived of his entire property by the king, who shall also cause his male organ to be cut off and cause him to be taken around on ass-back.

He who violates an unwilling woman by cunning shall be deprived by the king of his entire property, and expelled the country after his forehead has been branded with the figure of the female organ.

The punishment for violating an unwilling woman by cunning.

He, who has connection with a woman of the class to which he belongs, shall be fined 1000 *panas*.

For having connection with a woman of equal class.

The meaning is that he shall be fined if he do so by sending pimps, and so forth.

Explanation.

But if he thus misbehave as regards a *Sudra* woman he shall be fined 500 *panas*, and if he do so with regard to a woman of superior class he shall be put to death.

Or with a Sudra woman, or woman of a superior class.

If a person commit *(gurutalpaka)* adultery with the wife of his spiritual guide, and so forth, the figure of the female organ shall be branded on his body. If he be in the habit of drinking wine, the figure of a bottle shall be branded on him.

The punishment for a person committing adultery with the wife of his instructor, &c.

If he steal gold, the figure of the foot of a dog shall be branded on him.

For the stealer of gold.

If he murder a Brahmin, the figure of a headless Brahmin shall be branded on him.

For the murderer of a Brahmin.

YAGNYAVALKYA says, a fine of 1000 *panas* shall be imposed on one who has connection with a woman of the class to which he belongs.

For one who has connection with a woman of equal class.

And with a woman of inferior or superior class.

If he have connection with a woman of inferior class he shall be fined 500 *panas,* if with one of a superior class he shall be put to death.

How an adulteress shall be punished.

If a woman commit adultery, her ears and the like shall be cut off.

Explanation.

By the expression *and the like* is meant the hair, and so forth.

Vrihaspati on the punishment of an adulteress.

Therefore, where an adulterer shall be put to death, an adulteress, according to VRIHASPATI, shall be deprived of her ears, and the like.

Capital punishment for adultery with certain women and an unnatural crime with a cow.

VRIHASPATI says, if a man commit adultery with a woman who is impure and mean or who belongs to a superior class, or an unnatural crime with a cow, he shall be put to death.

Gurutalpaka defined by Nareda, and its punishment declared.

NAREDA says, by *gurutalpaka* is meant one who commits adultery with any of these twenty descriptions of women, namely, stepmother, mother's sister, mother-in-law, maternal uncle's wife, paternal aunt, paternal uncle's wife, friend's wife, pupil's wife, sister, sister's female friend, daughter-in-law, daughter, spiritual guide's wife, a woman of the same lineage, a dependant woman, the queen, a female ascetic, nurse, well-behaved Brahmini, or a woman of a superior class. For such a crime there is no other penalty than the excision of the male organ.

Explanation.

This penalty is for adultery in a private manner with such as have guardians.

Gurutalpaka defined by Yagnyavalka.

YAGNYAVALKYA defines *gurutalpaka* to be a man who commits adultery with his daughter-in-law, spiritual guide's wife, paternal aunt, mother's sister, maternal uncle's wife, or daughter.

The punishment of gurutalpaka.

The penalty for the abovementioned crime is death by the excision of the male organ.

For women, who willingly commit incest with persons of the same class.

If any of the abovementioned women, actuated by lust, willingly have incestuous connection with a person of the same class, she shall be punished like the man.

A Brahmin having connection with an unmarried Sudra woman, to be banished.

APASTAMBA says, if a Brahmin have sexual intercourse with an unmarried *Sudra* woman, he shall be banished.

How a Sudra, thus acting with a woman of any of the three superior classes, is to be punished.

GAUTAMA says, if a *Sudra* act in the abovementioned manner with a woman of any of the three superior classes, his male organ shall be cut off and his entire property confiscated.

The paramour to be put to death, &c., if the woman have a guardian.

But if the said woman have a guardian, the man shall be put to death and subjected to the other penalties.

The wives of such a Sudra to be doomed to slavery.

APASTAMBA says, the wives of a *Sudra* of the abovementioned description shall be doomed to slavery.

How such Sudra is to be put to death.

BAUDHAYANA speaks of the manner in which such a *Sudra* is to be put to death. He shall be covered with straw and burnt to death.

How a Sudra, who has connection with a Brahmin woman.

YAMA says, the king shall cause a *Sudra*, who has had connection with a Brahmin woman, to be dragged over red-hot iron and burnt to death with straw, wood, and so forth.

How a person who has connection with a woman of a superior class.

HARITA says that he, who has connection with a woman of a superior class, shall be bound by the king and put to death by being given as a prey to dogs. He shall then be burnt with wood.

How a woman who has connection with a man of an inferior class.

GAUTAMA says that a woman, having connection with a man of any inferior class, shall be put to death by being exposed as a prey to dogs.

How men of inferior castes who have connection with Brahmin women.

VASISHTHA says, if a *Sudra* have connection with a Brahmin woman, he shall be covered with straw and thrown into a fire. If a *Vaisya* do so with a Brahmin woman, he shall be covered with red *kusha* and thrown into a fire. If a *Kshatrya* act in that manner, he shall be covered with the leaves of reeds and thrown into a fire.

How such women shall be punished.

Such Brahmin woman, being mounted on horseback, shall be taken through the thoroughfares, her head shaven, her body anointed with ghee, her person exposed. She shall be released after suffering such punishment.

If a man of an inferior have connection with a woman of a superior class, both how to be punished.

If a *Vaisya* has connection with a *Kshatrya* woman, or a *Sudra* with a *Kshatrya* or *Vaisya* woman, both the man and the woman shall be punished in the abovementioned manner.

YAMA says, the Brahmin woman, who, being influenced by lust, has connection with a *Sudra*, shall be put to death by the king, by being exposed as a prey to dogs by means of the public executioners.

A Brahmin woman, who has connection with a Sudra, shall be put to death.

If she have connection with a *Vaisya* or *Kshatrya*, her head shall be shaved and he shall be caused to mount on ass-back.

If she have connection with a Vaisya or Kshatrya, how she and the man are to be punished.

VRIHASPATI says, the woman, who, coming to a man's house, entices him to embrace her, by touching his person, and so forth, shall receive the full punishment, and the man shall receive half the punishment.

If a woman entice a man, how both shall be punished.

After the nose, ears, and lips of the said woman have been cut off, and she has been taken through the thoroughfares, she shall be drowned, or exposed as a prey to dogs in the presence of several persons.

Such a woman shall be drowned or exposed as a prey to dogs.

VISHNU says, the woman, who does not love her impotent husband and commits adultery, shall be put to death.

A woman, whose husband is impotent, shall be put to death if she commit adultery.

KATYAYANA says, on the subject of fine, that dependant women shall not be liable to fines: such *as may be imposed on them* shall be levied from their guardians.

The guardians of dependant women shall be fined.

KATYAYANA says, if a woman, whose husband is in a distant country, be detected on her way to commit adultery, she shall be confined till his return.

How a woman, whose husband is absent, detected on her way to commit adultery, shall be punished.

It is said in the *Matsya Purana* that, if a man violate a woman, he shall be put to death but she shall not be blamed.

A man violating a woman, shall alone be punished.

INTERCOURSE WITH PROSTITUTES AND UNNATURAL CRIMES.

The punishment for intercourse with a prostitute kept by another.

VYASA says that he, who has intercourse with a prostitute kept by another, shall be fined fifty *panas*.

For forcible connection with her.

If he have connection with her forcibly, he shall be fined one hundred *panas*.

And for forcible connection with a maid servant.

YAGNYAVALKYA says, if a man have connection with a maid servant forcibly, he shall be fined ten *panas*.

For several persons who successively violate an unwilling woman.

If several persons successively violate an unwilling woman, each of them shall be fined twenty-four *panas*.

For unnaturally using a woman, or abusing, or having connection with, a female ascetic.

If a man use a woman in an unnatural manner, or if he so abuse, or have connection with, a female ascetic, he shall be fined forty *panas*.

For committing an unnatural crime with a cow or other animal.

NAREDA says, if a man commit an unnatural crime with an animal, he shall be fined one hundred *panas*; if with a cow, he shall be fined 500 *panas*.

For a man having connection with a very mean woman.

If a man have connection with a very mean woman, he shall be fined 500 *panas*.

For a Brahmin committing an unnatural crime with a cow,

If a Brahmin commit an unnatural crime with a cow, he shall be fined one *mohar*.

The fine of 500 *panas*, prescribed for committing an unnatural crime with a cow, is for *Vaisyas* and *Kshatryas*, for it has been declared above that a *Sudra* shall be put to death for such a crime; it is here said that a Brahmin shall pay a fine of one *mohar*. **Explanation.**

The fine of 500 *panas* is therefore intended for *Vaisyas* and *Kshatryas*.

If a Brahmin visit prostitutes, he shall be fined fifty *panas*. **The punishment for a Brahmin who visits prostitutes.**

The vile man, who has connection with a woman who has prostituted herself to many, shall be punished like one who has had intercourse with prostitutes, and not like him that has committed the crime with a respectable woman. **For a man who has connection with a woman who has prostituted herself to many.**

NAREDA says, if a man have connection with a woman with whom intercourse is forbidden by the Shasters, he shall be punished as a check on him. Penance is provided for his freedom from vice. **The reason for punishing a man who has improper connection with a woman.**

There is a text to the effect that the criminal, punished by the king, goes to heaven like virtuous men. **Punishment ensures salvation.**

Punished by the king means that the king caused the criminal to atone for his crime. **Explanation.**

This meaning is confirmed by the Section where the text occurs.

It is contained in the *Kalpataru*, Section "Mushalaghata," in the Chapter on the "theft of gold."

OF WOMEN AND OTHER MATTERS.

Women should always be kept in subjection.

YAGNYAVALKYA says, "women's fathers protect them in their childhood; their husbands protect them in youth; their sons protect them in age." In default of sons, their relatives should protect them; for they are "never fit for independence."

Duties of the father, husband, and sons of a woman.

VRIHASPATI says, if the father of a woman do not give her in marriage in proper time, if her husband do not have sexual intercourse with her after her menses, and if her sons do not support her, such a father and husband and such sons shall be disgraced and legally punished.

Women do not care for the beauty of men, &c.

Women do not care for the beauty of men and do not regard their age. Whether the latter be handsome or ugly, the former enter into sexual intercourse with them.

Characteristics of women.

In childhood they are bashful, in youth their bashfulness decreases, and in old age they consider their husbands no better than a straw.

How wives become disobedient.

As disease becomes incurable if it be neglected, so wives, if they be not checked, become disobedient.

According to Menu, what things appertain to women.

MENU has declared the undermentioned things to appertain to women: bed, ornaments, seats, love, anger, cunning, wicked deeds, and bad behaviour.

Such being the nature of women, men are to be particularly careful of them. Men to be particularly careful of them.

THE KING'S DUTIES.

Menu says, the king shall punish a person who does not perform his or her duties, whether that person be his father, spiritual guide, friend, mother, son, or priest. The king is impartially to punish all who neglect their duties.

Where a common person is liable to a fine of one *tola* of copper, there the king shall pay a thousand, which shall be thrown into water. For Gautama says, that Varuna is the god of punishment. The fine payable by the king.

DISHONESTY OF DEBTORS.

Menu says, if a debtor, who disowns his liability, be caused to acknowledge it by any means, he shall be fined five *per cent.* Punishment of the debtor who does not readily own his liability.

If, after every attempt, he do not acknowledge his liability and it be proved by evidence, he shall be fined ten *per cent.* If convicted on evidence.

FALSE EVIDENCE.

Menu speaks of witnesses.

According to legislators, false witnesses shall receive punishment, as follows, for the preservation of virtue and suppression of vice. False witnesses shall be punished.

If persons give false evidence through some inducement, they shall be fined 1000 *panas.* If they do so through ignorance, they shall be fined 250 *panas.* If they do it through fear, they shall The punishment for giving false evidence from various causes.

be fined 500 *panas*. If they act in the abovementioned manner for the sake of friendship, they shall be fined 1000 *panas*. If they are actuated by lust, they shall be fined 2500 *panas*. If they give false evidence through anger, they shall be fined 2000 *panas*. If they unconsciously perjure themselves, they shall be fined two hundred *panas*. If they ignorantly do so, they shall be fined one hundred *panas*.

Such punishment is for persons other than Brahmins.

If *Kshatryas*, *Vaisyas*, and *Sudras* thus give false evidence, the virtuous king shall punish them in the abovementioned manner and banish them.

A Brahmin who perjures himself shall be banished.

If a Brahmin give false evidence, he shall merely be banished.

Three kinds of fines. The equivalent of pana.

MENU says, 250 *panas* are called *(prathama sahosa)* primary fine ; 500 *panas*, *(madhyama sahosa)* medium fine ; and 1000 *panas*, *(uttama sahosa)* appropriate fine. A *tola* of copper is called a *pana*.

GIFT OR SALE WITHOUT OWNERSHIP.

The fine for a relative of the owner of an article, giving it away.

If a relative of the owner of an article give it away to some other person, he shall be fined 600 *panas*.

Any other to be punished like a thief.

If any other person act in the abovementioned manner, he shall be punished like a thief.

He who unwittingly sells an article of which he is not the owner, shall be punished.

According to this rule, he who unwittingly *(asyami vikraya)* sells an article of which he is not the proprietor, shall be punished. If he do it with a guilty knowledge, he shall be punished like a thief.

From this it is evident that if, in a family, a person sell an article belonging to his brothers, he shall be punished like a thief.

He who sells what is his brothers' shall be punished like a thief.

GIFTS FOR RELIGIOUS PURPOSES.

If a person take a gift for religious purposes, and do not so apply it, it should be taken back.

When a gift should be resumed.

If he through pride or avarice persist in declaring that he did apply it to religious purposes, the king shall fine him one *mohar*.

How a person, who falsely declares that he applied a gift to religious purposes, shall be punished.

The meaning is that, if the person have not applied the gift to religious purposes, the king shall cause him to return it. If the man promised to make the gift after performance of the ceremonies, he shall fulfil his promise. If the former take it, stating that he has performed them, he shall be fined one *mohar*.

Explanation.

THE LAW OF INHERITANCE.

OF PARTITION.

The period and rule of partition of heritage.

The proper period of partition of heritage is declared by Menu :—"After the death of the father and the mother, the brothers, being assembled, may equally divide among themselves the paternal estate; but they have no power over it while their parents are living."

Explanation.

Equally means in equal proportions; no deduction of a twentieth part being allowed for the eldest son, and so forth.

A deduction of a twentieth part of the heritage for the eldest son, &c.

While treating of heritage among sons, after their father's demise, Menu has allowed a deduction of a twentieth part (for the eldest), and so forth.

Implies inequality.

Then how can there be equal partition of heritage among the sons?

For what eldest son the additional share is allowable.

Let not such an objection be raised. For the deduction of a twentieth part, and so forth, is allowed in the case of such eldest son as is possessed of good qualities, or desires to receive the additional share.

Property, to which the father has the sole right, to be divided only at his pleasure.

Property over which the father has an independent right shall be divided at his pleasure only, while he is living. Therefore, his demise is essential to the partition of the abovementioned property. But what is the necessity for the demise of the mother? She has no right whatever over it.

When treating of the partition of heritage, SANKHA says that sons are not independent during the lifetime of their father. In like manner they are not so, as long as their mother lives. From this it may be assumed that she has a control over the estate.

Sons are not independent as long as their father and mother live.

No, for the preceding text is merely indicative of the praise of such a mother as possesses good qualities.

The text does not denote a mother's right.

How can dependence, with regard to the partition of an estate, upon a person who has no right over it, be consistent with reason?

Dependence as to partition of an estate upon a person who has no right over it, is inconsistent.

This is no argument at all. For the term paternal, being a conjunctive compound, means something belonging to both father and mother. It therefore also relates to maternal property. Hence the demise of the mother is necessary to the partition of her estate. With this view, MENU has made the foregoing provision.

Paternal means something belonging to both father and mother: the demise of the mother is necessary for the partition of her estate.

But it may again be urged that maternal property goes to daughters after the death of the mother, and, on failure of daughters, to their sons. Sons have no right to take it.

According to Nareda, sons have no right to maternal property.

According to NAREDA:—"Let sons divide the wealth when their father dies. Let daughters divide their mother's wealth, and, on failure of daughters, their male issue."

But, according to Menu, all the uterine brothers and sisters divide the maternal estate.

This text in no way debars any one from inheriting the maternal estate. MENU has spoken of joint succession in the following passage :—"On the death of the mother, let all the uterine brothers and the uterine sisters equally divide the maternal estate."

Explanation.

Therefore, brothers and sisters shall jointly divide the maternal estate.

Property independently held by the father shall not be divided in his lifetime.

From what has been said above, it is evident that the property which is independently held by the father, shall be divided after his demise, but in his lifetime it must remain intact.

Sankha on the point.

SANKHA confirms this by saying that "partition does not take place, if the father do not desire it, when he is old, or in his dotage, or is afflicted with disease."

Dotage defined.

Dotage means weakness of the mental powers.

When partition by a father is admissible.

If the father be alive and be without the above-mentioned complaints, and also willing, the partition is admissible. This will hereafter be explained.

Of united sons, the eldest may be the manager.

Or, after the demise of their father, the sons may live together, making the eldest the chief manager.

Menu on the point.

MENU confirms this by saying that "the eldest brother may take entire possession of the patrimony ; and the others may live subject to him, as to their father ;" or make him chief who is capable of business.

NAREDA speaks on the same subject :—"Let the eldest brother, like a father, support all the others, who are willing *to live together without partition;* or even the youngest brother, *if all assent,* and if he be capable of business : capacity for business is the best rule in a family." Nareda on the same.

Or let them divide the estate for the sake of performing religious duties. The estate may be divided for religious purposes.

MENU confirms this by saying—"Either let them thus live together, or, if they desire *separately to perform* religious rites, let them live apart : since religious duties are multiplied in separate houses, their separation is therefore legal." Menu on the point.

How are religious duties multiplied by partition of property ? VRIHASPATI speaks on this subject : "A single performance of the ceremonies of forefathers and of the worship of the deities and Brahmins may answer for brothers, who reside together and eat food dressed in the same place. In a family, the members of which live apart, these duties are separately performed in the house of each of them." Vrihaspati on religious duties.

Divided estates being the exclusive property of every heir, each may perform the ceremonies, sacrifices, &c., according to his own choice, without reference to the others. Hence partition multiplies religious performances. How partition multiplies religious performances.

OF PARTITION DURING THE LIFETIME OF THE FATHER.

When division may take place.

NAREDA speaks of the time of division among sons :—" When the mother is too aged to bear more sons, and all the sisters have been given away *in marriage*, and the father either refrains from pleasures, or withdraws from worldly concerns."

Yagnyavalkya on the division of self-acquired property.

YAGNYAVALKYA says :—" When the father makes a partition, let him separate his sons at his pleasure, and either *dismiss* the eldest with the largest share, or *if he choose* all may be equal sharers."

Explanation.

Pleasure applies in the case of self-acquired property.

Vishnu on the point.

VISHNU says, " when a father separates his sons from himself, his self-acquired property shall be divided at his choice."

Explanation.

Self-acquired property means such as has been gained by self-exertion.

Ancestral property recovered by the father when to be considered as self-acquired and when as common.

Likewise, any ancestral property recovered by the father shall, according to MENU, be considered as his self-acquired property. Because it is understood to be recovered without the aid of the ancestral property. But if it be recovered with the aid of the patrimony, it must be considered as common property.

Such property as is acquired or recovered by the father without the aid of the ancestral estate, shall be divided equally or unequally, or not divided at all, at his pleasure.

Property acquired or recovered by the father without the aid of the ancestral estate may be divided at his pleasure.

The partition of such property depends entirely on his own will, for the sons have no ownership therein.

Partition of such property depends entirely on his own will.

Menu says that, if a father, "by his own efforts, recover a *debt or property unjustly detained*, which could not be recovered before *by his father*, he shall not, unless by his free will, put it into parcenary with his sons, since in fact it was acquired by himself."

A debt or property recovered by the father, shall be divided according to his free will.

The meaning of the above is that if any property be taken away or seized by a stranger and recovered by the father, such property, even if it be ancestral, and also that which has been acquired by his own exertions, may be divided among his sons, if he choose, but not against his will.

Explanation.

The father has full dominion over the property of his father, which, being seized, is recovered by him by his own exertions, or over that which is gained by him through skill, valour, or the like. He may give it away at his pleasure, or he may distribute it. On failure of the father, the sons are entitled to an equal share of it.

Over what property the father has full dominion.

Seized means taken away by a stranger and not recovered by the grandfather through inability, but

Explanation.

recovered by the father. Such property and also that which is acquired by him through his ability may be distributed or given at his pleasure.

How property gained without making use of the ancestral estate, &c., shall be disposed of.

From what has been said, it is plain that any property gained by skill or exertion without making use of the ancestral estate, or any other means, and recovered without using the paternal estate, shall be divided or given at the pleasure of the father.

The power of the father over such property.

The father has full power to give a larger portion of the abovementioned property to his eldest son, or to take the greater portion of it for his own use, if he choose.

Self-acquired property may be divided at the pleasure of the father.

The unequal partition, referred to by YAGNYAVALKYA, applies in the case of the aforementioned self-acquired property. "When the father makes a partition, let him separate his sons *from himself* at his pleasure, and either *dismiss* the eldest with the largest share, or *if he choose* all may be equal sharers."

Explanation.

The abovementioned text relates to property over which the father has full dominion, for it occurs on the subject of self-acquired property.

When the wives of the father must have equal shares with the sons.

He (YAGNYAVALKYA) adds a special rule in the case of equal partition :—"When the father makes an equal partition among his sons, his wives must have equal shares *with them*, if they have received no wealth either from their lord or from his father."

Equal partition means that the wives who have received a separate property *(stridhana)* should be made equal sharers with the other wives. Where the father, giving smaller shares to his sons, takes the largest portion for his own use, he must give equal shares to his wives out of his own property. **Explanation.**

It is for this reason specially declared that equal shares shall be given to his wives, when the father makes an equal partition among his sons. **Equal shares shall be given to his wives, when the father makes an equal partition among his sons.**

HARITA says:—"If the father, after giving a small portion of the estate to his sons, and reserving the greatest part of it for his own use, become indigent, he may take back the portions given to them." **The father, on becoming indigent, may, in a certain case, resume his sons' portions.**

Indigent means poor. **Explanation.**

This text relates to self-acquired property.

Again:—"Let a father who makes a partition reserve two shares for himself." **On a partition a father may take two shares.**

SANKHA and LIKHITA say, if he (the father) be an only son, let him take two shares and the principal of the bipeds and quadrupeds. A bull shall be given to the eldest son, and a house, which is not the father's place of residence, to the youngest. **Allotments of sons.**

The conclusion is that the father shall take two shares and the best of the slaves and cattle for his own use. A bull shall be given to the virtuous **Explanation.**

eldest son, and a house, other than that occupied by the father, to the youngest, if he have good qualities.

When the father shall get a double share.

The father shall get a double share, when he is an only son of his father; for the above cited texts, being from the same root, may, consistently with brevity, be understood as referring to the same matter.

The condition (if the father be the only son) is not essential in the case of self-acquired property.

The foregoing rule relates only to ancestral property. The abovementioned condition (if he be an only son) is not essential in the case of the self-acquired property of the father.

Explanation.

Only means eldest, not one in number. Otherwise the words, eldest and youngest, would be inconsistent.

What additional property the virtuous eldest and youngest sons shall have.

Therefore, the conclusion is that the virtuous eldest and youngest sons shall have the bull and house respectively, besides equal shares with the other sons; and the father shall have two shares, with the aforementioned deductions.

How the father shall make partition, according to Apastamba.

APASTAMBA says, that the father, having satisfied the eldest son with one article, shall give equal shares to his living sons.

The son, but not the wife, of a deceased son shall share in the heritage.

From the word *living* it is to be understood that the wife of a deceased son shall have no share of the heritage, but her son is entitled to a share; because a son is said to be the soul of the father, and there is a text, by virtue of which a person is heir to his grandfather.

In the *Ratnakara* it is said that the word *living* applies to the father, and not to sons. Explanation.

This causes inconsistency, for the father, who makes the partition, is understood to be living. It is therefore unnecessary to apply the word *living* to the father.

Principal wealth signifies the best of all kinds of wealth.

DEVALA speaks of the precedence of sons: In classes other than the usual four, "*the precedence of sons is regulated* by the goodness of their disposition; and of twins *the eldest is he* who is first actually born. Among twins, to him, whose face *kinsmen* first see after his birth, belong *the privileges of* male offspring, the right of performing obsequies for his father, and *the honours of* primogeniture." Devala on the precedence of sons.

The forefathers of that son are exalted, who is born of parents of the same class, and whose face is first seen by kinsmen, and who is also senior in birth. The marks of the eldest son.

The conclusion, therefore, is that the first male offspring of a father and mother of the same class is the eldest son. Seniority of birth belongs to such a son, even if he be younger than the other sons of his father by his wives of different classes. The first male offspring of a father and mother of the same class is the eldest son.

MENU confirms this by saying:—"As between sons born of wives equal in class *and* without *any other* distinction, there can be no seniority in right of the mother; but the seniority, ordained by law, Menu on the point.

d 4

is according to birth." Therefore, in the case of wives taken from different classes even the last born son, by a wife of an equal class, becomes senior in birth.

How an eldest brother defrauding his younger brother shall be punished.

MENU says that "an eldest brother, who from avarice shall defraud his younger brother, shall forfeit *the honours of* his primogeniture, be deprived of his own share, and pay a fine to the king."

What allotments the eldest, middlemost, and youngest son are to receive.

"The portion deducted for the eldest is a twentieth part of the heritage with the best of the property; for the middlemost, half of that, or a fortieth; for the youngest, a quarter of it, or an eightieth."

What may be taken by the first born, if transcendently learned and virtuous.

"Of all the property collected, let the first born, *if he be transcendently learned and virtuous*, take the best article, whatever is most excellent in its kind, and the best of ten *cows or the like.*"

What article shall be allotted to the eldest, according to Baudhayana.

BAUDHAYANA says, one of the ten articles of the same kind shall be allotted to the eldest son, and his other brothers shall have equal shares with him. The sons are entitled to an equal share from their ancestral estate; but if one of them be transcendently learned and virtuous, he shall receive a greater portion of it.

Explanation.

The meaning of the above is that the eldest son shall receive a twentieth part of the ancestral estate besides his own share, if he be *very* qualified; but if he be *somewhat* qualified, he shall receive something.

DEVALA says "let the tenth part of the heritage be given to the eldest, who conducts himself according to law."

The virtuous eldest son gets a tenth part of the heritage.

According to HALAYUDHA and the *Parijata* this text is applicable in a case where the eldest son maintains the sacred fire, and is versed in the Shastras, and the others are possessed of no good qualities.

Where this text is applicable.

VRIHASPATI says: "sons, to whom equal, less, or greater shares have been allotted by their father, should maintain such distribution; otherwise they shall be deemed sinful."

Sons should maintain the distribution made by their father.

This relates to the self-acquired property of the father.

This relates to the father's self-acquired property.

MENU says: "if, among undivided brothers *living* with their father, there be a common exertion for common gain, the father shall never make an unequal division among them, *when they divide their families.*"

In what case the father should not make unequal division among his sons.

This text is applicable in the case of property which is gained by the equal exertions of all the brothers. There is therefore no inconsistency.

Where this text is applicable.

VRIHASPATI says that "the eldest, *or he who is pre-eminent* by birth, science, and virtuous qualities, shall receive two shares of the heritage; the rest shall share alike: but he is *venerable,* like their father."

What shares, according to Vrihaspati, the virtuous eldest son shall receive.

Where this text is applicable.

This text refers to such eldest brother as supports his younger brothers like their father.

What sons are entitled to a greater share.

All the sons shall receive equal shares of their paternal property; but such of them as are learned and endowed with good qualities are entitled to a greater share.

When the brothers of a co-heir shall get a share of the wealth acquired by him.

VYASA says, if a co-heir acquire wealth by employing the common horses, elephants, cars, weapons, or any other articles, and by his own valour, his brothers shall get a share of it; but he is entitled to a double share.

Explanation.

The meaning of the above is that if a co-heir acquire any thing by his valor but with help from the common stock, he shall receive a double share of it.

What co-heir shall take a double share.

VASISHTHA says, "he among them, by whom property is acquired through his own sole labour, shall take a double share of it."

Explanation.

This text is the same as the above.

When all the brothers shall receive equal shares.

YAGNYAVALKYA says, if the common property be improved, all the brothers shall receive equal shares.

How the shares of grandsons shall be regulated.

The shares of grandsons shall be regulated according to those of their fathers.

If the common property, &c., signifies that even if any co-heir improve it by commerce, agriculture, or the like, he shall not receive a greater share. It is to be here understood that this is applicable in a case where the other co-heirs have similarly augmented the common property ; otherwise it will be inconsistent with the text of VASISHTHA. Explanation.

GRANDSONS OF DIFFERENT FATHERS.

IF, on the death of brothers living together, their sons improve the common property by agriculture or the like, they shall not separately receive shares, but only the shares of their respective fathers. What shares the sons of deceased brothers living together, who improve the common property, shall receive.

NAREDA says he who manages the family business shall be supplied by his brothers or cousins with food, raiment, and beasts of burden. He who, being employed for the benefit of the family, promotes its temporal interests by agriculture, commerce, or the like, shall have equal shares with the co-heirs. Better food, clothes, and so forth, shall be given to him by his co-heirs in consideration of his exertions. The manager of the family business to get something more than his own share.

MENU says, "if any one of the brothers has a competence from his own occupation and wants not the property, he may debar himself from his share, some trifle being given him in lieu of maintenance." A trifle to be given to a brother, who has a competence, and relinquishes his share of joint property.

His co-sharers shall make him compensation out of their own shares, on division.

The brothers of that man, who is able to support himself by his own occupation and labour, and does not require his ancestral property but relinquishes it, shall give him compensation out of their shares of the property which they may divide among themselves.

Explanation.

HALAYUDHA says, the purport of the preceding text of NAREDA is the same with that of MENU, but in the *Prakasakara* the latter is thus explained.

An indolent partner shall not be allowed to enjoy the profit.

If, when partners are engaged in any work for the acquisition of wealth, one of them be indolent, he shall not be allowed to enjoy the profit; but his share of the principal must be given to him.

Who shall receive the share of a dead son.

KATYAYANA says, "should a brother *(anuja)* die before partition, his share shall be allowed to his son, provided he had received no fortune from his grandfather.

"That son's son shall receive his father's share from his uncle, or from his uncle's son; and the same proportionate share shall be allowed to all the brothers, according to law.

"Or, *if that grandson be also dead,* let his son take the share; beyond him, succession stops."

Explanation.

Anuja implies a brother.

His son signifies the son of a deceased brother.

No fortune means no portion.

What share shall the brother's son receive?

The reply of the sage to this question is, his father's share.

The brother's son shall receive the share of his father.

His son in the latter text signifies the great-grandson of him whose estate is divided. Hence, the estate of the owner shall be divided according to the number of his sons. Consequently, the share which is allotted to a son shall be received by his son or grandson but not by his great-grandson. This is applicable where the partners live together. The wife of a deceased son shall not therefore be entitled to a share, because such is not the rule.

Explanation.

DEVALA says, "partition of heritage among undivided parceners, and a second partition among divided relatives living together *after re-union*, shall extend to the fourth in descent: this is a settled rulo."

How far partition of heritage shall extend.

The partition of heritage shall extend from the original owner of the estate to his descendants in the fourth degree. This rule is also applicable where the divided relatives are living together after re-union, because the peculiar state of living together in the abovementioned text is mentioned.

It shall extend from the original owner of the estate to his descendants in the fourth degree.

"A share of the heritage shall be allotted with the brothers to the widows who have no offspring, but are supposed pregnant, *to be held by them* until they severally bear sons."

A share of the heritage shall be allotted to the widows who are supposed to be pregnant.

By *widows* are meant the wives of the deceased brothers. A share must be given to a brother's widow, who is likely to bear a son and, after

Explanation.

her delivery, that share belongs to her son; but if no son be brought forth, the said share shall be taken by her husband's brothers.

Vrihaspati on the shares of mother, step-mother, and unmarried daughters.

VRIHASPATI says on the same subject: "on the death of the father, the mother *(janani)* has a claim to an equal share with her own sons; mothers *(matara)* take the same share; and the *unmarried* daughters each a fourth of a share."

Explanation.

Mother (janani) means one who has male issue. *Mothers (matara)* means stepmothers who have no male issue. These females shall have equal shares with the sons.

The *unmarried sisters* shall receive a fourth part of the share of each of their brothers for their marriage.

Provision for the investiture and other rites of younger brothers.

NAREDA says, "For any of the brothers, whose investiture and other ceremonies had not been performed by the father in due order, the other brothers shall perform those ceremonies out of the paternal estate."

How the expense of their ceremonies shall be defrayed if no property of the father remain.

"Or, if no property of the father remain, the investiture and other ceremonies must be performed out of their own shares, by brothers, for whom those ceremonies have already been performed."

Childless wives of the father and paternal grandmothers are equal sharers.

VYASA says: "even childless wives of the father are pronounced equal sharers, and so are all the paternal grandmothers, who are declared equal to mothers."

YAGNYAVALKYA says, "of heirs dividing after the death of the father, let the step-mother also take an equal share." Yagnyavalkya on the step-mother's share.

OF EFFECTS UNDISTRIBUTED.

KATYAYANA says :—"Recovering what has been embezzled by any one *of the co-heirs,* let sons, after the death of the father, divide it equally with their brothers. An equal distribution to be made on the discovery of any fraud or mistake in the partition.

"If the parceners have secreted part of the assets from each other, or if any mistake have been made in the partition, on a subsequent discovery there must be an equal division of what has been restored *(or ill distributed)*: so BHRIGU has ordained."

OF A CO-HEIR RETURNING FROM ABROAD.

VRIHASPATI says :—"If a man leave the common family and reside in another country, his share must no doubt be given to his male descendants when they return. Be the descendant the third, or fifth, or even seventh in degree, he shall receive his hereditary allotment on proof of his birth and name." Who shall receive the share of a man who has left his country.

This text relates to those who return from a foreign country. Where this text is applicable.

"To the lineal descendants, when they appear, of that man whom the neighbours and old inhabitants know by tradition to be the proprietor, the land must be surrendered by his kinsmen." To whom the kinsmen of the proprietor of the land must surrender it.

OF PERSONS EXCLUDED FROM INHERITANCE.

A son who is not virtuous has no claim to the paternal estate.

VRIHASPATI says on this subject :—"Though born of a woman equal in class, one who is not virtuous shall have no claim to the paternal estate; it is ordained to devolve on those learned kinsmen who offer the funeral cake to the deceased."

Brothers addicted to vice lose their title to inherit.

MENU says that "all those brothers who are addicted to any vice, lose their title to the inheritance."

Explanation.

Addicted to any vice means devoted to any forbidden acts.

The right of inheritance of degraded persons is extinct.

SANCHA says: "of him who has been formally degraded, the right of inheritance, the funeral cake, and the libation of water, are extinct."

Explanation.

Formally degraded means "excluded from the joint libation of water."

Such a person is not competent to inherit paternal property and to offer the oblation of food and libation of water.

Persons excluded from a share of the heritage, according to Menu.

MENU says :—"Impotent persons and outcasts, persons born blind or deaf, madmen, idiots, the dumb, and such as have lost the use of a limb, are excluded from a share of the heritage.

"But it is just that the heir who knows his duty should give all of them food and raiment *for life* without stint, according to the best of his power: he who gives them nothing, sinks assuredly *to a region of punishment.*

Food and raiment should be given to such persons for life.

"If the eunuch and the rest should at any time desire to marry, *and if the wife of the eunuch should raise up a son to him by a man legally appointed, that son and* the issue of such as have children, shall be capable of inheriting."

The issue of such of them as have children may inherit.

Those who have lost the use of a limb signifies those who have been deprived of a hand, a leg, or any other member of the body. Such persons are not competent to perform ceremonies relating to the *Vedas* and *Smriti.* They are consequently not entitled to inherit paternal property. This is the correct meaning of the preceding text. But the offspring of all of them except the outcasts shall get the shares of their respective fathers in the inheritance.

Persons deprived of a limb cannot perform ceremonies relating to the Vedas and Smriti, consequently cannot inherit.

YAGNYAVALKYA says:—"An outcast and his son, an impotent person, one lame, a madman, an idiot, one born blind, he who is afflicted with an incurable disease, and the like, must be maintained without any allotment of shares."

What persons should be maintained without any allotment of shares.

He who is afflicted with an incurable disease means a person who is afflicted with leprosy or any such disease.

Explanation.

A leper and the like are not competent to receive shares of their paternal estate.

But their sons, if not disqualified, shall inherit.

"But their sons, whether begotten in lawful wedlock, or procreated by a kinsman on the wife duly authorised, may take shares, provided they have no disability."

Their daughters are to be supported.

"Their daughters must be supported so long as they be not disposed of in marriage."

Explanation.

Here the son of an outcast "begotten in lawful wedlock" is understood to be born before the degradation of his father from the class. But the other sons signify even those born after their fathers had become incompetent to inherit.

Daughters mean female children.

Disposed of in marriage means married.

Their chaste childless wives must be maintained.

YAGNYAVALKYA adds that "their childless wives, who preserve chastity, must be supplied with food and apparel; but disloyal and traitorous wives shall be banished from the habitation."

Traitorous wives signify such wives as try to administer poison, and so forth.

What sons, according to Nareda, cannot inherit.

NAREDA says:—"An enemy to his father, an outcast, and one who is addicted to vice, shall not inherit, though begotten by the deceased; much less if begotten on his wife by a kinsman legally appointed."

An enemy to his father means one who ill treats his father in his lifetime, or is averse to perform his obsequies when dead. Explanation.

"Those of the family who are afflicted with long and painful disease, an idiot, one who is insane, blind, or lame, should be maintained, but their sons are partakers of the inheritance." Persons who cannot inherit, are to be maintained.

Long disease means consumption, and the like. Explanation.

Painful disease signifies leprosy, and so forth.

Idiot means a person not susceptible of receiving instruction.

Devala says "when the father is dead *(as well as in his lifetime)* an impotent man, a leper, a madman, an idiot, a blind man, an outcast, the offspring of an outcast, and a person wearing the token *(of religious mendicity)* are not competent to share in the heritage. Food and raiment should be given to them, excepting the outcast. But the sons of such persons, being free from similar defects, shall obtain their fathers' shares of the inheritance." Devala on the persons who cannot inherit.

Here the word *dead* applies to that father who has lost the right of inheritance. Explanation.

A person wearing the token of mendicity means a professed devotee.

Defects signify such failings as disqualify a person to receive his share.

Vasishtha on the exclusion of devotees.

VASISHTHA says :—"They who have assumed another order, are excluded from participation."

Explanation.

Another order means the order "other than that of a housekeeper *or married man.*"

Katyayana on the point.

KATYAYANA says, that the son of a woman not married in regular order, and begotten on her by a kinsman, is not competent to inherit the paternal estate ; and so is an apostate from a religious order.

Explanation.

Marriage in regular order is lawful. The son of a woman who was married contrary to the regular order, and who is of the same family with her husband, and a person who has forsaken the order of an ascetic, are not competent to receive a share.

But a special provision has been made by KATYAYANA on behalf of the first.

When the son of a woman not married in regular order may inherit.

But the son of a woman not married in regular order may inherit property, if his father and mother belong to the same class.

Explanation.

The son of a woman who is not married in regular order and who belongs to the class of her husband is entitled to a share.

Recapitulation.

The summary of the above is this : a vicious person, one who is excommunicated from society for heinous crimes, an outcast, an impotent person, one who is incurably blind, or deaf, a madman, an idiot, a person who is dumb or destitute of limbs, a leper, an enemy to his father, one afflicted with consumption, an impostor, and a person who has relinquished his household order, are not competent to inherit property, but the sons of all of them except the outcast, if free from similar defects, are entitled to the inheritance.

PERFORMANCE OF CEREMONIES FOR BROTHERS AND SISTERS.

VYASA speaks of brothers and sisters, whose purificatory rites have not been performed :—" For any of the brothers, whose investiture and other ceremonies had not been performed, the other brothers, of whom the sacraments have already been completed shall perform those ceremonies *out of the paternal estate* : and for *unmarried* sisters, the sacraments shall be completed by their elder brothers, as the law requires."

Vyasa on brothers and sisters whose purificatory rites have not been performed.

NAREDA says :—" Or if no property of the father remain, the investiture and other ceremonies must be performed out of their own shares, by brothers, for whom those ceremonies have already been performed."

Nareda on the point.

YAGNYAVALKYA says :—" For any of the brothers, whose investiture and other ceremonies have not been performed *by the father*, those ceremonies shall be performed by brothers, of whom the sacraments have been completed ; and for their sisters, by giving a fourth part of their respective shares."

Yagnyavalkya on the point.

According to Menu, the unmarried daughters by the same mother are to receive a fourth part of the share of each of their brothers.

MENU says :—"To the *unmarried* daughters *by the same mother*, let their brothers give portions out of their own allotments respectively, *according to the classes of their several mothers:* let each give a fourth part of his own distinct share; and they, who refuse to give it, shall be degraded."

Explanation.

Their own allotments means the allotments of the brothers. Therefore, the meaning is that a quarter of the share ordained for a brother of the class to which she belongs, should be given to a maiden sister.

Property sufficient to defray the expenses of the nuptials should be given.

Here the mention of a quarter is not essential. Property sufficient to defray the expenses of the nuptials should be given, for this is ordained by VISHNU.

How the expenses of marriage and other ceremonies, are to be defrayed.

The expenses of the marriage and of other ceremonies of unmarried daughters, must be defrayed in proportion to the wealth inherited. The same opinion of the subject is held in the *Ratnakara* and by other writers.

OF PROPERTY SUBJECT TO PARTITION.

What property is divisible among heirs.

KATYAYANA says on this subject :—"What belonged to the paternal grandfather, or to the father, and any thing else, *appertaining to the co-heirs,* acquired by themselves, must all be divided on a partition among heirs."

Explanation.

Acquired by themselves means gained by the use of the paternal estate.

NAREDA says:—"What remains of the paternal inheritance, over and above the father's obligations and after payment of his debts, may be divided by the brothers, so that their father continue not a debtor." According to Nareda, after payment of the father's obligations and debts.

Over and above the father's obligations signifies "sums, of which payment had been promised by him." Explanation.

Therefore, after the payment of the father's debts, the residue should be divided among the co-heirs.

OF PROPERTY NOT SUBJECT TO PARTITION.

MENU says:—"Wealth, however, acquired by learning, belongs exclusively to him who acquired it; so does any thing given by a friend, received on account of marriage, or presented as a mark of respect *to a guest.*" Property acquired by learning is not divisible.

Any thing given by a friend means any thing gained on account of friendship. Explanation.

Received on account of marriage will be hereafter explained.

Presented as a mark of respect alludes to what is given to a guest on his arrival, to do him honor.

Nor property acquired without using the paternal estate.

MENU and VISHNU say that property, acquired by a brother through his labour, without using the paternal estate, shall not be given up without his assent.

Explanation.

Labour signifies service, and the like.

The above is merely an instance; for whatever is acquired, without employing the common wealth or estate, shall be the absolute property of the acquirer.

Vyasa on property received as gifts or acquired without the aid of the paternal estate.

VYASA says :—"What is given by the paternal grandfather, or by the father, as a token of affection, belongs to him *who receives it*; neither that, nor what is given by a mother, shall be taken from him. What a man gains by his own ability, without relying on the patrimony, he shall not give up to the co-heirs, nor that which is acquired by learning."

Explanation.

These two sorts of property are not liable to partition: property gained without the use of patrimony and that acquired by learning.

Property acquired by learning without any help from the common estate is not liable to partition.

In the *Prakasakara* it is stated that, if any property be acquired by learning without any help from the common estate, it is not liable to partition. But this opinion is not reasonable, for the two conditions laid down in the text become useless.

According to the Ratnakara, and some writers,

In the *Ratnakara* and by some writers the same opinion is maintained.

Here it may be argued that, according to the text of NAREDA, "A learned man need not give a share of his own acquired wealth, without his assent, to an unlearned co-heir: provided it were not gained by him by using the paternal estate."

A learned man not to give an unlearned co-heir a share of wealth independently acquired.

This text of NAREDA is applicable where the common estate is used for the purpose of acquiring learning as well as wealth.

Where the text of Nareda is applicable.

Consequently, if learning be acquired without using the paternal estate, and if any property be obtained by such learning, KATYAYANA, without mentioning whether the common estate has been used or not, says it is not divisible.

Property obtained by learning gained without using the paternal estate, is not divisible.

"Wealth gained through science, which was acquired from a stranger, while receiving a foreign maintenance, is termed acquisition through learning."

What is acquisition through learning.

From a stranger signifies from such a person as bears no relation to his co-heirs.

Explanation.

The same sage observes, "yet VRIHASPATI has ordained, that 'wealth shall be partible if it was gained by learned brothers who were instructed in the family by their father, or by their paternal grandfather *or uncles*; and it is the same if the wealth was acquired by valour, *or with assistance from the family estate*."

Wealth gained by learned brothers who were instructed in the family is divisible.

Science signifies both military and sacred science.

Explanation.

The meaning of the above is that wealth, gained by science, shall be divided amongst the brothers, provided *that science* was gained from the father and other co-heirs.

Gains of science described.

What is gained by the solution *of a difficulty*, after a prize has been offered, must be considered as acquired through science and is not included in partition *among co-heirs*. What has been obtained from a pupil, or by officiating as a priest, or for *answering* a question, or for determining a doubtful point, or through display of knowledge, or by *success in* disputation, or for superior *skill in* reading, the sages have declared to be the gains of science and not subject to distribution.

The same rule prevails in the arts.

"BHRIGU says that the same rule likewise prevails in the arts, for the excess above the price *of the common goods*," &c.

Explanation.

What is obtained by the display of superior knowledge in a particular branch of science, is the acquisition of learning.

By officiating as a priest means "received as a fee or gratuity from a person who employs him to officiate at a sacrifice."

Question means any thing proposed.

What has been gained as a reward for display of knowledge means what has been gained by one who shines in a learned assembly.

Superior reading means proficiency in learning.

Display of superior knowledge in a particular branch of science means proficiency in a particular branch of learning.

Wealth gained by science not to be shared with co-heirs, but with equals or superiors in learning.

KATYAYANA says, that "no part of the wealth, which is gained by science, need be given by a learned man to his unlearned co-heirs; but such property must be shared by him with those who are equal or superior in learning."

The cause of such division.

Here superior or equal learning is not the cause of the division of wealth, acquired by learning. Such a meaning renders the text obscure. If wealth, acquired by the learning of equals or superiors, be mixed together, it shall be divided; or, in other words, the mixture is the cause of such division.

In what case an ignorant man shall share in the wealth acquired by his learned brother.

Wealth, acquired by a learned man, whose family was supported, during his absence from home to acquire learning, by a brother, shall be shared with the latter, even if he be ignorant.

Summary.

The summary of the above is that, if a person acquire any property through learning, gained by obtaining maintenance from a stranger, it is called the acquisition of learning and is not liable to partition, provided his family were not maintained during his absence by any of his co-heirs.

Property gained by valour.

KATYAYANA says on this subject:—"When *a soldier*, despising danger, performs a gallant action, and favor is shown to him by his lord pleased with that action, whatever property is then received by him shall be considered as gained by valour. That and what is taken under a standard are declared not to be subject to distribution.

Spoil under a standard defined.

"What is seized *by a soldier* in war, after risking his life for his lord and routing the forces of the enemy, is named spoil under a standard."

Wealth received on account of marriage.

The same writer speaks of wealth which is received on account of marriage and which is not liable to partition:—

"What is received with a damsel equal in class, at the time of accepting her *in marriage*, let a man consider as wealth received with the maiden;" it is the best means of supporting life. Wealth, received with the bride, shall be considered as a marriage gift. With it ceremonies may be performed.

Property acquired by unlearned brothers shall be equally divided among them.

MENU ordains that, if all of them (brothers), being unlearned, acquire property *before partition* by their own labour, there shall be an equal division of that property *without regard to the first born*; for it was not the wealth of their father: this rule is clearly settled.

Explanation.

Labour means employment in agriculture, and so forth.

Equal means in just proportion.

Therefore, the deduction of the twentieth part is not applicable in this case.

GAUTAMA speaks of self-acquired property :—"The unlearned brothers shall take equal shares."

Gautama on the division of self-acquired property.

VASISHTHA says :—" He among them who has made an acquisition, may take a double portion of it."

Vasishtha on the point.

If any among the co-heirs living in union acquire any property by the use of the common estate, employing himself in agriculture, he shall have a double share, and the others a share each.

A co-heir, acquiring any property by the use of the common estate, shall have a double share.

VYASA says, that the brothers participate in that wealth which one of them gained by valour or the like, using any common property, such as a weapon or a vehicle : to him two shares shall be given, but the rest shall share alike.

Vyasa on the point.

Or the like signifies learning, which is the cause of self-acquired property, and which is to be considered as one of the means of acquiring such property as cannot be divided. From *the like* it is to be understood that valour and other qualities are employed. From the compound word *(samas)* valour, and the like *(saurjadi,)* another quality is to be understood.

Explanation

It has already been said that wealth, gained by valour and learning, is not liable to division, even if it be acquired by the use of the paternal estate.

A supposed inconsistency.

But it is here said that the division of such wealth may take place: consequently this is an inconsistency.

This is no argument.

Explanation. The former text is applicable in the case of that wealth, which has been acquired by valour and learning, and of which KATYAYANA speaks.

But the latter text refers to learning of another description.

SEPARATE PROPERTY OF WOMEN.

In treating of the distribution of a woman's peculiar property, the nature of it should first be explained.

Six kinds of property of a woman. It is thus described by MENU and KATYAYANA: "What was given before the nuptial fire, what was presented in the bridal procession, what has been conferred on the woman through affection, and what has been received by her from her brother, her mother, or her father, are denominated the six kinds of property of a woman."

Explanation. *Six kinds of property* means that there cannot be a less number.

What is property given before the nuptial fire. KATYAYANA thus explains the first three kinds. "What is given to women at the time of their marriage, before the sacred fire, is denominated by sages their property bestowed before *(adhyagni)* the nuptial fire."

What is given means what is presented by any person. Explanation.

In the same manner, "what a woman receives from the family of her parents, while she is being conducted to the house of her husband, is called the property of a woman given *(adhyabahanika)* at her nuptial procession. Property of a woman given at her nuptial procession.

Property of a woman given at her nuptial procession means any thing given by a person while she is proceeding the second time from the house of her father to that of her husband. Explanation.

Therefore, "any thing which is given to a woman by the mother or father of her husband in token of affection, and that which is given in return for her humble salutations, are called wealth gained by amiability." Wealth gained by amiability.

Amiability "consists in good temper, skill *in feminine arts*, and the like." Amiability defined.

What is *given in token of affection*, and "by the father or mother of her husband, to a woman who is endowed with good temper and other amiable qualities, and who humbly salutes their feet, constitutes the third sort of exclusive property." Third sort of exclusive property defined.

What is received from the mother, father, and brother, does not require any explanation. That which a woman receives for her consolation when her husband takes a second wife, is the seventh kind of peculiar property, and is thus explained by YAGNYAVALKYA:—"A woman, whose husband takes What a woman receives for her consolation when her husband takes a second wife is the seventh kind of peculiar property.

Yagnyavalkya on the point.

a second wife, shall have compensation for the supersession, if no property have been bestowed on her; but, if any have been given, she shall get so much as will make her share equal to that of the new bride."

Explanation.

When a man takes a second wife, his first wife is said to be *superseded.*

What a man gives to his first wife, at the time of his second marriage, is called *adhibedanika* or what is given to console her.

Vishnu on the property of a female.

VISHNU says:—"The property of a female is what her father, mother, son, or brother has given her; what she received before the nuptial fire; *or at the bridal procession;* or when her husband took a second wife; what her husband agrees should be regarded as her perquisites; what is received from his or her kinsmen as a gift subsequent to the marriage."

The perquisites of a woman described by Katyayana.

The six kinds of property here mentioned have already been explained. That which her husband agrees should be regarded as her perquisites, is thus explained by KATYAYANA.

"The small sums which are received by a woman as the price *or rewards* of household *duties, using household* utensils, tending beasts of burden, looking after milch cattle, taking care of ornaments of dress, or superintending servants, are called her perquisites."

The meaning of the above is that what the master of the house, pleased with the performance of the household business, gives to a woman, is her perquisite. Explanation.

"What is received by a woman after marriage, from the kinsmen of her lord, or those of her parents, is called a gift subsequent." What is a gift subsequent.

The peculiar property of women is thus explained. Explanation of peculiar property.

Saudayica is the name by which the different kinds of the peculiar property of women are known.

Katyayana says :—"That which is received by a married woman or a maiden, in the house of her husband or father, from her brothers or from her parents, is termed the gift of affectionate kindred." Gift of affectionate kindred defined.

By the words, *her husband*, are to be also understood his kindred. Explanation.

Hence, the meaning is, what a married woman or a maiden receives from her parents or their kindred or her husband's kindred is called the gift of affectionate kindred.

The means of subsistence and other kinds of women's peculiar property, will be described hereafter. The means of subsistence, &c., to be hereafter described.

The same writer states how it is to be used.

Katyayana on the use of the peculiar property of woman.

"The independence of women, who have received such gifts, is recognised in regard to that property;" for it was received through the kindness of the donors. "The power of women over the gifts of their affectionate kindred is ever celebrated, both in respect of donation and sale at their pleasure, even in the case of immovables."

Women can dispose of the immovables given by their husbands' kindred.

Women are competent to make gifts, and so forth, of the immovables given by their husbands' kindred.

Apastamba on the gifts of affectionate kindred.

APASTAMBA thus speaks of the gifts of affectionate kindred:—"Ornaments are the exclusive property of a wife, and so is wealth given to her by kinsmen or friends, according to some *legislators*.

Explanation.

Wealth given by kinsmen means that which is given at the time of marriage, and so forth, by kinsmen and the kinsmen of her parents or those of her husband.

Ornamental apparel worn by women during the lives of their husbands cannot be taken by the heirs of the latter.

MENU and VISHNU speak on the subject of ornaments. Such ornamental apparel as women wear during the lives of their husbands, the heirs of those husbands shall not divide among themselves; they who divide it among themselves fall deep *into sin*.

Any ornament worn by a woman with the consent of her husband shall be her property.

Any ornament which a woman wears with the consent of her husbands shall be her peculiar property, even if it have been not given to her. MADHATITHI declares that, according to the foregoing text of KATYAYANA, a woman is competent to give away or sell any immovable or movable property which she has received from her husband's kindred.

NAREDA says :—" Property given to her by her husband through pure affection she may enjoy at her pleasure after his death, or give away, with the exception of lands or houses." What property may be enjoyed by a woman at pleasure after her husband's death.

Consequently a woman can dispose of movable property which has been given her by her husband, but she can never dispose of immovable property. The same rule holds good in the case of *saudayica,* or the gifts of affectionate kindred. Explanation.

KATYAYANA says, that a woman, on the death of her husband, may enjoy his estate according to her pleasure ; but in his lifetime she should carefully preserve it. If he leave no estate, let her remain with his family. How a woman on the death of her husband may enjoy his estate and where she is to live.

A childless widow, preserving her chastity, shall enjoy her husband's property with moderation, as long as she lives. After her death, the heirs shall take it. A childless chaste widow shall, during her lifetime, enjoy her husband's property.

This admits of two meanings. The one is that, on the death of the husband, his property devolves on his wife, and becomes her own in default of other heirs. On the death of the husband without other heirs, his property devolves on his wife.

The other is that the property, which she enjoys with the consent of her husband in his lifetime, is to be regarded as her peculiar property. Property enjoyed by her with the consent of her husband is her peculiar property.

KTYAYANA says as to the first of these:—"Let a woman on the death of her husband enjoy her husband's property at her discretion."

This applies to movables.

This refers to property other than immovable.

How a woman shall enjoy immovable property.

The following provision is made for immovable property. Let a woman enjoy it with moderation as long as she lives. After her death, let the heirs take it.

Explanation.

Moderation means without much expenditure.

Childless widow means one who has no heir of her own.

The property protected in the lifetime of her husband.

On the second, it is said that "while he lives she should carefully preserve it," or, in other words, the property shall be protected in the lifetime of the husband. If her husband have left no wealth, the widow should live with his family.

Immovable property cannot be disposed of by the widow at her pleasure.

Hence the immovable property, which a woman gets after the death of her husband, cannot be disposed of at her pleasure.

Explanation.

The meaning of this is consonant with that of the husband's donation (which can only be enjoyed but not spent.)

The texts of KATYAYANA do not refer to the peculiar property of woman. The inconsistency owing to this is removed by the similarity of meaning.

As a woman cannot make a present of, or at pleasure dispose of immovable property, given to her by her husband in his lifetime, so she cannot dispose of any immovable property which she inherits on his death. A woman cannot dispose of immovable property inherited on the death of her husband.

The same opinion is maintained in the *Ratnakara* and the *Prakasakara*. So the Ratnakara and Prakasakara.

If the mother, on the death of her son, get his immovable property, she cannot make a gift of it, or dispose of it at her pleasure. Nor the immovable property inherited from her son.

DEVALA says, as to the property in question : Devala on the above.

" Food and vesture, ornaments, perquisites, and wealth received by a woman *from a kinsman*, are her own property ; she may enjoy it herself; and her husband has no right to it, except in extreme distress."

Food and vesture means " funds appropriated to her support." Explanation.

Ornaments means " ornamental apparel."

Perquisites means " wealth given to a damsel on demanding her in marriage."

Wealth received means " that which is received from kinsmen."

These are the several kinds of the peculiar property of women.

The property of a woman not to be used but for the relief of a distressed son.

"If he (the husband) give it away on a false consideration, or consume it, he must make good the value to the woman, with interest; but he may use the property of his wife, to relieve a distressed son."

Explanation.

The property of a woman should not be improperly given away or consumed without her consent, but it may be used for the relief of a distressed son. It is declared by the same writer that the husband has power to use it with or without the consent of his wife.

When the husband shall pay the principal only.

If the husband, "having obtained her consent, use the property amicably, he shall be required to pay the principal when he becomes rich."

The husband to refund the value of his wife's property at his convenience.

If the wife give her peculiar property through affection, when her husband is ill, or in danger, or has been confined by a creditor, he may give her the value of it when he pleases.

Explanation.

The meaning of the above is that if the wife, observing her husband's illness or the like, give her wealth, it may be re-paid by him at his pleasure.

When a husband is not liable to make good the property taken from his wife.

YAGNYAVALKYA says that "a husband is not liable to make good the property of his wife, taken by him in a famine, or for the performance of a duty, or during illness, or while under restraint."

Explanation.

While under restraint signifies while he is so ill that he cannot work.

KATYAYANA specially declares that money, taken by a man from his wife, for performing some imperative duty, when he has no means of doing so, shall not be repaid. But if the husband "have taken a second wife, and no longer give his first wife the honor due to her, the king shall compel him, by violence, to restore her property, though it was put amicably into his hands.

When money, taken from his wife is not to be repaid by a man.

When it is to be.

"If suitable food, apparel, and habitation, cease to be provided for a wife, she may by force take her own property, and a just allotment *for such a provision*; or she may, *if he die*, take it from his heir.

When a wife can forcibly take her own property, &c.

"This is a law of LIKHITA; but after receiving *her own property and just allotment*, she must reside with the family of her husband; yet, if afflicted by disease, and in danger of her life, she may go to her *own* kindred."

The wife after regaining her rights, must reside with the family of her husband.

When she may go to her own kindred.

"But a wife who does malicious acts injurious to her husband, who has no sense of shame, who destroys his effects, or who takes delight in being faithless to his bed, is held unworthy of the property before described.

A bad wife is unworthy of peculiar property.

"What has been promised to a woman by her husband, as her exclusive property, must be given by his sons as a debt of his, provided she remain with the family of her husband." It is not to be given, if she live with the family of her father,

Any thing promised to a woman by her husband as her exclusive property, must be given by his sons as a debt of his,

What is meant by "the honor due to her."

The honor due to her. This means that, if the husband do not visit her after the time of her menses and do not provide her with food and raiment, the wife has the right to demand her peculiar property from her husband, though it have been given to him at the time of his sickness or under similar circumstances.

Explanation.

After receiving, &c. Even if she receive her own property and allotments, she must reside with the family of her husband and not go to the family of her father.

Who does malicious acts injurious, &c. This shows that the kindred should demand the peculiar property from such a woman.

What has been promised to a woman by her husband. This passage does not require any explanation.

SUCCESSION TO A WOMAN'S SEPARATE PROPERTY.

How the mother's property is to be divided.

MENU says on this subject:—"On the death of the mother, let all the uterine brothers and *(if unmarried)* the uterine sisters divide the maternal estate, &c., in equal shares. It is fit that even to the daughters of those daughters something should be given, from the estate of their maternal grandmother, on the ground of natural affection.

Explanation.

Uterine signifies the offspring of the same father and mother.

Sisters. Only the unmarried ones are to be equal sharers.

VRIHASPATI confirms this, by declaring that "a woman's property goes to her children, and the daughter is a sharer with them, provided she be unaffianced; but, if she be married, she shall not receive the maternal wealth." Something should be given her that her feelings may not be wounded.

Vrihaspati's authority on the point.

To her children means to her sons.

Sharer with them, that is, an equal partaker, because no distinction is made.

Explanation.

If she be married signifies if *provided* with a husband.

Something, that is, in proportion to the estate.

GAUTAMA says that a woman's separate property goes to her daughters unmarried and unprovided for.

Who receive a woman's separate property.

Unprovided indicates misfortune, such as the want of son, husband, or wealth. This opinion is held in the *Ratnakara* and by some writers.

Explanation.

Even if the daughter as above described be destitute of a son, she shall receive a share from the maternal estate like the sons.

The daughter shall receive a share from the maternal estate.

MENU says:—"Property given to the mother on her marriage *(yautuca)* is the portion of her unmarried daughter."

The unmarried daughter inherits the property given to the mother on her marriage.

Yautuca.

Yautuca means property received at the time of marriage from parents, and such like.

Nuptial gifts.

VASISHTHA says, "let the females share the nuptial gifts *(parinayya)* of their mother."

"A nuptial gift *(parinayya)* means furniture, such as a mirror, combs, and so forth."

Who receive the residue of the mother's property after the payment of the debts.

YAGNYAVALKYA says, "the daughters share the residue of their mother's property, after payment of her debts, and so forth, and their issue succeed in their default."

The daughters shall divide their mother's effects, &c.

"Let the daughters divide their mother's effects, remaining over and above the debts; on failure of such, the (male) issue, that is, the sons, (in other words) their brothers, and their (daughters') sons shall inherit according to MENU."

Where the rule is applicable.

The foregoing rule refers to the property received by the woman, at the time of her marriage in the form denominated Brahma, and her (nuptial gifts, *i. e.*) furniture, combs, and so forth.

Who succeed on failure of daughters.

KATYAYANA says:—"But on failure of daughters the inheritance belongs to the son. That which has been given to her by her kindred goes on failure of kindred to her husband."

Married sisters shall share with kinsmen.

Married sisters shall share with kinsmen. This law concerning the separate property of a woman is ordained in the case of partition.

On failure of daughters, and so forth. The meaning of this is that the mother's estate, which consists in her furniture, nuptial gifts, as well as the gifts of parents, goes to her son, provided there be no daughters. Explanation.

The property, except the abovementioned articles, goes to the son and daughter after the death of the owner. This has been ordained before.

Given to her by her kindred. What is given by any one except the father, goes to both the brother and sister, but the latter, if unmarried, becomes an equal sharer. The sisters, if married, shall receive something from the estate. This is the signification of the text regarding married sisters. Married sisters shall receive something from the estate.

On failure of kindred, that is, in default of daughter's son and the like, the woman's property devolves on her husband. Explanation.

MENU says :—" It is admitted that the property of a woman married according to (any of) the ceremonies called *Brahma, Daiva, Arsha, Gandharba,* and *Prajapatya,* shall go to her husband, if she die without issue. But her wealth, given to her on her marriage in the form called *Asura* or either of the other two *(Rakshasa* and *Paisacha)* is ordained, on her death without issue, to become the property of her mother and father." The property of a woman married according to certain ceremonies shall go to her husband, on failure of issue. When her property goes to her parents

Without issue, that is, without children. Explanation.

Who, according to Gautama, shall get the sister's fee.

GAUTAMA says, "the sister's fee belongs to the uterine brothers; after them it goes to the mother, and then to the father." Some say that it goes to him before her.

Where this text applies.

This text alludes to property received at the time of marriage (in the form) called *Asura* and the other two.

Who shall take the wealth of a deceased damsel.

BAUDHAYANA says, "the wealth of a deceased damsel, let the uterine brothers themselves take; on failure of them, it shall belong to the mother, or, if she be dead, to the father.

ON THE DISTRIBUTION OF EFFECTS CONCEALED.

How effects secreted by one parcener from the others, and discovered after partition, are to be disposed of.

On this subject YAGNYAVALKYA says, "when effects secreted by one parcener from the others are discovered after partition, the co-heirs shall again distribute those effects in equal shares: this is a settled law."

A coparcener who conceals effects held in coparcenary cannot be charged with theft.

Partition being suggested as a matter of course, it is intimated by the enunciation of this text that the crime of theft is not committed by concealing effects held in co-parcenary. This is the opinion of HALAYUDHA.

Law of Bhrigu regarding effects, a part of which, being secreted is subsequently discovered.

KATYAYANA says, "if the parceners have secreted part of the effects from each other, or if any mistake have been made in the partition on a subsequent discovery, there must be an equal division *(or re-distribution)* of what is restored: this is a law of BHRIGU." Nor let a co-heir be obliged to make good what he had expended *before partition for the necessary support of his family.*

Equal division means that the division should be precisely similar. **Explanation.**

What he had expended, &c., signifies the concealed effects common to all.

Therefore, the meaning is that what has been consumed by a co-heir, he shall *not be required to make good.* **A co-heir shall not be required to make good what has been consumed by him.**

DISTRIBUTION AMONG BROTHERS UNEQUAL IN CLASS.

MENU says, "let the son of the Brahmin take four parts, the son of the *Kshatrya* three, the son of the *Vaisya* two parts, and the son of the *Sudra* a single part, if he be virtuous." **What the sons of wives of different classes shall take.**

It is said in the *Mahabharata* that the son of the *Kshatrya* wife shall receive four such parts of his father's estate, and he shall also take whatever implements of war belonged to his father, but the son of the *Vaisya* wife shall have three shares, and the son of the *Sudra* one share. **The division according to the Mahabharata.**

The estate of the *Vaisya* should be divided into five parts, four of which his son by a wife of his own class shall receive, and the remaining one shall be received by his son by a *Sudra* wife. **How the estate of the Vaisya is to be divided.**

Where this rule applies.

This rule applies where the Brahmin had married four, the *Kshatrya* three, and the *Vaisya* two wives from different classes. But if this be not the case, the separate share of a son of the wife different in class, should not be made from the said ten, eight, and five divisions.

Explanation.

Implements of war means horses, weapons, &c.

The estate of a Brahmin to be divided into nine parts.

VISHNU declares, "but if a Brahmin leave three sons and none by a *Sudra* wife, they shall divide the estate into nine parts."

Where this rule is applicable.

This rule is also ordained in the case of a *Kshatrya*.

The son of the Brahmin wife shall receive land received as reward for sacred literature.

VRIHASPATI says: "land received as reward for sacred literature must never be given to the son of the *Kshatrya* or other wife of inferior class: even if his father gave it to him, the son of the Brahmani wife may nevertheless *resume* it after his father's death."

Vriddha Menu on the point.

VRIDDHA MENU says: "the sons of the Brahmani wife shall take the land which descends as a holy heritage, but all the sons by women of the twice-born classes shall succeed to the house and field successively inherited from ancestors."

Explanation.

Decends as a holy heritage means, what is received for performing a sacrifice or imparting lessons in literature, or what is given as a reward.

Twice-born signifies the sons of the three classes other than the *Sudra*.

SANKHA and LIKHITA say :—" A son by a *Sudra* woman does not succeed to the paternal estate ; whatever his father gave him, that alone shall be his share ; but let the father also give him a bull and a cow, some black iron, and any black grain excepting linseed." **The share of the son by a Sudra woman.**

MENU says :—" But whether the Brahmin have sons or have no sons *by wives of the first three classes*, no more than a tenth part must be given to the son by a *Sudra* wife. **According to Menu, a tenth only is to be given to the son by a Sudra wife.**

" The son of a Brahmin, a *Kshatrya*, or a *Vaisya*, by a woman of the servile class, shall inherit no part of the estate *unless he be virtuous, nor jointly with other sons unless his mother was lawfully married :* whatever his father may give him, let that be his own." **When a son of one of the twice-born classes by a Sudra wife, shall inherit.**

Have sons means have issue by the wives of the first three classes. **Explanation.**

Have no son signifies have no issue of such kind.

Shall inherit no part of the estate, that is, even if the father be favorable to his son by a *Sudra* wife, he shall have no power to give him greater than the said tenth part. This is the opinion expressed in the *Kalpataru*. But a different opinion is held in the *Parijata*. A son by a married *Sudra* wife, though he be virtuous, shall receive the tenth part only of the paternal estate. **A son by a Sudra wife, though he be virtuous, shall receive a tenth only of the paternal estate.**

How the estate of a man who leaves no legitimate offspring shall be disposed of.

VRIHASPATI says, that "a virtuous and obedient son, born of a *Sudra* woman unto a man who leaves no legitimate offspring, shall take a *provision for his* maintenance, and the kinsmen shall inherit the remainder of the estate."

Explanation.

Who leaves no legitimate offspring, that is, who has no son by the wives of the first three classes.

Where this rule is applicable.

Kinsmen, first the nearest, and in default of them the remotest kindred. This rule relates to the child of an unmarried *Sudra*, for the text is laid down in the section treating of an unmarried woman.

When a son begotten by a Sudra on a female slave, may take a share of the heritage.

MENU says :—" But a son, begotten by a man of the servile class on his female slave, or on the female slave of his slave, may take a share of the heritage *if permitted by the other sons :* this is the law established."

Yagnyavalkya on the point.

YAGNYAVALKYA says :—" A son, begotten by a man of the servile class on his female slave, may receive a share by his father's choice, or, after the death of the father, the brothers shall allot him half a share.

A son of a Sudra by an unmarried woman may receive a share by the permission of his father, &c.

" A son of a *Sudra* by an unmarried woman may receive a share by the permission of his father; but, if the father be dead, he shall receive half of the share of his brothers who are borne by married wives.

When he shall take the whole.

" Should he have no brother, he shall take the whole, unless there be a daughter's son."

The meaning of the above is that the son of a *Sudra* by an unmarried woman receives the whole heritage, provided there be no son of married wives and daughters' sons. **Explanation.**

GAUTAMA says :—" Sons, borne by women in the inverse order of the classes, shall have a similar allotment to that of the son produced by a woman of the servile class. **The share to be received by sons, borne by woman in the inverse order of the classes.**

" A son begotton by a *Sudra* or other man of an inferior class on a *Vaisya*, or other woman of a superior class shall receive the means of livelihood, that is, stock for agriculture and the like, such as a plough, a ploughshare, and so forth." **A Sudra's son begotten on a woman of a superior class shall receive the means of livelihood.**

ON THE PARTICIPATION OF SONS BORN AFTER A PARTITION.

SONS born after a partition are of two kinds, namely, the one is *the son who* at the time of partition is *in the womb,* and the other, the son *conceived* and born after the partition. **Two kinds of sons born after partition.**

YAGNYAVALKYA speaks of the first :—" After a division, a son born of a woman equal in class claims partition *of the original estate ;* or a distribution shall be made of the present wealth, exclusive of *subsequent* income and *past* expenses." **A son born of a woman equal in class claims participation of the original estate, &c.**

Claims partition, that is, is competent to receive a share. **Explanation.**

Of the present wealth means out of the present wealth visible, or both visible and invisible.

Exclusive of subsequent income, &c., that is, excluding the subsequent increase and what has been consumed by the brothers.

A son born after partition, being virtuous shall receive his share of the whole estate, &c.

HALAYUDHA is of opinion that "a son born after partition, being virtuous, shall receive his share of the whole estate; that is, of both sorts of property, forthcoming and not forthcoming; but one deficient in good qualities shall only receive a share of the present wealth."

Who shall give a share to the sons born after partition.

VISHNU says :—" Sons, with whom the father has made a partition, should give a share to the son born after the distribution."

This text is differently explained.

This text has like the preceding two significations.

What share shall be received by a son, born after a division.

Of the second, that is, the son born after the partition, MENU says :—" A son, born after a division, shall alone take the paternal wealth, or he shall participate with such *of the brothers* as are re-united with the *father*."

Explanation.

As the son, who is in the womb at the time of partition, receives his share from the brothers, so the son born after partition does not receive it from them, but shall have only the share of his father.

This meaning is derived from the word *alone*.

When the father's share shall be delivered to the son born after partition.

Here it is to be understood that if, in the life-time of the father, the sons desire to have their share and the father be also anxious to reserve his share, then the father's share should, after his death, be delivered to the son born after partition. But if the father, after division, being re-united with his own brother, or sons, die, the son born after partition shall receive his father's share from the re-united persons or co-heirs.

VRIHASPATI says:—"The younger brothers of those, who have made a partition with their father, whether children of the same mother or of other wives, shall take the father's share. The younger brothers of those who have made partition with their father shall take the latters' share.

"A son, born before partition, has no claim on the paternal wealth; nor one, begotten after it, on that of his brothers." A son begotten after partition cannot claim the wealth of his brothers.

Younger brothers means that if, after the partition, many sons be born, they shall still have the share of their father. Explanation.

A son born before partition, that is, he who is separated from his father.

All the wealth which is acquired by the father himself, who has made a partition with his sons, goes to the son begotten by him after the partition. Those born before it, are declared to have no right; as in the wealth, so in the debts likewise, and in gifts, pledges, and purchases. All the wealth acquired by the father after partition goes to the son thereafter begotten by him.

They have no claims on each other, except for acts of mourning and libations of water. The reciprocal claims of sons born before and after partition.

Summary.

The summary of the above is this, that a son, who is in the womb at the time of partition, and is born after it, shall receive his equal share from the separated co-heirs out of their estate. But he, who is *begotten* and born after partition, shall only get the share of his father. This is the opinion of MENU and other legislators.

OF SONS.

Twelve kinds of sons, described by Yama.

YAMA says :—" Twelve sons are named by sages, who know the principles of things. Among these sons, six are kinsmen and heirs; six not heirs, but kinsmen.

"The first is declared to be the son begotten by a man himself *in lawful wedlock;* the second a son begotten on his wife *by a kinsman;* the third is the son of an appointed daughter; thus have the learned declared the law.

"The fourth is a son by a twice-married woman; the fifth, a son by an unmarried girl; the sixth a son of concealed birth in the husband's mansion: these six give the funeral cake and take the heritage."

What sons are only kinsmen.

" A son rejected *by his father or mother*, the son of a pregnant bride, a son given *by his natural parents*, a son made through adoption, and fifthly a son bought, and *lastly* he who offers himself of his own accord.

"These six being of mixed origin are kinsmen, but not heirs *except to their own father.*"

NAREDA says :—" A son begotten by a man himself *in lawful wedlock,* a son begotten on his wife *by a kinsman,* the son of an appointed daughter, the son of an unmarried girl, the son of a pregnant bride, and a son of concealed birth, a son by a twice-married woman, a son rejected, a son given *by his natural parents,* a son bought, a son made *by adoption,* and a son self-given, are declared to be twelve sons.

Nareda on the point.

" Among these, six are heirs to kinsmen, six not heirs but kinsmen ; their relative rank corresponds with the order in which they are here named.

The relative rank of these corresponds with the order in which they are described.

"On the death of the father they succeed in their order to his wealth ; on the failure of the best and the next best, let the inferior in order take the heritage."

On the demise of the father, they succeed in their order to his wealth.

The meaning is, on default of each preceding, the next succeeding in order is entitled to the property.

Explanation.

MENU says :—" Of the twelve sons of men, whom MENU, sprung from the Self-Existent, has named, six are kinsmen and heirs, six not heirs, except to their own father, but kinsmen."

Of the twelve sons, six are kinsmen and heirs and six not heirs except to their own father.

Who are kinsmen and heirs.

The son begotten by a man himself *in lawful wedlock,* the son of his wife, and so forth, a son given to him, a son made or adopted, a son of concealed birth, or whose real father cannot be known, and a son rejected, and so forth, are the six kinsmen and heirs:

Who are only kinsmen.

The son of a young woman unmarried, the son of a pregnant bride, a son bought, a son by a twice-married woman, a son self-given, and a son by a *Sudra,* are the six kinsmen but not heirs to *collaterals.*

To what sons participation of wealth belongs.

BAUDHAYANA says:—"Participation of wealth belongs to the son begotten by a man himself, and so forth, the son of his appointed daughter, the son begotten on his wife, and so forth, a son given, a son made by adoption, a son of concealed birth, and a son rejected by his natural parents.

To what sons consanguinity denoted by a common family appellation belongs.

"Consanguinity, *denoted by a common family appellation,* belongs to the son of an unmarried girl, the son of a pregnant bride, a son bought, a son by a twice married-woman, a son self-given, and a son of a *priest* by a *Sudra.*"

Devala on sons.

DEVALA enumerates the son of the body, the son of an appointed daughter, the son of a wife, the son of an unmarried girl, a son of concealed birth, a son rejected, the son of a pregnant bride, a son by a twice married-woman, a son given, and so forth, a son self-given, a son made *by adoption,* and a son bought. He then adds:—These twelve sons are considered as offspring *by birth or adoption;*

namely, sons begotten by a man himself, sons begotten by another, *but fathered by him*, sons acquired, and sons by their own consent.

Among these, the first six are kinsmen and heirs, the other six inherit only from their own fathers. The rank of sons is distinguished by the order in which they are enumerated.

The first six are kinsmen and heirs, the other six inherit from their fathers only.

All these adopted sons are pronounced heirs of a man who has no son begotten by himself; but, should a son of his body be afterwards born, there is no larger portion for them, by reason of seniority.

Adopted sons are heirs when there is no son begotten.

" Such among them as are of the same class *with that son* shall have as their share one-third of the property, and so forth ; but those of a lower class must live under him with clothes and food only."

The share of adopted sons, if a son be afterwards begotten.

VISHNU enumerates the real legitimate son, the son of the wife, the son of an appointed daughter, the son of a twice-married woman, the son of the unmarried daughter, the son of hidden origin, the son received with a pregnant bride, the son given, the son purchased, the son self-given, the son rejected, and the son obtained in any manner whatsoever. He then adds, " Of these, the first in order is the most worthy : he only is entitled to the estate, but he should support the rest."

Of the twelve sons, the first in order is the most worthy, &c.

The first is the son begotten by a man himself on his own wife, *(or the son of the body, for this agrees* with VASISHTHA) ; the second is the son of

Explanation.

a wife, begotten by a man of equal class on *a widow duly appointed;* she who is given in marriage by her father with a declaration in this form, "her son shall be my son," as well as she, who having no brothers, is so appointed to raise up a son to her father, though not yet given in marriage, is an appointed daughter, *and considered as the third son;* the fourth is the son of a twice-married woman; the fifth, the son of an unmarried girl; the sixth, the son of concealed birth, (he is the son of him on whose wife he was begotten); the seventh is the son of a pregnant bride, (and the son of a woman espoused while pregnant is the son of the man who marries her); the eighth is a son given, and becomes the son of him to whom he is given by his natural father or mother; the ninth, a son sold; the tenth, a son self-given, (he is the son of the man to whom he gives himself); the eleventh is a son rejected, (being forsaken by his father or mother, he becomes the son of him by whom he is received); the twelfth is a son any how produced irregularly, (and he is also called *Sudra*, *or a son by a Sudra*).

Others say that the son made is the 12th, and the 13th is the son by a *Sudra*.

According to Vishnu, the next in order becomes heir and presents funeral oblations on failure of the preceding.

On the subject of dispute, VISHNU says:—"Of the son begotten by himself, the son of a wife, the son of an appointed daughter, the son of concealed birth, the son of an unmarried girl, the son of a twice-married woman, the son given, the son purchased, the son made, the son self-given, the son of a pregnant bride, the son rejected, the next in order becomes heir and presents funeral oblations on failure of the preceding."

YAGNYAVALKYA says :—"The legitimate son is one procreated on the lawful wedded wife. Yagnyavalkya on the twelve sons. Legitimateson.

"Equal to him is the son of an appointed daughter. Son of an appointed daughter.

"The son of the wife is one begotten on a wife by a kinsman of her husband, or by some other relative. Son of the wife.

"One secretly produced in the house is a son of hidden origin. Son of hidden origin.

"A damsel's child is one born of an unmarried woman; he is considered as the son of his maternal grandsire. Son of an unmarried woman.

"A child begotten on a woman whose *first* marriage had not been consummated, or on one who had been defloured *before marriage*, is called the son of a twice-married woman. Son of a twice-married woman.

"He, whom his father and his mother give for adoption shall be considered as a son given. Son given.

"A son bought is one who was sold by his father and mother. Son bought.

"A son made is one adopted by the man himself. Son made.

"One who gives himself is self-given. Son self-given.

A child accepted, while yet in the womb, is one received with a bride. Son of a pregnant bride.

Son deserted. "He who is taken for adoption, having been forsaken by his parents, is a deserted son.

The order in which they inherit. "Among these the next in order is heir, and presents funeral oblations, on failure of the preceding."

Explanation. The legitimate son is first. Here the *lawful wife* is a woman of equal tribe espoused in lawful wedlock: a son begotten by himself on her is the first legitimate son, because the author says that one produced on the lawful wedded wife of equal tribe is called legitimate.

The second son. The son of an appointed daughter is second.

The third son. The wife's son *(Kshetraja)* is third. If the husband of the wife be anxious to have the son, the aforesaid son may belong to him; and if the procreator also claim the abovementioned son, he may belong to him: but if both of them be anxious for the issue, that offspring may be considered as the son of two fathers.

A son of two fathers.

The fourth son. The son of hidden origin is the fourth, but he must be begotten by a man of a tribe equal to that of his mother. He shall belong to his mother's husband.

The damsel's child. The damsel's child is the fifth; he is the son of his maternal grandfather, provided the grandfather be childless: but if his mother's husband be childless, he shall belong to him.

The sixth son. The son of a twice-married woman is the sixth he is the son of that person who will afterwards marry his mother.

The son given is the seventh; he becomes the son of his adopter. The seventh son.

The son bought is the eighth; for he is sold by his father or mother by receiving wealth, and is acknowledged by the childless buyer as his own son. The eighth son.

The son made by the person himself is the ninth. He is one who willingly becomes the son of a person who, having no issue, is anxious to get a son, and answers in the affirmative when he is asked by the intending adopter whether he likes to be his son or not. He is the son of the adopter. The ninth son.

The son self-given is the tenth; he, being bereft of father and mother, or abandoned by them through anger and so forth, willingly goes to a person by saying, "let me become thy son." The tenth son.

The son received with a bride is the eleventh; he is accepted while he is "yet a fœtus in the womb of his mother;" he becomes the son of the bridegroom. The eleventh son.

The son rejected is the twelfth; he, having been discarded by his father and mother or either of them, through poverty and the like, is taken for adoption and becomes the son of the taker. The twelfth son.

VRIHASPATI says, "One alone, namely, the son of the body, is declared to be owner of the wealth *left by his father*; an appointed daughter is equal to him; but the other sons shall only be maintained. Vrihaspati on the son entitled to the wealth of the father.

Menu on the point.

MENU says, "The legitimate son is the sole heir of his father's estate; but for the sake of innocence, he should give a maintenance to the rest."

Explanation.

For the sake of innocence, means for the sake of kindness.

Maintenance means livelihood.

When the legitimate son and the son of an appointed daughter, inherit equally.

If the son of an appointed daughter be first born and the true legitimate son be born subsequent to him, an equal partition should be made between them.

Menu on the point.

MENU ordains on this, "A daughter having been appointed, if a son be afterwards born, the division of the heritage must in that case be equal, since there is no right of primogeniture for the woman."

Katyayana on the shares of the legitimate son, and of other sons.

KATYAYANA says, "If a legitimate son be born, the rest are pronounced sharers of a third part, provided they belong to the same tribe; but if they be of a different class, they are entitled to food and raiment only."

A legitimate son, though last born, inherits the whole estate *minus* the shares of other sons.

This share of a third part is for the *Kshetraja,* or the son of a wife, according to the text of the *Brahma Purana*:—"The son begotten by a man himself *in lawful wedlock,* even though last born, shall enjoy the whole of the estate; let the son of a wife begotten *by a kinsman* obtain a third part as his share, and the son of an appointed daughter a fourth."

Some legislators are of opinion that the preceding text relates to the given son who possesses virtuous qualities. Where the text is applicable.

Premising the adopted son, VRIHASPATI says, "If a legitimate son be born subsequent to the adoption of one, the latter shares a fourth part, provided the estate have not been expended in pious acts." When the adopted son shares a fourth part.

Pious acts means sacrifices and so forth.

MENU and other legislators have said that, notwithstanding other kinds of sons, the legitimate son alone receives the whole estate of his father, but they have also declared that the other sons are sharers of the estate. To remove this contradiction it must be understood that, if the legitimate son be virtuous, he shall receive the whole estate without giving a share to the others; but if he be void of good qualities, and others possess them, they are entitled to have their respective shares, as has been stated above. Inconsistencies reconciled. A virtuous legitimate son receives the whole estate of his father; in any other case, the other sons sons divide it with him.

The inconsistency in the rule that the son of the wife and the son given shall receive more or less from the estate, may be removed by *observing* the distinction of good and bad qualities.

The inconsistency in the texts of VISHNU and YAGNYAVALKYA, regarding the performance of religious ceremonies, will be removed by *observing* the distinction of good qualities or vices, or recognising their rights alternatively.

Sons born of the same mother by different fathers receive the estates of their fathers.

VISHNU says, on partition between two sons born of the same mother, by different fathers: "Sons born of the same mother by different fathers shall receive the estates of their respective fathers."

Childless persons alluded to elsewhere.

The description of childless persons has been given in the *Shradh Chintamani*, and it is therefore not necessary to dwell any more upon the subject.

A son informally adopted does not inherit.

The son who is adopted without observing the rules ordained is not competent to have a share, because he is not to be considered as a real son.

ON THE SUCCESSION TO THE ESTATE OF ONE WHO LEAVES NO SON.

Order of succession to the wealth of a person who leaves no son.

VISHNU says:—"The wealth of him who leaves no male issue goes to his wife; on failure of her, to his daughter; if there be none, to the mother;* if she be dead, to the father;* on failure of him, to the brothers; after them it descends to the brothers' sons; if none exist, it passes to the kinsmen *(bandhu)*; in their default to relatives, *(saculya)*; on failure of these to the fellow-student; for want of these heirs the property escheats to the king, excepting the wealth of a Brahmin."

Kinsmen signifies *distant* kindred.

Explanation.

Relatives means those who are descended from the original stock.

* In other compilations these clause are transposed.

Vrihat MENU says, "The relation of the *sapindas*, or kindred connected by the funeral oblation, ceases with the seventh person; and that of *samanodakas*, or those connected by a common libation of water, extends to the fourteenth degree, or, as some affirm, it reaches as far as the memory of birth and name extends." Who are sapindas and who samanodakas.

After the fourteenth degree descendants are said to be of the same *gotra*, or "the relation of family name." Who are descendants of the same gotra.

Who leaves no son means who has no son, grandson, or great grandson. Explanation.

The right of performing funeral obsequies is settled according to the following authority: "The son, the son of a son, and the son of a grandson;" hence their right of inheritance, which is similar to the right of performing funeral obsequies, is likewise established. Therefore, in default of a great grandson, the estate devolves on the widow. The widow's right to inherit.

Vrihat MENU says:—"A widow, who has no male issue, who keeps the bed of her lord inviolate, and who strictly performs the duties of widowhood, shall alone offer the cake at his obsequies, and succeed to his whole estate." Description of widow entitled to succeed.

VRIHASPATI declares:—"Although distant kinsmen, although his father and mother, although uterine brothers be living, the wife of him who dies leaving no male issue shall succeed to his share. If the wife die before her husband, she shall receive his Vrihaspati on the point.

consecrated fire. If not, the widow faithful to her lord, shall take his wealth; this is a primeval law.

Religious duties of the widow who inherits the estate of her husband.

"Taking his effects, movable and immovable, the precious and base metals, the grains, liquids, and clothes, let her cause several *Shraddhas* to be offered in each month, in the sixth month, and at the close of the year.

Her duties towards her husband's kindred.

"With food and other things consecrated to the gods and the manes, let her honor paternal uncles, spiritual parents, daughters' sons, the offspring of her husband's sisters, and his maternal uncles," old men, helpless persons, "guests and females of the family."

Kinsmen who become her adversaries, shall be punished.

"Those near or distant kinsmen who become her adversaries or who injure the woman's property, let the king chastise by inflicting on them the punishment of robbery."

Explanation.

Here by the mention of the *Shraddhas* that a wife must perform, it is meant that she shall also perform the ten *Shraddhas* of her husband recently deceased, and also celebrate the obsequies annually, and take the whole estate of her lord. What has been said above is applicable in the case of a husband who has taken his share from his co-heirs.

The rules apply where the husband lived separate.

Faithful to her lord means chaste. Faithful wife does not here signify one who burns herself on the funeral pile of her husband, for she cannot then inherit her husband's estate. Therefore the conclusion is that, in the absence of a great grandson of her husband, the chaste wife is entitled to receive his estate.

Rule where the husband was unseparated.

SANKHA speaks of cases where the husband lived with his co-heirs :—" To the childless wives of brothers and of sons, strictly observing the conduct prescribed, the proprietor of the estate must allot mere food and old garments which are not tattered."

Harita on the right of widows.

HARITA says, " A woman widowed and young is untractable ; but separate property must always be given to women that they may pass their destined life."

Argument on the application of the text.

BALARUPA is of opinion that this text alludes only to a woman whose husband was re-united with his co-heirs.

When the husband dies without partition with his co-heirs, he has no share at all : what then could his wife receive ? It cannot be argued that she is entitled to a share like her husband, because there is no authority for this ; nor should it be argued that the preceding texts are authority for her receiving a share, because they merely allude to the separate property of a husband.

Right of posthumous sons of brothers separated.

Therefore VASISHTHA directs that " partition of heritage *take place* among brothers, *having waited* until the delivery of such of the women as are childless *but pregnant*."

Explanation.

At the time of partition a share must be reserved for the sons of widowed wives of the brothers, who are pregnant by their husbands, until the delivery of children; and if no male issue be produced, the abovementioned shares should be taken by them, that is, by living brothers; and it has been distinctly explained in the *Ratnakara* and other works.

The widow has but a life interest in her husband's estate.

Thus it is said in the *Mahabharata*: "For women the heritage of their husbands is pronounced applicable to use. Let not women on any account make waste of their husbands' wealth."

Explanation.

Here *waste* means sale and gift at their own choice.

Daughters inherit on failure of widows.

On failure of wives, the heritage devolves on the daughters, according to the preceding text of VISHNU.

Nareda on the ground of the daughter's right.

NAREDA also says:—"On failure of male issue, the daughter inherits, for she is equally a cause of perpetuating the race; since both the son and daughter are the means of prolonging the father's line."

Menu on the point.

MENU says:—"The son of a man is even as himself, and the daughter is equal to the son; how then can any other inherit his property, notwithstanding the survival of her who is as it were himself?"

Vrihaspati on the point.

VRIHASPATI says:—"As a son, so does the daughter of a man proceed from his several limbs; how then should any other person take her father's wealth?"

But what kind of daughter is competent to receive her father's heritage, is declared by the same author.

Description of daughter competent to inherit.

"Being of equal class and married to a man of like tribe, and being virtuous and devoted to obedience, she (namely, the daughter,) whether appointed or not appointed to continue the male line, shall take the property of her father who leaves no son, *nor widow*."

BALARUPA is of opinion that the maiden and unmarried daughters take the heritage successively. PARASARA says:—"Let a maiden daughter take the heritage of one who dies leaving no male issue; if there be no such daughter, a married one shall inherit."

The respective rights of the maiden and the married daughter.

Here it should not be argued that the aforesaid authorities are only intended for the right of the *appointed* daughter; for, in the preceding text of MENU, from the term *unappointed* it is to be understood that the daughter was neither appointed nor intended for appointment. Yet *appointed* should not be here spoken of, because MENU has declared that "such a daughter receives an equal share with the son."

Explanation.

In default of the daughter, the mother succeeds to the estate; according to the authority of VISHNU, and VRIHASPATI also has declared thus:—"On the decease of a son, who leaves neither wife nor male issue, the mother must be considered as heiress, or, by her consent, the brother may inherit."

In default of the daughter, the mother succeeds to the estate.

Explanation. *Her consent*, that is, the mother's consent. By the term *mother*, the father is also meant. Hence, according to the *Parijata*, her *consent* means the consent of the mother and father.

The daughter's son is the next heir. VRIHASPATI says: "as the ownership of the father's wealth devolves on her, although kindred exist, so her son likewise is acknowledged to be heir to his maternal grandfather's estate."

Menu's authority. MENU says :—" Let the daughter's son take the whole estate of his own father, who leaves no *other* son, and let him offer two funeral oblations, the one to his own father, the other to his maternal grandfather."

Where these two texts apply. Those two texts obtain in default of mother and father. For the right of succession of wife, daughter, and others, has been stated successively.

The paternal grandmother succeeds in default of the mother. MENU says :—" Of a son, dying childless *and leaving no widow, the father and mother* shall take the estate, and the mother also being dead, the paternal grandmother shall take the heritage."

Explanation. The meaning is that as, on failure of daughter and others who succeed before her, the mother is the successor, so the paternal grandmother inherits in default of kinsmen. It is stated on authority that, on the failure of the mother, the property devolves on the father and other kinsmen nearest in degree.

The father's right to succeed. In default of the mother, the property goes to the father, according to the authority of VISHNU.

MENU ordains:—"Of him who leaves no son, the father shall take the inheritance or the brothers."

The right of succession of he brother has been settled by the authority of VISHNU. The brother's right to succeed.

GAUTAMA says, "The wealth of deceased brothers goes to the oldest."

MENU says, "To the nearest *Sapinda* the inheritance *next* belongs." The right of the sapinda.

APASTAMBA says: "The effects of him, who leaves no male issue, are received by his nearest kinsman; on failure of him by the remote one; in default of him by the spiritual preceptor; after him by the pupil." The right of the spiritual preceptor and pupil.

YAGNYAVALKYA says: "A wife, daughters, both parents, brothers, their sons, kinsmen sprung from the same original stock, distant kindred, a pupil, and a fellow student in theology; on failure of the first of these, the next in order shares the estate of him who has gone to heaven leaving no male issue. This law extends to all classes." Yagnyavalkya on the order of succession.

Both parents. Here a doubt may arise as to the order of succession. To remove this, the following explanation will suffice: the mother, and, on failure of her, the father, because this text has the same origin with that of VISHNU. Explanation.

Their sons means brothers' sons.

Leaving no male issue means having no son, nor son's son, nor grandson's son.

Who shall take the property of a man dying separate from his co-heirs on failure of male issue.

KATYAYANA says :—" If a man die separate from his co-heirs, let his father take the property on failure of male issue; or successively the brother, or the mother, or the father's mother."

Explanation.

Here the altercation is decided in this manner : the property acquired by the father devolves on him, and that which is acquired by brothers and others shall be shared by them.

Paithinasi on the point.

PAITHINASI says :—" The effects of him who leaves no male issue go to his brother; on failure of brothers, his father and mother shall take the heritage."

Devala on the point.

DEVALA says :—" Next, let brothers of the whole blood divide the heritage of him who leaves no male issue, or daughters equal (as appertaining to the same tribe); or let the father, if he survive, or *half* brothers belonging to the same tribe, or the mother, or the wife, inherit in their order. On failure of all these, the nearest of the kinsmen succeed."

Explanation.

Equal (as appertaining to the same tribe) refers to the brothers of the whole blood.

Brother belonging to the same tribe, signifies the sons of the stepmother.

To remove the inconsistency between the texts of VISHNU and YAGNYAVALKYA, HALAYUDHA states that the phrase *in order,* in the text of DEVALA, applies to the order of succession as settled by YAGNYAVALKYA.

It appears also that the author of the *Kalpataru* is of the same opinion, because, citing the text of DEVALA, he quotes the texts of VISHNU and YAGNYAVALKYA. But it is not well settled, because DEVALA, leaving the order of succession declared by himself, explains it by taking the meaning of the order of succession mentioned by others. It is improper to depend upon what is in the possession of others by leaving that which is at our control. Even if this be done, contradiction in the passage of PAITHINASI cannot be removed.

The order of succession of Yagnyavalkya and Vishnu refers to ancestral property, and that of Paithinasi to other property.

Therefore, it is concluded in the *Ratnakara*, that the order of succession mentioned by YAGNYAVALKYA and VISHNU obtains in property acquired by forefathers, and in other property the order of PAITHINASI and others obtains.

Baudhayana on the point.

BAUDHAYANA says: "On failure of kinsmen connected by the funeral cake, kinsmen allied by family shall inherit; in default of them, the spiritual preceptor, the pupil, or the priest hired to perform sacrifices, shall take the inheritance; and lastly, on failure of them, the king.

When cognate kindred shall inherit.

"In default of kinsmen allied by family," the (*bandhu*) cognate kindred shall inherit, as stated by YAGNYAVALKYA.

Three sorts of cognate kindred.

Cognate kindred are of three sorts, namely, a person's own, his father's, and his mother's, who are thus specified:

Who are a person's own cognate kindred.

"The sons of his own father's sister, the sons of his own mother's sister, and the sons of his own mother's brother, must be considered as his *own* cognate kindred."

His father's cognate kindred.

"The sons of his father's paternal aunt, the sons of his father's maternal aunt, and the sons of his father's maternal uncle, must be deemed his *father's* cognate kindred.

His mother's cognate kindred.

"The sons of his mother's paternal aunt, the sons of his mother's maternal aunt, and the sons of his mother's maternal uncle, must be reckoned his *mother's* cognate kindred."

Explanation.

These should inherit according to their order.

The king is the ultimate heir of all but Brahmins.

BALARUPA is of the same opinion. In default of the said heirs the wealth goes to the king, excepting, however, the property of a Brahmana.

Menu on the point.

MENU speaks on this: "The wealth of a Brahmana shall never be taken as an *escheat* by the king: this is a fixed law; but the wealth of the other classes, on failure of all heirs, the king may take."

Devala on the point.

DEVALA says: "In every case the king may take the wealth of a subject dying without an heir, except the estate of a priest; for the property of a Brahmana dying without an heir must be given to learned priests."

Without an heir means without one who is entitled to inheritance.

Vrihaspati on the point.

VRIHASPATI says: "The king takes *as an escheat* the wealth of those *Kshatryas, Vaisyas*, and *Sudras*, who leave no son, nor wife, nor brother; for he is lord of all."

BAUDHAYANA says, that poison destroys only him who takes it, but holy property kills a son and a son's son; the king shall not therefore take the property of a Brahmana. Why the king shall not take the property of a Brahmin.

SANKHA and LIKHITA say, "The property of a learned priest descends to the Brahmanas, and not to the king." Brahmins get the property of learned priests.

Therefore the summary of the abovementioned heirs is this; first, the son; on failure of him, the grandson; in his absence, the grandson's son; on failure of him, a chaste wife; in her default, the daughters; in their absence, the mother; in her default, the father; and in his default, the daughter's son; and in default of him, the brother; in his default, the brother's son; and on his death, the nearest kinsmen; in default of them, the remotest kindred according to their order: in default of all these, the nearest *saculya*; on failure of them, the remotest *saculya*; in their absence, maternal uncles and others. But on failure of all these heirs the king inherits, except the property of a Brahmana, which goes to another Brahmana. Summary.

YAGNYAVALKYA says: "The heirs of a hermit, an ascetic, and a professed student are, in their order, the preceptor, the virtuous pupil, and the spiritual brother and associate in holiness." Who are the heirs of a hermit, an ascetic, and a professed student.

"Order," that is, the inverse order. Therefore, the preceptor takes the goods of the professed student, who passes away his life in the abode of his spiritual preceptor. The property of an ascetic is taken by Explanation.

his pupil. The property of a hermit is taken by one of his fellows.

Persons who have left the household order cannot inherit.

There is no probability of ascetics and hermits getting the paternal wealth, according to the following text: "Persons who have left the household order are incapable to receive a share: a hermit is allowed to collect food for his support for a year; and an ascetic has his property, such as a copina, or piece of cloth worn over his privities, and the like."

Exceptions to the rule as to escheats.

SANKHA says: "The inherited property of a woman must not be seized by the king, nor the *acquired* effects of an infant, nor the wealth of a woman received in the six modes of acquisition, nor the patrimony of an infant."

Explanation.

The six modes of acquisition have already been explained, that is, "what is given before the nuptial fire," and so forth.

How long the king should keep the property of an infant.

MENU says, that the king should guard the property which descends to an infant by inheritance until he return from the house of his preceptor, or until he have passed his minority.

RE-UNION OF SEPARATED PARCENERS.

Re-union defined.

VRIHASPATI says: "He is said to be re-united who, having made a partition, lives again, through affection, and so forth, with his father, his brother, or his paternal uncle.

"Our property shall be common to all." This kind of agreement is called re-union, and this is to be known by their jointly carrying on any trade, because re-union depends upon the mutual use of the said property. Evidence of re-union

If one of the re-united persons have acquired, acquire, or shall acquire, any property, it shall be common to all the parceners. Therefore, after partition, the re-union of wealth with the father, brother, and paternal uncle, is called re-union. This is the opinion given in the *Prokasakara*. But this opinion, according to the author of the *Ratnakara* and others, is erroneous; because, from the import of the term "again," it is clear that, after partition, the mere making of the wealth of the parceners common to all is called re-union. Therefore re-union is possible with any of the co-heirs. But the terms *father, brother, uncle*, in the preceding text, are superfluous. Modern legislators are of opinion that mere mixture of wealth is called re-union. Therefore, the first principle of re-union is the common consent of both the parties; and it may either be with the co-heirs or with a stranger after the partition of wealth. Explanation. The first principle of re-union is the consent of the parties.

But it is not fixed that re-union should take place after partition. If this opinion be granted, re-union cannot take place with a brother born after partition. It may be said that re-union cannot take place with such a brother. This cannot be granted, because re-union with such brothers takes place. If any of the co-heirs be a minor, and be separated by the consent of the mother, re-union may likewise take place with him by the consent of his mother. How re-union with minor co-heirs takes place.

SUCCESSION TO PROPERTY OF RE-UNITED PARCENERS.

No right of promogeniture at division by re-united brothers.

VRIHASPATI says :—"If brothers, who have made a partition, become through mutual affection re-united, and *again* make a division of their joint property, the first-born has no right to a larger portion.

The disposal of share of a deceased brother.

"Should any one of them die or any how seclude himself from the world, his share shall not be lost, but devolve on his uterine brothers.

When his sister may take his share.

"But his sister is next entitled to take the share. This law concerns him who leaves no issue, nor wife, nor father, nor mother.

"That re-united parcener, who singly acquires wealth through learning, valour, and the like, shall take a double share, and the others each a share."

Explanation.

In a case of re-union, the eldest shall not get a larger share.

But some difference as to the wealth acquired through knowledge and so forth, is explained by the author himself.

Any one: if any of the re-united parceners cannot receive a share, through his death or secession from the household order, his share shall not be lost. Who then shall receive his share? In reply to this question the sage declares that it devolves on his uterine brothers, that is, those with whom he was re-united. This text consequently

Menu's authority.

coincides with that of MENU: "But his uterine brothers and sisters, and such brothers as were re-united after separation, shall assemble and divide his share equally."

The meaning is that a uterine brother, who is not re-united, shall not receive a share. Explanation.

Some legislators explain the above in the following manner :—If, after the re-union of co-heirs, a portion of whose property was divided and the amount of each co-heir's share was only fixed, one of them die, leaving no son, wife, mother, or father, his *entire* share shall be taken by his uterine brothers who were united with him. Another view of the case.

By the division of a portion is to be understood that of the entire property, in the same manner as the whole of the rice in a vessel at the time of cooking can be said to be boiled by seeing only a portion of it. Explanation of the same. The rule, that the uterine brothers shall receive the share of one who dies without leaving a son, wife, brother, or father, which has been mentioned above, is applicable in a case like this. Application of the rule. This cannot be the case; for division cannot be said to take place when only the amount of shares is fixed. For that is known to the co-heirs even before partition. But actual division takes place when the co-heirs come to know the very things which each of them shall receive as his share. Wherein actual division consists. It cannot take place unless the articles that will fall to their share are precisely denoted, in the same way as cows are divided by taking hold of their horns. Therefore, on the death of the original owner, the right of co-heirs to the entire property becomes extinct, or is reduced, and causes the right of them to their respective shares. This is the essential feature of separation.

Partition may be of two sorts, namely, the one in which the property remains entire, but the profit Two sorts of partition.

of it is divided among the co-heirs. By the other, the property is divided into as many shares as there are co-heirs.

A man shall, after re-union, give a share to a born uterine brother, and take that of one who is dead.

YAGNYAVALKYA says that a man shall, after re-union, give a share to a uterine brother who (jatta) is born, and take that of one who is dead.

Explanations.

HALAYUDHA says that born (jatta) means living.

Others explain the abovementioned text in the following manner :—If, after the re-union of a father with his son, the former, having begotten another son, die, the first son shall give the share of the father to the last born son.

If one of two re-united brothers die, the surviving one shall receive the property of the other. But where there is re-union among step-brothers and, uterine brothers, the uterine shall receive each others' shares.

Hence, sons re-united with their father shall receive his share even if he have sons who are separate.

Consequently, sons who have re-united with their father shall receive the share of the latter, even if he have sons who live separated. For it is a general rule, that those who live together have a title to the share of such of them as die. Those who are re-united after partition and re-united uterine brothers shall get each others' shares.

Re-union between father and son.

Re-union can also take place between father and son. It is also proper that the title of sons to the estate of their father should cease after the division of property, and should revive upon their re-union.

From the text of VRIHASPATI, to the effect that re-united brothers receive each others' property, when they leave no son, and so forth, the decision that re-united sons only shall receive the property of the father cannot be correct. *The foregoing doctrine controverted.*

The foregoing argument is untenable; for the text of VRIHASPATI is applicable where sons are born after re-union. *Explanation.*

The conclusion is, that sons born after partition shall receive the share of their father, who is re-united with his other sons. In default of sons born after partition, re-united sons or brothers or any such shall get it, and sons who live separated shall have no title to it. *Conclusion.*

MENU says, that sons born after partition shall either get the share of their father, or share the property of those who live with him. *Menu on the share of sons born after partition.*

From the concluding portion of MENU's saying it is manifest, that sons born after partition get the entire property of their father, and that, in their default, it is received by those who were re-united with him. Therefore the rule, that sons born before partition have no claim to paternal property, and that those born after it have an interest in it, is also reasonable. *Explanation.*

It might be argued from the above that, if a man, who has made partition with his sons, re-unite with his brother and die without leaving any sons other *Inference that a re-united brother shall get the property, and* not sons who live separate.

than those who are separated, the re-united brother shall get his share, to which his sons have no claim. There can be no objection to this.

Re-united step-brothers shall take each others' property.

A uterine brother, even when separated, shall inherit, but not a separated step-brother.

YAGNYAVALKYA speaks of cases where the step-brothers are re-united and uterine brothers live separated. Re-united step-brothers, but not brothers who live separated, shall take each others' property. A uterine brother, even when he is separated, shall have the property. But a separated step-brother cannot get it.

The reason of this rule.

It may be said that the re-union of step-brothers, and the birth of uterine brothers from the same womb, are the source of their right of inheritance.

Explanation.

The preceding text does not admit of the meaning that step-brothers shall not receive each others' property, even when they are re-united, for then re-union becomes unnecessary.

The re-united have a title to each others' shares.

NAREDA says, that those who are re-united have a title to each others' share. In default of them, their sons obtain the share. In their default others *(other kinsmen)* who are re-united get it.

Explanation.

The meaning of the first half of the foregoing passage cannot be that every one must remember, at the time of re-distribution, what he had at the time of re-union. The entire property having become common by re-union, such an injunction would render the meaning of the text obscure.

SANKHA says, if one of the re-united brothers die without leaving a son, or become an ascetic, the rest shall divide amongst themselves all his property, with the exception of what belongs to his wife. These heirs shall have to support his wives for life, if they be chaste. If they prove unchaste, *even* their peculiar property shall be forcibly taken away.

Disposal of the property of a re-united brother, who dies without leaving a son, or becomes an ascetic.

An unchaste woman has no rights.

If the deceased brother leave any unmarried daughter, she shall be supported, till her marriage, out of his wealth. Her husband shall afterwards support her. Therefore, the unchaste shall not only not be supported, but any property given her out of affection shall be forcibly taken away. The expenses of the support and marriage of the unmarried daughter shall be defrayed out of her father's estate.

Explanation.

KATYAYANA says, those who are re-united get each others' property. This rule holds good with regard to those who lived separated. In default of sons, those who are re-united shall get each others' property.

The re-united are reciprocal heirs.

The meaning of the latter part of the text is that, when a re-united man has no sons, his property shall then be taken by those who are re-united with him.

Explanation.

The summary is, that if any one die after re-union, his property devolves on his living sons, grandsons, or great grandsons, born after partition. In their

Summary.

default, the widow who observes all the sacred rules of widowhood, and gives up the eight kinds of sexual gratifications, shall get it; and the other widows who are chaste shall be supported but shall not get any share. The unmarried daughter of such proprietor shall be maintained out of his property till her marriage, the expenses of which shall also be defrayed out of it.

The father of the deceased is also to be maintained.

If the proprietor leave a father, the latter shall be maintained out of his property, like his chaste wives.

In default of other heirs, the property devolves on re-united co-parceners.

In default of the aforesaid heirs, the entire property of the said proprietor shall devolve on those with whom he was re-united.

On re-union between step-brothers and uterine brothers, the latter get each others' property.

If there be re-union between step-brothers and uterine brothers, the latter shall get each others' property.

Surviving step-brothers and uterine brothers equally share the property of re-united step-brothers.

If there be re-union among step-brothers only, and the uterine brothers remain separated, the step-brothers and the uterine brothers shall equally share the property of the deceased brothers.

The survivor gets the whole.

If only one survive, he shall get the whole.

Division of property, acquired after re-union by learning, and added to the common stock.

If any one acquire property after re-union, by learning and so forth, and add it to the common stock, he will get two parts of it, and the others shall get only one part each.

RIGHTS OF FATHER AND SON IN ANCESTRAL PROPERTY.

It is declared in the work called *Prakasa* that immovable and biped property, even if it be self-acquired, cannot be sold or given away without the consent of the sons. They who are born, they who are yet in the womb, and *even* they who are not yet conceived, require paternal property for their maintenance. Therefore, it is improper to deprive them of it.

Immovable and biped property, even if it be self-acquired, to be disposed of with consent of sons.

None to be deprived of paternal property.

As a special case, the proprietor can give away, sell, or mortgage the immovable property, on any crisis, for the support of the family, and principally for religious acts. When any common danger happens, or when a daughter of the family is to be married, and the like, even the divided immovable property can be given or sold, by a person who has become separated.

When the proprietor can dispose of immovable property.

All co-parceners have an equal claim to immovable property, whether they be separated or live together. Therefore, one of them is not competent to make a gift of, mortgage, or sell it.

Why one of the co-parceners cannot dispose of immovable property.

The purport of this passage is, that the property, which has been only nominally divided, remains common to all the heirs. Therefore a single person is not its absolute master. If the entire property be divided, his act, whatever it be, is lawful.

Explanation.

Some thus explain the foregoing passage. In order to remove any doubt as to a division having

Another explanation.

taken place, the consent of the divided co-parceners shall be taken when the gift, mortgage, or sale of the immovable property is made.

Illustration from the mode in which transfer of land is made.

The passage, *which declares* that land goes to another person's possession by the following six ways,—consent of the inhabitants of the village where it is situated, that of kinsmen, that of the chief of the district, and that of shareholders, and the gift of gold and water,—means that the consent of the inhabitants of the village where the land is situate, of the kinsmen, and of the shareholders, is necessary for making the gift known to all. The consent of the chief of the district is necessary for removing any dispute with regard to boundaries.

Why the consent of the inhabitants of the frontier is necessary.

Why gold and water are presented.

The object of the gift of gold and water is *to evince* that, *though* land cannot be sold, but may be mortgaged by consent; yet if, notwithstanding this prohibition, and the blessing and enjoyment of paradise which await both him that gives and him that takes land, there be any necessity for a sale, it shall be sold in the form of a donation, by giving gold and water on the land.

ON THE ASCERTAINMENT OF PARTITION.

How doubt regarding partition among co-heirs is to be removed.

NAREDA says, if there be any doubt with regard to partition among co-heirs, it may be removed by kinsmen who are the witnesses to it, by the partition deed, and by distinct income and expenditure, and so forth.

When the brothers live together, only one of each set of religious ceremonies is performed by all of them. But after partition they separately celebrate religious rites. Divided partners give or receive things in mortgage, separately perform ceremonies every new moon, and so forth, and contract or give loans, without consulting each other.

Divided brothers can be witnesses to the concerns of each other, can be sureties for each other, can make or receive presents; but undivided ones cannot do so. Those who perform the abovementioned deeds out of their own stock, shall be known as separated, even if there be no partition deed. Divided brothers can be witnesses as to each other, and act independently.

When one becomes a witness and another contracts a debt or becomes surety, or when one grants and another receives a loan, they are known to be separated. Partition denoted by transactions with each other.

YAGNYAVALKYA says that, if there be any doubt about partition, it may be removed by kinsmen witnesses, the partition deed *(yatuka,)* different houses and fields. Yagnyavalkya on the removal of doubt about partition.

Yatuka means separate. It is derived from *ya* which means *unmixed*. Explanation.

The purport of the above is that the aforesaid transactions cannot take place without partition. Therefore partition will be determined by them.

Mutual transactions denote separation of interests.

Brothers, husband and wife, father and son, are not competent to be each other's sureties or witnesses, or to contract debts between themselves when they live together.

There should not be division between husband and wife.

APASTAMBA says, that there should not be division between husband and wife.

From this it may be argued that no mention can be made of it.

Explanation.

The argument is unreasonable, for both the husband and the wife should maintain the sacred fire; from this ceremony it appears that they have an equal right to this, or, in other words, there can be no division. The man who makes *Yaga* being invested with the *mekhala*, or sacred threads made of *kusa*, and his wife being invested with the rope with which the ploughshare is tied, their priest shall complete it. The wife shall look at the sacred *ghee*, and the husband shall bind the *Veda*. According to these *Vedic* rules, both the husband and the wife have an equal claim to matters concerning the *Vedas* and to ceremonies prescribed in the *Dharma Shastras*, to marriage and to daily domestic duties. And both of them equally enjoy God's blessing and suffer the consequences of his displeasure.

For these reasons, the doctrine that husband and wife have no division of property cannot be correct.

APASTAMBA's text refers only to ceremonies and *yagas*. He has concluded with saying that, after marriage, husband and wife have an equal title in all acts, and are equally heirs of God's blessing, and equally liable to His displeasure. Where Apastamba's text applies.

The title of the wife to property is mentioned in the work called *Adhikarana*. Hence she may claim partition with her husband. The title of the wife to property is supposititious.

This is not actually the case. For wife, slave, and son have no property of their own. From this it must be known that the wife has no right to property.

In the *Adhikarana* her title to *join in* the religious ceremonies of her husband is merely mentioned. Her title to religious ceremonies with her husband is only mentioned.

It is said in the *Ratnakara*: That division of property may take place between husband and wife, appears from the following text: "Wives should be made equal sharers." The Ratnakara on the point.

VRIHASPATI says: Divided partners separately acquire wealth and spend it, contract debts or lend money, and purchase or sell things. The meaning of this is that those who purchase things from, or sell them to, each other, are understood to be separated. How divided partners may be known.

DUTIES AND RIGHTS OF DIVIDED PARCENERS.

Nareda on the duties of divided share-holders.

NAREDA speaks of these in the following manner :—If any have several sons, and these do not re-unite after partition, they shall separately perform *Dharma, Krya, Karma,* and *Guna.*

Dharma, Krya, Karma, Guna, defined.

Dharma means the daily duties, such as hospitality, and the like.

Krya means contracting debts or lending money, and so forth.

Karma means the support of the family, and so forth.

Guna means service.

Divided partners can dispose of their property at their pleasure.

Divided partners are competent to give away, sell, or to do what they please with, their respective property, for then they have become its lords.

OF THE VALIDITY OF MORTGAGES.

YAGNYAVALKYA says, that in matters of dispute what is last done is valid; but in cases of mortgage, gift, or purchase, what is first done is valid.

In mortgages, &c., what is first done is valid.

Dealings of the same kind are here understood.

Hence VRIHASPATI says that, if a person, taking a loan, *payable* with interest at the rate of two per cent, finally agree, from some unavoidable circumstances, to pay interest at five per cent, the latter rate shall be valid.

The rate of interest finally promised obtains.

Both these transactions being about interest, they are of the same kind.

Explanation.

The last transaction is, as a rule, valid. But cases of mortgage, and so forth, are exceptions to it. Consequently, an article which has been mortgaged, given, or sold, for the second time, shall be returned.

An article mortgaged, &c. a second time, shall be returned.

Further, if an article be sold after it has been given to another, or be given after it has been sold, the sale or gift shall not be valid. For how can he, who has no proprietary right in an article, sell or give it to another? Therefore, the law is that the sale or gift of an article by one who is not its owner is null and void.

The sale or gift of an article already given or sold, is not valid.

For want of ownership.

The last transaction is valid.

VRIHASPATI says, that the first rule becomes invalid after the passing of a second, and so forth. In the same manner, the validity of the last transactions is greater than that of any preceding one.

The mortgage of a deposited article or the sale of a mortgaged one, is valid.

If a person mortgage a deposited article, or sell a mortgaged one, the last act is valid.

Deposit defined.

Deposit means the act of keeping any thing in the care of another mortgagee.

Mortgage defined.

Whereas *mortgage* signifies the act of placing it with another, as if he were its owner. Of these two mortgage is the more valid. Sale and other acts are more valid than mortgage, since ownership is thereby destroyed.

Mortgage is not so valid as sale.

As mortgage does not extinguish the proprietary right, it is not so valid as sale.

The first sale is valid.

Sale, and so forth, being the extinguishment of the proprietary right of the vendor, if he re-sell an article the first act shall be valid.

The first mortgage is valid.

Mortgage, and so forth, do not extinguish proprietary right. But if an article be at the same time twice mortgaged, the first mortgage shall be valid.

Acts which extinguish ownership invalidate others.

Acts that extinguish ownership invalidate those that do not.

These rules are derived from practice.

This is the purport of all that has been said above: such is the manner, it is observed in the *Ratnakara*, in which men act in such cases.

VRIHASPATI says that, if an article be mortgaged, sold, and given away, on the same day, and if a doubt arise as to whether the sale, or mortgage, or gift first took place, all three acts shall be valid. The two interested parties shall divide the article, in proportion to the money they have paid, and the third to his share. These three parties shall equally divide the disputed property.

Vrihaspati declares simultaneous sale, mortgage, and gift of the same property equally valid.

HYLAUDHA says, the mortgagee's share is not valid, because the mortgage itself is not valid.

Halayudha's opinion is against the mortgagee.

GAMBLING WITH DICE AND LIVING CREATURES.

MENU says, that gambling with inanimate things, such as dice, and the like, is called *Dyuta* and that with animate objects called *Samahvaya*.

Definition of terms.

VRIHASPATI says, that legislators define *Samahvaya* to be the act of causing birds, sheep, deer, and the like, to fight, by laying wagers.

MENU says, Both these kinds of gaming are open robbery; consequently the king shall always be careful to check them.

Menu's denunciation of animal fights on wagers.

The king shall punish those who engage in and those who encourage such amusements.

The actors and abettors to be punished.

Punishment is also to be inflicted on those *Sudras*, who invest themselves with the sacred thread of the twice-born classes.

Sudras, likewise, who assume the sacred thread.

KATYAYANA says, that persons should never engage in gambling with dice: it inflames avarice and

The evils of gambling with dice.

anger, is the source of evil, is cruel, destroys human wealth, and gives birth to quarrels, as poison comes out of the mouths of serpents. The king shall therefore check it in his kingdom.

Gambling tolerated, under rules, for the arrest of thieves.

VRIHASPATI says, that MENU has forbidden the amusement because truth, purity, and wealth are destroyed by it. Others have made provision for it for the arrest of thieves. Government officers may take part in its proceeds and conduct it. YAGNYAVALKYA says, gambling with dice should be allowed under the superintendence of a Government officer, in order to find out thieves.

This rule also applies in the case of animal fights.

This rule is also applicable in the case of the amusement called *Samahwaya*.

Rules regarding the wagers laid.

VRIHASPATI says, If the dependants of a *wealthy* man be defeated in promoting the amusement, the latter shall pay the amount of the wager. The wager should be publicly laid.

Fraudulent gamblers to be banished. Secret gamblers to be punished.

Those who fraudulently gamble with dice shall be banished. NAREDA says: He who gambles with dice without the king's knowledge, shall not get the stake of the game, nay he shall be fined.

Explanation.

Wagers laid for amusement in a game, without the king's knowledge, shall not be *allowed to* be received by the gamblers, who shall moreover be fined.

If the game was carried on with the knowledge of the king, the stake shall only once be allowed. Authorised games.

But if eatables be staked, they shall be allowed once. Eatables staked.

Persons may at times gamble for amusement; but they shall not be allowed to addict themselves to it. Addiction to gambling prohibited.

VRIHASPATI says, the king shall punish those who gamble to cheat others, those who embezzle revenue, and those who deceive the public. They who gamble to cheat others, &c., shall be punished.

VISHNU says, the hands of those who are addicted to gambling with dice, for the sake of cheating others, shall be cut off. The hands of gamblers to be cut off.

The thumbs, and the fingers adjacent to them, of those who gamble under any pretence, shall be cut off.

YAGNYAVALKYA says, the king shall banish these two sorts of persons after having branded them. Such persons shall be banished.

The abovementioned punishments are to be inflicted according to the nature of the crime. The punishments to be suited to the crime.

PUNISHMENT THE SUPPORT OF LAW.

The punishment of disobedience.

KATYAYANA says: "He who does not obey the laws enacted by the king shall be condemned by all and punished by the king."

The quality of punishment.

MENU says, "In the beginning God created punishment, which is the protector of all creatures, like *Dharma*, the son of the Almighty and His glory."

It keeps all in the path of duty.

From fear of punishment, all objects, whether animate or inanimate, can be enjoyed, and all remain in the path of duty.

Punishment should be appropriate.

Taking into proper consideration the country, time, means of learning, fit punishment is to be inflicted on evil-doers.

The might and benefit of punishment.

Punishment is the king himself, the head and ruler, and security for the four *Ashrams* and for *Dharma*.

The effects of punishment.

It governs all subjects and defends them from danger. It watches the sleeping. Lawyers call it *Dharma*. When it is inflicted after proper consideration, it renders satisfaction to all. But when it is inconsiderately inflicted, it becomes the destruction of all things.

If the king through negligence do not punish the guilty, the powerful oppress the poor, as fishes are roasted by being pierced with spits, and as the crows take away the bread of *yagas*, and the dogs lick the ghee of *yagas*. None can have power over another, and the good gradually become bad. *The effects of the impunity of crime*

Men in general are submissive to punishment. Innocent men are rare. The whole world has become a place of enjoyment owing to the fear of punishment. *Punishment promotes the happiness of the world.*

The deities, demons, celestial musicians, fiends, birds, and snakes, promote the happiness of this world through fear of punishment. *By it the deities and superior beings promote the happiness of this world.*

When punishment is unjustly inflicted or not inflicted at all, all classes addict themselves to wickedness, all rules are reversed, and all persons become avaricious. *Evils that arise from the want of it.*

When dark-hued and red-eyed punishment goes about for the destruction of wickedness, the people do not become unhappy. *The benefit derived from it.*

If a king, who speaks truth, administers impartial justice, is intelligent, and versed in the ways of acquiring virtue and wealth, and of enjoying happiness, justly impose such punishment, his virtue, wealth, and happiness increase. *The greatness of the just king.*

If a king be addicted to enjoyment through mental weakness, he is ruined by punishment. *The ruin of the weak king.*

Justice essential to punishment.

Punishment is invincible. Men who have not been able to control their minds, cannot inflict it.

The ruin of the unjust king.

Punishment ruins a king who is void of virtue, together with his friends, that is, his sons.

The king "who allows oppression, shares the crime."

If a king do not protect his subjects, he participates in a sixth part of the crimes committed by his people.

By protecting his subjects, he gains a share of their virtues.

If he duly protect them, he obtains a sixth part of the virtue gained by his subjects by the study of the *Vedas*, by making *yagas*, gifts, and religious services.

Such acts are equivalent to the most valuable daily sacrifices.

If the king protect his subjects, conformably to the *Shastras*, and execute those who are worthy of capital punishment, he will have daily performed sacrifices the fee of which is a lakh.

The king has the sole right to punish.

It has been said that the king alone has the right of inflicting punishment.

The spiritual happiness of the king who suppresses wickedness.

That king shall obtain a seat in the kingdom of *Indra*, in whose kingdom theft, adultery, abusive, rashness, and oppression are unknown.

The king who performs his duty is the king of kings.

It is the duty of a king to check the abovenamed evils in his kingdom. That king who performs his duty becomes the king of kings, and is praised by the whole world.

INDEX

OF

NAMES AND MATTERS.

ERRATA.

Page 8, line 7,		for Harida,	read Harita
„ 36, „ 14,		„ their,	„ the
„ 39, „ 28,		„ it,	„ them
„ 106, 166		„ Vas	„ Vyasa
„ 151, „ 4, from	below,	„ or,	„ and
„ 293, „ 11,		„ unmarried	„ married
„ 295, „ 3,		„ he,	„ the
„ 317, „ 9,		„ Hylaudha,	„ Halayudha
Preface, *p.* xi, note, *line* 20,		„ became	„ because
„ lxvii, „ 7,		„ eir	„ their
„ lxix, „ 19,		„ but often	„ but too often
„ lxxii, note, *last line*		„ he	„ the

A few other *literal* errors, and as well as *discrepancies* in the mode of writing proper names, will doubtless be perceived and corrrected by the careful reader.

CPSIA information can be obtained
at www.ICGtesting.com
Printed in the USA
LVHW110932160522
718424LV00013B/93

9 783375 003418